'Ewa Which Way is an important addition to "the other side of Hawai'i" fiction that has flourished over the past twenty years, joining the compelling novels, short stories, and non-fiction of Lois-Ann Yamanaka, R. Zamora Linmark, Chris McKinney, Mark Panek, Alexei Melnick, Lisa Linn Kanae, Lee Cataluna, and many others. But Tyler Miranda has given us a an intimate, painful yet riveting portrait of a family in crisis, and a moving account of the lengths that Landon, the older boy and our guide into this world, will go to protect his troubled brother Luke and himself. Though cruelty and neglect are everywhere, there are no villains here, and Landon's desperate, often futile attempts to save everyone would be tragic if the novel's conclusion wasn't so brave and affirming. *'Ewa Which Way* is an honest, carefully crafted, powerful, and unforgettable novel of Hawai'i today.

—Craig Howes, co-producer of *Aloha Shorts*

Miranda's narrator is that child you know, the quiet one you've worried about, the boy with eyes that have seen too many sad things. Miranda takes the reader into the world of that wise-eyed child, and it is a place of fierce love, broken dreams, and beautiful imagery. This is an uncommon story about common people.

—Lee Cataluna, author of *Folks You Meet in Longs* and *Three Years on Doreen's Sofa*

'Ewa Which Way brought back all of my memories—both good and bad—of growing up in Hawai'i. The voices in Tyler Miranda's story are brutally honest. His writing does not apologize for being real. I was completely engaged and rooted for these two unlikely heroes until the very last page.

—Wendie Burbridge, writer of the "Five-0 Redux" for the *Honolulu Star-Advertiser*'s *The Pulse*

This novel centers around the idea that children hear and see the world as children do, and that adults are often so wrapped up in their own needs and feelings that they have no way to understand what their children need. Landon, the central character in the book, is dealing with a new, almost alien, neighborhood, with a mother who is wrapped up in her own past mistakes and mishaps and a father who has no sympathy for any of it: his wife, his sons, even himself. All he wants is to be out of it all. This is a story about Hawai'i and a story about all of us, no matter where we grew up.

—LaRene Despain, Emeritus Professor of English, University of Hawai'i at Mānoa

'Ewa is pronounced "ev-ah" in Hawaiian and defined by Mary Kawena Pukui and Samuel H. Elbert as:

1. vs. Crooked, out of shape, imperfect, ill-fitting.
2. (Cap.) n. Place name west of Honolulu, used as a direction term.

Pukui, Mary Kawena, and Samuel H. Elbert, eds. *Hawaiian Dictionary: Revised and Enlarged Edition*. Honolulu: University of Hawaii Press, 1986. Print.

‘EWA WHICH WAY

a novel by

Tyler Miranda

ISBN 978-0-910043-87-8

This is issue #101 (Spring 2012) of *Bamboo Ridge, Journal of Hawai'i Literature and Arts* (ISSN 0733-0308).

Published by Bamboo Ridge Press
Printed in the United States of America
Indexed in the Humanities International Index
Bamboo Ridge Press is a member of the Council of Literary Magazines and Presses (CLMP).

Typesetting, design, and cover art: Wayne Kawamoto
Author's photo by Christie Miranda
Back cover photo of author at age 12 by Portrait World, Inc.

Bamboo Ridge Press is a nonprofit, tax-exempt corporation formed in 1978 to foster the appreciation, understanding, and creation of literary, visual, or performing arts by, for, or about Hawai'i's people. This publication was made possible with support from the Mayor's Office of Culture & the Arts (MOCA) and the Hawai'i State Foundation on Culture and the Arts (SFCA), through appropriations from the Hawai'i State Legislature (and by the National Endowment for the Arts [NEA]).

Bamboo Ridge is published twice a year. For subscription information, back issues, or a catalog, please contact:

Bamboo Ridge Press
P.O. Box 61781
Honolulu, HI 96839-1781
(808) 626-1481
brinfo@bambooridge.com
www.bambooridge.com

5 4 3 2 1 13 14 15 16 17

for my brother Todd

Kids always think they know best. Remember how certain we were that there couldn't possibly be an adult who understood what we were going through? Parents were always too busy, too tired, too . . . distracted. Once we believed that parents couldn't be trusted, it set us free.

But that's not it entirely, is it? As kids, we think that running away is a perfectly fine approach to dealing with problems. As if some primal law is still hard-wired along the strands of our infant DNA. Why else do we run from one another, wildly fleeing the one who's IT? Why do we run away from home, only to get to the end of the block before turning back? Why do we indulge in roller coasters and surfboards and fast cars? Escapism. Freedom. Ascension. A million moments that stitch together this primitive truth in a human being. Yet, somehow, we figure out that if we want to make it in the long run, at some point, we have to stop running.

Which brings me around to the point of all this. I was twelve when I first considered suicide. It was November of 1982, a year or so after my family moved back to 'Ewa Beach. My parents were still married then, but what that really meant was that my little brother and I had only each other to rely on. I don't remember at what point I took it upon myself as the older brother to make sure he made it through. I just believed it was my job to save him. Right then, I was certain there wasn't an adult alive who could help. I can still remember the moment before I jumped, the wind so hard the rain felt like God's own tears falling sideways. A million little moments had unraveled and just come crashing down on me. And as I stood there, I thought I had it all figured out.

ONE

1

When I was small, we all sat in the crying room at church. Our Lady of Perpetual Help was the only Catholic Church for miles. Every Sunday after moving back to 'Ewa Beach, we'd be in that soundproofed room behind the last row of pews: Mom, Dad, me, my little brother Luke, and the other families with small children. In the crying room, people could be as noisy as necessary. Babies screamed. Parents scolded. Everybody made noise. Well, everybody except me and Luke.

Mom used to let me and Luke play with our *Star Wars* toys at church. But if we got too loud, she'd *pssst-pssst* us, like how our neighbors on Pupu Street, the Peraltas, called their children. When we looked, she had the handle of a thick, wooden spoon inching out of her purse like a lightsaber igniting. If we didn't knock it off, and quick, we got a spoon-end stinger on the back of our hands. After a couple of times, both Luke and I chose more, uh, appropriately.

Then one day, Mom declared me and Luke too old for the crying room. After that, we all sat together in pews. She said we kids had to learn more about our religion. That meant all toys stayed at home. It was high time we learned about the Father, the Son, and the Holy Ghost. About gospels, original sin, and temptation. We couldn't do that playing with *Star Wars* toys.

Star Wars is the best movie ever made. Hands down. When it first came out, Mom said I had *Star Wars* on the brain. Riding in the car to Longs, window down, wind through my hair: a trip to a galaxy far, far away. Washing dishes with caked-on scraps from dinner: an escape from the Death Star's trash compactor. Helping Mom weed her rose bushes, with my fingers molding soft earth: an endless trench to make an attack run through, with gun turrets and laser fire everywhere.

Mom and Dad liked *Star Wars*, too. Dad even said we'd go see *The Empire Strikes Back* soon. It had already been out for a while. Mom said she knew that George Lucas was Catholic 'cause of the aliens. How else did he dream up all those creatures in the Cantina? She said they came straight from the *Book of Revelations*. Dad said *Star Wars* wasn't about some silly, drunken aliens. He said *Star Wars* was about good versus evil. Period.

If I had to pinpoint it, though, what I loved the most about *Star Wars* were the spaceships. Luke Skywalker's X-Wing, Tie Fighters, the *Millennium Falcon*, Imperial Star Destroyers. Good guys or bad guys, I didn't care. I loved the final scene in the movie. X-Wings and Tie Fighters, dogfighting over the Death Star, corkscrewing through yellow-orange explosions. Lighting up the heavens, even if only for a moment.

Why spaceships? 'Cause of hyperspace, of course. Only a *Star Wars* ship could do this. It sped up so fast, the cockpit filled with long, taut needles of starlight that stretched closer and closer, until finally, the ship slingshotted like a rock from a rubber band. And then it was gone.

Toby Ka'ea was the only church friend I actually hung out with outside of church. We met in Mrs. Kepple's Sunday School class. Both of us wore collared shirts and long pants, and we sat with seven other kids our age. We were both drenched in sweat as Mrs. Kepple explained Bible stories. We both doodled in our Sunday School workbooks while we pretended to be good Christian boys. When Toby saw my surfer on a flat horizon, he added in waves and rocks to make it more dangerous. From then on, Sunday School was fun.

Mom believed once I got home from school with Luke, I needed to stay put. There was no reason to go anywhere. Didn't I have chores and homework to do? When she was too preoccupied, I just snuck out. But other times, I had to beg to hang out with Toby. The first time I asked if I could go to his house, Mom asked me his last name. When I told her, she looked at me funny and said, "Ka'ea? Is he Hawaiian?" Then she grilled me. *Who* were his mother and father? *Where* did they live? *What* did they do? She even asked if Toby was religious.

I wasn't sure which question to answer first. "Um, Toby's half-Okinawan/half-Hawaiian. Him and his modda live just up da road, on da ocean-side of Pupu Street, and—"

Mom stopped me. "Hold on. It's just him and his mother? No . . . father?" She squinted, suspicious now.

"Dey go church just like us," I offered.

Then Mom got really nervous. "*What* church?"

"Our church," I said simply. "Our Lady of Perpetual Help."

Mom was quiet as she considered. Finally, she sighed. "Toby must be a very nice boy. You can go over today, Landon, but on Sunday, you have to introduce me to the Japanese lady—I mean, to his *mom*. Okay? And make sure you're back before dinner."

Toby's mom was so different. She asked *how* my family was doing, not *Who? Where? What?* She offered me afternoon snacks like apples, Jell-O, or Lay's Potato Chips, while Toby and I watched cartoons on TV. She asked if I wanted to stay for dinner, if I liked 'Ewa Beach, and listened to my responses. She asked if I liked school and what my favorite subject was. She even asked what I wanted to be when I grew up. When I said I didn't know, Mrs. Ka'ea smiled kindly. "Landon, all you have to do is reach for the stars and your dreams can come true."

As he drove away from church, Dad was pissed. "Dat priest is fulla shit. No way I going pray to no saint fo' in-ter-seed." Mom was about to say something, but Dad just kept right on. "And no cut me off, Minerva. Just 'cause you talk mo' fancy dan me, no give you da right. It says 'em, right in da Bible. We no should pray to nobody but Jesus."

Mom exhaled loudly. She waited until we turned off Pohakupuna Road onto Hailipo Street to make sure Dad was finished. "Leonard, why are you *bucking* your faith? That's what the church says we should do. Who are you to challenge the Roman Catholic Church? Such a Doubting Thomas. *They* go back until the days of Jesus. That should be good enough for you."

Mom and Dad didn't look at each other during this. Eyes straight ahead. Luke just watched Pupu Street blur by his window. He had no clue what *this* was.

Dad snorted angrily. "Minerva, I can quote da Bible too: 'Thou shalt not have any graven images.' Yet da Catholic Church get plenny Mary statues lying all over da place. Not supposed to be li'dat. Dey no do ev'ryting da Bible say. No good dat."

Mom folded her arms and snickered. "'Ye of little *faith*.'"

"Gimme a break," Dad snapped, and the car fell silent. We passed the Fishers' and the Chings' properties which were ocean-side, across the street from ours. After passing the Higas next door, we turned into our driveway. Farther down the street, next door to the Chings and across the street from the Peraltas, I saw Mr. Gomes shooting his driveway down with a water hose. When we first moved back to 'Ewa Beach, he'd wave whenever he saw one of us. But now he didn't look up, and he didn't wave anymore either. Come to think of it, his son Preston didn't come over anymore to see if I could play. And that came only after a few weeks. I wondered if all our neighbors felt the same about us, wanting nothing to do with the DeSilvas. Dad's voice brought me back to the car. "'No one comes to da Fadda, except through da Son.' And you know dat's word fo' word, Minerva. How you going con-tra-dick me on dis one?" And that was the end of it. Dad killed the engine as if to punctuate his point, and Luke jumped out of the car first, still clueless.

For the first time since mass, and only for a moment, Mom and Dad made eye contact like the way they did in church. Our priest, Father Thomas, asked husbands and wives to look at each other, to truly see each other. He had them repeat the prayer for married couples during which husbands and wives promise to honor one another. Only for a moment did they get back there, where they truly saw. And then it was broken. The four of us were out of the car, headed for the same house. Home from church but so far apart.

Mrs. Ka'ea said that whenever we saw a shooting star, to close our eyes, take a deep breath, and make a wish. But not to tell anyone or the wish wouldn't come true. 'Ewa Beach nights were always warm. Thick salty air. I went out in the backyard after everyone was asleep. At night, the healthy patches of grass got cool and damp. When I took off my shirt and lay on the soft, brisk green, my skin exploded in goose bumps. Under a sky full of stars, I thought about what Mrs. Ka'ea said. Each pinpoint could be a wish. I inhaled the rich possibility of it and smiled. Every so often, I watched an airplane rumble from one end of the Milky Way to the other, heading for the airport in a brilliant streak of light. But still no shooting stars.

I heard Luke in our bedroom, so I peeked around the corner. He knelt in front of our bunk bed and held aloft a small bowl of Nilla Wafers. "Forgive us our trass-passes, as we forgive those who trass-pass against us. Like Darren Furtado and all his punk friends. Even if I hate their guts. For dis da gospel according to me, Luke. Glory to you, Lord. Dis my body which will be given up fo' you." He ceremoniously set the bowl down just like our priest, took a Nilla Wafer out, and just as impressively placed it in his mouth. "Do dis in memory of me."

When Dad came home from work, he told us to get ready quick 'cause he already got tickets for *The Empire Strikes Back*. Mom asked how he had the money to buy tickets. She hoped it wasn't from the grocery money. No answer. Dad said it again. *Hurry up and get ready.*

Luke and I both decided which two *Star Wars* action figures to play with in the car. Luke Skywalker in his white desert-planet clothes and Darth Vader in his black breathing suit. Blue lightsaber versus red. We planned to take turns beating up Darth Vader in the back seat. Once we were ready, we sat on the beat-up love seat by the front door, waiting for Mom and Dad.

Dad came out first, black and white aloha shirt with red hibiscus and a faded pair of jeans. As he went out to warm up the car, he said we might as well load up too. Mom was almost ready. But twenty minutes, three horn-blaring blasts, and a slew of *gunfunnits* later, and Mom still wasn't in the car. Dad grumbled to himself, obviously irritated. "I swear, she betta not say she kissing dat damn crucifix by da front door again." Dad snickered, having thought of something else. "No, dis time she prob'ly making sure those god-awful damask drapes, or whateva da hell kine expensive shit she bought, is closed *properly*." Dad shook his head, as the possibilities seemed to spiral out of control the longer he waited. "How da frick dat even make sense?" Finally, Dad turned off the engine. He dug his elbow into the armrest and leaned his head into his hand. That was when I felt it start to build. Meanwhile, Luke had a mean lightsaber battle going on beside me in the back seat.

There was any number of tasks that could've kept Mom from being in the car already. Like polishing the three-foot brass candlesticks flanking the love seat in the living room. Or wiping the foot-high porcelain angels in front of those. Or vacuuming the shag carpet so there were no footprints when we left, only lines. But then there was the dust quotient on the base-boards. The sheen of the bathroom floor. The orderliness of the kitchen. The distractions were endless. Mom and Dad had fought about this before. She claimed that when we left to go out, the house—and all its . . . Portuguese ephemera—should be spotless. Which was really funny 'cause everything we had was old and ratty. No matter how much we cleaned, the brass would forever be tarnished, the nap on the love seat stained and threadbare, and the porcelain chipped. But none of those were really why Mom wasn't ready yet.

Mom only *said* they were. The truth was she didn't want Dad knowing she still took forever to paint her face. The problem was that Dad knew Mom's ruse, and it pissed him off even more.

When Mom finally got in, Dad gunned the engine without a word. Nothing was said until we were already on the freeway, heading for the Cinerama in town. "I was in the middle of, uh . . . marinating the pork butt in your favorite—ketchup sauce and stewed tomatoes." Dad just shook his head. "I was, Leonard. I had to finish it before we left. It needed twenty-four hours to sit. Otherwise, we couldn't eat it tomorrow."

Dad stared straight ahead. "I seen da meat in da fridge, Minerva," Dad chided. "Was already pau before I came home."

Mom was silent for a moment, perhaps constructing a new lie. But when she spoke, it was clear she knew she had been caught. "So, how do I look then?" Mom asked, as innocently as she could. She wore a blue mu'umu'u with white and yellow plumeria, white heels, long glossy nails, and a ton of makeup. Dad side-eyed her, then drove on. "Don't you like the way I look?" The tension got stronger, the breathing shorter.

"Dammit, Minerva. We going movies, not one fancy restaurant, five-course meal. Why you gotta make all li'dat? No matter how much powder you slap on, your face not going be white like one *haole*. You not from da mainland. You one Portagee from 'Ālewa Heights, fo' Christ's sake." Dad rapped the steering wheel with an open palm. "Shit, look me. I neva even shave. And, you, wit' your clown face. You make me look like one bum."

Mom huffed. "I'm only dressing up for you. The least you could do is appreciate it. It took me forty-five minutes to get ready."

"I know." Two opponents, words drawn, burning each other in quick slices.

Forty-five minutes late meant we had to wait in a line that already wrapped around the Cinerama and along the parking lot. Our seats were lousy, off on the far right and almost in the back. As the 20th Century Fox fanfare played, Dad muttered something about broads.

When the movie was over, I felt scared. I didn't expect that ending. Luke Skywalker made me afraid in a way that hurt. Not just butterflies in your stomach kind of hurt, but the deep, down kind that bubbled over like foam and made you sick.

How could Darth Vader be Luke Skywalker's father? Both of his parents were dead. Besides, Luke Skywalker was the good guy. He flew an

X-Wing. He blew up the Death Star, for crying out loud. He was going to be a Jedi Knight.

As I got into Dad's Chevy, I apologized to my brother. But Luke gave me a weird look. "What fo'?" he asked, puzzled. "I liked da movie. Was good, except fo' da part wen Luke get his hand chopped off. But I no care," he yelled. "I going be one Jedi!"

So many things Luke didn't understand. If he only knew why I said sorry or why Luke Skywalker screamed *no* after his hand was sizzled off. It was like he *knew* Darth Vader told him the truth. And if my brother understood that, he'd be afraid too. Like me.

Our Lady of Perpetual Help was blazing hot Sunday morning. The four of us sat in a pew near the windows in the back, Dad on one end next to Mom, then me, and then Luke. People fanned themselves with hymnbooks and missals. Our priest, Father Thomas, had sweat spots that formed on his cloak. We had just read from the missal, and he was explaining what today's scriptures meant. How we needed to know the word gospel meant *good news*, but how we also needed to ask ourselves why. We needed to keep our eyes open, to be able to receive the good news of Jesus Christ and how He had saved us. Mom listened close, eating it up.

Before Father Thomas sat to meditate, he'd always end his sermon with, "Let us pray."

As if on cue, Luke slowly produced Luke Skywalker and Darth Vader action figures and began playing with them on his lap. The sanctuary was quiet, except for the spit-filled lightsaber battle Luke had full-on gotten into. "Whuzsh . . . Zsheew! 'I am your father.' *No!*"

In a flash, Mom whipped out her wooden spoon, reached over me, and smacked the back of Luke's hand so hard he yelped. Everyone in the church looked toward Luke, who was looking at Mom, who had not only tucked the spoon away but also had her index finger up to her mouth while she stared straight ahead. That meant Luke had better not make another peep or he was really going to get it when we got home. People gave us stink looks and shook their heads at us. People in stuffy mu'umu'u and slacks, and it felt like all of them were looking at my brother. I wanted to yell at them to mind their own business. To leave my brother alone.

Suddenly, Father Thomas snapped everyone back to attention: "Let us together proclaim our profession of faith." The congregation stood, and like the push of a button, words droned from everyone's mouths. A dry, hot hum rose toward the rafters.

Luke had both action figures taken away for that. Mom said it was for being so damn inconsiderate. Didn't he know church was not a playground? People went there to learn about God, not to be disrupted by a disobedient child. God must be so disappointed when children weren't interested in learning about Him. Luke concentrated on his hands, as he rolled each palm into the other on his lap.

Later on, before we went to sleep, Luke hung his head over the edge of our bunk bed. "I no get it, Landon. So confusing. I swear, Fadda Thomas wen' say, 'Let us play.'"

I wanted to laugh but held it in. So young and so confused about so many things. "You mental, Luke. He said, 'Let us *pray.*' Not *play.*"

Luke was quiet for a moment. "'Ewa Beach is junk. Why we no can play no more?"

"'Cause, Mom said no bring toys to church no more, dat's why. Period." He had to learn, sooner or later.

No response. Luke craned his neck toward Mom and Dad's room. "You tink God disappointed wit' me?"

"I dunno, Luke. Maybe. I mean . . . I dunno. Get plenty people not listening in church. How many times da guy in front us wen' yawn. His wife, digging her eyeball ev'ry couple minutes. And their tree kids, finga wrestling so much must of had one tournament in their pew. Dey get nerve looking at you like you not paying attention. But not just dem, get plenty more people not listening. So, da way I figga, get plenty people He disappointed wit'. Not just you."

Luke considered this and then lay back on his bed. He was quiet for a couple of minutes. "I not going bring toys to church no more. I going do my best fo' try learn too." From the way he said it, it sounded like a mission. A Jedi's mission. He curled up on his side and tried to find the right spot. In a couple of minutes, he was asleep.

When the house was quiet, I went outside to lie in the refreshing prickle of damp, cool grass. *The Empire Strikes Back* was still on my mind. I tried to figure out this whole Luke Skywalker/Darth Vader thing. If Luke Skywalker was half Darth Vader, it meant he was half evil too. That tripped my mind. How was something both good and evil, both light and dark at the same time? I realized that was what scared me the most. I wanted to scream *no* as loud as I could and run away from what might be true.

All of a sudden, I stopped. Hold on. If Jesus was half His Father, and His Father was good, did that mean Jesus was half evil too? Was his mother Mary the evil half?

And then I saw it, like an idea stretched bright across the black sky. My first shooting star. I took a deep breath. I closed my eyes and began a wish that felt more like a prayer:

For Mom and Dad, to hear the good news and to look at each other more.

For Luke, to be less confused. To learn the way things were now that we lived in 'Ewa Beach.

For me? Nothing. I was blank, so I thought fast. I kept my eyes pinched shut 'cause I wanted my wish to be good. I heard an airplane pass overhead. And then it came. For me, I wished to be able to fly. Just once. Like in an airplane or an X-Wing. But even better: to be completely free, so I could soar through the air with nothing to be afraid of.

I opened my eyes to red and blue dots. Eventually, the stars fell back into place like I had just come out of hyperspace. Like I was right where I belonged. Under a million stars.

2

"Don't forget to use Clorox for the whites, Landon," Mom yelled from the kitchen, where she talked on the phone with her only sister, Aunty Selma.

Clorox? I hadn't used Clorox once. Tide always got the stains out. Well, almost. After a moment, I called dutifully back. "Okay, Mom."

Once we moved back to 'Ewa Beach, I learned the power of Tide. Every day after school, I loaded dirty clothes into the beat-up Whirlpool Grandma gave us. A few weeks before, Mom and Dad had a mean fight 'cause we went a week and a half without clean clothes. Why should *he* have to wash clothes? Didn't he have to work all those extra hours 'cause of the promotion he took? Well, didn't he know *she* was busy doing everything for the house? Cooking, cleaning, taking care of the kids, shopping. Somewhere in the middle of all the mudslinging, Mom had her revelation. Since I was almost out of elementary school, I should have more responsibilities.

We didn't have a dryer yet, so I had to line dry clothes in the backyard. I hung each shirt, panty, and sock, wet and limp, with clothespins. Dad said maybe in a couple of months we could afford a reconditioned dryer from the used appliance store. But no matter, 'Ewa Beach was hot compared to 'Ālewa Heights, so clothes dried right away.

Sometimes, Luke sat on the outside basin and dangled his feet, while I stuffed clothes into the rusty Whirlpool. He chewed his nails and crunched them into bits, as he complained about 'Ewa Beach. After moving back, it seemed like it was all he did. And lately, it had been getting worse. How hot it was. How he hated 'Ewa Beach Elementary School. How Mrs. Shelley, his third grade teacher, always called on him, making him look stupid in front of everyone. How he hated Pupu Street 'cause there were no kids his age to play with. Then he fell silent again. Nail bits were slid to the tip of his tongue and spat toward the fence.

There was a commercial for Rinso I liked with this old Asian husband and wife. The wife bugged her husband to tell her how he got their clothes so clean. He looked at the camera from behind his newspaper with a grin and said, "Ancient Chinese Secret." The wife harrumphed but found out that it was actually Rinso. They both laughed as she shook her head.

While we ate dinner, I asked Mom if she knew how I got the clothes so clean. She looked blankly at me. "I no can tell you," I said. "Ancient Portagee Secret." I busted out laughing so hard I almost choked on the peas in my mouth.

Dad and Luke both laughed, too.

But Mom didn't. Instead, she shook her head. "How many times do I have to tell you, Landon? We're Portuguese, not Portagee. You sound so low-class when you speak like that."

Then Dad shook his head, too.

When Dad got home, he headed straight to the bedroom to take off his work clothes. That meant three more things to wash: aloha shirt, slacks, and a thin, white undershirt. When he emerged, he looked more relaxed in his *boro-boro* shirt and shorts. Pukas and all. His usual stop, before he headed to either the green recliner in the living room or to his workroom, was the kitchen for something to drink. Sometimes it was a tall glass of ice water or a can of Bud from the fridge. Other times it was his short glass of Jack Daniel's. He said it took the edge off. Mom didn't look at him while she poured the brown liquid from the bottle. Without a word, Dad took the glass to his workroom to tinker with his radio-controlled car. Later, Mom told Aunty Selma on the phone that Dad never even said thank you.

I collected the shirt, slacks, and undershirt from their bedroom and put them in the bathroom hamper. I glanced out the bathroom door to make sure no one was coming, then lifted Dad's shirt and inhaled. It burned from my lungs down to my stomach. It was a mixture of Brut, sweat, and VO5 hair oil. And even though it reeked from a long day, it still smelled right.

Toby invited me to hang out with him after school. He and some of our classmates were going to McDonald's. Since his mom wouldn't be home until almost four, Toby said he always killed time at 'Ewa Beach Shopping Center.

Even if I wanted to, I told Toby I couldn't go, 'cause once the dismissal bell rang, I was supposed to meet Luke *immediately* at his classroom. Mom said this was 'Ewa Beach, after all, and it was safer if we walked home together. But when I got to Luke's classroom, he wasn't there. Without looking at me, Luke's haole teacher, Mrs. Shelley, said real sassy to check the office. Then she ignored me.

Luke was outside the office on the concrete. He was dirty. Really dirty. It looked like he had rolled around in the dirt mounds behind the third grade wing. His new school shirt and shorts were full of pukas.

As I got closer, I noticed his lip was swollen. When he saw me, he struggled to his feet. He wouldn't even look at me. Without a word between us, we headed home.

The afternoon seemed to get a little hotter. "You like me kick their asses?" I asked. I knew it wasn't just one guy. Besides, I was big for my age while Luke was small for his. It wouldn't take much for a sixth grader like me to scare the crap out of a few third grade punks.

"No, 'cause den I going be one chicken," Luke said. "No can handle, gotta call my big brudda." My poor Lego-building, non-athletic brother, and here he was, trying to act macho.

I exhaled tiredly. "Mom gotta go office, meet with da principal?" He nodded. "Dat's da third time since da school year start, Luke. She going be pissed. Plus, almost all da new clothes from Sears all bust up already."

Luke's head hung low. "I know."

We shuffled along and kicked up dust. "What dey bugging you fo' anyways?"

It took him a moment, but when he spoke, it was like waves crashing against rocks, spilling over. "'Cause I look haole. Ev'ry day, da same ting: 'Haole Boy, gimme your lunch money,' or 'Haole Boy, no look at me li'dat. I going broke your white ass,' or 'Tink you so smart, ah, Haole Boy, wit' da nice clothes? Answer all da time. Like make us look stupid, ah?'"

I didn't know what to say or how to help. I searched the ground for answers, but there was only heat that rose from the asphalt. It burned as it slid up my shirt.

Luke prattled on, almost as if he couldn't stop. "Today, I wen' get so fed up, I wen' snap at Merril Puncion in class. Afta he make one sly 'Haole Boy' comment at me, I scream at him fo' shut up before I broke his ass. Right in front Mrs. Shelley. And den, wen she writing me one note fo' da office, Darren Furtado and all his boys whisper back and forth and eyeball me, only 'cause Merril one of his boys too, ah? It no even matter I Portagee just like Darren. Dat's wen I seen him lip 'afta school' at me. But dey wen' jump me recess time instead." A moment passed. "I hate 'Ewa Beach. I like go home."

"How many was?"

"Four. But no do nothin', 'kay?" He waited for me to say something.

That was when I began to feel my brother in me. The pull of Luke's eyes, the pull of a brother I sometimes didn't understand. At once screaming for help but pushing away, desperately needing help but even more than that, needing to tough it out. I wanted to reach for him, but he was so far away.

All I knew was I had to clean him up when we got home.

In silence, we rounded the corner of Hailipo Street onto Pupu Street, past houses with overgrown bougainvillea and empty gravel lots full of weeds. We walked up the driveway to our house. Mom was outside on her hands and knees, pruning one of her rose bushes. "Hi, Mom," we both chimed in together. She responded without looking up, focused on the next snip. A rose clipping fell on the grass next to her knee. She didn't see us go in the house.

In the bathroom, I cleaned Luke's lip and cuts with Bactine and then I put him in the shower. I made piles with his clothes and the laundry from the rest of the house. When I opened the back door to load up the washing machine, I heard: "Landon?" Luke's head stuck out of the shower curtain. "Why we gotta stay here fo'?" His question, so pure, so simple, so far away from ʻEwa Beach. I knew he'd like nothing better than to go back to ʻĀlewa Heights, back to a familiar place with people he knew. Back to rainy nights and dew on the grass in the morning.

I shrugged my shoulders and shook my head like I didn't know why.

It was bound to happen, I guess, but hiding things became easy. Mom used to grill me about my dirty clothes. She used to give full-on twenty questions: Where'd you go? Why'd you go there? What were you doing? Who'd you go with? You're not supposed to go anywhere after school. Just bring your brother straight home. Haven't I told you all kinds of hoodlums roam around ʻEwa Beach?

But since the laundry became my responsibility, I started surfing behind my friend Toby's house. I explored the storm drain down the road. I didn't realize it passed right by our house and dumped into the ocean. I even burned some of the trash behind the garage. Mom never saw and never knew. Dad's paint thinner and lighter fluid were easy enough to find, plus the hotel matchbooks he brought home from work conventions were always scattered about. Come to think of it, if Mom was on the phone when Luke and I got home from school, there was a good two hours before I had to be inside, looking like I was doing my homework. The key: make sure the chores were done first. Chores, then homework, Mom said. A couple hours later, when Dad pulled into the driveway, Mom got off the phone and started dinner, like she slaved over it for hours. Only then did she check on me and Luke. And she was always amazed at how much homework I had.

Ever noticed how clean clothes right off the line smell?
Hot and alive like ʻEwa Beach. Mountain fresh like ʻĀlewa Heights.
Restored, but not really.
A hot so painful it was exhilarating.
Then back to normal.
Well, almost.

Luke often helped me fold laundry. We sat on my bed and pulled tightly on shirts. All the wrinkles had to come out. Mom said it was embarrassing to walk around with wrinkles in your clothes. Well, then there must be a ton of shame people at ‘Ewa Beach Elementary School.

"You know what I miss, Landon?" Luke suddenly asked.

I glanced at Luke and shook my head. I knew what was coming.

"I mean, besides my friends up on Skyline Drive back home?" Luke turned two socks inside out and squished them into a ball. When I didn't respond, he answered himself. "I miss da rain. Da way would hit da tin roof. Like one thousand birds running across da sky. Rememba playing in da rain? I miss how cool would get. Too hot ‘Ewa Beach, yeah?"

I nodded and smiled weakly. I missed it too.

After first recess, my teacher Mrs. Kato sent me to pick up the projector from the library. At this time, the younger students had just started lunch. All the students were supposed to walk single file to the cafeteria across the younger students' recess field. Two classrooms of kids filed out of the third grade wing and headed toward the cafeteria. A couple seconds later, my jaw dropped when I saw my little brother dart out of his classroom, running full blast across the field. Behind, four other third graders, all bigger than Luke, chased after him. Mrs. Shelley yelled from the classroom. She screamed that my brother was going to the office again for insubordination. All at the same time, I wanted to leave the projector where it stood and shoot across the field. I wanted to tackle those punks, to help Luke.

Everything seemed to stop. I wanted so desperately to do something, but I didn't move 'cause I knew Luke didn't want me to.

I finally exhaled when Luke reached the lunch line way ahead of the others. I didn't realize I had been holding my breath. When Luke got there, the boys all stopped running and started walking. I watched to make sure they left him alone. Right before Luke went into the cafeteria, I noticed he didn't have his shoes on.

Then it hit me: why his socks had been so dirty.

After school, I didn't even bother to stop by Mrs. Shelley's room. I headed straight for the office. Luke was outside on the ground again. He got up slowly when he saw me. The first thing I noticed: he wasn't dirty. Good. That meant they didn't jump him.

We walked for a while. Usually, Luke said something by the time we got halfway down Pāpipi Road. But today? Nothing.

I decided to break the silence. "I neva go Mrs. Shelley's room, Luke. I knew you was going be at da office."

Nothing. We just kept walking.

"I seen you running to lunch today."

Luke's head hung a little lower. Still nothing.

I looked down and grinned. "I neva know you run dat fast." He looked up and searched my face to see what I meant. Finding it, he smiled faintly, proud of the compliment. "Why dey chasing you, Luke?"

It took him a couple of minutes, but he eventually let it out. "Mrs. Shelley, dat's why. She so stupid, she dunno what go on in her own room. She no even know what 'haole' mean. She tink Darren guys calling me somethin' nice. And wen dey call her 'da bestest haole teacha dey eva had,' so dumb, she tink dey being nice too.

"She always collect our lunch money first ting in da morning, yeah? But lunch time, wen she give us our money back, and ev'rybody trying fo' get one betta place in line, she neva hear Darren or one of his boys tell me fo' give him my lunch money. Ev'ry day, da same ting. So ev'ry day, I run out da door before Mrs. Shelley say, 'cause if I get to da caf' before Darren guys, dey no can do nothin' to me. All Mrs. Shelley do is make one scene from da classroom 'cause she tink we playing around. So, either I do dat, or I no eat."

"And you run betta without shoes?" I asked, although I already knew the answer. "What, you just kick 'em off and go? No time fo' da socks?"

He nodded, as his chest started to heave. It was easy to see he wanted to cry, but he held it in. "I hate dis place," he said suddenly. "I like go home."

It was so hot that by the time we got home, both of us were sweating. We went straight to doing chores. Cleaning bathroom day. I grabbed the Clorox, Ajax, Scotch-Brite scrubbers, and Pine-Sol. Shiny porcelain as well as fumes that burned our noses.

When Mom finally left to go to Foodland, I told Luke to forget about his chores 'cause I had a surprise for him. I stood him in the middle of the front yard with his eyes closed. Then I uncoiled the water hose and turned it on full blast. I aimed it high into the air, so the water fell like rain over Luke. At first, he was surprised, but then he closed his eyes, angled his head upward, and just stood there. He spun around and around, swatting at the glistening crystal drops, trying to catch some in his mouth. He washed his hair with both hands. And for the first time that day, he was smiling. He wasn't thinking about Mom and Dad at the principal's office. Or about the need to sprint just so he could eat lunch. He wasn't thinking about 'Ālewa Heights 'cause, at that moment, he was finally on Pupu Street.

Warm water fell from an old rubber hose like liquid sunshine. Droplets pelted the ground like a thousand pattering feet, but sadly still kicked up mud that clung to my brother.

I knew it wasn't home, but it was the best I could do.

3

Mom could spend the entire day out in the yard with her rose bushes. Hours later, her sweat-soaked work clothes were covered with mud, and her arms and nose were sunburned. She called it relaxing. It sounded more like chores to me.

Mom liked to get me and Luke outside on the weekend. Luke and I used to get up early on Saturday mornings to watch cartoons in the family room. First off, at seven o'clock, *Looney Tunes*. We busted up laughing so much that, pretty soon, Mom woke up, and the next thing we knew, we were on garden patrol. We tried to laugh . . . softly. But that didn't work either. We lasted until seven-thirty, eight max. After that, we just slept until Mom yanked us out of bed.

Mom had different color rose bushes in the front yard. Yellow was for friendship, Mom said. White, for purity. Red, for love. Mom said variety was the spice of life.

"What's spice?" Luke asked, as he plucked at leaves snagged in the aloe vera plant.

"Spice is *flavor*," Mom replied, excited that at least one of her kids finally took an interest. "Spice is what makes everything taste better. It makes things more interesting."

"So if I put Lawry's garlic salt on da grass, I going like mowing betta?" Mom smacked my head for the wise-ass remark, but I didn't care. The slap was worth it. I didn't just dislike yard work, I hated it. With a passion. Plants grew just fine on their own. I preferred Dad's B.O. undershirts, muddy floorboards, and grease-encrusted dishes. Anything but squatting over anthills full of red drones, or digging in mud for a single blade of grass that, for whatever reason, just shouldn't be there. I figured if God wanted rose bushes to grow in clean, free-of-any-green mud, He wouldn't have created weeds. Clearly, that deserved another slap.

Mrs. Kato assigned our class a project today. A three-part assignment that should take a couple of weeks to complete. There was a written report, a project board with display, and an oral presentation. Moans came from all corners of the room as she revealed the amount of work involved. We had to interview family members and write a one-page report. We had to draw, color, cut, and paste. We also had to get up in front of everyone and make A. But the loudest moan came from me when I heard the title of the project: "My Family Tree."

Mrs. Kato handed out a poster board and rubber band to each of us. On the chalkboard, she drew an example of what a family *tree* looked like. I cringed at the word. She sprinkled boxes all over branches and told us that those were for names of family members. I sank deeper into my chair as she explained. It was going to be a long two weeks.

Mom said rose bushes needed strong roots before they produced choice flowers. But instead of flowers, she often used the word *offspring.* Flowers, trees, plants, any living thing needed to root in one place before it could shine for all the world to see. Before making a family of its own. Mom said when she talked to her rose bushes, it helped them to really dig in deep.

On her hands and knees, juicy mud clinging everywhere, Mom whispered sweetly, "How do you like that, my darlin'? Lots of water for you." She whipped around and yelled, "Luke, stop fooling around with that water hose and bring it over here. What the hell are you spraying it into the air for?" She snatched the black rubber hose from Luke. Mom turned back to her roses, her voice instantly soft. "It's hot and dry over here, isn't it, sweetie? Not like 'Ālewa Heights." It was so embarrassing. Mom, in the front yard, was talking to a plant. I glanced at Luke. He was on his knees, wide-eyed, as he silently soaked up the honey in her voice.

Fujioka's, or the *plant farm* as I called it, was near Arakawa's and the sugar mill in Waipahu. This was where Mom got all her plants. From rose bushes to tulips, orchids to bird of paradise, I had never seen so many plants in one place before. When we turned onto Waipahu Street and drove toward Kamehameha Highway, Mom called out loudly, "We're almost at Fujioka's!" She was trying to make it exciting for us. When there was no response, Mom spoke again. "It's the closest to Heaven on Earth that any of us will ever get." I glanced at Luke in the back seat, and his expression said it all: eyes rolled so far into his head he didn't even have eyes anymore, just two white bulbs. He was just as thrilled to be going to the plant farm as I was.

Going to Fujioka's meant a more-than-three-hour adventure. Unlike *Gilligan's Island* where there were lagoons to swim in, cocktails to be sipped, and shade to nap in once it got too hot, at Fujioka's there was nothing to do but look at plants outside. Mom would pick us up after school and go straight there. And, after a three-hour tour, she'd speed back to 'Ewa Beach with the new plants and try to get dinner ready before Dad got home. Which she never did.

Luke and I slowly made our way to the back of Fujioka's. There was a showplace area in front next to the house where the old Japanese couple lived. Directly behind was a huge, wild yard. It was so quiet back there. Trees on all sides, mazes of plants that grew in the ground, and all the way in the back, a greenhouse filled with potted infant plants. And, right around four o'clock when the sun went down, it cast spindly shadows so long they looked like people.

The old Japanese lady watched me and Luke like a hawk. When we stared at the chrysanthemums, she made like she was watering them. If we checked out the Pele's Hair, she came by with a spray bottle. Everywhere we went in the backyard, she was right there. As if we might stuff plants in our pockets. And heaven forbid if Luke touched something. "You break, you buy," she scolded, as Luke pulled his hand away. I wanted to ask how you break a star fruit tree, but instead, I told Luke we needed to find Mom already. When we left the plant farm, three new potted plants sat next to Luke in the back seat. No one bothered to ask the names.

The family tree project was almost as painful as helping Mom with her flowerbed. My tree with boxes came out looking like a gnarled connect-the-dot activity. Pencil scratches and eraser burn-marks covered the poster board. I had to re-draw my tree three times 'cause at first, I only included Mom, Dad, me, and Luke. But after I interviewed Dad, I needed boxes for Mom's sister Aunty Selma and three more sets for Dad's relatives in Waipahu and ‘Ewa. And after I talked to Mom, I realized I had forgotten Grandma, Dad’s mom who lived in ‘Ewa Beach, too. I never knew there were so many branches on my tree.

Mrs. Kato explained the pecking order of relatives. She said the oldest, our grandparents, went on the bottom ’cause that was how trees got strong: through their roots. Mrs. Kato explained that all we needed to do was to work our way up the tree, from roots to leaves. So, our parents as well as our aunties and uncles went right above our grandparents, our cousins right above our aunts and uncles, and us above our parents.

My tree only had a few people to connect in order to get to me. For the first time, I felt relieved. Renton Velloria and Vicky Lau, two others who shared a table with me, had about the same number of names as me. But Boris Puinip, our fourth table member, had so many, there wasn’t enough space on his poster board for all the boxes. Mom said it was no wonder, ’cause he probably had twenty aunties and uncles from Manila who lived in the same house with him.

On the coffee table at home:

Better Homes and Gardens from three years ago. The only subscription Mom ever ordered from Ed McMahon. Spread out like a fan of money. We never won the million dollars.

The book *Tess of the d’Urbervilles*. Mom’s favorite since high school. She went on and on about how she always wanted a horse, or how she always wanted to live in a mansion or a castle, just like in the book. Or how, even though we were Catholic and not supposed to believe in reincarnation, she suspected she had been royalty in a former life. Whenever she started, I picked up *Better Homes and Gardens* and pretended to read the articles on gardening.

A coffee mug with *#1 Mom* on the side. Luke and I bought it from Woolworth’s for Mother’s Day last year. It was funny. Mom never gulped from it. She always took long sips with her pinky finger up in the air.

A potted plant. She referred to it as a *centerpiece.* A new one appeared every two weeks ’cause its predecessor always died, no matter what Mom did.

Mom said the thorns on a rose helped to protect it. She snipped a young, unopened red rose and placed it in a vase on the end table in the living room. I wasn’t sure why, but the rose bud fascinated me. There was a twisting spiral of red veins, like angry lightning that wound higher up the petals, as though squeezing it shut, but at the same time, trying to pry the flower open. As I stared, it seemed the bud actually pinched itself closed, not letting anything in or out. When Dad walked in from work, he moseyed past the end table and shook his head.

Mrs. Kato was stressed out 'cause nobody brought in a draft of our written report. She didn't seem so gung-ho about our project anymore. "How can you do oral reports next week if you don't have your written draft today?" she asked. "Don't you all know how important this assignment is?" Mrs. Kato caught herself, swallowing down her frustration. She took a deep breath. When she spoke next, her voice wavered with emotion. "Stop what you're doing, everyone. I want to tell you a story."

The class fell silent, able to at least comply with something.

Mrs. Kato asked how many of us knew what World War II was, and when only a handful of us raised our hands, she explained it as the darkest chapter in human history. She laid it on thick. Nazi Germany, the Holocaust, Pearl Harbor, the Atomic Bomb. Millions dead. I looked around and saw a range of expressions on my classmates' faces. Fear, anxiety, confusion. It was sad too 'cause there were others that were losing interest, as if what Mrs. Kato was saying couldn't possibly have anything to do with them. Mrs. Kato must have sensed that too 'cause she brought the issue back to the bombing of Pearl Harbor and what happened next. "My Japanese grandparents were taken from their homes against their will, along with their children who were American citizens, and placed in an internment camp. Just because they looked like the enemy." She waited a moment, staring as the faces of disinterested students comprehended the injustice of what she was saying.

"Just 'cause dey was Japanee?" Afa Palaipale asked.

Mrs. Kato nodded. "My mom and my dad were only teenagers at the time, a little older than all of you. They both met in the Honouliuli Internment Camp—"

Renton Velloria broke in, shocked. "Honouliuli? Like da road fo' go Waipahu?"

Mrs. Kato smiled and nodded again. "The camp was on the Waianae side of that road, just mauka of H-1. It was called Hell Valley because it was so hot. Imagine waking up one day, living behind barbed wire, being watched by someone with a gun, living in nothing more than a plywood tent." Mrs. Kato paused, as she now had everyone's attention. It was one thing to listen to bad things that had happened to someone else, but another entirely when it happened to someone you knew and liked.

"I never knew what my family had gone through until I had to do this very assignment almost two decades ago. When I was young, my mom and dad never said a word about Honouliuli because it was too sad to talk about. They said they weren't ashamed, that they understood, but they also made a promise not to let that place determine their future either." Mrs. Kato had the class riveted. "Can you imagine falling in love in a place as awful as that? When I asked them about it, both of my parents remembered the same story fondly. They weren't supposed to do it, but they snuck to the aqueduct and engraved each other's name into the stone, as a promise to marry. But do you know *why* they did it?" The class was silent, waiting on her every word. "Sure, it was a way to rebel against the unfairness of being there, to make a mark that would last long after they had left Honouliuli. But they said they did it because it gave them hope. By proclaiming their love on something as life-giving as a waterway, and to have the mark be permanent, it made their future together that much more real to them." Girls in the class sighed, saying how romantic that was. "That's why this assignment is so important, class. It can tell you where you came from. Who you are. *What* you are. It might even help you choose where you'll live and work when you're all grown up." Mrs. Kato winked.

Mrs. Kato said what she should do was call our parents 'cause none of us had our written drafts for our project, but instead, she extended the deadline. Also, she decided to let us read our written reports in place of our oral one. But she made it clear: if we didn't finish by next Monday, she'd be making phone calls.

What to write? I didn't think there was anything interesting to say about my family, not like Mrs. Kato's. Mom told me Dad's side of the family came from the Madeira Islands to work on the plantations. She said his great-grandfather rose up as a big-time luna. And, when he was too old to work anymore, the plantation boss gave him two homesteads, one in 'Ewa and one in Waipahu. "Free land," Mom said. "Just spread out and settle. It didn't matter if it was out in the boondocks, right?"

When I asked Dad, he said to write about how I didn't have grandparents from Mom's side . . . anymore. He told me to ask Mom for the details.

See? Nothing interesting. In fact, both Mom and Dad made snide remarks about their past as well as each other's family, like they were trying as hard as they could to forget it all. I thought back to the promise Mrs. Kato's parents made each other, engraving it in stone. For a moment, I wondered what had brought my parents together in the first place and what kind of promise they had made. I was confident it wasn't made in rock. Sand, maybe.

Mom still talked to her rose bushes in the front yard: "My little babies, reaching toward Heaven. I have to be careful I don't drown you. But it's so dry, isn't it? Here, wrap your arms around this stake. It'll help you to grow straight and tall. What? You love me? You're so sweet, my darlin' red. I love you too. You always grow beautiful reds for me. Even in 'Ālewa Heights. So sweet. So *thoughtful*. Even though your roots weren't strong and the soil not healthy enough, you still grew a flower for me."

The day before my project was due, Mom said Luke and I didn't have to walk home from school 'cause she'd pick us up. Damn. That meant only one thing: the plant farm.

All the way down Fort Weaver Road toward Waipahu, nobody spoke. I didn't look forward to the rest of the afternoon. I glanced in the back seat. Luke had already wilted.

I thought about my project. I wondered what I should do about the paper I had yet to write. When we turned onto Waipahu Street, I asked Mom why we didn't have grandparents from her side. Silence. She looked straight ahead. The car spat gravel as we skidded to a stop in the Fujioka's driveway. "You want to see them?" she said tersely. My eyes were wide as I nodded yes. She hurried into the plant farm and returned with a small pot of white roses.

Mom said we'd go back to Fujioka's later. Off of Waipahu Street, we turned left onto Kamehameha Highway and drove for some time in silence. Eventually, we headed down a long, winding road. Lots of trees hung over the asphalt and blocked out the sun.

The road ended at a cemetery called Mililani Mortuary. Mom looped around the statue of Mary and parked next to a lush, grassy field. The first thing I noticed was that the air was cool. Mom took the pot and slammed the door. "Come on," she said. "You wanted to see your grandparents." Luke and I followed slowly behind, careful not to step on any headstones. In the middle of what seemed like an arbitrary row, Mom stopped and set the pot down. She ran her fingers on the grass. There was one small, in-ground headstone:

VERNON SAMUEL BODE and MINDY SARAH BODE
July 17, 1929-December 28, 1969 and April 3, 1935-December 28, 1969
Husband and Wife To Each Other
Father and Mother To Two
Travelers In This Lifetime

No one said a word. How did they die? What happened? I watched a tear slide down Mom's face. She turned to me. "Your grandparents are dead, Landon. You can put that in your report." Her face turned hard. "It's time to go." She yanked Luke's hand toward the car.

"How did Grandma and Grandpa die, Mom?" I really wanted to know.

There was no answer for a long time. Once in the car, Mom wiped away more tears. "Maybe later, Landon. You're too young to understand now." And that was the end of it.

Mom's eyes were so full she just didn't see me. Something happened on December 28, 1969, and she didn't want me to know yet. But I was pretty sure I already understood. December 28, 1969, was only a few days before I was born.

When we got to Fujioka's, Mom told me and Luke that we had better behave. Luke and I wandered to the backyard 'cause Mom was going to be a while. Not two minutes, and the old Japanese lady was already following us. Luke and I ended up in front of the greenhouse and were about to enter when she shouted frantically. "You no go inside! Baby plant. Very delicate." I looked into the greenhouse while Luke pulled on my hand. Inside, there were rows and rows of little, green, box-shaped pots. The old lady scuttled in front of me to block my view.

I strained to see past her. "Do those plants eva come out of da pots?"

A pause. She seemed to look at me for the first time. She glanced into the greenhouse before she spoke. "Yes, ev'ry time. Always take out. Or roots no grow. No go come strong. Take out wen strong, plant in ground. Always."

And just like that, plants and Mom made sense to me. I told the old lady thank you and meant it. Also, for the first time, she didn't follow us.

We found Mom by a hāpu'u fern. She was talking again: "I'm going to bring you home too. That's only two this time. He bought movie tickets with money we didn't have."

On our way home, I sat back, the wind in my hair. My project no longer swirled in my head. I knew my family tree and what I had to write.

I finished my written report at eleven-thirty. Dad was already asleep. Mom's drooping voice came into our bedroom. I knew she stood in front of the end table by the hallway. She apologized to the rose bud for cutting it too soon. And then she scolded herself. She shouldn't have brought the rose bushes from ʻĀlewa Heights. The soil here was too dry. She always drowned them, so the roots didn't take hold. She said she wanted to give up already. "Not even noticed once. Like you weren't even there." She slid the vase off the table.

After Mom went to sleep, I retrieved the rose clipping from the trash. The bud hung limply, dead long before it bloomed. Funny, the thorns didn't do one damn thing to protect it.

The classroom was always crazy on report days. Nobody wanted to make A, but it was so shame, we all knew we were about to anyway. Boys and girls pointed at each other and silently mouthed how bad the others were going to mess up.

Mrs. Kato pulled names from a hat, and the first person to give an oral report was Jason Jones, a haole boy. Blonde hair, blue eyes, from Mississippi. He was very quiet and didn't have friends. His poster board was so shame, only had him, his mom, his dad, and his aunty. Four skull-and-crossbones were at the roots for his grandparents. He said he didn't have any other family 'cause his dad was in the military at Iroquois Point. His family was always moving around. When he finished, there was only a sprinkle of claps. Mrs. Kato was one of them.

Next to go was Afa Palaipale. A Samoan kid, big for his age just like me. Whenever it was time to play basketball, kickball, football, or any other team sport, both Afa and I were chosen as captains, 'cause nobody wanted us on the same team. His report was better, and only his dad had been left off his poster board. He said his mom didn't tell him why his dad was in O-triple-C, Oahu Community Correctional Center. There was more applause this time.

I had to go third. The sweat trickled down my back as I carried up my supplies. As I set my project up, whispers went around the classroom. Once my classmates saw my poster board, whispers melted into laughter. Then the teasing began: "So mental. Da assignment was My Family Tree, not My

Family *Trees*. Two-for-one special?" "What two trees doing holding hands?" "Why you get one dry, shrivel flower? No can afford one real one, DeSilva? Plus, should be tree, not flower." I swallowed hard and sucked everything down. For a moment, I wanted to run. From my project. From my tree. I was ashamed of what I was. Their words felt like ants crawling all over me. But somehow, I took a deep breath and said above their noise:

"I get two trees instead of one 'cause one wen' die. Da roots from my modda's side all dry up like dis flower. But my fadda's side wen' grow strong. Get my grandma and my aunties and uncles. Lucky ting, 'cause at least my modda can make offspring too, ah?" The class fell silent. Mrs. Kato was nodding yes. "My fadda work Waipahu now, and my modda stay home, taking care all of us. I wen' put my fadda and modda at da top of their own tree, not me and my little brudda. My fadda's tree get strong roots, and my modda's one stay holding on, always reaching up to Heaven. Da End." I packed up my stuff as quickly as possible. The class was quiet. They weren't sure if they should they clap or not. I didn't care. I was just glad to be done.

Mrs. Kato asked me to stay in when the recess bell rang. "Where are you and your brother on your poster board, Landon?"

Damn. She wouldn't ask unless I was going to get a bad grade. "On da side of da trees get two leaves floating in da air. Dat's me and him."

"Why aren't you both *on* the tree?"

I knew it. Bad grade. She didn't ask anyone else any questions. "We no stay on da tree 'cause if you no more place fo' your own roots, you not going be able fo' grow. Plus, nothin' going grow in 'Ewa Beach."

Mrs. Kato gave me a strange look and then dismissed me. I already knew I was going to get a *D* or *F* for this project. I felt it in my bones, but I didn't care. As I ran out to recess, I felt it burn like the first time all over again, and I meant it. I hated plants. With a passion.

4

Whenever Dad's side of the family had an all-day potluck, 'Ewa Beach Park was where we went. It was at the end of Fort Weaver Road, just before Iroquois Point Naval Installation. There was a basketball court as well as a large field perfect for soccer practice. Beyond, the shore was speckled with rocks, and waves washed up the sand and tumbled limu back and forth. The wind was always thin and unpredictable. Loud, happy Portuguese people commandeered all the space under the pavilion. Three hibachis grilled at the same time, four coolers were filled mostly with beer, and worn rubber slippers were scattered all over the place.

Mom always invited her sister, Aunty Selma, to come to these potlucks. Dad's side didn't mind. "More da merrier," Uncle Sonny said drunkenly, as he kissed Aunty Selma on the cheek. She pat-hugged Dad's younger brother on the back, wearing her thin smile. Mom and Aunty Selma then sat by themselves on one of the park benches near the basketball court. Their plates were loaded with kal-bi ribs, barbecue chicken, and sushi. They usually ate and whispered about how obnoxious Dad's side was. And then they laughed like sisters.

This potluck was for Uncle Vincent and Aunty Abi's daughter Amy who finally got engaged. They wanted to welcome her fiancé into the family. "Da best way fo' open up your arms is wit' plenny beer and ono pupus!" Uncle Vincent called out. Uncles raised their drinks and whooped, despite the conversations they were in. Bottles were drained, and so another round got passed. Aunties shook their heads but smiled the whole time.

Suddenly, Uncle Vincent produced his guitar, strummed it loudly, and cried out, "Time fo' Chamarita!" A chorus of cheers erupted as men and women began partnering up. "Amy," Uncle Vincent scolded playfully, "get your man out there on da dance floor. Dis one ancient Portagee courtship rich—" He paused for a second, confused, knowing what he said didn't sound quite right. He was going for the word *ritual.* But once everyone realized he had misspoken, and most likely 'cause he was happily drunk, the pavilion exploded in laughter. "Yeah, yeah, yeah," Uncle Vincent said, knowing he earned that ribbing. He took a sip from his can of Bud and played on, as men and women danced around in a big circle. Somehow, they all knew the steps, even though nobody got it right every single time. They were too busy laughing and teasing one another. They danced toward the middle, then went back out, and then repeated that same move so many times I lost count. All of us on the side clapped to the beat, trying to help the dancers keep time. Eventually, they re-partnered and started the Chamarita again.

As I clapped along, I smiled 'cause everyone was just having fun. It was nice. When I looked around, though, I saw Mom and Aunty Selma way over on the park bench glowering at us. Well, *almost* everyone was having fun.

Maybe this Portuguese dance was just too . . . Portagee for them. But if that was the case, what really was the difference?

Whenever Dad's side of the family had a *technical* problem, they called Dad. In high school, auto, metal shop, and wood shop were the only classes Dad could get *A*'s in. Grandma said Dad struggled with his other courses 'cause he couldn't use his hands. She said he once took apart her toilet, but before she found him, the house had flooded. Growing up, Dad always challenged himself. He always tried out things he learned at school. He constructed cages for their animals outside. He put together transistor radios and rebuilt engines. Eventually, he even designed the addition to Grandma's house. She said Dad was always reaching for the next goal.

Mom said Dad's persistence was a sickness. She claimed Dad just couldn't say no to his family. Whether it was Aunty Abi's broken phone jack, Uncle Sonny's rabbit ears on his TV, or Grandma's ancient icebox, Dad just drove over after work with his toolbox. No questions asked.

The best time, however, to pick Dad's brain was at family potlucks. When pupus went around, people talked to Dad. They tried to be sly, but he knew what they were about. When Aunty Abi brought him sashimi, she also asked why her phone didn't stay plugged in. When Uncle Sonny handed Dad the bowl of tako poke, he also slipped in questions about TV reception. But Grandma didn't have to bring Dad food. As soon as she shuffled over, he made room for her. Not even a minute later, and he had already promised to check her icebox after the potluck. Grandma said it again, loud for everyone to hear: "My boy, he so *good* wit' his hands."

It seemed Dad was always busy with some project. His most recent one required a huge antenna to be built in the backyard. At its tallest, the antenna rivaled the Norfolk Pine in the front yard. Inspecting it from below, Mom said the monstrosity was out of place, like our very own Eiffel Tower. She muttered something about money as she stormed off toward the kitchen.

Once the antenna went up, Dad sat in his workroom, setting up his new toy: a ham radio. He said it was like a telephone. But instead of only being able to talk with one person, a ham radio had hundreds of frequencies to choose from.

I was confused. "So you can talk wit' twenny people at da same time?" I asked.

"Dat's right. Sharp, ah, you boy? You can talk to people on da odda side of da world, all at da same time." His voice rose and fell with so much energy. He was so into it, just like a kid.

Since setting up the ham radio, Dad didn't seem to mind waiting for dinner. Sometimes, from our room, Luke and I listened to his booming voice. "Come in. Come in. Dis KH6JE. Anybody there? KH6 Juliet Echo. Dammit. What da hell I doing wrong?" Both Luke and I laughed quietly over our homework. Dad was frustrated over another toy he hadn't quite figured out yet. "Hello, anybody out there? Anybody copy?" He pounded the table in his workroom so hard it jerked me and Luke from our homework.

Dad brought home a black male kitten after he fixed Aunty Abi's phone. It rested in his arms without squirming. Scrawny and long-backed, its scared, yellow eyes darted about, blinking fast. Dad wiped at globs of makapiapia in the corners of its eyes, and the black, slinky body vibrated richly.

After dinner, Dad explained about the kitten. As he was driving home on Fort Weaver Road, something flew at his windshield from the direction of oncoming traffic. For just a moment, he saw it was a paper bag duct-taped into a tight roll. He swerved hard and slammed on the brakes, losing control of the car. The Chevy one-eightied onto the shoulder and almost plowed into the sugarcane field. He said he sat there for a while as he caught his breath. Just when he figured he was okay, someone tapped on his window and scared the shit out of him. A guy had stopped to see if Dad needed help. But before he left, he handed Dad the rolled-up paper bag. He thought that when Dad lost control of the car, the roll had flown out on its own.

Dad rubbed his brow, looking a little green. "Wen I open da bag, I almost vomit right there. Get two baby cats all twist and bloody, da eyeballs gone from da socket, jelly around da puka. But underneath, get dis little one squirming, meowing fo' help." We all looked at the kitten who slept on Dad's lap. "Was so sad, I wen' straight to my modda's house and bury da odda two, and den clean dis one up." Dad stroked the kitten. It swiftly focused two tiny, yellow slivers on Dad. He cupped the kitten with both hands and held it up. A quiet *meow* for Dad.

Dad made a friend all the way in Australia. The man's name was Romeo Ellison. Just like Dad, he built his own ham radio from scratch and had been broadcasting for weeks without success. They both said it was lucky they found each other.

After work, when six o'clock rolled around, Dad called us into his workroom. He reminded me and Luke not to touch anything, not to talk, not to sneeze, and if we had to fut, for God's sake, to get the hell out of the room. At first, it was pretty cool to talk to someone on the other side of the world. But what *talking* amounted to was me and Luke saying *Hi* when Dad told us to. Otherwise, we just listened to Dad and his friend Romeo. But I have to admit, Dad laughed a lot every time he and his friend talked. He sipped from his short glass of Jack Daniel's, then set it down and laughed some more. Like he was in a whole different world.

Something weird about Romeo was that he always said "Cheers" and "Mate." Dad laughed when I asked about it at dinner. "Cheers is like *hana hou,* or *right on,*" he said. "Like one toast from your favorite brew. Cheers, brah. You know?" He gulped down some rice. Mom watched him closely. "And Mate is like in cowboy movies wen John Wayne go, 'Well, *pard-ner.*' Like he saying you his friend."

I was still confused. "But why Mate? Why dat word?"

Dad shrugged and downed the last of his afternoon drink, chasing the rice.

It was Mom who answered. "It's because Australians were criminals at one time, and the continent was their prison, Landon." She first looked at me, then slowly at Dad. "Together, they were sent to Australia by boat. So they developed a habit of calling each other Mate." She watched Dad the entire time she explained this to me.

Dad breathed deeply. "Yeah, mate. Like one shipmate. Like I sailing away, ah?" He shook his head, looked down, and then kept eating.

We chose to name the kitten Zork, after Dad's favorite computer game. And from the get-go, it was clear: Zork was Dad's cat. In the early evening, Zork waited by the front door. As soon as Dad came home, Zork slid along Dad's legs, his motor running.

Mom watched from the kitchen. "Who needs a dog when we have a cat like that?"

Dad bent down to scratch behind Zork's ears and all down his neck. Dad mumbled that even though Zork was a black cat, no way he was bad luck. Zork stood on hind legs and reached with both front paws, begging for more. After another moment of behind-the-ears bliss, Dad made for the bedroom to change, as Zork's lithe black body sauntered at his feet.

A call sign was a person's name on the radio. Dad's call sign was KH6JE. He repeated it over and over when broadcasting. "KH6JE. KH6 Juliet. Echo. Is *anybody* there?" It sounded cool, like *Star Wars* language. But the part that confused me was the end: Juliet. Echo. Why didn't he say "Jell-O-Egg Roll" or "Jumping-Energy" or "Jelly-Éclair?" When I asked, Dad just laughed. He explained that before talking on the ham radio, everyone had to re-learn the alphabet. Each letter only had one word used to describe it. Otherwise, it was too confusing. Thousands of people would describe the same letters differently. Juliet and Echo were the letters J and E in the alphabet he had to re-learn. Easy.

Easy for him. "Not confusing fo' learn all those new words?" I asked.

Dad shook his head. "J is fo' Juliet, right? Just like *Romeo and Juliet.* And E is fo' Echo. 'Cause wit' da mic, sometimes my voice make one echo. Like was there, but not really."

Mom didn't like the ideas Dad got from his friend Romeo. She said even the man's name made him sound fishy. Romeo probably had no responsibilities and didn't even go to church. Dad was Catholic, after all. How could he even mention superstitions or luck? It had to be his friend. Dad never wanted to go to Australia before. He'd never talked about camping in the outback, in some godforsaken bushes, with no showers or toilets. And he definitely never talked about skipping out on work to hike up Diamond Head. "He used to talk so little, for so long," she said to herself, stirring a pot of curry. "And now I wish he'd just be quiet again."

Sunday afternoon on the roof, Dad told me about sound waves while we did maintenance on his antenna. "Sound waves just like water waves you see at da beach. But invisible. Da radio shoot sound waves into da air and catch 'em through da antenna." What? Dad saw that he just flew way over my head with that. "Okay, imagine one fishing hook. Dat's da antenna. Get bait on top, right? Dat's da voice going out. It saying, 'Eat me.' Den, wen da fish bite, da hook pierce da buggah and you reel 'em in."

I squinted, as I struggled to understand. "But how can if da voice invisible?"

"Wen you fish, you can see underwater? Invisible, but da hook still going catch, right?"

I slowly nodded yes, the idea still foggy.

Dad stepped off the roof so that one foot was on the antenna and the other was on the tarpaper. "Okay, nevamind da whole fish ting." He twisted bolts then checked to see if they were tight in place. "Right now, I talking to you, right? You can hear me, ah? Tink about it. You can see my voice? Invisible, right? Same ting. Dis antenna shoot my voice out there and my friend on da odda side of da world catch 'em. Like he get one big ear." We both laughed.

"So was like one echo," I said, "there, but not really." I took the slip-joint pliers from him, then handed him both a screwdriver and a ratchet wrench.

"You sharp, ah, boy?" Dad winked. "Almost as sharp as dis wrench, but still sharp."

But I finally understood. The afternoon got long, but I didn't mind. I grabbed tools when Dad asked for them and listened to a couple of new jokes. He told me about echoes and about how George Lucas made laser sounds for *Star Wars*. How Lucas took a hammer or a metal pipe and pounded different surfaces until he found the right sound. Sheet metal, stop signs, telephone support lines. Dad drifted to other topics, like when he was young, how he'd surf at 'Ewa Beach Park from sunup to sundown. But somehow, he always came back to his toys: the antenna, the ham radio, his call sign. "Was easy fo' rememba my call sign 'cause I rememba da story *Romeo and Juliet* from high school. Piss me off, da ending. Da two family's kids all maké at da end, like dey doom from da get-go. No matter how many times I wen' through 'em, freshmen year den sofmore year again, I always hope da ending going change. I know what going happen, but I still like 'em survive. Like somehow *I* going change 'em. But no can. Was written in da stars."

When Zork caught a brown field mouse, snuck it into the house, and placed it on Dad's lap at dinnertime, Dad lost it. And Zork got his first lickens.

Mom told Dad to calm down. It was just a mouse. "Why are you so upset? I thought you two were buddies."

Dad looked at me then at Mom. He held Zork by the scruff of the neck. "I neva free dis guy so he can go trap and kill odda animals."

Mom made a face. "He's just an animal himself, Leonard."

Dad looked away, while his eyes danced like quick paws. And then I saw it: another glance at me, one that lingered, a look much heavier than any I had seen before.

"Zork's just doing what comes natural," Mom said simply.

Dad exhaled and then scowled. "I know."

When Luke and I got home from school, Mom was on the phone with Aunty Selma. Mom's voice was almost a whisper. Then, without warning, a side-splitting laugh echoed through the house. Only Aunty Selma made Mom laugh like that.

As Mom talked on the phone, she handed me and Luke two slips of paper: our chores. Laundry for me and raking leaves for Luke. Luke stomped toward our room. He hated this part of the day. But I waited while she talked 'cause I wanted to hang out with Toby after I was done. But I didn't dare interrupt her, or else all hell would break loose. Both Luke and I knew better. We already knew how rude we were, how inconsiderate, how we had no manners whatsoever. She showed me her index finger, as if to say, "Just one more moment."

Mom talked about how if Dad wasn't helping out his degenerate family with all *their* projects, he wasted his time talking with his friend Romeo. And how Romeo must be rich and single, with all the time in the world to play with his toys. And that was another thing. How silly, two grown men, still playing with toys. She thought boys were supposed to outgrow those things. Aunty Selma said something that made Mom laugh again.

"By the way, Selma, do you want to come to another of Leonard's family gatherings? Please? I know, you're right. It *is* shameful. Total brownies. That's why Portuguese have a bad name. But I can't endure another afternoon all by myself. Yep, same place. God knows. You know that bunch, any excuse to throw a party." That was when I grew tired of waiting. I decided to just sneak out. She'd never even know I was gone.

When I finished my chores, I met Toby at his house. At school, we had talked about exploring the storm drain that emptied into the ocean near my house. We wanted to see how far under Pupu Street it went.

Just outside the storm drain, trickles of murky water splashed from the maw of the tunnel onto the rocky shoreline. We slowly climbed into the huge concrete tube. It was so big that we both easily stood upright. The salt air and sewage mixed into a stink only bearable in small breaths. We used Mrs. Ka'ea's flashlight to see. Every so many feet, there were rays of light that shot down like laser beams from the pukas in manholes and from drainage openings.

Dad had always warned me and Luke not go anywhere near storm drains or sewers. No matter what. There was no way to know what was down there. Or worse, *who*. But since we moved back to 'Ewa Beach, I hadn't been listening very well.

It was crazy how much junk got trapped down there. Empty McDonald's paper cups and Styrofoam Big Mac containers, as well as house stuff like broken picture frames, splintered shelves and cabinets, and curly-cue telephone cords. There were hubcaps, flabby inner tubes, and a huge stop sign. The trash formed two banks through which a thick rivulet ran. The flashlight beam faded into the black, the darkness so thick it seemed to swallow light itself.

"Hello?" Toby called into the darkness. His voice repeated three, four, five times. Hello? Hello? Hello? No answer. Honestly, I was thankful for that. I felt the darkness all around me as Toby's voice faded. Toby inhaled and then belted out louder than before. "Anyone there?" Four, five, six times, as it melted into the dark. There? There? There?

"Nah, Toby, cut it out." He aimed the flashlight at me. I pointed at the light that stabbed through a manhole above. "You no like nobody hear, ah?" Mainly I was worried about Mom. Then Dad. And then my ass 'cause it would get kicked from here to the next universe.

"What'chu scared fo'? Nobody going hear. Besides, only you and me down here." He kicked a paper cup into the trickling liquid, inhaled again, and before I could stop him, he yelled into the darkness. "Welcome to McDonald's. Can I help you?" His voice boomed back and forth. It echoed deeper, farther away. Help you? Help you? Help you?

"Help me," someone muttered not a few feet away from us. It wasn't Toby's voice, and it wasn't mine. For a moment, we just stood there. What the hell? I hoped it was just our minds playing tricks on us. But then we heard it again, stronger than a whisper, like Igor from *Frankenstein*: "Help me." And then, suddenly, the voice was all around us. Help me. Help me! HELP ME! The echo was darkness itself, and we were trapped as we slid down its throat.

There were never two people who ran as fast as Toby and I did that day. We ran back the way we came and didn't stop until we got to his house. Our slippers and feet were covered in sludge, our legs splattered in brown, and our chests heaved in fright. Outside his house, Toby realized he didn't have his mom's flashlight anymore. And we weren't about to go back to get it either.

When we finally caught our breath, Toby and I agreed not to tell anyone, especially our parents, about the storm drain. Otherwise, we'd both be grounded and confined to the house for the rest of this lifetime and the next. But even more so, we swore never to tell anyone about the voice we heard. The sick sound of it, like a trapped animal in the darkness, reaching out in echoes for help. It was our secret. Help me. Words that only we could hear.

Words like Dad said were there, but not really.

5

Sometimes Luke was not all there. Mom told him to rake leaves into piles in the backyard, and he'd pick them up leaf by leaf. If Dad told him to help Mom carry in groceries, he grabbed items from the brown paper bag instead of bringing in the whole package. If Mom told him to scrub the toilet, even though he did it before with a bristle brush, he grabbed one of our toothbrushes. Like he knew he'd get busted but did it anyway.

This time it was his Lego. Dad told Luke a thousand times, plus head-cracks, not to play with Lego in the living room. Either Luke had the deafest ear God ever gave someone, or he was plain stupid, 'cause he was in the living room again. With his Lego.

Luke's latest project was an attempt at a spaceship. He was almost finished, and I had to admit it looked pretty good. There were sixteen places for *Star Wars* action figures to sit in: gun turrets, the bridge, the cockpit, the cargo hold. When I reminded him that we didn't even have sixteen action figures, he said he knew. What, did he expect company, or something?

Mrs. Kato explained that our school's open house night was right before Halloween this year. A little late, but that was just how things worked out. She had a number of activities planned in preparation for our parents' visit: writing assignments; a display of the best work done in class so far; and classroom decorations that included banners, streamers, party hats, and a festive door contest. She wanted us to come together and think up the zaniest, craziest, most original door design ever. The classroom with the best door in school won a pizza party from Pizza Hut. Mrs. Kato gave a pep talk that worked. She said that she knew we could win 'cause we were so talented. She wanted our door to be so attractive it invited people right inside.

Things Luke did without thinking through:

Stood on the glass-top coffee table. Two, side-by-side glass plates. He said he just wanted to see what it felt like. After Mom checked him for cuts, his okole got rearranged with the yardstick. The welts on his ass and legs were so bad, he had a hard time sitting anywhere for a week. We got a solid-wood coffee table after that.

Wrote on the Chevy's vinyl upholstery. Large black letters in El Marko ink on the back of the long front seat: *L-U-K-E.* He had no explanation for that. After using the belt, Dad told Luke he was the stupidest criminal ever born. It took Luke two weeks to finally get it.

Stole Mom's prized Hershey's Kisses treasure chest. It wasn't much, just a plastic box that looked like a house. It had a silver-and-gold frame with clear plastic to see through the panels. Oval jewels in red and blue all over. But Mom said it was for her *treasures.* When Mom asked where it was and Luke said he didn't know, I knew he was in for his biggest lickens yet. For the last three days, the treasure chest had been under my bottom bunk.

I thumped the underside of his bed with my foot. "Luke, what'chu doing? You going get us both in even more trouble if you no give Mom back her stuff."

"I dunno where stay," Luke said innocently.

What the hell was he trying to accomplish? I had to make him see. "Dummy, I know was you. No can be me 'cause I know *I* never put 'em underneath my bed."

"I not one dummy, Landon. And I not stupid."

"Den, what? You trying fo' make Hershey squirt on your underwear like last time? No more Kisses in da box anymore. Besides, your ass was grass fo' dat one."

Luke was quiet for a moment. "I just like looking at 'em."

"Well, you betta do somethin' quick, or I going tell, 'cause I not going stay grounded much longer while you fut around. Just put 'em back in Mom's room already. No need tell."

The next day, Luke set the treasure chest back on Mom's nightstand. The only problem: Mom was changing in her room when he did that. Busted.

I got to watch *Leave It To Beaver* at Toby's house. It was easy to imagine Luke as Theodore, arguing with a friend about the huge bowl on the billboard, whether or not there was actually a ton of Zesto soup making the steam that rose from it. Luke would be dumb enough to scale the billboard to prove his point. And then not be able to get down.

And when Luke was finally rescued, after inconveniencing as many people as possible, Mom and Dad would hug Luke instead of getting angry. They'd give him a lecture about safety. About how worried they were. About taking dares and being wise enough to know better. The lesson would make it through his thick skull as people looked on and nodded approvingly. I imagined that was the end of the episode. And that Luke finally got the message.

One day left and our class was almost finished with the last of the decorations. Luke said his class had been finished for the past week. Since his class was done, they had been making silly jack-o-lanterns out of empty milk cartons. Square jack-o-lanterns? When I pointed this out to Luke, he got salty and told me to shut up.

The scene we created for the door decoration contest was a surfer with a big smile and shaka. Above him was a white box for his words: "We're surfing into the new year! Welcome, all!" So far, our door was the best in the sixth grade wing. Our door was three-dimensional, like the surfer was really sliding down the wave, ready to splash water on whoever dared to enter. We made all the props as a class. Some of us colored Glad Wrap with marsh pens to make blue water. Others rolled Reynold's aluminum foil to make all the body parts. Mrs. Kato said that was why we were going to win the pizza party. We worked together as a team, and the result was beautiful. Plus, with an open door, everyone would feel right at home.

When Dad came home from work, Luke brought his Lego starship into the living room. So it was no surprise that when Dad rounded the corner, he stepped on a piece. It was also no surprise that Dad hopped on one foot and held the other, swearing first at the pain, then at the coffee table his shin rammed into, then at Luke for how asininely stupid he was and how he had the most sonofabitchiness deaf ear he had ever seen in a jackass of a human being. What was a surprise: the blood that seeped through Dad's fingers, dripping from his heel. When Dad saw it, he whacked Luke so hard on the head that Luke tumbled toward the front door. And with one swift kick, the starship was blasted into bits. In slow motion, flying Lego squares showered across the room at Luke. He reached up as if to stop it from happening. Colored plastic pieces zipped by in a blur and pelted the door. For a moment it sounded like rain. Dad yelled at Luke to wise up. And to clean up his damn mess.

On Saturday, while Mom and Luke weeded the flowerbeds, Dad and I hung a screen door. For a while now, Mom had bugged Dad to get one. Mom said the house would be so much cooler. I was just happy I didn't have to mess with her plants.

Dad talked as we worked. "Wit' one house, can count on one ting: always going break. Dat's why you need tools. Eh, you listening, or what?" I looked at him and nodded. He pulled the trigger on the power drill, threading a screw into wood. "'Cause wen you come older, tings going break, and *you* gotta figga how fo' fix 'em yourself." The power drill whined, once, twice, then jerked to a stop. "There," Dad said, as he winked at me. "Screwed."

Mom, Luke, and I went to Luke's third grade open house first. His teacher Mrs. Shelley talked real slow in a mainland accent. In other words, boring. I made eye contact with Luke and pretended I was falling asleep. Luke giggled. He whispered that Darren Furtado and his boys now called Mrs. Shelley the best haole teacher *in the world*. When Mom caught us, she elbowed me and glowered at Luke. We both pretended to listen after that. I almost fell asleep for real.

Luke's classroom door was all hamajang. It looked like kindergarten work. Cotton balls, red and green construction paper, and glitter swirled over a family of elf-people who wore snow clothes and pointy ears. Luke said Mrs. Shelley wanted the theme to be "Dreaming of a White Year." As if it ever got cold enough to snow in 'Ewa Beach. Besides, it was Halloween, not Christmas. He said the class complained so much she changed it to "Mrs. Shelley's Little Helpers." I shook my head and wondered if some of Luke's mental-ass ideas came from her.

Only six families came to Mrs. Shelley's open house. When it was over, she stood by the door and said she just loved her students as well as teaching in 'Ewa Beach. Right. Like she was so clever. We weren't that stupid. We knew a fake smile when we saw one.

Mom talked real proper to Mrs. Shelley. In the same kind of voice she used on the phone. "Hell-o, Mrs. Shelley. I'm doing fine. And you? Smashing. Yes, it *is* wonderful meeting outside of the principal's office." They giggled like Mom and Aunty Selma did.

By the time we got to my classroom, there was no room to sit. Most of my classmates and their parents had shown up. Mrs. Kato was already into her speech, giving it her all: "Please know your children worked very hard on this project. They wanted to show you how far they've come this year. They really are a talented class, and I'm so proud to have this bunch of kids. Now, parents, our door is always open. If you like, come down and spend the day with us." Groans came from various parts of the room. "We're one big *ohana*, working together and helping each other out. So, please, if you ever have any questions, or want to spend the day, don't hesitate, no be shame. Just call me up and let me know you're coming. No problem."

Mrs. Kato talked with parents in her shorts and the school's logo-embroidered polo shirt, laughing, joking, making sure they all felt welcome. Parents looked over their children's shoulders at the class display for how and where their son or daughter fit in.

But Mom barely said two words to Mrs. Kato. This was their conversation:

"Hello, Mrs. DeSilva, I'm so glad you could make it. Great to finally meet you."

"Yeah . . . hi, Mrs. Kato. Good to meet you too." What, no *smashing*?

"Landon's such a great help. I wish I had a dozen students just like him."

"Fo' real?" Mom looked down at me for a moment. "Nah, he one good boy. He listen *most* of da time." What was she doing? She never spoke pidgin.

"Only you tonight? Mr. DeSilva couldn't make it?"

"No, just us. Their fadda's working late tonight, but he going be home soon, so we gotta go. He like dinna ready wen he come home. Sorry."

And that was it.

In the car, Mom raved about Mrs. Shelley. Her nails, her dress, her make-up, and what a perfect smile she had. Such nice teeth. Mom said Mrs. Shelley must really take care of herself.

Then Mom talked about the school. How low-class it was in 'Ewa Beach and how Mrs. Kato practically begged parents to get involved. Mom said Mrs. Kato had no shame wearing a wrinkled shirt and shorts when addressing a room full of strangers. So unprofessional, speaking her half-pidgin broken English. Mom laughed derisively. "Her classroom's an *ohana*? And *no be shame*? No wonder the schools are so terrible."

My blood boiled. Mom didn't have to talk about Mrs. Kato like that. "Why you talk pidgin too, den?" I asked. That should hit home.

Mom side-eyed me and shook her head. "You think I don't know how *fo' talk*? I grew up on this island too. I know how to *speak* pidgin. I just choose not to." Mom snorted. "I know the proper time and place, Landon. Something you and your brother don't."

So many things I wanted to say. What about our class coming together 'cause of Mrs. Kato? What about all our hard work? What about our door decoration? As we pulled into the driveway, I decided to just keep my mouth shut. Mom hadn't said one word about the door.

I was so angry I wanted scream. Even though I couldn't articulate why I was so upset, I knew what it felt like. Mom was so . . . fake. And to someone nice like Mrs. Kato. But on the other hand, Mom was nice to someone fake like Mrs. Shelley. Suddenly, something dawned on me, and it made me sick. "So it's okay if *you* talk pidgin, even if you Portuguese?"

Mom was halfway out the car. She turned back and scrutinized me. "For your information," she said shortly, "when I do speak pidgin, it's to help others *who speak pidgin* understand better." She slammed the door.

Sure it was, Mom. I had suddenly understood why she had a problem with the word Portagee. It had nothing to do with *being* Portuguese, and I realized it must kill her that we had to live here on Pupu Street. It was all just an excuse to hide what she really thought of people like Mrs. Kato or the Chings across the street or the Peraltas next door or, hell, all of 'Ewa Beach for that matter. Mom believed she was somehow better than everybody.

On Halloween, I sat in the front yard while Mom took Luke trick-or-treating. Usually Dad would, but he had been working late for the past couple of weeks. She gave every excuse not to go: 'Ewa Beach was dangerous at night, the candy might be poisoned, Halloween went against the Catholic Church. But when Mom saw Luke by the front door ripping pieces from his sad milk carton jack-o-lantern, she gave in.

Before she yanked him down the driveway, she gave me a saimin bowl full of Milky Way Fun-Size bars. Then she turned off all of the lights. She locked the front door, slammed the screen door shut, and told me that was all the candy we had to give out. So when the bowl was empty, go in through the back door but don't turn on the lights. Or else kids would be coming by all night, crying trick-or-treat. What did they think, that we were rich, or something?

A lot of kids and parents walked past our house without even stopping. Even though I sat on the curb, they walked right past. I must've looked like a kid taking a break in front of someone's house, examining my hoard of treasures. But when I glanced over my shoulder, I understood better: our lights were off and the door was closed.

No one was home, got it? Don't even bother.

I opened a Milky Way and bit off a piece. I looked up at the stars, and let the bite of chocolate melt in my mouth. It got quiet. I watched all kinds of aliens, goblins, ninjas, and sports figures trick-or-treat around our house. Floating by as if weightless. I looked up. There was so much space and so many stars up there. I inhaled deeply and felt as quiet as the sky.

So when Mom's voice echoed down Pupu Street, I really heard it. So did everyone else, like the Higas next door and the Fishers across the street. Heads turned to watch. She rounded the bend and pulled Luke by the ear. She yelled that he didn't deserve to go trick-or-treating 'cause he kept pulling stupid crap like this. Mom took Luke inside, flung him into our room by the ear, and slammed the door. Then she yelled at me for not passing out all of the candy. What the hell was I saving it for? Damn, selfish kids.

As Mom rammed dishes around, slammed cabinet doors, and got dinner ready, she told me what happened. Everything had been going fine until they went to Mrs. Souza's house. Mrs. Souza was this old widow with wrinkly, transparent skin, the type that spent Sunday mass on her knees, rubbing rosary beads together. And she always had kind, Christian words for everyone.

"That stupid jackass kid," Mom said, "started singing the trick-or-treat song. And there were so many people there, and mostly from church too, mind you. He just moseyed through the crowd, all eyes on him because he was singing like a fool. 'Trick-or-treat, smell my feet, give me something good to eat. If you don't, I don't care, I'll pull down my underwear.' And if I didn't want to die right there when he did."

My brow furrowed. "Wen he did what?"

She exhaled deeply. "Pull down his underwear. In front of everyone. And if that wasn't bad enough, his BVD had a huge, brown stain on the bottom." Mom buried her face in her hands. "It's like he waits for the worst, the most inopportune moment, to do something. And that's when he opens his mouth."

In our bedroom, Luke worked on his newest Lego project: a house. So far, there were three bedrooms, a living room, a family room, a bathroom, and a kitchen. On the bottom, the foundation was a thin, green sheet of Lego, with tracks of interlocking plastic pieces that outlined each room. Luke sat on the carpet and stared at his project, as though calculating the size of each room, the number of windows needed, the location of doors in and out. He snapped pieces together and took them apart. He said it had to be just right.

I still thought about Halloween. "You gotta wise up, Luke. So dumb. Why you always try fo' get in trouble?"

He snapped a piece into place and when he spoke, he didn't look at me. "Shut up. I not dumb. I know what I doing."

"Yeah, right. You only wen' pull da trick-or-treat stunt 'cause Mom wen' take away your *Star Wars* people in church. You trying fo' get even."

"Oh, yeah? Try look unda da bed." He pulled off a Lego and held it between two fingers. He rotated it as though deciding where it should go. "Try look, smarty-pants."

Way under my bunk were his Luke Skywalker and Darth Vader action figures. I was surprised. "Mom neva give you these back. Luke, how you wen' get 'em?"

"Eh, whop your jaws, Landon. Now *you* da dumb one, so shut up."

I didn't expect this. And whatever it was, it needed to stop. "Who you tink you? Little punk. Maybe you not dumb, and maybe you no try fo' get in trouble, but you damn well no tink before you open your mouth and let everybody see inside. You tink I going keep quiet and get in trouble fo' you next time? No way." I chucked his figures at the Lego house foundation.

Big, sad eyes. "Sorry, Landon."

"You betta be. I dunno what you tinking or what you trying fo' prove. But keep your mouth shut and open your eyes. You and me, Luke, we bruddas. We gotta stick together."

Head low. A long frown. "I know."

Toby and I ate chocolate chip cookies at his house, sat in front of the TV, and drank ice-cold glasses of milk. Just like they did in *Leave It To Beaver*. Mrs. Ka'ea baked the cookies, filled the glasses when we got there, and told us to hurry before the show started. We watched Eddie Haskell and Wally Cleaver eat their cookies in a town much cooler than 'Ewa Beach. They talked about what a screw-up the Beaver was. We laughed more than they did.

"Just like your brudda," Toby said. "Luke DeSilva: *Da Portagee Beaver*." Then he laughed more than I did. When Toby realized, he stammered. "Eh, sorry, Landon. I neva mean . . . you know—"

I stopped Toby so he didn't have to explain. "Nah, no worry. I know. He always mess up. My fadda had fo' get six stitches on his foot. It's like Luke *trying* fo' get in trouble."

The episode wound up with Ward Cleaver explaining proper behavior to the Beaver. And then it ended. Right there. No head cracks, no cusswords, no carry-over to the next show.

The theme song played and two brothers made trouble to each other as they walked home from school. The street was Pine or Grant Avenue, not Pupu Street, and the weather was always comfortable. The brothers ran to the tree in the front yard, chased each other, and raced toward the house. They knew the front door was open. They knew homework came before chores and playing. So when they yanked the knob and flew in, they weren't surprised. Even their friends knew: the Cleavers' front door was always open.

Exactly how it should be.

6

Even if it was November, 'Ewa Beach continued to get hotter. I found myself with my eyes to the sky a lot lately, hoping for something to help cool things off. Outside doing yard work, sweat and mud dripped like coffee down my face. When Mom saw I was drifting among a few white clouds, she yelled at me to finish raking. She could use a hand with the flowerbed.

Mom wore a big lauhala hat, the kind usually found over haole heads on vacation. Mom's face was shaded from the scorching sun as her fingers danced in and out of wet soil. She gave me a look that said I'd better light a fire under my ass and speed things up.

The sun cooked my arms red as I stuffed a Hefty garbage bag full of frayed ti leaves and crunchy money tree blades. I glanced up at wisps of white clouds. What I wouldn't do for a couple of thick, juicy clouds, black and heavy with rain. And then I was floating again.

Suddenly, Mom yelled at me. Damn, I had to find a way to cool off.

Zork slept on the green-and-yellow linoleum in the kitchen. He purred softly when I ran my fingers through his black fur. Thin slices of yellow eyes peeked out from the membrane then slowly rolled back. Since the mouse episode, Dad said Zork wasn't allowed outside anymore. He didn't want Zork to pick up any *bad* habits. What Dad didn't know was Zork knew how to get out if he wanted. He'd lean against the frame of the screen door until it popped open, then he'd slide slowly out.

Zork slept under the kitchen table where it was cool. Salt air wafted through the windows like a whisper. Sometimes he jerked awake, a couple blinks to find himself, then scurried to the front door. He sat and pawed at the screen, responding to whatever woke him. After a while, he went back to the kitchen and curled up around the cold metal of a chair leg. His head sank to the cool linoleum again. It seemed like Zork had it all figured out.

It was getting harder to sneak away to go hang out with Toby 'cause Mom enlisted me and Luke for dinner duty. She said she was too busy, that she needed the help. Besides, since we were getting older, we should know how to cook and clean. Not like *someone* she knew. I complained so much that Mom stuck me with sanitation services. I had to wash dishes as they were dirtied, take out the kitchen trash when stink and full, and sweep or mop when she or Luke spilled something. Luke's job was to help her cook. What a crock.

Mom showed Luke the art of cooking as she knew it:

> Rule #1: Start off with Wesson Oil, no matter what you were cooking. Mom had a hoard of Wesson bottles under the stove. If it was meat, she said to fry it. But first, lube the pan really well so that the meat browned without burning the pan.
>
> Rule #2: If the dish didn't taste right, add some AJI-NO-MOTO. The MSG crystals tasted good when we shook them into our hands and licked them off. But we had to be careful; if Mom saw us, we should expect at least a head crack for such low-class behavior.
>
> Rule #3: Presentation was everything. If the food didn't look good, it wouldn't taste good. She said it didn't matter how long it took. Never do anything half-assed.

Tonight, Mom made hamburgers and French fries. She greased the pan and seasoned the patties with AJI. Luke's eyes focused on the pan, the rising steam and breathing bubbles. Then came the French fries. Pale sticks that looked like pasty bodies sliding into the pool with a hiss.

When Dad came for his Jack Daniel's, he exhaled in disappointment. "Come on, Minerva. Not hamburga and fries *again*. Wen you going make Portagee bean soup, or *asuda*, da one you put da boil egg in da vinegar-tomato sauce, or . . . ooh, *pastéis de bacalhau*?"

Mom kept her eyes on the bubbling fries. "I'm not making codfish cakes, Leonard. Last time, the house stank for a week."

Luke just watched the fries turn a golden brown.

Dad groaned as he poured whiskey into a glass. "What about *casilla*, den? Da one wit' blood sausage? You neva make my modda's recipe long time." He capped the black-labeled bottle and stood there, flicking it with his finger. "You said you was going *try*," he said sullenly.

Mom scooped fries from the oil and set them on a plate lined with Scott towels. "I don't want to cut up pork hearts and livers, Leonard. Not to mention, I hate *morcela* . . . Black Pudding, whatever it's called. And don't you find it just a little disgusting, eating *morcela* after it's melted into the sauce? It's like drinking all that blood from the sausage." Mom made a sour face.

"But dat's why *casilla* taste so good."

Mom shook her head as she slid more pale potato sticks into the oil. "I'm not making *that*. Besides, it's not even called *casilla*. It's *cozido à Portuguesa*. My grandmother used to make a similar stew. Thank God my mother stopped that tradition." Mom used the scooper to submerge all the fries, unaware how tense Dad had become. "Peasants only ate it because everyone was so poor back then, Leonard. It's not like cozido's a delicacy. People were just making use of whatever scraps they had lying around—"

Dad interrupted her. "But why I no can call 'em *casilla*? Hah? Dat's what my modda call 'em."

Mom stirred the bubbling fries and snickered. "Yes, but she also makes tuna *sang*-wiches." Luke chuckled at the word, drawing Mom's eyes. She smiled at him. But if Mom had looked at Dad, she would've seen the whites of his eyes, a death stare of disbelief. "I'm telling you, Leonard. It's *cozido*, not *casilla*. Over time, it turned into *casilla* the same way the word Portuguese turned into Portagee, the way *açorda* turned into *asuda*. Too many lazy tongues weren't corrected." Mom inspected a scoop of fries, oblivious to how her words had been taken.

Suddenly, Dad slammed the bottle of Jack Daniel's onto the counter, demanding everyone's attention. He stood glaring at Mom, his face so furiously red he was unable to utter even a single word. Finally, he stormed out of the kitchen, sloshing brown liquid from his glass.

Mom glanced at Luke, grimacing. "Oops," she said. She sighed tiredly and scooped out another batch of glistening fries.

For the last few days, Luke did his homework outside. After chores, he took his math workbook, his composition notebook, and his pens out back. He lay belly down on the lanai with a glass of yellow liquid. Whatever it was looked good, especially since it was so hot. Must be Kool-Aid lemonade. Or maybe Mom bought Mountain Dew. I ransacked the refrigerator as well as the kitchen cabinets but found nothing. That little stinker must've hidden it.

"Do not hide," Father Thomas bellowed, "in the shadows of sin. *That* is the black temptation of hell. God sacrificed so much that we, His children, may live in the light. All we must do is turn away from the darkness and we will be blessed. The marks of hell are upon us, but those scars will be removed, if we just believe." In Our Lady of Perpetual Help, Father Thomas stood before the congregation but hardly moved. Sweat dripped down his old, white, translucent forehead and slid onto his collar. When he got really excited, though, he talked with his hands. And then we really saw it, sweat spots under his arms halfway down his robe.

Mom and Luke focused on the sermon. They soaked up every word despite the heat in the room. But Dad shook his head more than usual today. I knew what that meant.

While he ate lunch at home, Dad finally said what was on his mind. He didn't look at Mom when he spoke. "I said 'em before, and I going say 'em again. Dat priest is fulla shit."

Mom rolled her eyes and shook her head. She set her coffee cup down, steam curling like fingers. "Not again, Leonard. When are you going to just believe that—"

Dad chewed between rants. He took a sip of ice water. "Damn haole, preaching to a bunch of dark-skin local people. Who he tink him?"

I had never thought about that before, how a priest might offend the congregation. I figured that church was just . . . church. Heaven, hell, temptation, salvation. I never heard Father Thomas talk about haoles or locals, only God's children. Why was Dad so mad?

Mom sighed. "Leonard, those were today's scriptures. They were about burning in—"

"Dat's right, burning. Damn guy, can see right through his pre-ju-diss ass—and sweating so much, he must get one hand in hell already. If you ask me, he da one burning, not me."

Mom took a deep breath. "Leonard, Father Thomas didn't mean anything by it."

Dad scoffed, as he taunted Mom. "Oh, he *Fadda Thomas* now. What, you guys friends? You pals wit' da haole?"

Mom struggled to breathe evenly. "I don't know why this is such a problem. If you just gave your priest half a chance—"

Dad interrupted viciously. "Why you force me fo' go church anyways, Minerva? I already get enuff haole shit fo' deal wit' at home." Dad stopped suddenly. Once he realized what he said, he looked away bitterly.

But there it was, the accusation ringing between them like so much white noise. Dad wasn't really upset about church or even what Father Thomas said. This was about Mom.

Mom just stared darkly at Dad, fuming. Finally, she went to eat in the kitchen without another word.

Dad didn't watch her go. His eyebrows hung dark, like heavy clouds ready to explode.

Every day after school now, Luke was outside with golden drink in a glass. And he kept playing dumb too, like he didn't know what I was talking about. When I asked him where he hid the Mountain Dew, Luke made a face. "Dis not Mountain Dew," he said without looking at me. I was about ready to blast him. But then I noticed he wasn't wearing a T-shirt, as his sweaty body sprawled under 'Ewa Beach's unforgiving sun. His skin was so light. And red now, too.

Toby and I straddled his surfboards in the ocean behind his house. Aaah . . . the glorious Pacific Ocean. There weren't many waves today, but I didn't care. Waves splashed cold water, up and down. I practically had to beg Mom to let me out of the house. I just had to be home in time to help with dinner, which meant I only had about an hour. At least I got to cool off.

My mind started to drift again: the lulling swells, the empty blue sky, the wind more like a spray. A smell both salty and sweet. Every few moments, the sun intensified, and water dried into crystals on our skin. The tingle of hot water and cold heat. And with every splash, goose bumps dazzled across our arms, as our feet dangled into the dark, deep, blue water below.

"What'chu tink, Landon?"

I had been so enchanted by the water Toby's voice startled me. He sat there staring, waiting for an answer. "Uh . . . what'chu said?"

Toby rose then fell with each wave. "About Jason Jones and Afa Palaipale? What'chu tink? Jason coming school tomorrow, or what? I be so shame if I got *my* lip all buss up."

Then I remembered. Toby meant the two boys from our class. "I dunno. Jason wen' get his ass kick pretty good."

Toby snickered. "What a dummy. Afa same size as you, Landon, plus Afa Samoan. Jason dumb he wise off to Afa, especially 'cause he one small, runt haole."

I felt the boil start within me. "Nah, but why Afa gotta do dat fo'? Jason neva know what *mahalo* mean wen somebody *say* 'em. He thought Afa calling him rubbish, like on one trash can." I instinctively thought of Luke.

"Eh, if Jason no can figga *mahalo* mean 'Thank You,' he *should* get his ass rearrange. I like tell him, 'Learn how tings is ova here or go back home, *haole*.'"

Up, down. Rising and falling. I didn't know if I agreed with Toby, but I wasn't about to say anything. A lone cloud slid in front of the sun and cast a shadow that made us both look up. It was thick and juicy, dark in the middle but also ringed by a glow of white.

When Luke and I got home, Mom was stuffing Scott towels into a small cardboard box. She fiddled with something inside. Mom told us that earlier Zork had let himself out again. She watched him run around the backyard, nap in the shade, and chase bugs. And then for a long time, she didn't see him until he suddenly showed up at the front door, moaning with something clenched between his teeth. She said she flinched when the thing in his mouth began thrashing about. But Zork just held on, his yellow eyes focused on her. "He caught this," Mom said, and then she showed us the freakiest thing ever: a white mynah bird.

Mom said it was an albino. Both Luke and I had no clue what that meant. She said most living things could be born albino if something went wrong when they were still in the womb. The skin came out pale, the hair white, and the eyes pink. She also said albinos had poor eyesight.

Even though the bird was cute, it gave me the creeps. Luke just stared at it. When Dad discovered Mom wanted to keep it, the look on his face was classic. "What . . . eva, Minerva."

Dad was so tired after work that he didn't even ask how the bird found its way into the house. He just wanted a drink and to go sit down. Nobody explained that Zork had caught it. That would've meant the damn cat had been outside. Whenever Zork pawed at the screen door, Dad either yanked Zork away or tapped Zork's okole, both of which he did with his foot. Neither gentle nor vicious. Needless to say, Zork had avoided Dad more and more. Zork watched and waited, unsure of which mood came walking through the door.

Holding the bird up to her face and gazing into its pink eyes, Mom named the bird Rosie.

When I found Luke convulsing on the lanai outside, I yelled for Mom. His back was fried red, the color of Mom's roses. He was sprawled on his side, teeth chattering, and his skin was slimy and thick from sweat and body oil. We all loaded into the car and flew to the doctor's.

Five hours and two IV bags of fluid later, Luke slept peacefully in his bed. It was almost nine o'clock at night when Mom finished preparing dinner. Her voice floated in like steam. "That's what I said, Leonard. Three hundred ninety dollars for the hospitalization."

Dad's voice was tired, reproachful. "We no can afford dis, Minerva. You know dat. You suppose to take care da kids. Tell da damn kid fo' put on one shirt, fo' Christ's sake."

"Leonard, don't take the Lord's name in vain—"

Dad screamed like a frustrated animal. "No change da subject! You always talk fancy around da problem and muddy up da whole ting. Plus, no bring God into dis. Dis about you not doing your job. Like dis food, what fo' gotta fry 'em fo' so long? Why gotta be *just right*? Presentation no make sense, Minerva! Take so damn long da way you do 'em. Just slap 'em together. All going da same place."

When I heard Mom washing dishes, I ventured out to the kitchen. The hot water was on full blast, and Mom sniffled. I grabbed the dish towel to help dry dishes. Dad came in and poured a glass of Jack Daniel's. No ice. Dark brown liquid swirled around the lip of the glass as he walked away. Mom dug at the inside of her mouth with her tongue. I wanted to say something, anything, but instead, I just wiped the warm, wet dishes Mom handed me.

Luke's back was still warm. Since he had sunburned himself face down, he reminded me of a penguin: pale, soft-fleshed belly covered by a dark, tight-fitting coat. Except his burnt skin wasn't black. It was purple, like the Japanese eggplant growing next door in the Higas' vegetable garden. He sat Indian-style on the floor in front of my bunk, as I rubbed Noxema into his skin. I swirled globs of cool, white cream onto his back, and he shuddered slightly. I tried not to pop the fizz of sweat bubbles that pimpled his thick, purple flesh.

Luke was the first to break the silence. "Landon? You mad at me?"

I sighed tiredly. "I not mad, Luke. But you gotta use your head. Mom and Dad been fighting, you know." Luke's head sank low. He knew. "Plus, you wen' scare me. I no like lose you. You my little brudda. Da only one I get."

Luke was quiet for a moment, as though he considered what I meant. "Sorry, Landon. I not going do dat again." After rubbing Noxema into his back, I wiped my hands on a Scott towel. Luke chuckled. "I guess I neva shoulda use oil, huh?" he asked, looking up at me.

I cocked my head, my eyebrows raised in curiosity. "What . . . oil?"

"Wesson Oil, from da kitchen. I wen' pour 'em in one glass and bring 'em outside. And den I rub 'em on my skin wen I do my homework."

Wesson Oil . . . not Kool-Aid lemonade, or Mountain Dew? Wesson Oil. My thoughts boiled until they were just steam, as they found their way out of my mouth. "Luke, what da hell you tinking? Dat's fo' cook *food* wit', not sunbathe. You lucky you neva cook fo' real."

But that was when it all came out. Luke told me how he thought that if he got darker, Darren Furtado and his boys might believe he wasn't haole, that he really was local. So that they'd leave him alone. But then, at church, he remembered our priest, Father Thomas, said that we shouldn't get too dark, or else we were going to burn in hell. So, when Mom showed us how to darken meat without burning the pan, Luke figured he had the perfect plan.

"I not dark like you, Landon. I seen da odda six-graders. Dey *like* you. Dey no tell you fo' shut your mouth, fo' no even try talk pidgin, Haole Boy." He bit his upper lip and flared his nostrils. Then he frowned and looked me straight in the eye. "You tink God going let me burn?"

"I dunno, I tink you wen' burn enough already, what'chu tink? You pretty crispy, ah?" Luke nodded slowly, his bottom lip long. "But you eva pull one stunt li'dat again, you no need worry about Darren Furtado, 'cause I going kill you myself." I pretended I was mad for a moment but then let a smile slip along the corners of my mouth. Luke hugged me hard before he clambered onto his bunk, glossy-Noxema back and all.

As Luke's rhythmic breaths floated down, ideas splashed hotly across my mind: albino, sin, haole, Wesson Oil, and sunburn. All mixed into a pasty purple-whiteness on my brother's back. A flight of faces blazed by with each new idea: Luke to Jason to Mom, then Toby then Afa and then Dad. After a while, I decided to just get up. I went to the kitchen to try to cool off.

I sat on a chair at the kitchen table, vinyl sticking to my skin. The drapes fluttered inward like labored breathing. I lay my head down and rested on my cheek. Zork purred softly under the table, sliding between my legs. Then he jumped onto the kitchen table and tiptoed around my face, his motor still running. When I lifted my head, Zork hopped from the table to the kitchen counter. He sauntered from one end to the other, paced in a circle, then sat. His yellow slivers sparkled in the dark. He let out a soft meow, as if calling me closer.

Zork sat facing Dad's bottle of Jack Daniel's on the counter. I ran my fingers through his fur as he stood and rubbed himself against the bottle. Without warning, he darted from the counter and flew onto the table, like he wanted me standing there alone. He curled into himself, eyes blinking back at me. I glanced at Dad's bottle of Jack Daniel's. Why not? I grabbed Dad's short glass and filled it to the lip with dark brown liquor. I held the glass up and inhaled. It was sweet and strong, singeing my nostrils like vapor from hot liquid. It was a smell I took in again, a smell I instinctively named *sin*. After a moment, for the first time, I took a sip.

A spray of heat against the back of my throat made me cough hard. But then cold replaced the heat. I felt a chill all over. Was that why Dad drank this? I took a deeper sip and clenched my teeth. This time, I held the cough in. The burn flooded down my throat, chased by a blizzard of cold air. I filled my mouth then, emptying the glass, and swallowed the fire down. I felt it burn hotter than any day outside doing yard work. I expected the cold to follow, but it didn't. Instead, the fire in my stomach grew hotter, quickly moving up my neck. When it hit my head, my stomach went numb. For a moment, I figured I must've just cooked myself too.

I looked back at the table. Zork meowed for me. To come? I washed the glass and put it back in the cabinet. The numbness clawed up my chest and, at the same time, sauntered down my legs. The heat in my head was gone. And so were the words, the ideas, the faces. They were all gone. I rested my cheek on the cool table, and I thought I felt happy in this empty place. The next thing I knew, Zork was sliding back and forth across my scalp. It was funny. I couldn't tell if he was purring or if the vibration came from inside my head. Sinking deeper, softer into the refreshing black, it all made sense. This was why Dad needed Jack Daniel's to relax. This was cooling off. And then it happened, a steady rhythm of cold waves finally came down, at last washing away each thought like an ocean of shadows crashing over me.

7

We all wished the embarrassment were over. Picture taking at school was always painful. We sweated in our Sunday best all day long and tried to keep our hair in the right place. While the photographer fiddled with the camera, we had to stay frozen, stretch the fakest smile possible, and whine *cheese*, only to have to repeat the process. And if that wasn't bad enough, if we forgot a change of clothes, tough luck. We had to suck it up until we went home.

This was how picture taking went: two months ago, the photographer came and made us pose, freeze, and then whine. We all thought it was done. But then the photographer called up Mrs. Kato and told her there was a . . . problem. Mrs. Kato was unbelievably pissed when she saw Afa Palaipale sticking middle finger above Renton Velloria's head. Renton looked like *My Favorite Martian*. Above Renton, Afa's big, shameless smile radiated under his spiky hair.

So we went back to the auditorium. We waited while the photographer counted to three. Everyone was in the picture except Afa who sat on the side and stuck middle finger again. The flash popped fast like lightning, but this time, Mrs. Kato saw.

She yanked Afa by the ear to our classroom. As she wrote a note for the office, she let him have it. "Why are you trying me, Afa? I already talked to your mother about this. The rules are on my side. You want to keep *playing*, you're going to lose every time." Afa made a sassy face as he strutted away, the note flying between his fingers. At the time, maybe Afa forgot he was Samoan. Mom said Samoan parents got so embarrassed when teachers called home that the parents would ensure proper future behavior by *reminding* kids they weren't so tough. Mrs. Kato shook her head and muttered. "We'll see what your mom thinks about that face as well."

A couple of days later, Afa finally returned to school. The first thing he did when he walked in the door was address Mrs. Kato. "Good morning, Miss. I sorry fo' being disrespeckfo." His voice was flat and practiced, and his eyes were low and defeated. He tiptoed toward his desk, his back stiff, ass tight. He couldn't even sit without wincing.

It was clear to everyone. Game over. Mrs. Kato: one. Afa: zero.

The score was tied. Dallas Cowboys: 35. Pittsburgh Steelers: 35.

Sunday after church, Dad sat on the edge of his recliner and yelled at the TV. He called the referees fat, blind, good-for-nothing zebras. "I sick and tired of da damn refs. Why da refs no let 'em play? Dey know da rules. Just piss 'em off more. Try look." Players pushed and shoved until the officials jumped in to separate them.

But the referees didn't see players from both benches fly onto the field. Black jerseys and white jerseys headed straight for each other, two colors blending in a way they weren't supposed to. The referees scattered as a full-blown fight erupted. Dad got into it and yelled at the TV again. "No back down, fricken panty!" He thrust himself into his recliner then flipped the footrest up. He looked at me and then pointed at the TV. "Look dat Cowboy panty, da one in da white. Dat big, tree hunnerd pound one. Look him backing away from da Pittsburgh guy. Same size as him. So dis-gusting. Neva back down, and neva take crap from nobody."

After everyone was asleep, I lay outside, looking at the stars. But what I realized was how loud the night was. Crickets droned in a quiet, endless purr. Insects crackled next door in the Peraltas' bug-zapper. Occasionally, moths fluttered, wings snapping crisply in the air. Then, from somewhere close, there was a cat's cry. A soft siren at first, but it stretched into a long and steady whine. The wild tone intensified, growing deeper, closer. The cry amplified into a warning, then louder still into a threat. Then there was a second cat. The howls swelled desperately high. And then, for a moment, there was silence. Suddenly, the two snarling voices exploded into one dizzying screech that wailed across the night sky.

Toby and I defined the game as the following: on our surfboards, we both had to start off at the same place in the ocean. We had to first pick out and then catch the same wave. If he didn't catch it, and I did, I scored a point, and the same for him if I didn't. If we both didn't catch the wave, there were no points either way. However, if we both caught the same wave, the contest really began. The first person to fall or bail off the board lost a point while the other scored a point.

Toby said he got the idea from his cousin Chaz who he borrowed the surfboards from. His cousin raced cars near Helemano. On Kamehameha Highway, Chaz and his friends raced downhill toward Haleiwa. They started from the same place on Kamehameha Highway and waited for a car heading uphill toward them. When they saw lights flickering in the distance, they took off. Toby said the game was called *Chicken*. The object was for the guy on the right side of the road to not allow the car on the left, the one with oncoming traffic, to get in front of him. If the guy on the right failed, he lost the race and the hundred bucks he put in. The guy on the left had to either outrace the guy on the right and zoom in front of him, or stay on the road and force the oncoming car to pull off the road. But if he chickened out and pulled off, he'd lose the race and his fifty bucks. When I asked why one guy had to risk less than the other, Toby said simply it was 'cause the guy on the left had more to lose.

Toby called our surfing game Chicken of the Sea, or COTS. He said it needed a code name 'cause his mom would kick his ass if she knew what we were doing. I hated to think what my parents would do. What was so *Chicken* about COTS? When we both caught a wave, we surfed straight toward eight-foot-high lava rocks that made up most of the shore on Pupu Street.

The first few times, I lost bad. Toby had been surfing since he was small, but I only started after I met him. He was surprised how quickly I caught on. He admitted I could take off, drop in, pump, and cut back pretty good for someone who'd just started.

Toby teased me that I was Rory Russell, always second place to him, Gerry Lopez. Toby slid along the water so easy, I imagined he really was Gerry Lopez. Fast and sleek, a master whose board barely touched the water. Race after race, we shot toward the rocks. And race after race, I always bailed first. I didn't trust myself. Plus, I didn't want to bust Chaz's Lightning Bolt surfboard. So, I was always the chicken of the sea, reeling in the board by the leash.

But I didn't care. It was on these days that I imagined flying. The sun burned the tips of the water white as we raced toward the shore. The wind sped past and pulled my skin taut, as I pressed onward. At times, it felt like I was actually rising out of the water, taking flight, if only for a few moments. And then I bailed.

Dad called to say he got four Pioneer Chicken Monday Night Specials for dinner, one for each of us. A thigh or a drumstick, plus a biscuit, mini-tub of gravy, and coleslaw. After Mom hung up, she just sat there and breathed heavily. Then she dialed Aunty Selma. "Leonard says one thing and does another. 'I'm buying dinner,' he decrees, like I should be thankful. This, after he lectured me about wasting money."

As we watched Monday Night Football, we yanked off strips of greasy meat while Dad did Howard Cosell commentary. Bits of crunchy brown skin shot out of his mouth onto his white undershirt. Mom looked at him and rolled her eyes, exhaling in disgust. By the end of the first quarter, Dad had enough crumbs on his belly to snack on until halftime.

During commercials, Dad prattled, to no one in particular. "Afta I pick up dinna, I was coming home and wen' turn off Fort Weaver onto Pāpipi Road, ah? As I driving pass Barney's, I be damn if I neva seen da worse ting fo' happen 'Ewa Beach. Get one sign fo' McDonald's Big Mac right in front Barney's." Dad noticed the crumbs and picked at them, placing them in his mouth between statements. "Damn haoles, trying fo' run us local guys outta biz-ness. Dey get so much money, dey do whateva dey like. Dey make up da rules as dey go." He popped the last of the crumbs into his mouth.

Mom waited until the game came back on before she stood and walked slowly in front of the screen. When she spoke, her voice was sassy. "I guess all's fair in love and war, huh?" Then Mom strutted away toward the kitchen. She didn't give Dad a chance to reply. It was a game they both knew how to play but each with their own rule book.

Luke made eye contact with me. "Who at war?" he whispered.

Dad watched Mom and shook his head. He exhaled darkly, then sank back into his chair.

Whenever Zork saw Luke coming, he darted away as fast as four legs could scurry. So Luke resorted to cunning. He tiptoed while Zork slept under the kitchen table. Luke thought he could surprise Zork, but Luke always bumped into something and gave himself away.

Chasing didn't work and neither did baiting. Zork was too smart for that. Luke reminded me of Wile E. Coyote from *Looney Tunes*. Luke tried chasing Zork, only to end up stubbing his toe on the end table in the living room, tripping, and crashing into the wall. The hanging crucifix bucked on the wall and then rattled back into place. It looked like Christ took a shot at Luke, kicking at my idiot brother as he crumpled to the floor in a heap. But the family picture fell, and the glass shattered. That stunt got Luke two head cracks: one for stupidity and the other for running in the house. Luke also tried putting Meow Mix cat food in his hand and sitting down in front of Zork. So mental. Zork just sat and stared at Luke with blank eyes that really said, *Do you think I'm that stupid?* When Luke chomped on the nugget to show Zork just how ono the food was, Mom cracked his head for being so damn low-class. Meow Mix nuggets flew across the floor. Mom yanked Luke to the kitchen cabinet to clean up the mess he made from scooping out the cat food in the first place. She told him while he sniffled to think about it. The damn cat already knew what the food tasted like. Zork wasn't going to risk capture for that. While Mom scolded Luke, Zork feasted on the scattered Meow Mix nuggets as though they were the spoils of some great contest. Crunching each nugget slowly, Zork savored victory and licked his chops.

Undeterred, Luke set up a big cardboard box in our room. He said he saw this on *Looney Tunes*, when Elmer Fudd put a carrot under a box with a stick to hold it up. And when Bugs Bunny went for the carrot, Elmer Fudd caught him under the box. Luke somehow forgot that getting caught was all part of Bugs Bunny's plan.

Watching Luke from my bed, I shook my head. "Luke, wen you going learn? You not going win. If da cat even tink you get somethin' up your sleeve, he going steer clear of you."

Luke frowned and made a face at me. "You watch, Landon. I going get 'em."

My poor brother. "You going about it all wrong, Luke. All you tink about is you. You gotta tink about da cat. Cats need space. From da time Zork been small, you always like touch him, pet him, hold him. You been irritating him his whole life. You gotta leave him be, so he come check you out." Luke's eyebrows furrowed. He didn't believe. "Come, try watch."

I took Luke to the living room and told him to stay by the hallway door. Then I just sat lazily on the couch. A couple minutes later, Zork flew onto my lap, his head twisting to the side for scratches and his motor running full blast. I smirked at Luke.

Luke took a deep breath and leaned against the hallway door. I stopped petting Zork and pretended to fall asleep. At last, Zork lost interest in me and eyed Luke who acted like he didn't care. Zork walked in circles around the room, slowly sauntering closer. But Luke was so desperate, he reached out and scared Zork away.

I shook my head. "Why you rush fo'? You eva tink what'chu going do once you catch him? If you tink you just going hold him, tink again. He going fight like hell fo' be free. He no trust you, Luke. I told you da rule. You gotta give him space. Wen he trust you, den he going come around all da time. You going see."

In the Foodland parking lot, Mom, Luke and I saw two old men arguing over the way one of them parked. There was a Portuguese guy and a Hawaiian guy, both about the same age. The Portuguese guy was pissed 'cause the Hawaiian guy, in his beat-up Maverick, parked too close to his shiny Lincoln Continental. The Maverick was definitely crooked, its rear end over the line. The Hawaiian guy got futless and made like he was going to ram his car door into the Lincoln's glossy paint job. Then the Portuguese guy waved his hands wildly and threatened the Hawaiian guy, that he better not swing the door if he knew what was good for him.

Mom shook her head as we crossed the driveway into Foodland. She said it was embarrassing, how those men were so ignorant they didn't even care people were watching. I looked back. The two guys were in each other's faces. Mom huffed loudly. "You know, it takes a bigger man to walk away from a fight. But I doubt *those two* ever learned that. Two grown men. It's so disgusting."

Luke laughed so hard when Tweety outsmarted Sylvester. It was always the same, Sylvester with his complex plans that never worked out. Sometimes the cat got close, even trapping Tweety beneath his paws, but Sylvester never caught Tweety for good.

Luke imitated his favorite *Looney Tunes* pair, switching from one voice to the other:

He made the nasal voice as well as the speech impediment. He pretended to bring a huge mallet down onto Sylvester's head. "Take dat, you mean ol' pooty-tat." Then Luke switched to Sylvester. He acted dizzy, rolled his eyes, and massaged the imaginary lump on top of his head. And when he spoke, it was with lots of spit, thick from the front of his mouth. "Thufferin' thuccotash!" And then he passed out, just like the foiled cat. Luke lay on the ground and enjoyed every moment of Tweety's triumph. At least he wasn't thinking like Elmer Fudd anymore.

From the family room, I watched Zork in the living room, frozen under the birdcage, his eyes glued on Rosie. This was no cartoon. Zork's tail swept slowly back and forth. Rosie fluttered in her cage when Zork's head jerked. Looking at both of them, I'd put ten bucks on Zork any day.

Some days, Mom made strange foods with dinner. She made all the usual main dishes: pork butt with stewed tomatoes, beef curry, fried noodles with Spam. But every so often, she also threw in an off-the-wall dessert. Plus, she said we had to try it at least once, or else we'd never know if we *really* didn't like it. Luke thought Mom's worst surprise dessert was what she called Ants on a Log. Seriously? Celery, peanut butter, and raisins? Luke actually threw up later that night, convinced there were stringy legs that swished around in his stomach. But to me, Mom's worst dessert was Pineapple Royale. A pineapple ring on the bottom, covered by a slice of cheddar cheese, topped with a glob of Best Foods. She said it was a delicacy. But I said it was disgusting. Mom shook her head at me. "You just don't have any culture yet, Landon."

Forced to take that jab from her—and about my open-mindedness no less—I suddenly felt very . . . wicked. "Why, dis one *Portagee* dish?"

Mom huffed, irritated, "Stop calling us *that*. How many times do I have to say it? We're Portuguese, not Portagee." Silently, I laughed to myself. Mom didn't get it. She didn't know I was calling Pineapple Royale low-class, using the word Portagee the way *she* meant it. "And, no, this isn't a Portuguese dish—" She stopped abruptly, like something had just occurred to her. She scooped another glob of white mayonnaise onto perspiring cheese. "Actually, I don't know for sure. It might be. My mother taught me how to make this when I—" She stopped once again and glanced sharply at me. The few times Mom started to talk about her deceased mother, my grandmother, she always stopped herself.

"Wen what, Mom?" All traces of my wickedness were gone. I really wanted to know.

Silence. Mom's jaw flexed as she considered. But she just glanced at me then slapped more mayo onto sweaty cheese. She wasn't about to say more. Clearly, she had said enough.

So unfair.

Luke was so white it was disgusting. Ever since he told me about not fitting in at school, I mentally compared us. His hair and eyes were a lighter brown. His voice was squeaky-thin, and his eyelashes were longer. Definitely lighter-skinned than me. I never really noticed before.

Luke wanted to stay home and play with Lego instead of sneaking away with me in the afternoon. He was really into his new project. With his spaceship blasted into bits, he snapped pieces into place as he erected his Lego house. Three layers of multi-colored blocks already made up the outside walls. So Filipino, I told Luke. "Who you going sell dat to, da Peraltas next door? Dey already get one house and just like yours. Da buggah all red and yellow and their fence green." I laughed and kept folding clothes on my bed. Luke stuck his tongue at me. So I ribbed him again. "Ho, easy wit' da colors. Who like live in one book-book house li'dat?"

Luke ignored me and grabbed our Han Solo and Princess Leia action figures. He told me that *they* wanted to live in his house. Ever since we saw *The Empire Strikes Back*, I had to remind Luke that he needed to get the love-triangle straight. He liked to pretend that Luke Skywalker and Princess Leia had something going on, but I reminded him that she told Han Solo she loved him. Luke had a hard time arguing with that. He told me that one day, Han Solo and Princess Leia would be really happy in his house. Maybe he had finally accepted it.

There were no inside walls yet, only a bit of furniture, some of the appliances, and one lonely bed. There wasn't even a front door to the place. I didn't have the heart to tell Luke that if Han Solo and Princess Leia lived in that house, they weren't going to be too happy. Princesses liked to live in castles, not houses.

Han Solo and Princess Leia walked around the house and talked in Luke's voice:

"Isn't dis house beu-ti-full, hunny?" Han Solo said, all lovey-dovey.

"It's perfeck, dear," Princess Leia replied sweetly.

"Isn't it great dat we get tree open rooms?"

"Why is dat, dear?"

"'Cause wheneva we fight, get one room fo' go to. Wit' tree rooms, I no need leave fo' cool off. Can stay right here." Han Solo hugged Princess Leia.

"Dat's right, dear, now I no need worry about you driving. And I no need block you so you no leave da house. Going be so nice." Princess Leia sighed in appreciation.

Two action figures strolled through an empty house, saying nothing, yet their words were loaded with meaning. I watched Luke, how he was completely lost in what he was doing. I wondered just how much he understood. And for a moment, I felt so sad I almost cried.

Zork sauntered into our room and sat down next to Luke. His tail swept back and forth at the tip, as he watched Luke's hands on the action figures. At first, Luke didn't even notice Zork. Zork perked at Luke's voice and cocked his head as though listening.

"You no play fair, Leia. You gotta play by da rules," Han Solo said. "We no need fo' talk about ev'ryting. I just like get away. But you always trap me. I need space . . . "

Luke finally noticed Zork next to him. Zork let out a long, soft meow. Neither of them moved. They just sat there, looking at each other. Suddenly, Luke shot out his hand to try to grab Zork. But the cat was too fast. Zork leapt across the Lego house, feet barely touching plastic. Zork scurried for freedom while Han Solo and Princess Leia were knocked about, landing in different parts of their house. All Luke could do was watch.

When Mrs. Kato told the class that we were playing flag football in P.E. today, the boys went nuts. The first order of business was to determine the red team captain and the blue team captain. Whispers went around the room while we were supposed to be doing math work, and it was settled. It was no surprise. Afa Palaipale and I were captains. So we jan-ken-poed at lunch time to see who chose first. Afa won and chose Renton Velloria. Red with him. I chose Toby Ka'ea. Blue with me. Preston Pascua, Erwin Bolosan, and Freddy Campos, all red. Jared Matsumoto, Garrick Yee, and Manford Castillo, all blue. But then, it always came down to two: Boris Puinip and Jason Jones. A small Filipino boy or the haole boy.

Boris had a rice bowl haircut and wore a huge wooden cross that hung from twine around his neck. He always wore long black pants and a thin, long-sleeved, white shirt. Boris could run like hell, but since he was so small, he couldn't hold onto the ball to save his life.

Jason had blond hair and blue eyes. He talked with a funny accent and said he came from Mississippi. He was actually pretty good at baseball, football, and basketball. But he hardly talked anymore. When he first came to 'Ewa Beach Elementary School, he told us about the places he had been, about all the friends he had on the mainland, and about all the toys he had. Pretty soon, no one liked him 'cause it sounded like he was bragging. Everyone stopped talking *to* him and started talking *about* him. He was so stuck-up. He only wanted to make us look stupid. Damn haole, he thought he was better than us. And at the same time, Jason stopped talking to us too, sensing without really understanding what had happened around him.

With flag football, though, it never failed to come down to two: Boris, red. Jason, blue.

Almost everyone went barefoot when we played flag football. Before we started, as if adhering to an unspoken rule, we took off our shoes and slippers and left them in a pile on the basketball courts. We all knew that bare feet would dig into the dry dirt the best. Then we used some slippers from the pile to indicate the two end zones and the sidelines in the dusty field.

The rules: each team only got four downs to score before the ball changed possession. The defense had to count *three Mississippi*'s before they rushed. The defense only had to pull one flag to get a player down. And every touchdown was worth seven points.

Dust clouds swirled with heat from the dirt-packed ground, like steam from a frying pan. The sun burned down, and even before we started, faces were already streaked with sweat and speckled with mud. Everyone was jittery, eager to start as the pressure mounted. Mrs. Kato flipped a coin to see who received first. It came up heads: Afa won.

The game was a blur of red and blue, of dust and heat, of offense and defense. Actually, very little defense. Afa's team scored right away. Then my team scored. They scored again, and then we did. Back and forth we ran, fighting, scrapping on every down. Suddenly, Mrs. Kato blew the whistle, 'cause school was almost over. But the game was tied: 35-35. Mrs. Kato told us to pack the flags and the ball into the P.E. equipment bag. She strolled toward the storage room, umbrella shading her from the sun.

We all knew a football game couldn't end in a tie. It wasn't right. Then, as if we were waiting for the justice of it, someone yelled, "Last point wins!" And since the rule had been spoken, it became official. Afa's team had the ball, and they had scored on every possession. What we needed was defense. So I changed positions with Toby and told him to cover Renton Velloria for the pass. I took the line to rush the quarterback. Someone had to stop Afa.

Down, he looked left. Set, looked right.

Hike! *One Mississippi!*

Red scrambled onto our side, blue covering.

Two Mississippi!

Afa was still looking. Everybody must be covered.

Three Mississippi!

I rushed Afa and lunged for his red flag. He saw me coming, pulled back, and let the ball fly. But instead of reaching for his flag, I jumped, and as the football left Afa's hand, I clipped it. It egg-wobbled in slow motion, as it fell through the rising dust. Everyone was frozen, eyes glued to the dropping ball. Except Jason. The heat stopped, the sweat stopped, the dust stopped, even the ball looked like it was suspended above the ground. And, in full stride, like a lightning bolt, Jason scooped the ball just before it hit the dirt and sped across the goal line in a blur.

Touchdown. Last point won. 42-35.

My team jumped and cheered, high-fiving with sweaty hands. We congratulated Jason. *That was unreal! Awesome catch! You saved the day!* The moment swirled around Jason, faster and faster, and even though my feet burned, the ocean of blue I was caught in felt good.

But then Afa broke in. "You fucking cheating haole!" At once, everything stopped. Afa's voice still hung, ringing red in the air. He pointed at Jason. "Da ball touch da ground, so incomplete, not touchdown. Fucking haole cheata, like make me look bad, ah?" Afa was already swelling in size, sucking deep breaths and puffing himself up. Jason backed away, not wanting to get caught in this. "C'mon, stinking cheata. We go beef." Afa pushed Jason and the boys circled up, trapping them in. That was when I started to feel it.

On a day so hot it caused blisters, I felt the icy sweat of something I couldn't name if I wanted to. But it certainly grew as Afa pushed Jason again. I could hear my father's voice, telling me not to back down and to never take crap from anybody. I didn't even hear the others chanting anymore, only their lips moving in silence: *beef, beef, beef.* Afa pushed Jason hard so that he fell in the dirt. The cold sank deeper and deeper, hitting bottom somewhere then shooting up. I rationalized what I saw and tried to convince myself to stay out of it. I had more to lose. But Afa's body flexed over Jason, his fists clenched, his mouth twisting around the only two words that were fair to him: *fight me.* Something within me broke as Afa wound up to kick Jason who was helpless on the ground. I felt an ice-cold rush that made me act.

Before I realized what I had done, I found myself rolling around with Afa in the dirt. Football, Afa, Jason, red, blue. It was all a blur.

Then Afa was yelling at me. Why?

"You like beef instead, Landon? C'mon throw, I waiting. C'mon!" He was screaming, like a wounded animal. Things were speeding up.

Why was Afa yelling? And then it came to me. I tackled him, that was why.

Afa puffed out his chest, inches away from mine. "What, Landon? You one panty too? C'mon, we go beef!"

Had I actually tackled him? And then it clicked: I stopped him from kicking Jason. I turned back to Afa. He saw something that made him back up, but he continued to rant. I held my stare, just waiting for him to do something. He called me every name in the book 'cause I wouldn't take a swing. There were so many things I wanted to do, so many ways I wanted to hurt him. What kind of person would kick someone on the ground? My chest heaved and my teeth ground, as I imagined spiking him into the dirt like a football. Like what he just did to Jason. I felt it all boiling within me: I wanted to be *disgusting.*

Suddenly, the icy cold dissipated. And all that was left were Mom's words, telling me it took a bigger man to walk away from a fight.

Then everything stopped. I took a deep breath. "I going back class," I finally said. My feet backed away before I even knew what I was doing. Afa *bawk-bawked* like I was the one scared, and the other boys shook their heads at me. Everybody was going to talk, like Afa already was. Word would spread, and I knew I was about to be named the sixth grade chicken.

At this point, I didn't even remember why I stopped Afa from hurting Jason in the first place or why I held back from cranking him after. If someone came at you, weren't you supposed to stand your ground? We were supposed to never back down and never take crap from anybody. But we weren't supposed to fight either. That was how it worked.

Funny, I didn't feel like the bigger man. In fact, I felt smaller. I glanced over my shoulder. I felt smaller than Boris Puinip over there, laughing at me, the newborn chicken. I turned toward the classroom and melted under the laughter. And as I walked away, I didn't get it. I didn't back down and didn't fight, but I felt disgusting anyway.

8

The fights were getting louder. Pupu Street was usually quiet, but at night, between swells of ocean waves smashing against rocks, Mom and Dad's voices rose and fell like explosions. From where they were, they didn't hear the cleansing symphony of the tide. They didn't hear how soft the breeze was that floated in through the kitchen window. They didn't hear crickets singing to each other in voices that gently rippled and washed.

They didn't hear anything. But I did. I heard it all from our darkened bedroom.

Dead bolts slid, hooks-and-eyes jiggled, and door handles unlocked. Front doors creaked open. The Higas and Peraltas on either side of us. The Fishers, Chings, and Gomeses across the street. I looked outside at the silhouettes glaring from their doorways. I watched figures quietly cross the street to talk about us. Porch lights were eclipsed, as our neighbors' shadows whispered among the breeze. I listened to their not-so-silent protest. How inconsiderate we were, how ignorant. We should know better. Didn't we know to keep it down after it got dark?

Our neighbors' words kept me up at night, long after everything was over. Hiding in my room, I tried to escape what our neighbors thought of us. But it didn't matter. Even if I'd turned out the lights and kept as still as possible, their whispers were still there, as trustworthy as shadows, and they felt like only one thing: shame.

"Animals have no shame. Especially male animals," Mom said, as she looked from the kitchen. Zork pawed at the screen door with eager eyes. For the last twenty minutes, a painful, hot cry had stretched over Pupu Street. Another cat, somewhere not too far, had its siren on full blast. Mom held the receiver next to her ear, pinched between her shoulder and neck. "Can you hear it? Yes, it's another *wonderful* aspect of living in 'Ewa Beach. One of the neighbors' cats must be in heat. Ours is at the door right now, itching to go outside. I know, Selma. God knows I know." Mom laughed thinly. She glanced at me, but then immediately looked away. "I know it's natural, but these animals should be fixed. Then there wouldn't be any more problems."

And with that, the screen door hissed shut. I only glimpsed Zork's body streaking away.

Just like when it was time to help Mom with her rose bushes, I made myself as scarce as possible when she headed to the bathroom. Even there, she'd find something for me to do. And I'd have to do it right then. Like go in there when she was taking a crap to empty the trash can or to grab her a new roll of toilet paper or to take her clothes and throw them in the washer. So disgusting, but I stopped asking why it had to be right then. If I did ask, when she came out of the toilet, she made me select a chili pepper from the bush outside and then squished it on my lips, forcing me to swallow it for being so disrespectful. Did I really think my shit didn't stink?

But the worst, the absolutely rock-bottom of gross was when she told me to take her wadded-up-in-toilet-paper tampon from the bathroom to the kitchen rubbish. So shame. She said she didn't want to leave it in the bathroom trash bin. Instead of asking why she didn't just take it to the kitchen herself when she was done, when I'd see her head to the toilet, I suddenly became the model subordinate. I'd find something to do, even head to the corner of the lot to pluck those damn ti leaves from the aloe plant I kept forgetting about. Then, I played deaf.

Unfortunately, Luke hadn't learned to make himself scarce when Mom headed to the bathroom. In our room, he somberly confided in me. "I tink somethin' wrong wit' Mom. In da batroom, she wen' call me and tell me fo' take dis . . . *ting* to da kitchen. Was all wrap up in toilet paper. So I neva tink nothin'. I just thought was rubbish.

"But on da way to da kitchen, da buggah was getting all warm through da toilet paper. So above da trash can, I wen' open 'em up and look inside. Ho, at first, I almost wen' throw up right there. All bloody and juicy, get meat and strings all ova. And da smell, was so hauna. Was so stale like da time I wen' keep da gecko fo' couple months and da buggah started fo' rot, you rememba? But den, my eyes got stuck on 'em, like I no could stop looking. And after, start looking cool, like my toe, da time I wen' stub 'em on da sidewalk. Was all hanging and pink underneath. But den, I thought about Mom. I rememba dis blood came from her. And den I came scared." There was a long pause. His eyes were teary. "Is she going die?"

My face was puckered, as though I had sucked on something sour. "Luke, you not suppose to open 'em up. Just take 'em and throw 'em away."

Luke's expression was pained. "But how come she bleeding, Landon?"

I considered how to answer this. I breathed deeply. "'Cause she get her rags. Ev'ry girl going get 'em wen dey old enough. And afta dat, going happen ev'ry month. Dat's da start of how babies is made. I was all gross-out when Mrs. Kato wen' show us the *Miracle of Life* film last quarter."

"But if somebody lose too much blood, dey die, Landon. Dat's what dey taught us wen we wen' fire station fo' field trip. You sure she not dying, Landon?"

"I know sound like no fit da rules, but I not lying, Luke. Mom not going die. I promise." From the look on his face, I could tell Luke still didn't believe so I offered a suggestion. "Before you get all bent out of shape, wait one month. Mom going stop asking you fo' take dat crap to da kitchen, but den, out of nowhere, she going call you fo' do 'em again. So, no worry, okay? I *promise* she going call."

Our Lady of Perpetual Help echoed with Father Thomas's words: "It's a sin, a cardinal sin, mind you, to engage in fornication before marriage. And it goes without saying that it is also a sin while married. Marriage is the union that God has set up to yoke two unlike parts together. For man and woman to finally unite in harmony under God's holy law. In today's scriptures, Samson was weak when it came to women. To think that one of God's strongest warriors succumbed to his lust is almost unfathomable. He was not able to control himself and, therefore, failed as a leader to the Israelites. Who did he hurt? Himself, yes. But also his people. And because of a woman? No, because of his lust. Samson forgot he had the responsibility to lead by example. And because of his lack of foresight, Samson not only brought about his own downfall, but scattered the Israelites like seeds across the earth.

"And how about David? One of God's greatest kings. Even he was not free from this temptation. His premarital affair was like a disease, eating away at his endeavors. Remember, a lustful heart leads to impetuous actions, compelling an otherwise obedient servant to make rash decisions. David thought he'd right a wrong by marrying Bathsheba after his premarital weakness. The problem was that he already committed the crime and so was infected with the *disease*. It didn't matter if David married her after the fact. His sin already corrupted his moral and spiritual fiber. David was reduced to shambles as a leader and destroyed not only his family but the nation of Israel as well. And to think that it all started from one flicker of temptation.

"You see, once the choice is made, we can never go back. Are you Samson? Or worse yet David? Look within and be honest as to who is looking back at you. And if it's Samson or David in your reflection, you may be asking if there is any hope. Two words: Jesus Christ. Christ died for us all, and He's your way back to God. In Samson and David's days, while burnt offerings and sacrifices begot forgiveness, there still were consequences. Prices needed to be paid. Christ paid the ultimate price so that we wouldn't have to, so that we might live.

"Look inside, everyone. Look deep. Do you see it? The decay that is waiting to be healed? Christ wants to help you get rid of that. Let us pray."

Father Thomas sat down to meditate. The congregation quietly waited except for some ladies who fanned themselves with the missal. For the first time, I noticed my family sat in a different configuration than normal. Mom usually bent over backward to make sure she sat next to Dad, then me, then Luke. But today, Mom was on one end of the pew and Dad was on the other. Luke and I were between them: me next to Dad, Luke next to Mom.

And for the first time, I felt it, like the delay of an ant bite. The prick of something close, something hot, something that was there all throughout church. It pulled my eyes toward Dad's face. And for the second time in my life, I saw it, Dad's furious stare upon me. Tucked tight in a side-eye, his look screamed words only he could hear. His face was taut and his teeth ground away enamel, crunching thoughts only he could swallow.

Luke and I downed Fruit Loops while watching *Looney Tunes*. When Tweety dropped an anvil on Sylvester's head, Luke laughed so hard he snorted milk into his nose and launched cereal back into his bowl. He was lucky Mom didn't see that. I shook my head. Sylvester stumbled while stars circled in front of his eyes, a lump already growing between his ears. "Thufferin' thuccotash." The dizzy cat's expected coda brought another round of laughter from Luke.

After Sylvester and Tweety, it was Bugs Bunny and the Tazmanian Devil's turn. Luke thought it was great how Bugs Bunny tricked Taz when he dressed up like a girl Tazmanian Devil. Bugs Bunny had the whole ensemble: the skirt, the high heels, the lipstick. Bugs Bunny even spun around fast, snorting and grunting just like Taz.

After he slurped down his milk, Luke got up and whirled around the family room. I warned him to knock it off, that he just drank milk, that he might throw up. But Luke wouldn't listen, just kept spinning around and around. By the way Luke wobbled, the room must have started to blur. And sure enough, he tripped, stumbled, and crashed to the family room floor. Where did this come from? Lying on his back, Luke wore a stupid grin on his face, like he had gotten away with something. "Landon, I tink I seeing stars."

Later, Mom took us to Foodland to pick up groceries for dinner. When we approached the checkout line, Luke stopped at the magazine rack to peek at some of the naughty ones like *Hustler* and *Playboy*. Mom saw him and smacked his hands away from the plastic partition.

Mom eyed Luke, and when she spoke, her voice was solemn. "Watch out, or else, if you keep looking at *those* magazines, you're going to get Star Eye."

Luke glanced at the magazine rack again as he rubbed his hand. "What's Star Eye?"

Mom waited a moment, a slight grin on her face. "Star Eye is what happens when little boys see something they're not supposed to."

When Mom was paying, she told me to find Luke 'cause we were ready to go. I didn't need to go very far. He was at the magazine rack, gazing at the cover of *Penthouse*. The cover girl was in a skimpy Dallas Cowboy cheerleader outfit, complete with blue and silver tassels, two six-shooters, white boots, and only two blue stars covering the tips of her chichis. Luke gazed and breathed through his gaping mouth as though trying to swallow her with every breath.

I told Luke to put the magazine back on the rack 'cause Mom said we were ready to go. But he ignored me and kept consuming every inch of her. So with one hand, I yanked the magazine, and with the other, I pushed Luke away. I put the *Penthouse* back where it belonged.

As we walked, Luke adjusted himself down there. "What'chu did dat fo'?"

Gripping his arm tightly, I pulled Luke toward the entrance where Mom waited for us. "'Cause you getting Star Eye, hard head."

Luke glanced down at himself and then frowned. "I no more Star Eye," he whined.

We were almost to where Mom was standing. "You like bet you getting Star Eye?" I asked, as I pointed at his crotch. "You seeing stars *and* you growing one lump just like Sylvester." Luke looked at himself again, and then at me.

When we got to the entrance, Mom sighed impatiently. She looked at Luke and then addressed me. "Where was he?"

But before I could answer, Luke broke in excitedly. "Mom, try look Landon's pants! We get two Star Eye now!"

I turned on Luke, horrified. "*Shut* up!"

For a moment, Mom just stood there, staring blankly at us. "Oh, my God," she said, mortified, then stormed off toward the car.

When Dad saw Zork outside the screen door, he pointed in disbelief. Something flashed over his eyes, and as the words for it slithered across his lips, he mouthed his thought silently. Dad beelined for the screen door. Before Zork could slide into the house, Dad seized him by the scruff of the neck and held him high above the ground.

Dad sneered as he held Zork's taut eyes up to his. "Fucking, dumbass cat. You sticking your dick somewhere you not suppose to. You making more problems dan you worth. But instead of beating you, I going do you one favor. I going save you from yourself." Dad took Zork to the bathroom, flung him in, and slammed the door shut.

Dad yelled for me to get his toolbox. When I returned, he was at the front door muttering. "Damn cat, so fricken stupid. Just no can fight da urge. No shame, ah?" With his drill, Dad made a tiny hole in the metal of the screen door as well as in the wood of the door frame. He selected a screwdriver.

"What'chu doing, Dad?" I asked.

"Putting one hook-and-eye on dis damn door. Dis going end right now." He manually twisted the hook into place on the screen door. Then he slipped the screwdriver into the eye and turned until the metal loop was snug in the wood. Then he tested it. "See, da male part go in da female part, and just li'dat, pau, she catch. Problem solved."

Later that night, Zork sat by the front door and pawed at the screen, looking out at the street. He meowed softly as though calling to the warm 'Ewa Beach night. The chirping of crickets, the crash of waves, and the rustling of leaves came back, seeping through the screen like lonely whispers from a restless lover. Zork stared at me with heavy, furious eyes, and at once I knew the problem was not solved. I'd seen that look recently, coming more and more from Dad. And that was when it hit me. Zork wasn't ashamed, he wanted out . . . just like Dad.

9

As much as I didn't want to believe it, there were some things we just couldn't stop. Mom said we couldn't stop the sun from rising, so why fight it? She always had some saying when she wanted us to do something. When Luke and I pretended we had deaf ear: *I've got the hammer and the nails*. Even after threats, if we still hadn't moved, she said like Dirty Harry: *Go ahead, make my day*. But the worst, when Mom was sick and tired of talking to us: *Wait until your father gets home*. I pulled Luke outside, even if he was playing with Lego. I pulled him outside, not 'cause of the lickens, but 'cause of what Mom's complaints to Dad might start.

The things I wished I could stop:

The grass from growing. This included not only grass, but all plants, all leaves, and all weeds. No more hot afternoons outside mowing, raking, or weeding. No sunburns, no mud, no stains to get out. Mom said the grass was always greener on the other side. I looked at our yard, then at our neighbors'. Their yards were as burnt as ours.

Getting sick, or anything that made me have to stay home. Ukus, stomach flu, ear infection, pink eye. No more sweating in bed or medicine that made me want to vomit even worse. Mom said that cough syrup was for my own good. So I slurped it down, feeling it ooze into my stomach and then spread out. And I still felt like throwing up.

The fighting and the spanking. Mom and Dad yelling about money, about the rules, about the house. Mom and Dad hitting me. Mom and Dad hitting Luke, even if he sometimes deserved it. No more shame, no more Jack Daniel's, no more crying. Mom said we should never go to bed angry. Recently, I hardly slept at all. There'd be no more spacing out or listening to our neighbors outside my window.

I wished I could stop the words. The voices were loud and clear: Chicken. Panty. Never take crap from nobody. All's fair in love and war. It takes a bigger man. I wanted to stop the words that kept me up all night.

Words that had become a part of me. Words that everyone saw, like dirty laundry with stains so deep no amount of Tide could get it clean. Mom said that sticks and stones may break my bones, but words would never hurt me.

Sorry, but you were wrong, Mom. Words got into my head and then multiplied. They seared through the night. They ricocheted and at the same time infected. They echoed through every part of me. Words made me think of flying like never before.

But Mom also said to be careful what you wished for 'cause it might come true.

Watching Luke gave me something to do at night. His body stretched across the sheets, eyes shut, chest rising and falling in perfect rhythm. I wondered what it was like to be in his head. What it sounded like, if it was quiet. I wondered if he dreamed, with who and where he drifted off to so peacefully. I wondered when he was going to realize his clothes were getting small on him, that his bed was getting smaller too. His calm body sprawled out in different directions, his arms and legs like tentacles, and he covered more of the bed than ever before. I wondered sadly if Luke knew how bad it would feel when he did realize, when he understood everything that went on around him.

Zork knew he wasn't getting out. Lately, instead of just sitting in front of the screen door, lightly pawing at the air, he locked his claws onto the screen and pulled. Back and forth, on his hind legs, his body jerked, yanking as though to save his life. He let go and slumped down, his claws sliding back into skin. After a moment, Zork approached the door and rubbed against it. Then he snuggled his head into the corner of the door frame and pushed against the screen. The hook-and-eye jiggled but held tight. He pushed for a few seconds before he stood on his hind legs and grabbed onto the screen again. Zork was yanking violently by the time I lifted him off the screen. I cradled him as he looked up at me. He let out a sound so sad that it wasn't a meow at all. It was more like a word, a moan from somewhere deep within his body.

I sat down in front of the screen with Zork on my lap and scratched behind his ears until he purred. "I sorry, Zork. I wen' help Dad put dis on." He looked outside at the still sky. "I know how you feel, all cage-up, no can go hang out wit' your friends." Zork feverishly watched some birds fly by. "But please no hang out by da door. And no yank on 'em if Dad home. Bum-bye he going give you *hell* fo' real." Zork looked up at the word. Eye to eye, we stared at each other. Like a flicker, he saw it in me and I in him. He meowed softly then started rubbing his head up and down my hand. I swear, this cat understood.

After hearing about me and Afa, Mrs. Ka'ea had Toby invite me for dinner. She had him ask me while we were at school. Somehow, she got our phone number, called Mom, and cleared everything so that I could go over right after I walked Luke home from school. First, there were cookies and milk on the table. And after, if we wanted, we could surf or watch TV for an hour while she got dinner ready. With every bite of chocolate and every swig of milk, I thought how nice it must feel to be Toby. To have this waiting for him when he came home every day. To live with the ocean right outside his window, where he saw and not just heard it. To come home to rich and creamy treats instead of chores. To be so lucky and not even realize it. Every day.

When we came back from surfing, we washed up for dinner. At the table, Mrs. Ka'ea talked to me as she set down dishes. "You're a good boy, Landon. I invited you over 'cause I wanted to thank you." I felt strange inside, scared and cold in the pit of my stomach. Hearing her say thank you was like getting tumbled underwater and not knowing which way was up. "Toby told me what you did for Jason, the cute, little, haole boy in your class. Children can be so mean to each other, acting out everything they see." I felt the cold welling inside. I wanted it to stop. The words were rising. "I try to teach Toby not to be just a mindless follower, satisfied with being like everybody else." She scooped macaroni salad, rice, and barbecue meat onto our plates. But now, my appetite was gone. I wanted her to just please stop. "By helping Jason, you taught Toby a very important lesson. Right, Toby?" He nodded, chewing on meat. I hadn't even touched my plate. Mrs. Ka'ea smiled and patted my head with her hand. It was a cool, soft pillow. "Thank you, Landon, for being such a good friend to my son. Now, eat up."

After that, I didn't feel like eating 'cause I knew what Mrs. Ka'ea was really saying. She wanted Toby to be more like me. And with that thought came an icy realization. If Toby had tried to help me with Afa, Toby might have become Afa's target. I'd never expect that of Toby. I was as big as Afa. Toby was much smaller. Besides, it was *my* fight. Not Toby's.

Suddenly, I wanted to tell Mrs. Ka'ea everything. About the words, the name-calling, the chicken noises. How they were clinging *to* me and *within* me, eating me from the inside out. I wanted to tell her that every day, Afa talked shit about me, claiming that I was too afraid to fight him. I wanted to explain how whenever I raised my hand to answer a question, I had to listen to clucking noises from Afa's side of the room and everyone giggling at me. Did she really want Toby to be in that position or to have only slept eight hours in the last three days? I didn't.

The more I thought about it, though, the more I wanted to rest my words . . . somewhere. I *wanted* to let them out. Not just for Toby, but for me as well.

But not yet, not now. Instead, I slowly swallowed it all down with food. Every ounce of shame, every word with every bite, thinner and thinner, until there was only a plate, scraps of chewed gristle, and thoughts of just how lucky Toby was.

My first thought was: no fucking way. On my bed was the flashlight Toby and I lost in the storm drain a couple months ago. I recognized it immediately. I glanced around the room with one thought: Luke. He was asleep and he looked all right. Everything seemed to slow as tingles from the back of my head fell like icy ocean waves down my spine. Questions branched out and infected every thought: who, what, when, how? It wasn't Luke. He wasn't with me and Toby when we dropped the flashlight in the storm drain. No one saw us except . . . and then, two words echoed, like whispers that splintered across my mind. *Help me.* Was it the man whose voice we heard? It couldn't be. I looked about the room as I tried to deny it. How did he get in here? Was Luke asleep when he came in? Another wave of realization hit. I started this. My breathing became short. I went to the living room and sat down on the sofa. This was my fault.

I felt heavy. Like sinking. I knew I shouldn't have gone into the storm drain.

I was falling fast. Falling hard. I needed to guard the front door.

What did I do?

Suddenly, I stood up. I glanced about, realizing I must have passed out. Then I remembered why. I hurried to our bedroom, not sure if I was hoping the flashlight was still there. I didn't know what would be worse. But when I looked around the corner, I knew the answer. Shit. How the hell could a flashlight get up and walk off my bed?

Luke's chest rose and fell in complete rhythm. I felt a little better for that. Then I tore around the room, looking for any sign, any clue left by whoever or whatever was in our room. In the closet, nothing. On the window sills, nothing. Under my bunk, nothing, only Luke's Lego house, his *Star Wars* figures, and torn pages from his composition notebook. I examined my bed sheet. Nothing. Not even the wet, stink, rotten smell of the storm drain.

I already knew that whoever put the flashlight on my bed was the same person that whispered in the storm drain. I knew he had been in our room while my brother slept. That was the worst, as I thought of *him* so close to my brother. It wasn't fair. I started this, Luke didn't.

I felt myself go hard inside. I had to tell Toby. We had to go back there.

I stared out at the yellow spill of streetlight. Palm tree branches danced in the wind as shadows slipped in and out of everything, playing tricks on me. With teeth clenched, I whispered through the screen, "I may be one chicken, but you not going mess wit' my liddle brudda. I can stay up all night, so no even try sneak in here no more. Leave us da fuck alone."

Our science teacher Ms. Shimizu left us hovering above our own petri dishes. We did an experiment on how fast mold can multiply. Before we started, she showed us slides on how once a germ got into something, it grew and grew until whatever it ate ran out of material for the germ to consume. Mrs. Kato grossed out in the back of the room. She didn't want anything to do with the experiment. She said it was *bachi*, like asking for bad luck. Through the plastic cover, the black stain grew outward on a piece of bread, chomping away at every flake of white.

At home, Luke showed me a magnifying glass he stole from Ms. Shimizu's class a couple of weeks ago. He said Ms. Shimizu took his class behind the third grade wing to look for insects. She gave each student a magnifying glass, told them to find an insect, and then to draw it. Luke said the magnifying glass made things so clear that he couldn't resist taking it.

"What'chu mean, you no could resist? You one klepto, or what, Luke? You betta give 'em back bum-bye you get Ms. Shimizu in trouble." He looked at me through the magnifying glass. "Besides, you start stealing, you going turn rotten and wind up in jail." Luke squinted, then blinked his distorted eye behind the lens, a swollen black pupil in the middle of white jelly.

Warm brown liquid splashed as Dad plopped two ice cubes into his glass. Dad did this almost every day now. Before, he took the glass to his workroom or to the family room to watch TV. But now, he sat out back in the lawn chair and faced the backyard. No one talked to him until after he had his Jack Daniel's, or else we were going to hear it. "What, boy? I no can relax two minutes before I gotta do somethin'? Frick, you sucking me up, brah."

After Dad went outside, I marked his bottle of Jack Daniel's with a red ballpoint, hiding the ink on the black of the label. It was my own little experiment to gauge how much Dad drank. I needed to estimate how much could be missed. And so far, he hadn't caught me.

Dad didn't play with his ham radio or radio-controlled cars anymore either. He was so tired that when he came home, he just burned out with Jack Daniel's and sometimes numbed himself to sleep with just a few glasses. On the phone, Mom told Aunty Selma that it was so typical of men. They got some crazy idea under their skin and obsessed over it, like a precious ham radio. But when they finally got it, they lost interest. And then whatever it was that they just *had* to have would lie rotting on the side. What a waste.

Mom told Luke the Portuguese sweet bread better not go to waste. A few days ago, when Mrs. Shelley called to remind Luke to bring in the money for his fundraiser tickets, Mom almost blew a gasket. For one thing, she had no clue Luke committed to sell ten tickets. Seriously, when did Luke think he was going door-to-door? Second, Mom hated *pão doce.* Bloated yellow bread baked in a pie tin? Sweaty and puffy like a pregnant woman? No, sir-ee, she said. Only good, old-fashioned white bread for her. And, third, if Luke didn't turn in the money, Mom would look bad in front of Mrs. Shelley. And that was not going to happen. Therefore, since Luke was foolish enough to volunteer in the first place, Mom said *he* had to eat all the sweet bread before it went bad. All ten tins. No cereal for breakfast, just sweet bread. No rice or potatoes for dinner, just sweet bread. And if he wanted a snack after school? Yep, sweet bread.

By day three, Luke was tired of the fluffy goodness. From the get-go, I *helped* by doubling what he ate. Mom never said I couldn't, and I loved *pão doce*. But together, we had only eaten five of the tins. The remaining discs of sweet bread rested on the kitchen table, still wrapped in plastic and twist-tied.

At breakfast, Luke just sat and stared tiredly at the loaves as though they were mocking him. "Why Mom had fo' buy all of 'em?"

I opened a loaf and ripped off a piece of sweet bread. I put it on a plate and set it before Luke. "'Cause, Mom neva like look like one brownie to your teacha." I glanced sharply at my brother, realizing what I said. But it was too late to take it back.

For a moment, Luke considered and then moaned wistfully. "Ooh, brownies. How come we no could sell brownies? Sound good, ah?"

I looked at Luke for a moment, while I suppressed a laugh. Then I nodded as solemnly as I could, trying to mask my relief with empathy. It wasn't too hard, though. Chocolatey treats were a lot better than what I said. I ripped off a piece of sweet bread and sighed heavily.

Toby and I sat next to each other in Sunday School and scribbled notes so that our teacher Mrs. Kepple didn't see. Mrs. Kepple was this fat, old, local lady who had a haole last name. Dad said sarcastically that she was just like him, another Portagee who married haole. When I asked how he knew Mrs. Kepple was Portuguese, Dad snickered that the size of her ass gave her away, just look at all my Portagee Aunties. He also bet me that, in thirty years, Mom would look like Humpty Dumpty, too. But then he said, joking aside, for as long as he had gone to Our Lady of Perpetual Help, Mrs. Kepple was just a typical, bubbly, Portagee lady, not like Mom and Aunty Selma who both had the personality of a whoopee cushion. When Dad finally stopped laughing, he said Mrs. Kepple was happy, just kind of . . . mental. And I could see that. When she talked, she really got into her Bible stories, gesturing with her hands a lot. Today, she was busy talking about Adam and Eve: "People only talk about how Eve brought about the downfall of man. They talk about *her* responsibility, like it was only *her* fault."

Our faces were bright, listening. Toby and I just kept writing on the sly.

Me: *You neva guess what happen.*

Mrs. Kepple got really excited. "Adam had a brain. Did Eve shove the fruit in his face? Did she hold a gun to his head and force-feed it down his throat?"

Several kids winced. Was Mrs. Kepple talking about a gun?

Toby: *What?*

"If he ate the fruit, it's his fault too, yeah? But that's not how the story goes, so women get a bad rap. How fair is that?"

Eyebrows furrowed as expressions soured.

Me: *You rememba da flashlight we loss in da storm drain?*

"Okay, try wait. I wen' lose my train of thought. Try wait. Okay, Adam and Eve. Eve was his wife, ah?"

Faces cringed. Mouths open, dull stares.

Toby: *Yeah, my mom still salty I loss 'em.*

"And she came from Adam, from his rib. So, she was a part of him, from the inside out."

Heads shook, and foreheads creased.

Me: *I seen 'em in my room three nights ago.*

"God said she completed Adam. She was his companion to walk around paradise with."

Toby: *Yeah right. Good one.*

"And God gave one simple rule. Don't eat the fruit."

Me: *Promise da buggah was lying on my bed.*

"But human beings are funny, you know. You tell them do one thing, they're going to do the other. Just to try, 'cause it must be good, yeah?"

Toby: *So give 'em back so my mom stop asking fo' 'em.*

"So, Eve, fighting against her curiosity, tasted the fruit. But who knew it was her for sure? It could have been Adam that took the first bite."

Heads went down on tabletops.

Me: *I wen' pass out and den da buggah not there wen I woke up.*

Mrs. Kepple sounded ticked off. "I bet Adam took the first bite and got Eve into this mess. Sounds like something a man would do. They start it, and then we gotta pay for it."

Toby: *Now I know you lying.*

"You know, 'cause men wrote the books, ah? Change the story here. Change a little there. And make *themselves* look better." Mrs. Kepple waited for the idea to click. No luck.

Me: *PROMISE I wen' SHIT my pants wen I seen 'em. WAS ON MY BED BUT NOT THERE WEN I WOKE UP.*

"Okay, wait. Try wait. The fruit . . . the fruit. Oh yeah, the fruit. What's important is the fruit."

I looked around. No one had a clue what she was talking about.

Toby: *So where da ting stay den?*

"The fruit was from the tree of knowledge of good and evil. When the fruit got eaten, that was the problem. Was like the fruit was rotten."

Some kids looked out the windows now.

Me: *I tink da guy from da storm drain get 'em. I like go back and look fo' 'em.*

"It's like if you ate something bad. Like it was stuck in you for a few days. It's going to make you sick, ah? All it takes is one bad *apple* to spoil a whole bunch."

Whispers went around about how gross Mrs. Kepple was.

Toby: *Wen?*

"Same thing. The fruit made Adam and Eve sick. They saw everything differently. It was like a disease growing inside them. Paradise wasn't paradise anymore 'cause they knew too much."

We all sat there like child zombies, staring blankly.

Me: *Today.*

"It was like once a bite was taken, they couldn't stop. But it didn't matter, 'cause one bite was all it took and they were never the same."

Faces became desperate, itching to leave when the church bell rang.

Toby: *No can today my mom taking me town wit' her fo' work or somethin'. Sorry.*

"Wasn't that an interesting story, boys and girls? Now, please take out a sheet of paper or open your notebooks. I want you to write down all of the things that your parents warned you not to do that you've done. Don't worry, I'm not going to look at this list, and neither are your parents. It's for you. I want you to take this paper and pray that Jesus removes all of the apple seeds that are growing inside you."

Mrs. Kepple began walking around, so Toby and I stopped writing to each other. We fumbled for our notebooks and pretended we had listened the whole time. Mrs. Kepple told us to hurry 'cause our time was almost up. Before we left, she wanted us to have a list of things we had done that we shouldn't have.

Where to start? My pencil on the paper, I thought of all the rules I had tested since moving back to ʻEwa Beach. My eyes went blank, as I started floating away . . . on the ocean, under the stars, in the kitchen. I could hear the night wind, churning words as I unscrewed the cap on Dad's whiskey bottle. The promise of cool numbness. I didn't want to write. The room was getting warmer. I looked at the clock. It was almost time.

Mrs. Kepple came near. "Come on, Landon," she said cheerfully, "don't you want Jesus to get rid of all those apple seeds?" She said it all happy, as if that made the shame go away.

Then it locked tight, right in my stomach. I felt sick, like when I had food poisoning. I put my pencil down. "No. I no like write."

"Come on, Landon. It's not that bad. Just one thing then, before the bell rings. You have to tell Jesus so He can help you. You have to come out and say it."

Couldn't she see? It was all over my body. "I know 'em already. I no like write 'em."

"Just one thing, Landon. Okay? Take your time."

Just thinking about it made me sweat, as the heat boiled within. From somewhere deep, a thought swirled upward. I looked at her and whispered like in confession. "I . . . I take Dad's Jack—" I choked on the hot words inside.

"You what?" she whispered, crouching. "You take your dad's jack? His . . . money?"

"No," I said, as I searched for the words just within my reach. Deep down, I wanted to confess, to let it out. This was my chance to be free from sin. Why fight it? One less word.

Suddenly, the church bell rang. The sound spiraled away and took us with it, like seeds trickling through fingers.

By Sunday afternoon, even I was tired of eating sweet bread. It was day five, and we still had two loaves left. On the way to her bedroom, Mom saw us at the kitchen table and reminded Luke to eat up. She said if he knew what was good for him, he better not let either of the loaves go bad. Luke and I watched her go. When Mom was out of sight, he took one of the loaves and placed it tin-side-down on his head, like a golden hairdo. "Who dis, Landon?" he asked. Then he flashed a sassy face and stroked the sweet bread as if it were coiffed oh-so-fashionably. And when he spoke, it was in his best rich-lady's voice. "I take five hours fo' get my Portagee beehive ready. Nice, ah, Leonard?" I wanted to laugh, but he paused, reached up, and ripped a hole in the plastic wrapper. Still fiddling with the loaf on his head, he pretended to suffer an affront. "How come, Leonard? You no like da way I look?" Then he savagely yanked down a fistful of sweet bread and chewed on it the way a cow would grass.

I busted out laughing, but then remembered Mom was just down the hallway. "Luke, you betta knock it off," I said, chuckling. "Mom see you do dat, you going be in worse trouble."

Maybe it was 'cause he had an audience, or maybe just that he was finally enjoying his sweet bread penance, but Luke couldn't stop. "Nah, who *dis*?" he said, as he stood. He took the loaf from his head and the one from the table, turned around, and positioned them on his ass, one on each cheek. Then he started dancing about, the two tins clinking against each other as he sashayed into the kitchen and back. "Look me, I doing da Chamarita! I doing da Chamarita!" he said in Aunty Selma's tangy voice. "At least I do 'em da *right* way, ah? Not like da DeSilvas. What a como-shen! Da way dey do 'em is just noise."

Luke and I laughed so hard we couldn't breathe. But what he did gave me an idea. I told Luke we had been going about eating the sweet bread all wrong. What we needed to do was make getting rid of it a game. The rules would be simple: each person had to use the sweet bread loaf or a ripped-off piece or even just the tin, and pretend that it was something else. "For example," I said, picking up one of the loaves from the table and making it fly above us, "look da Portagee UFO!"

Luke's face lit up. "So what happens if I no can tink of somethin'?"

"Afta five seconds, if either one of us no come up wit' somethin', we gotta eat one piece sweet bread. Dat way, we going be pau wit' da two tins in no time."

Luke thought about it. He grabbed both loaves, placing them to his ears. "Help me, Obi-Wan Kenobi," he said, mimicking Princess Leia's distress, "you're my only hope."

Luke had caught on quickly. For an instant, I thought about what Mom might say about playing with food but figured we were most likely safe. I really didn't think she considered *pão doce* food. I placed the tin on my wrist and held it there, pretending I was reading something. "Right now, it's, uh, four o'clock."

Luke smiled. He held the loaf above him and fanned his shirt. He wiped at his face as though he were sweating. "Ho, da hot. We baking out here in da sun, ah?"

Back and forth we went. The sweet bread loaves became clever things like the Olympic event discus, the Eucharistic body of Christ, a solitary cookie left alone with a conflicted Cookie Monster, and even Christ's halo from *The Last Supper*. But they also turned into Luke squatting over a golden pile of shit, pretending to upchuck a mound of vomit, and threatening to squeeze a swollen pimple all over the kitchen table.

But I didn't care. Luke and I were having too much fun. In spite of all the laughing, all it took was twenty minutes and the sweet bread was gone.

The opening of the storm drain jutted out from a slope of rocks and dirt. Above it, rocks had been cemented, defining the foundation height for properties on Pupu Street. Below the storm drain, the rocks extended like a platform then dropped eight feet, straight down into the ocean. It was funny, I lived on the one street in 'Ewa Beach without sand, just a hard, cold shoreline of rock.

The storm drain seeped a thick brown liquid. The sludge emptied onto the pocky shelf of rocks, filling small tide pools as it made its way two feet forward before spilling over the edge. I stood at the opening and peered deep into the maw of the tunnel, trying to work up the courage to go in alone. Waves crashed behind me like a heavy heartbeat, the cold spray dazzling the skin on my neck. Or was that just fear as it settled?

I wanted to go in, but my feet didn't let me. A numbness started to grow. I knew I could do it if Toby were here. Another wave smashed below and wet my shirt from behind.

Staring into the dark, I felt something inside me. There was so much noise from the ocean, but inside the storm drain, nothing. A swollen silence in the dark. It echoed all over me, climbed up my legs, slid under my clothes, reached toward my throat, and made it hard to breathe. I stepped back and sat on one of the clean rocks. I took a few deep breaths.

The storm drain seemed to stare back at me now. The blackness was an enlarging iris that ate away at the whitish-gray concrete lip. It got bigger by the moment. I looked away. I couldn't do it. I just couldn't go in.

I heard Afa's voice. *Chicken. Panty.*

Mom said: *Never put off for tomorrow what you could do today.*

But I also knew there were some things we just couldn't stop. And maybe it was an excuse, and maybe I was chicken, but for some reason, I already knew that I'd see the flashlight again. So why bother to go in there?

As I turned to go, I noticed something beneath the mouth of the storm drain. Most of the rocks on either side were black and dead. But just beneath the storm drain, though, healthy triangular piles of opihi and barnacles grew upward from the rocks, splashed by the thick brown trickle. Sponges of different colors also grew around the craggy mounds like fields of Lego surrounding church spires. It was fascinating. Red, orange, and yellow patches somehow flourished. And all from brown sludge. I thought about what Mom always said. If that wasn't making the best out of a bad situation, I didn't know what was.

After the cops left, Dad went to the kitchen to drown himself in more Jack Daniel's. Mom stared out at Pupu Street from the kitchen table. He walked right by, the fight obviously done for tonight, and parked himself in the family room where Luke and I sat quietly on the sofa.

Dad swallowed a sip with his teeth clenched, as his face wrinkled into a sneer. He side-eyed us. Luke and I tried not to watch him. Our heads hung low, and our hands were on our laps. He took another sip. Dad rocked back and forth in his recliner. Another sip. Almost to the bottom of the glass, Dad looked at me, and when he spoke, he slurred. "You getting pretty big, ah, Landon? You get good fingas, ah? Good at pressing buttons, ah, you?" What? He wasn't making sense. Maybe he was drunk. "What you looking at?" He wasn't tired anymore, just mad. And he looked at me funny again. "What you like? You no tink you did enuff already?" Words came off his tongue as if thrown.

"I dunno what—"

Dad sat forward menacingly. "What? What you said? You like me whip you wit' da belt? Go ahead, one more word. Dat's all it take and I break your fingas so you only hear one dial tone. You get one big mouth and plenny words, dat's how I know was you." He was at the edge of his seat, just waiting for another opportunity. So far in now, it was as if he didn't know how to stop. One hand gripped the glass and the other was a twisted fist that dug into the armrest. I looked down, finally understanding. Calling the cops. He knew. My stomach knotted around everything that wanted to come into my eyes. But was it really that bad? I only wanted them to stop fighting. Surely he could understand as much. So why was he looking at me like that? What else did I do?

Dad finally sat back in his chair and aimed his bloodshot eyes at the ceiling. He inhaled deeply and closed his eyes. A few minutes later, he was asleep, drifting on some strange tide.

This time, my body didn't buckle when I saw the flashlight, glowing in the on-position on my bed. I scanned the room for any sign from whoever put it there. Nothing.

The easy rhythm of Luke's breathing sounded peaceful, like the ocean. Must be nice.

I looked back at the flashlight. It was a sign, an intrusion, a taunt from someone. Whatever it was, it needed to stop, and it needed to be now. I had to do something about it. I had to take a stand. So I walked to my bed and picked up the flashlight. The smooth, clean plastic made my heart pump fast. I tucked it under my shirt and then lay face-up on my bed. I folded my arms tight and sank my head deep into my pillow. If whoever had taken the flashlight wanted it back, he'd have to pry it from my arms.

I knew there were some things we just couldn't stop, but whatever the outcome, either way, this one was coming to an end.

And somewhere between thinking about the right words to say and about deep-rooted seeds and about a flashlight digging into the flesh of my chest, I drifted off to sleep. I figured why fight it? And when I woke up, I realized I had slept through the entire night, not waking up until morning for the first time in three weeks. There were red, fleshy lines blossoming into a bruise on my chest from the flashlight I still gripped. As I lay in bed with the morning sun filtering in, I smiled, staring at the ceiling. It was so quiet and peaceful. I didn't know how long the feeling would last and honestly, I didn't care. It just felt nice not being the chicken for once.

10

Mom said it wasn't only how hot you cooked something, it was how long you left it in one place before you stirred it up. You didn't want to burn anything. When we got back from Foodland, Mom and Luke roasted popcorn. Mom bought the tinfoil pan of Jiffy Pop popcorn, the kind that needed to be held on the stove and shaken every so often. Ever since we saw *The Empire Strikes Back* and ate a large tub of popcorn, Luke had bugged Mom for more. Whenever she did get popcorn, Mom and Luke practically ate the whole thing by themselves.

When it was ready, Mom whisked the cover away and loaded a chunk of Imperial margarine into the pan. It steamed as the yellow block melted onto white lumps.

Luke said that besides eating popcorn when it was all juicy and full of salt like at the theaters, the best thing about popping popcorn was when the kernels first started snapping. Mom let him shake the pan. It didn't matter if he got violent and turned it upside down 'cause it had a lid. Luke said he liked to grip the handle while the tin throbbed, sputter-jolting with each blossom of popcorn. "Sound almost like one heartbeat, Landon. Nah, like one car motor having hard time start. Nah, like Zork purring, if he not ready fo' you pet him." Where did he get this from? I didn't ask 'cause Luke was having so much fun. He shook the pan, along with the rest of his body in a strange third-grade dance, so I had to just shake my head and laugh instead.

The paper wrapper on each crayon crackled from the point of light Luke directed. He played with his stolen magnifying glass every chance he got. He sat outside, cracking his knuckles from one hand on the sidewalk while holding the glass steady with the other. After a while, he switched. The paper ignited, as flames ate their way outward, burning into black flakes. Suddenly, they got picked up by the wind and were gone. Luke did this with several crayons from his sixteen box of Crayolas. He did red, yellow, orange, green, blue. He burned each label off and watched the flames lick everything away.

When there was no more paper to burn, he focused the sunlight on the clump of half-melted crayons on the sidewalk. At first, he kept the light in one place, but then he moved it around as though he were drawing on the twisted bodies of crayons. The colors bled into one another, a warm dizzying swirl that made a psychedelic puddle on the concrete.

I told Luke that I needed help wiping the windows. But he was so into what he was doing that all he did was raise the magnifying glass to his face and look at me through it. And honestly, that was beginning to irk the shit out of me already. Whenever he didn't want to do something, he lifted that damn thing over his eye, blinking slowly while squinting the other eye, and pretended he was deaf. He acted so dumb that sometimes I felt like really cracking his head. This time, however, I told him that if he didn't quit, Mom was going to see.

He aimed the glass back down. "She only going scold me, den go back inside da house."

"So you like her snap? Why you trying fo' irritate her?"

He lifted the magnifying glass back up to his eye and stuck his tongue out at me. "'Cause wit' dis I can see more clear." His distorted eyeball blinked through the glass.

"You no see shit, brah. If you not working, Mom going blame me, and I going get it too."

Luke already aimed his beam of light back on the lump of melted crayons. He sat there, waiting for Mom to see him, like he was trying to get busted. After a few minutes, he peeled the gnarled, crayon carcass off the concrete like burnt crust from a pan. He held it up in the air like a priest, two hands around the bottom end, and chanted. "Our Father who *Art* in Heaven." He turned around and looked at me. A thin smile crept onto his face, like he had just been caught doing something wrong. Before I could say anything, he broke the silence. "Get it? Art?" He held his crayon wafer toward me, as though in offering.

I looked at Luke and wanted to laugh, wanted to fall on the ground and laugh so hard I pissed my pants. But another part of me couldn't figure my brother out. Was he *that* off?

I rolled my eyes. The blob in his hands was a swirl of colors fanning outward from a core, like looking at a hurricane from above. I met Luke's gaze. His devious smile faded as he lifted his eyebrows meaningfully. I honestly wasn't sure whether or not something was there, or if there was just something *wrong* with him.

Mom's temper made her talk to herself as she hung the family picture on the living room wall. Ever since Luke chased Zork, crashed into the wall, and made the picture fall, the frame didn't quite hang the same. When the picture hit the floor, the wood bent and the glass shattered. Mom mumbled aloud about Luke:

"Sometimes I wonder about him, like maybe he should be in special ed. God forbid one of *my* kids ends up in there with all the dummies. But he's so . . . " Mom trailed off. She exhaled loudly. "And that's another thing. The one family picture we've got is now ruined. There's no reason why we can't have more. 'What fo'? I no like look at da past. Always look ahead.' Sure, Leonard, whatever you say. What you mean is you're cheap and stingy." She stepped back and examined the picture. She adjusted it left, then right. "And if you didn't get so worked up and unable to control yourself . . . " she said, trailing off again, and then snorting sarcastically.

Mom stepped back, inspecting the frame, making sure it was just right. Her face was red and flushed. It looked like something was building up, like she was ready to explode. But she didn't. She just let out one word, really just a whisper, before heading to the kitchen: "Perfect."

After Dad passed out in his recliner, his mouth hung open, catching flies. Luke circled around with magnifying glass in hand. Luke went real close to Dad's body, like he was doing some kind of an experiment. One enlarged eye, one scrunched eye. Up Dad's arms, across his head, deep into his hair, around his face, back and forth on his stomach. Catching Luke's attention, I lipped the words: *What'chu doing?* Luke put his finger up to his mouth. We both knew that if Dad woke up, he was going to pop his top and lick Luke for making fun of him.

Later, while doing my Social Studies homework, I asked Luke if he had shit for brains. He said he was only observing Dad. "Inspector Clouseau, what'chu *observing* Dad fo'?" I asked. "You one scientist, or somethin'?" Luke began laughing to himself. "What's so funny?" I snapped.

"Scientist . . . Sigh-ant-is," he said slowly between chuckles, sounding it out for me, as if that made a difference.

I just stared at him, my aggravation clear.

He tried to explain through his giggling. "And one odda word fo' Dad is Pop, right?"

After a moment, I snapped again. "So?"

"Scientist Pop. Scientist Dad. Sigh-ant-is . . . POP!" Luke busted out laughing and curled up on the ground. He started burning out, doing donuts on our bedroom floor. His face red and teary already, he held his gut while going in circles.

I could do nothing but look. Whatever the joke was, I didn't get it.

In December, ‘Ewa Beach finally got a little cooler. For the last couple of days, it had been cold enough in the morning to grab a sweater for school. But by the time first recess came, it was already too warm to keep it on. At least we weren’t sweating in the afternoon anymore.

What I noticed most was how cloudy it got in December. Ripples of clouds floated as though undulating across the sky. Some were thick and dark, some white and fluffy. Once in a while, a storm came off the ocean, and then the sky was gray all morning long until the storm clouds burned off. But the closer to the end of the year it got, the more clouds that formed and the more rain that fell.

And when it rained, it came down heavy. Not like in ‘Ālewa Heights, where the rain was like birds’ feet tickling the rooftop. ‘Ewa Beach rain was thick and loaded, like slaps from Dad.

And with rain came thunder and lightning. Quick snapshots of light, almost too fast for the eye to see, followed by distinct crackles that rumbled up and down the street.

I looked at the sky and knew. The rain was coming. Maybe that was a good thing.

Luke wadded a small pile of crispy leaves then set it on fire with magnified light. Brittle skeletons blackened into flakes and fluttered away on the wind. He crumpled his bad-grade assignments and charred lines onto the paper. The heap ignited. Small flames licked upward, quickly running out of room to grow before dissipating. With the same magnified light, he drew on Dad’s plywood, scorching hot silhouettes of insects and animals onto the hard surface.

I found Luke outside on the concrete sidewalk, looking down at the ground through the magnifying glass. He sat motionless, as he held the handle still. As I got closer, I realized he focused the light on ants. He waited for an ant to come into range then followed the skittering body a few inches with the glass. The ant ran around, faster and faster, in circles, trying to escape the spotlight. The body shook, tweaking a little, before it sounded as though it exhaled in defeat, and then: POP! The ant exploded on the sidewalk, leaving not much more than a clear liquid stain and body parts on the concrete.

Luke sat there, like he was king, as he followed ants that dared come within his sight. Like in *Clash of the Titans* when the gods played around with people's lives, Luke sat there, watching without thinking twice. On second thought, I didn't think he was watching at all. He was *listening.* He winced with a subtle twitch every time an ant bubbled, sighed, and popped.

Toby and I didn't look before we leaped. It was so humid that all we cared about was getting into the water and onto our boards. Everything had been going fine until we both caught a killer wave. I wiped out first, naturally, but then Toby did right after. And that was when, through the sound of whitewash cycling, I heard Toby's board snap. The thud was so distinct, like a brittle, hollow bone popping in two. Toby told me after that when he tried to drop in on the wave, he wasn't sure what happened, but the wave kept gaining on him, sucking, pulling him up the face, until he went over the falls. But as he fell off, the wave somehow spat his board downward instead of outward, pinning it under the lip and then crunching it at the bottom.

Toby cussed about how pissed his cousin Chaz was going to be. One of his favorite boards, his trusty Lightning Bolt, gone in the blink of an eye. Toby said this was big-time *bachi.*

To me, this was more than mere . . . bad luck. It was a sign. We had to be more careful.

Outside on the concrete sidewalk, Luke was burning stuff again. I didn't see what he got out of it. He crouched over the magnifying glass and focused the light on something. I opened the screen door and went over to the front of the yard where Luke sat. When I saw what he was burning, my eyes almost popped out. Luke had the family picture on the sidewalk, the one Mom fussed over so much, magnifying glass hovering over it. The paper started to curl at the edges and was so soft from the heat that the front had dimpled from the textured surface of the sidewalk. But over Dad, around his entire body, Luke sizzled long streaks. The paper was black and bubbled like popcorn. I yanked the picture from under the magnifying glass.

"What da hell you doing, Luke? Mom going broke your ass. You know dis one of da few pictures we get of da family. Now it's all ruin. What'chu tinking?" I imagined the moment Mom saw this. I could hear her screaming already.

"I wanted fo' draw," he said as he looked away, his voice not even convincing himself. "But if Mom find 'em, I going tell her I was only trying fo' look at 'em betta."

What the fuck? If Mom found it? I wanted to say everything but couldn't. I wanted to knock some sense into him but didn't. I couldn't do anything but shake my head and stare blankly at him, so frustrated that I squeezed him tight with every thought.

I looked back at the picture. Over Dad, in black, bubbling, burn marks: antennas, fangs, oval body, and six crispy, bony legs.

Luke stood next to me and pointed to his drawing. "Get it? Sigh-ant-is-Pop?"

"Scientist Pop? What da hell you talking about? You going get us both in trouble wit' dis. Take dis and hide 'em whereva you so good at hiding stuff." I slammed the picture into his chest and yanked him toward the house.

Walking toward the front door, though, was when I felt it. Something was coming closer, something I couldn't stop no matter how hard I tried. Everything slowed with each step we took toward the house. Out of nowhere, dark clouds crept in front of the sun, blanketing the entire sky. On the inside of the screen door, Zork's elongated body clung to the mesh, jerking, yanking to be free. Dad's Chevy pulled in, lurching up the driveway, tires pinching asphalt to a stop.

In between moments, I felt it inch closer. Its legs crawled all over me, tickling, propelling me toward the house. Something said to not stay in one place, but at the same time, to grab Luke and to take cover. There was a flash of light too fast to truly see and a loud boom that chased it. Lightning, thunder. The sound echoed in my head, speeding everything up as it bounced back and forth. I flung Luke into the house and told him to hurry. Then I peeled Zork off the screen door and tossed him skittering into the house.

Right then, something deep within snapped, the slow-motion and the speed gone. For a moment, it was calm again. I watched Dad slam his car door. The sky was dark. There was another flash of lightning with thunder rumbling behind. Everything settled, and it was hot.

The rain was coming.

It was pouring outside when Mom told Dad that he had been drinking too much lately. From that, they got into another long, drawn-out yell fest in the kitchen that lasted two hours. From the moment they started fighting, Zork had waited at the screen door, skittishly trotting back and forth. Rosie fluttered in her cage. Luke and I sat on the love seat in the living room, just watching. The rain hadn't let up at all. In fact, with all the lightning and thunder, it sounded like it was getting worse.

Mom told Dad he didn't even talk to us anymore. He didn't do anything but sit outside after work, eat dinner, then fall asleep. They went around and around. Dad argued that he spent so many hours at work, and this was the last thing he needed. He downed his second glass of Jack Daniel's in Mom's face.

"Do you know how much whiskey costs, Leonard? All that money you claim we don't have, just being drunk away. What about a dryer? I've been line-drying clothes since we've gotten here." She had been line-drying clothes? Mom always took credit for the house stuff we did. "Also, why in the world did you need a ham radio? That monstrosity of an antenna is still sitting outside the house. What a waste of—"

Dad cut her off as he poured another glass of Jack Daniel's. "No even talk, Minerva. No even try. I told you wen I agree fo' take da promo-shen, 'cause of da long hours I gotta put in, da bonus money was fo' my projecks. We wen' move back here fo' save money. Period. Rememba? Closer to work, save time, save gas. So no ack. I can choose how I like spend 'em."

Zork's head jerked as though listening, then he crept to the other side of the living room.

"So easy for you. You change the rules whenever you want. Leonard the Dictator, right? Absolutely no fairness. And besides, you are the one who shouldn't *ack*. You wanted to come out here to be closer to your family. The job was an excuse. Did you ever think about me? That I might want to stay close to my sister, to the only *family* I have left?"

The word set Dad off. "Da only *family* you got? What da fuck me? What about my modda? She always treat you like one of her own. You rememba? I neva want *dis*. You did."

Zork trotted back to the screen door, sniffing the wet, shifting, evening air.

"Great, just perfect. So what are you saying, Leonard? You want a *divorce*?"

And for the first time, there was silence. Such a powerful word. It was powerful enough to stop the hurtful words coming out of both of their mouths. Dad looked long and hard at Mom, his chest heaving with breath. "I gotta get outta here," he said.

Zork sauntered to the other side of the living room again.

Dad made to go, but Mom stepped in front of him. "Don't leave, Leonard. I want to talk about this. You're scaring me. What's going on in your head?"

Then Rosie started chirping.

Dad tried to move around Mom, as his third glass of Jack Daniel's swirled about, some of the liquid swashing out. "Get outta my way, Minerva," he warned.

Zork ran at the door then stopped, his head jerking about, inspecting something outside.

"You've drunk too much, Leonard. You're not going anywhere. Give me the glass."

A strong wind blew, a peal of thunder in the background.

Dad yanked the glass away from Mom, spilling more whiskey. And when he spoke, his voice was hard. "Minerva, you cornering me like you always do. I just like be alone right now."

Zork looked toward the kitchen, and then tiptoed back to the other side of the living room. He looked straight at me.

Mom stood in Dad's way, blocking him from the living room. "No, Leonard. Just give me the glass first." I saw Dad's eyes over her shoulder. They were focused on me. Mom was still pleading. "Just give me—"

That was when Dad snapped. "Get outta my fucking way!"

Out of the corner of my eye, I saw Zork run full-blast toward the screen door, his yellow eyes glinting. But this time, he didn't stop. He flew straight into the screen door, ripping a hole at the bottom where there was no metal frame. The impact was so loud that it startled both Mom and Dad. I jumped off the couch and hurried outside after Zork. Down the sidewalk, in the pouring rain, I ran into the street. Zork galloped full-speed down Pupu Street. I yelled his name over and over, but he didn't look back. Not once.

Zork's body got smaller as snapshots of lightning popped off. Each picture a little less than the one before. Thunder echoed from somewhere near, a billowing thick roll that drew Zork farther away from Pupu Street.

And the rain kept coming.

TWO

11

It was almost Christmas, with all of its surprises. That meant no school, no homework, and thankfully, no Afa Palaipale. I was so sick of his stinking chicken noises. Everywhere I went, he was there. To lunch: *bawk-bawk-bawk-bawk*. To the bathroom: *bawk-bawk-bawk-bawk*. To line up for our field trip: *bawk-bawk-bawk-bawk*. When Afa caught me off guard, I felt my gut tighten up, and I'd just stand there. I waited for him to do something. But he just blocked my way, telling me to make the first move. So we stood frozen like two statues, eyeing each other. And after all that, nothing happened. At least not yet.

Since Christmas break started, I was glad I didn't have to deal with any of Afa's shit. Two whole weeks of peace and quiet. Less words to deal with. But then, a sound so sweet and clear drifted in from the kitchen:

On the first day of Christmas
My true love gave to me
A partridge in a pear tree

Mom's voice poured out words so free and light. The sound always caught me and Luke off guard. And it didn't matter she couldn't sing that well. Whenever Mom started, Luke and I knew Christmas was near. First, the rusted tree stand came out, then the red-velvet tree skirt, and the leftover rolls of wrapping paper from last year. The plastic snowman almost as tall as Luke followed, along with half-empty cans of spray snow, strands of tinsel, our nativity scene, holiday stencils for the living room window, hanging ornaments, and flashing tree lights.

Mom was so into the season, she even offered me and Luke Christmas treats. "Do you guys want some egg nog?" she asked. "I found it on special at Foodland. It was really cheap, so you can have more than one glass if you want." It was hard to say no to that, especially since Mom was in such a generous mood. Plus, when Dad was at work, Mom whipped out the goodies: fruitcake, candy canes, gingerbread, and butter cookies in the shape of tiny Christmas trees. She said she loved Christmas, and the food! Oh, the food! It reminded her of when she was little. Luke consumed whatever Mom offered. He ate everything, extra sweet and sugary, smiling the whole time. As for me, I liked most of it, but I honestly couldn't see what Luke saw in fruitcake.

But when Dad came home, Mom slid everything away 'cause he didn't like *any* of it. Dad said Mom's Christmas food was too haole for him. He said he'd take anything over gingerbread again, like andagi, mochi, or manju. "Ooh, what about malasada?" Dad asked, almost salivating. "Dat's one good Portagee treat. Ono at Christmas time, you know."

Mom covered the fruitcake and slid the entire container in the cold oven, out of sight. "Malasadas were made before Lent, not Christmas," Mom said plainly, "so that all the *indulgences* in the house, like lard and sugar, were used up by the time Fat Tuesday rolled around." Mom turned and was surprised by Dad's dejected expression.

Dad snorted. "Why tradition even matter, Minerva? Not like you going make *vinha d'alhos,* and dat's Christmas food," Dad said sulkily. "I mean, shit, my grandfadda guys was poor, but dey still kill one whole pig Christmas time. What, we got nothin' fo' celebrate?" Dad marched off to their bedroom. Mom watched him go. Dad hadn't said two words to anybody since their last fight. He also had been coming home so late from work he hadn't touched his Jack Daniel's either. From the front door, he'd head straight to shower. By the time he came out, dinner would be ready, so he'd eat and then go to bed, only to have to repeat the cycle again the next day. Mom stared after him with a miserable, little lopsided pucker to her lips.

Dad hadn't even commented on the living room decorations Luke and I did, not that I thought he would. We even went so far as to stencil the picture window with the words *Walking in a Winter Wonderland* in thick, fluffy, snow letters. The only thing missing was a Christmas tree. Dad usually had something to say about the living room being so mainland-ish, so haole. But not this time. He walked right through the living room like the decorations weren't even there. Or worse, like he wasn't.

Luke said it was worse to know a gift was bad and still have to open it, than it was to rip it open and find out he got a bad gift. "At least wen you ripping into da buggah, can be almost anythin'. But if you know da buggah bad, you still gotta open 'em and ack surprise. So fake. I rather be surprise. Good or bad. What'chu tink, Landon?"

Where did he come up with this stuff? "I tink you one in-grate, Luke. How you tink people feel if dey knew what'chu tinking? I no tink dey eva give you one present again." I didn't tell him I knew exactly what he meant. I didn't want him thinking it was okay to think that way. Grandma always gave us Fruit of the Loom tank tops or ball-hugger BVDs that never fit. We might need those . . . garments, but going for an all-day trip to J.C. Penney's with Mom, just to exchange underwear, was more torture than it was worth. Besides, Luke probably wanted the entire army of G.I. Joe's he had talked about. I wanted to tell him to get real and listen to what Mom and Dad had been fighting about. He'd get something, just not *all* the toys on his wish list. But I didn't say anything. I figured it couldn't hurt to let him dream a little more.

Luke was quiet for a while then started up again. "So, is it betta fo' know what you going get, or what? Even if da buggah good?"

Since he wasn't talking bad about anyone's gifts and since he wasn't going to let these asinine questions go, I decided to indulge him. "If you like feel all jittery, then wait fo' Christmas. No sneak looks, and no try guess what da buggah is. Wait fo' open presents. 'Cause just like on *Candid Camera*. You seen people's faces wen dey get surprise? You tink dey like dat? No way. If dey knew before hand, dey coulda breathe easy and relax. But no, dey get thrown off, and sometimes dey even like cry. I take knowing all da way. No surprises fo' me."

Luke didn't say anything for a while, but then he dropped his head over the side of the bunk. His hair clung to his head in mid-fall, as his face turned red. "I would tell you what you going get from Mom and Dad if I knew, Landon."

Luke's words hung in the air between us, like little gifts to hold onto. Just when I thought he didn't get it, Luke said something that made me realize he wasn't so young anymore. A part of me wished he'd never grow old enough to *see*. But another part knew better. I smiled and thanked him, knowing it was just a matter of time.

Mom smiled while she sang. She leaned close to Rosie's cage, and let her voice rise and fall. Then Rosie began too. When Zork was still around, Rosie just stayed quiet, trying not to attract the cat's attention. But ever since Zork ran away, Rosie became more vocal. She flapped her wings and sang all the time now, feathers floating softly to the ground around her cage.

All day long, Mom pretended she was Karen Carpenter. She usually started off with "I'll Be Home for Christmas." She sang this one slow and drew out the last words so that the lines almost hovered breathlessly in the air. Then she moved on to other Carpenters' Christmas songs like "Merry Christmas, Darling" and "Winter Wonderland." She belted out lyrics, like she was the one excited for the twenty-fifth. Sooner or later, though, she moved to other Karen Carpenter songs. Like "There's a Kind of Hush" and "Top of the World." But whenever she sang these, her work pace steadily slowed down as she drifted off. It was when she sang "Hurting Each Other" that Mom stopped moving altogether. Her voice was weak, and her eyes went blank. She stared off into nothing, her attention wafting away as though along the melody of her voice.

I hadn't seen Zork since he ran away. None of our neighbors had seen him either. Luke and I put up LOST CAT posters at Foodland and at church, but no one had called. Whenever I thought about it late at night, the image that flashed was of Zork as he galloped away. Freeze-frame after freeze-frame from the lightning, farther and farther away.

Dad was so mad he kicked the metal door frame, which dented it. Zork had ruined the mesh of the screen door, and Dad had to re-screen it now. He muttered about that damn, good-for-nothing animal, only after one thing. Good, now Zork was someone else's problem.

That night, I watched from outside as the rain fell like heavy words all over me. Dad cursed the cat he originally saved, the cat that was once his buddy. Through the screen, Dad looked at me like he had before. Heavy and loaded. There had been too many times he'd done that in the last few months. I wondered if he was still mad about the time I called the cops. But something about his eyes suggested it was worse. And not knowing made me nervous inside. I wished he would just say what was on his mind already. But I also knew I had to be careful what I wished for. It might come true.

When we were ready to look for a tree, we all loaded up in Dad's red Chevy Nova. Mom already knew what stores we were going to hit that night. Woolworth's, Foodland, and GEM. I didn't know why. Every year, the place we got our tree from was Pearl City Holiday Mart.

Mom took more than a *long time* when looking for a tree, just like at Fujioka's or when returning Christmas presents. She took so long I expected Dad to grumble how tired he was after a long day at work. How one tree was the same as the rest. How he had to get up early, so she needed to hurry up. Whenever we went to get our tree, Dad was always in a rush.

When it came to stuff like dinner, Mom at least pretended to hurry. But with a Christmas tree, she didn't even flinch. She was on a mission. Our job was to march out tree after tree, so she could inspect them. She made her fingers into an L-7 and appraised our models through her viewfinder, as though she were a photographer. Luke's trees never got chosen, probably 'cause he had to stick to the smaller, scrawny ones. And when Dad impatiently discarded his tree and stormed off to look for a new one, Mom remained surprisingly upbeat. She turned to Luke who displayed another sad three-foot specimen. "Your father will just have to deal with this," she muttered and then indicated *no* to Luke's offering. "It's only once a year. After all, it is *tradition*." Mom suddenly stopped, as the word fluttered in the air around us. Tradition. Mom looked after Dad and exhaled heavily, a glum smile across her face.

At the end of the night, we still hadn't found our tree. But it somehow didn't matter. The next day, Mom was still singing.

On the other side of the house, the sound of the vacuum thundered over Mom's voice. The chores had been a lot lighter since vacation started. All Mom wanted me to do was to dust and then vacuum her room. When I got to the closet, I knew the routine: turn off the vacuum; pull everything out, including shoes, boxes, and bags; and vacuum the carpet underneath as well. As I removed the boxes from the closet, I noticed one I had never seen before. It was heavy but flimsy as it was so old. I studied the shelf and noticed a void. I looked back at the box.

A large, Stayfree cardboard box with incredibly dusty panels. It must have been up there for a long time. And in big, black El-Marko ink on the side of the box: *MOM'S PICTURES*. I was confused 'cause it didn't look like Mom's handwriting. But then my eyes went wide when I realized something else. Mom always said how she wished we had more pictures. I tiptoed down the hallway and peered toward the kitchen. Mom was on the phone with Aunty Selma. I hurried back to their bedroom and turned the vacuum back on. Then I slid the panels open.

In the box, lots of old, yellow, crinkly papers. Recipes. There was one for Old Fashioned Butter Cookies and another for Mindy's Fruitcake. I rummaged deeper, searching for the pictures. Under the recipes were the faded, empty envelopes that once held developed photos. A lot of envelopes were from Longs Drugs, but all of them were for a customer named Mindy Bode. For a moment, I went blank. But then the name clicked. I recognized it from the graveyard. Mindy Bode was Mom's mom. The dates on the envelopes ranged from the late forties to the late sixties. I dug some more. Under the empty envelopes were heaps of pictures.

I picked up one.

A tall, slender man and woman, arms around each other, waving a pennant with words I can't make out, standing in front of a sign that says 'Honolulu Stadium.' They're dressed like rabid sports fans. Matching clothes. Very good-looking.

The years whispered words into my ears: Grandma and Grandpa. The date on the back of the picture was 1967.

I grabbed the next picture.

The same couple, my grandma and grandpa, but younger, and there's a young girl standing between them, holding hands with them. Smiling wide, missing a tooth, and not much older than Luke. They stand with a huge Mickey Mouse in front of the most well-groomed patch of flowers I have ever seen in my life. Taking in the entire picture at once, the word 'Disneyland' can be seen behind them.

The year was 1958. I didn't recognize the little girl until I covered her hair with my finger. I saw Luke's eyes, his nose, his wide smile in hers. That little girl was Mom.

I snatched up another picture.

Grandma and Grandpa stand with a teenaged Mom outside Honolulu International Airport. The three of them smile, trying to look happy. Grandma and Grandpa pose, arms around each other's waist, but neither of them touch Mom. Instead, Mom is frozen next to them, holding herself, hands gently cupping her enlarged belly.

The date: 1969. I dropped the picture, as an icy flood of emotion cascaded over me. But before I picked up the photo again, I knew. As I stared at Mom, I had a hard time breathing 'cause for the first time in my life, I saw myself in her. Surprise.

For the last few days, Mom left letters for Dad on the kitchen counter. On single sheets of folder paper, love notes from her to him. When Dad woke up and went for coffee in the kitchen, the letter sat in his empty mug, like a mystical, rolled-up scroll. He always stood there and read it. Then he'd fold it up and tuck it in his work slacks, sipping coffee as he headed out the door. Dad never acknowledged me in the dark, as I ate breakfast at the kitchen table.

One letter slipped out of his pocket and landed on the floor in the living room. But he just walked out the door and left. Once he drove down Pupu Street, I retrieved the letter and checked if Mom was awake. Then I took it to me and Luke's bedroom to read.

To My Dearest Love,

Thank you for last night. It's been so long since we've played like that. I can't remember the last time. You made me feel like a young woman again. Like those times you used to come over late at night to my parents' house in 'Ālewa Heights. You used to call out in little meows (your secret call) until I heard you. Do you remember that? How we used to laugh when you finally got into my bedroom? Sometimes you were outside for an hour or more because my mom or my dad kept checking on me. But you just stood there frozen in the moonlight like a beautiful statue. Waiting there, so faithful, so reliable. I remember thinking how lucky I was to have you. And that's just how I feel now. And when you took me from . . . well, you know, I couldn't help but purr like your little pussycat again. It brought back so many memories of our early days. The days before we got married. Thank you for giving us one more try.

XOXO
Your Kitten,
Minnie

While Mom cleaned Rosie's cage, she let Rosie climb on the outside. She pulled newspapers out, changed the water and seed dish, and sprayed down the bars. Mom hummed Carpenters again. Rosie cocked her head, pink eyes blinking, and watched Mom.

I had been thinking about the pictures I saw. "Mom, you ever wen' go Disneyland?"

Mom side-eyed me, her head in the cage, looking out from between the bars. "Yes, I went with my mom and dad when I was young. Why?"

I knew from her anxious tone that what she was really trying to find out was if I knew something I shouldn't. But I was ready. "Toby told me. He said his cousin just wen' come back from da mainland and showed him a bunch of pictures." I waited for her reaction.

Mom considered and then went back to cleaning the cage. "Disneyland was fun. The People Movers, 20,000 Leagues Under the Sea, and the Space Rockets were my favorites. But to me, the airplane was the most fun. It's like you're the boss. You can watch a movie, listen to music, call the stewardess for more soda, and it doesn't cost a cent more. You eat with silverware, but that's only when you travel in first—" She suddenly stopped. She stared at Rosie on the cage in front of her. Mom blinked twice, before glancing back at me. She smiled tightly. "Maybe one day we'll go to Disneyland, Landon, so you can fly in an airplane too." And that was it. She put her finger out for Rosie and then returned Rosie to her perch in the cage.

I closed my eyes with the image of Mom still stained in my sight. Every time I got close, she sailed away as fast as she could, taking everything with her. My mother, the person who had already flown and loved to fly, would rather lock up her memories in a cardboard box than share them with me. Mom pretended to be blind and cut herself off from her roots, and me from mine.

That was why I wasn't putting the three pictures back. Ever. I figured that if they helped her fly, maybe they'd help me too.

After we finally got a Christmas tree, I helped Dad load it onto the roof of his Chevy. The tree was wrapped in plastic netting, bound up tight like a snared animal. We tied it down for the trip home on Fort Weaver Road.

Dad drove with his left arm out of the window and his right one on the steering wheel. After the couple of hours it took Mom to finally choose a tree, his body language was pretty normal. He had wanted to go home a long time before. Mom was usually irked with Dad and would sit on the far right of the long front seat. But not tonight. Mom sat in the middle, very close to Dad. She rested her head on his shoulder.

I inhaled deeply and for the first time in months, there was no shame, just the fresh, thick smell of pine. I leaned my head back and craned my neck so I could see out the rear window above. The top of our Christmas tree hung off the roof and was set against the backdrop of the night sky. Streetlights flashed by. Pine needles seemed to break free and soar away, as if from the tail of a great green comet. And then, suddenly, Mom started singing:

Gone away is the blue bird
Here to stay is the new bird

Mom's voice was so light and free, it was a current of soft, feathered words. And then something even more unexpected happened. Mom leaned over and whispered demurely to Dad. "How about I make *vinha d'alhos* tomorrow?" Dad glanced at Mom who was staring back intently. Surprised, Dad drove on, but he smiled and nodded eagerly. Mom rested her head on his shoulder once again. After a moment, Dad murmured the way Zork purred when he was happiest. I closed my eyes like a shutter and imagined the flash.

Mom wrapping herself around Dad, intertwining her roots, holding on even though knowing how to fly. And Dad right where he should be. Luke snoring lightly, and he would always be able to. And there I am, perched but hoping to God the new bird stays.

I opened my eyes and leaned my head back again to look at the tree and the sky and the strobe of streetlights. It all blurred so fast it reminded me of flying, of spreading my wings and letting go. But instead, I held onto the snapshot burned across my mind, of my mother and father together in the front seat. Happy 'cause of something so simple as the promise of *vinha d'alhos*. Wine, vinegar, garlic, and pork had suddenly become so much more than just the ingredients of a Portuguese dish. They signified that, we too, had something to celebrate.

I sat there, knowing this moment was an unopened gift. And even though I didn't know if the surprise would be good or how long it would last, since there was a chance, my choice was clear. I held onto the present. I held onto the gift of this moment with both claws clinging tight.

12

Letting go was sometimes hard. When Luke was a baby, he didn't want to give up his *ne-ne* bottle. Even if it was empty, he didn't release his grip. And heaven forbid trying to pry it from his white-fingered death grip. His face swelled red as he prepared to explode. If Mom snatched it from him, he raised hell until she either gave him back the bottle or until he wiped himself out. Mom had to bribe him with Lego before he let go of his bottle for good at nearly four years of age. Holding onto something became a habit, I guess.

Just like Toby's flashlight. It had been over a couple of months since the *Help Me* man put it in my room. That was what I called him now. I didn't know if he was a ghost or a real person, but every night, after Luke's breathing became regular, I tucked the flashlight under my shirt. I wrapped my arms around myself, digging the flashlight deeper into flesh. I was beginning to think it actually helped me to sleep.

Some nights, it took longer to drift off, so I just hugged myself in the dark. The streetlight threw a bright rectangle against the far wall and on part of the floor. I'd watch as the Norfolk Pine swayed in the wind and cast images in our room like shadow puppets. They took on all kinds of shapes. Sometimes the shadows were people, swaying back and forth as though merely drunk. At others, they were monsters, staggering as though infected. But then the beam from Toby's flashlight would erase the whole show, proving nothing was there.

That was why I didn't want to give it back to Toby. But I finally decided that, after all, the flashlight was his mom's. Even though a part of me wanted to keep it, there was another part that didn't want anything to do with it anymore. Having it around was only asking for trouble.

When I finally returned it, Toby laughed. He said his Mom had already bought another one. "What took so long?" he joked, taking the flashlight from me.

I considered telling him how I went to bed with it every night, how I prodded my skin with it to sleep better, how I expected an eventual confrontation with the *Help Me* man, and how I wanted to make that guy pay for sneaking into our room. But instead, I simply shrugged my shoulders and told Toby I forgot.

As we ate cookies at Toby's house, the flashlight sitting safely on his kitchen counter, something came loose inside. After letting go of the flashlight, I felt lighter somehow. Like wind slipping by. Like surfing. Letting go felt free.

Luke's Lego house looked almost done. The walls were eight to nine blocks high, and every room was furnished. He had what seemed like all the comforts of home, from chairs to the normal appliances, from bedrooms to a kitchen. He even had stuff that we didn't, like a garbage chute. Luke said he saw it on TV. He thought a garbage chute was really cool 'cause we could just slide everything down in one place, no problem.

Luke showed me the *map* of his house he drew in his marble composition book. Dad would call it a floor plan, but I didn't say anything. Luke said he drew it in Mrs. Shelley's class when she talked about geography. She told them stories and showed them where the events took place on the world map. Luke said the most recent story was about the Seven Cities of Gold. He got the idea to draw the map of his house while spacing out somewhere in South America.

I had to admit it was a pretty impressive house. Luke wanted to build a removable roof, in order to easily get to his *Star Wars* action figure residents. "Bum-bye dey going get stuck inside," he said. "But I no mo' nuff Lego fo' build da roof. See?" He showed me his almost empty suitcase of Lego, as he blinked his eyes innocently. Just listening to him, I almost expected what came next. I nodded and just went back to folding laundry. "But if . . . *you*—"

I cut him of before he even began. "No even ask, Luke."

He made a face. "Why? You could ask fo' both of us—"

"'Cause my birthday is fo' *my* wishes, not yours. Besides, going be like Christmas. Tink I going waste my one wish on Lego?" Luke wrinkled his lips and pouted. "You going get your birthday couple months. Ask fo' more Lego den." I watched my brother's eyebrows get heavy, as he folded his arms. It was just like Christmas morning when he opened gift after gift of tee shirts, underwear, and socks. He got one toy gift from Mom and Dad: a plastic sand castle set, complete with yellow shovel, blue sand bucket, and red tower moldings. The sand castle set was on his wish list, but probably number thirty-one.

He frowned and exhaled bitterly. "Christmas was betta at 'Ālewa Heights."

I hadn't heard him complain about 'Ewa Beach for a while now. He tucked his hands under his armpits and buried deep within himself.

Christmas sucked, true, but I didn't tell him that. I even felt the sand castle set was an all-time worst gift nominee, but I didn't dare breathe a word of it either. Instead I just shook my head at him. "Why you pouting? You da one ask fo' eighteen billion gifts. How dey suppose to know which one you *really* like? Besides, open your eyes. We no more dat much money."

Luke perked up. He looked at me as though something had just dawned on him. "Dat's *it*. All I need is liddle bit money. Den I can go Woolworth's and pick up couple boxes—"

It was my turn to make a face, then scoff. "Get real. Where you going get money? If Dad get problems making more, how you going?"

Luke wasn't even listening to me. He moved around *Star Wars* people inside the house, his eyes wide with thought. "If I not going get what I ask fo', den I going buy 'em myself," he mumbled, as he laid Princess Leia and Han Solo on the same bed in one of the rooms.

I shook my head again and went back to folding clothes. Why was it so important that he absolutely had to have Lego? Luke reminded me of Dad when Dad wanted a new toy.

Luke built something out of the remaining Lego pieces. I watched him as I finished folding the laundry. He made a little Lego box. He snapped it into the closet right beside Han Solo who relaxed on his bed. "What's dat?" I asked, as I walked past him.

Luke smiled cleverly. "A treasure chest. X mark da spot."

Digging in the moist dirt of an empty flowerbed, Mom's hands seemed to know exactly what to do. With a steady flow from the water hose, Mom made craters in the soft earth. She said 'Ewa Beach hadn't been very nice to her *babies*, her precious rose bushes. The sudden change in weather now that it was January must have shocked them 'cause many of the plants withered in the mounting heat. Some bushes had even died. So, today, she said we were going to start replenishing her *stock*. Mom dropped a little chicken manure and fertilizer in the wet soil and then placed a couple of seeds into each hole. She piled dirt quickly on top of the seeds. She said not many people grew roses this way, but this was a trick she had learned a long time ago.

I looked at the packet the rose seeds came in. My brow furrowed. "Mom? Dis says should be cooler fo' da plants germinate," I said.

Mom snatched the packet away from me. "Don't worry about that. Don't you think I know what I'm doing?" she said defensively.

Honestly? No, I didn't. I was going to tell her no wonder her rose bushes died. She was doing things the hard way. But I decided to keep my mouth shut. I didn't want to play with plants any more than I had to.

Luke asked Mom how plants grew. Mom explained that when seeds were planted in the ground, the soil fed the seeds and made them grow into a plant. Luke's lips pinched together. He didn't get it. "So da seeds alive wen dey come outta da package?" he asked.

Mom's brow furrowed as she thought. "Well . . . no, I guess. But something *magical* happens when you place them in the ground." She smiled and playfully smudged dirt on Luke's face.

Mom told us to wash off and then roll up the water hose. Since the water hose was one of those fifty-foot jobs connected to the spigot on the side of the house, it took me and Luke a while to coil it up. After we cleaned off, I went to the front to ask Mom if we were done. Mom kneeled in front of the flowerbed and whispered into the soil. "Please grow. Please stay alive. Grow for the four of us. I'm sorry for everything. Please grow and give me a sign that you're still listening." Mom patted the ground over each pile, the dirt as smooth as freshly filled graves.

Since some of the rose bushes Mom brought from 'Ālewa Heights died, I imagined the seeds as they sprouted into new bushes, twisting toward the sun at full speed like on the science films they showed us at school. For a moment, it was amazing to me how something that wasn't alive, that was buried deep in the ground, could still live. Not that these seeds ever would. Mom only cared *if* the seeds grew, not *why*.

I started to notice that when people lied, or when they didn't want to tell the *whole* truth, the corners of their lips curled and their hands fidgeted. They occasionally swiped at an uncontrollable itch on the nose. Their head tilted to one side, as their forehead got smooth. And the telltale sign of deceit: their eyes were never still. Those people never looked straight at other people, eyes always dancing around the subject. And their eyes never rested until the lie was forgotten about.

This all happened very fast, all within a moment.

So I had to watch, or else I wouldn't know the truth.

Mom didn't let go very easily. Whenever Luke asked a question about why we had to stay in 'Ewa Beach, Mom scratched her nose. When he asked if he could get a box of Lego at Woolworth's, she didn't look at him but still told him no. Whenever Luke asked her something, he never watched. He didn't see Mom bury things deeper.

For the last two Sundays, Dad hadn't come with us to church. Mom said he shouldn't miss church. He was the very one who needed to go. Dad only sank deeper into his recliner in front of the TV, making it clear what he intended to do.

All the way to church, Mom grumbled about doing everything by herself now, about how she couldn't believe Dad was slipping, how she thought he had really changed. We arrived at the back pew almost twenty minutes after mass started 'cause Mom had tried to get Dad to come. The scriptures had been read, and Father Thomas was already into his sermon.

Before we did the profession of faith, Father Thomas called up kids who were in first communion class. As they stood before the altar, he read a prayer over them. Suddenly, Mom leaned over and whispered in my ear. "You already had first communion, right?" I shook my head no. She exhaled tiredly, and her gaze fell to her lap. Her folded hands were limp on her dress. She touched her wedding ring gently, tracing over the diamond with her index finger. Onto her lap, a tear soaked into the flower print. "Please, Mama?" she whimpered to herself.

After the other kids went out to study for first communion, and after we said the profession of faith, one of the speakers recited the prayers. He started off with, "For our community, that we may come to know the needs of our brothers. We pray to the Lord." Then we needed to respond with, "Lord, hear our prayer." This part of mass always took a long time, going back and forth between prayers, one after the other. Of course, we could speed things along by saying all the prayers at once and then praying to God, but I didn't say anything 'cause I didn't want to get slapped for being irreverent.

The speaker always finished with a prayer for all the things listed in our parish book of intentions and for all of our own personal needs. We were supposed to close our eyes and pray for those. Instead I snuck looks at Mom and Luke. Both of them had their eyes squinted shut. I bet money Mom asked for forgiveness 'cause I hadn't had first communion. I peeked at Luke and smiled. So earnest. I bet he was angling for Lego. Then Father Thomas asked us to pray for the soul of Christina Salvador. When he said this, Mom dropped onto the kneeler quickly and clasped her hands together in prayer. She always got weird when she heard someone died.

"Christina has been laid to rest, but not forever," Father Thomas said. "She lays only for a moment until she can share in the riches of eternity. Pray for her as she joins our Heavenly Father in the gift of everlasting life, as we all join in the unending hope of rising again with her. Please remember Christina as well as the rest of the Salvador family in your prayers this week. And for all those prayers spoken or unspoken, we pray to the Lord."

Mom stood right on cue and said with every one else, "Lord, hear our prayer."

Behind our pew in the back of the church was an array of candles set in blue and red glass holders. Before we left, Mom gave me and Luke a quarter to put in the padlocked offering box. She said the three of us would each light a candle for Christina Salvador. She dropped her coin in, and it landed with a metallic splash. I did the same. We both lit a candle. But when it came to Luke, though, he didn't just insert the coin. He gazed wide-eyed at the quarter, rotating it between his fingers. Mom told him to insert the coin. By the time he finally realized we were waiting on him, Mom just pointed to the collection box. Luke whined that he was just admiring how shiny the coin was. His eyes aimed everywhere but at Mom's face, his lip curling thinly. It wasn't hard to guess what was on his mind. He slowly reached, dangling the quarter over the slot. If Mom wasn't there, I honestly wasn't sure he would've actually let go of the coin. There were so many possibilities. He'd be a little closer to his goal, and it was hard to ignore that. But when Mom smacked his head for fooling around at church, his fingers instinctively released the quarter. And when it hit other coins at the bottom of the box, I swore it sounded like Lego.

Outside in the backyard after church, I listened to Mom scrub the lanai while I raked money tree leaves. Peeking at her, I watched as she moved around almost desperately on her hands and knees with what Luke and I called the coconut brush, trying to get a mud stain out of the concrete. The coconut brush was about a foot long altogether, just like a regular brush with a handle, but the bristles were made from coconut husk fibers. Mom said her father had *fashioned* it himself a long time ago. Whenever she felt a stain just had to go, she always reached for the coconut brush.

I leaned against the rake, watching Mom as she scrubbed relentlessly. It was weird, as if she were possessed, scouring so vigorously she was already sweating. "I tink you got 'em, Mom. Bum-bye you going set da concrete on fire," I joked.

Mom stopped, looking up. She glanced back down at the area she had been scrubbing. She indicated for me to come and have a look. "See how white and clean that gets? All the brown mud is gone." She stared at the spot and inhaled heavily, trying to catch her breath.

I looked at the coconut brush. "Why you do 'em *dat* way?" I asked quietly. "We get one push broom, and plenty soap and water."

Mom glanced at me and then considered. "My grandmother used to do it this way in the plantation days. In fact, all the women and children in the Portuguese camp would scrub the wooden sidewalks so much it turned the wood white."

The question left my lips before I realized what I was asking, and how it could be taken. "How come you do dis if you no like Portagee stuff?"

Mom appraised me. "First of all, stop calling us *that*. We're Portuguese, not Portagee. And what Portuguese stuff don't I like?"

I considered how to respond. I hadn't meant to accuse Mom, but it was something I had wondered. Just where was the line she had drawn? "Um, you no like da food, like *casilla* or *vinha d'alhos*. Wheneva Grandma make one plate fo' us, you throw 'em away. All da Jesus paintings Grandma made fo' us, you got rid of those too. I know you got four gold crucifix pendants as gifts dat you neva worn. You no like do da *Chamarita*, or sing or clap wit' ev'rybody—" I suddenly stopped. I could have continued, but Mom's expression was so twisted I didn't want to.

Tears had begun to stream down Mom's face. Her lips pulled into a miserable pout. She held up the coconut brush, as if to show it to me. Then, without warning, she stood up roughly and hurled the coconut brush against the house. Wiping her face, she stormed inside and slid the family room door shut so hard the glass rattled in place.

Rain hitting a tin roof, the scuttle of a thousand birds across the sky. I had forgotten how soothing 'Ālewa Heights was. Aunty Selma's living room drapes fluttered in gentle breaths of turquoise fabric, like hair floating underwater. Whispers of soft wind made the living room feel cool. Luke lay on the sofa with arms behind his head, his chest rising and falling just right. And to think I was getting used to 'Ewa Beach.

Aunty Selma invited us over for dinner. And just like the last couple of times at church, Dad didn't come. Mom was in the kitchen with Aunty Selma. They sat at the table, as the scent of sizzling salmon seemed to swim into the living room. Mom was still crying. From the moment Aunty Selma asked where Dad was, Mom started bawling and hadn't let up. They tried to keep their voices down so we didn't hear, but Mom was almost hyperventilating.

"I-don't-know-where-he-is-Sel-ma." Each word came slow, between heaves.

I peeked in the kitchen and saw Aunty Selma hand Mom a wad of Kleenex.

"There, there, Minerva. I thought things were starting to turn around for you two. You said you were starting to see the old Leonard. Like you resurrected him from the dead." Mom blew her nose. "So *every* night he comes home late?" Mom nodded. "But he says he's *working*?" Another nod. "You know . . . " Aunty Selma said, trailing off. Her loaded words seemed to hang in the air between them.

Mom hyperventilated again. "He-doesn't-want-*it*-any-more. He-comes-home-drinks-then-goes-to-bed. Noth-ing." She tried to say more, but couldn't. The words were too heavy.

Aunty Selma moved her chair closer to Mom's. "There, there, Minerva. Don't cry. Everything's going to be all right. Don't cry." With one arm draped over Mom's shoulder, Aunty Selma rubbed Mom's back tenderly.

"I-am-alone-with-the-kids-all-the-time. He-never-helps. I'm-afraid-he-wants—" Mom made a squeak I had never heard before and then muffled the rest between her hands. As Aunty Selma tried to comfort her, Mom belted out, "He said *divorce* again!"

Aunty Selma came to the kitchen doorway and told me to take Luke outside to play. When I said it was raining and there weren't any toys here, she gave me stink eye. She told me to go to our old house downstairs, whatever. Just make sure we came back in about thirty minutes. Dinner should be ready by then.

Aunty Selma's house was right above our old house on Skyline Drive. The property was actually a big hill with two separate houses built one on top of the other. Our house, hidden from the road 'cause it was completely under Aunty Selma's, faced away from Skyline Drive, looking over Honolulu Harbor and Sand Island. Farther in the distance toward Diamond Head were the buildings of downtown Honolulu.

I took Luke downstairs for a few minutes. It felt strange being back. The patter of rain as it massaged the ground. It was wonderful, like hearing it for the first time. I closed my eyes and inhaled: wet, soft, cool. Aaah . . . 'Ālewa Heights.

Then I remembered what I used to do alone on days like this. I decided it was high time I shared it with Luke. I grabbed Luke's arm and yanked him upstairs. I dragged him to the dead end side of Skyline Drive where there was a graveyard just below Natsunoya Tea House. Pu'ukamali'i Cemetery was very old, with wild grass growing everywhere. Some headstones were cracked while others had fragmented into rubble. I always thought it was so sad that no one ever came to visit, as if this place and all the people in it had been completely forgotten. So, whenever I needed to get out of the house, I went there.

The graveyard was quite high up, so standing there, taking in the view of Honolulu Harbor and Sand Island, I always felt calm. Complete, somehow. On a ridge between two valleys, it felt as if I were in two places at once. I liked not having to choose sides. Plus, in a graveyard, I could think 'cause it was always quiet.

Luke and I lay down, each on two sides of the same tawny, weather-beaten headstone:

TOMÁS KANALUA
CPL 1 HAWAII INF
WORLD WAR 1
MAY 26, 1897 to MARCH 11, 1929

Rain spooled down in long, thin strands like tears. Looking above into the fading gray light, I told Luke about the times I used to come here late in the afternoon, and how I would get busted, 'cause when I went home I was soaked. I told him about how it made me feel to lie here, not caring if I got lickens or not. How I'd take this cemetery any day over a church 'cause it felt like I could talk straight to God being so high up, with nothing but clouds and sky in between.

Luke propped up on one elbow and eyed me curiously. He had that wrinkled-forehead look again. "You like be wit' dead people instead of at one church?"

Orange light broke through the gray and matured into a softer blue, almost silver. Stars poked through the clouds and into the twilit sky. I pointed up. "Look all those stars, Luke. Listen how quiet. How dis place not more holy dan one . . . building?" I waited for him to respond. When it was clear he had no answer, I went on. "Besides, Luke, dead people not going bother. It's da living ones you gotta worry about. Look," I said, indicating a broken headstone.

Luke thought for a bit and then nodded. He rested his head back on the grass.

I leaned back as well and inhaled this moment with Luke, taking the silence and the rain and peace deep inside to that place where prayers were felt and not just thought. Please, God, no matter how hot it was going to get at home, let Luke remember it too. Then I closed my eyes and heard the refrain from church: *We pray to the Lord. Lord, hear our prayer.*

When Mrs. Ka'ea heard the timer go off on the stove, she rose from the kitchen table she had been working at all afternoon. After she pulled out a steaming dish from the oven and set it on a trivet, she sat back down at the table. Since Toby was still in the bathroom, I went over and sat at the kitchen table too. Mrs. Ka'ea glanced at me for a moment, smiled, then looked down. She shuffled through a pile of papers, occasionally jotting down notes on a yellow legal tablet.

"Is dat fo' your work, Mrs. Ka'ea?" I asked. She looked up and nodded yes, then right back to reading. "And you gotta bring work home?" She nodded yes again and scribbled down something. "What'chu working on?"

Mrs. Ka'ea put her pen down gently and set the stack of papers down as well. "I can see I'm not going to get much work done," she said good-naturedly. She smiled and reached over to ruffle my hair. "But that's okay . . . this time." She winked, and the whole time she spoke, she looked me square in the eye. "Since I'm a paralegal, I have to prepare these papers for court."

My brow furrowed. "What's a para-leego?"

Mrs. Ka'ea smiled. "A *paralegal* is someone who helps a lawyer prepare certain legal documents for when that lawyer goes to court. Do you know what a lawyer is?"

I nodded. "I seen *Kramer vs. Kramer*." And then I remembered. "Lawyers is mean."

Mrs. Ka'ea considered. "Uh . . . the one I work for does practice family law."

I scrunched my forehead. Something sounded suspicious. "What's *family* law?"

"Well, it's how we figure out separations, divorce and custody issues, annulments—"

I cut her off. My heart pounded. "Just like *Kramer vs. Kramer*?"

Mrs. Ka'ea paused a moment, as though testing words before she spoke. "Yes, Landon. What you saw was family law. There was a separation and divorce, then a custody battle. But you have to understand, lawyers aren't *mean*. They're just fighting for the parents. Because both parents usually want the child to live with them."

All of a sudden, I froze. Two parents fighting for one child? What happened when there were two kids? It was one thing when it was a movie, but another thing entirely when I thought of me and Luke. "Do dey always give da kids to da modda, like in da movie?"

Mrs. Ka'ea smiled. "No, not always. Mothers are usually more involved in their children's lives than fathers, so we do see it a lot. But sometimes, it's the father. Other times, one child wants to stay with one parent, and another child wants to stay with the other. It just depends. That's what lawyers help parents figure out."

I felt cold. "You mean da kids no always stay together?" The question came from deep down and was really only one precious word: *Luke.*

"Sometimes, Landon. Sometimes the court finds one parent not fit to take care of the children. I've even seen a few times when children were taken completely away from their parents and put into foster homes, then eventually put up for adoption. When that happens, it's rare for siblings to stay together. People usually only want to adopt one child."

My head spun, and words got caught against the walls of my mind as they went around and around: divorce, custody, adoption. From the moment they left Mrs. Ka'ea's lips, I knew they'd get under my skin and haunt me like our neighbors' whispers.

Mrs. Ka'ea must have seen my panic. She reached out and rested her hand against my cheek. "Family law and lawyers are not all bad, Landon. I mean, adoption can be a very good thing. And it makes me happy."

I thought back to the movie, the yelling, the arguing, the anger. The way the people behaved was so shame. It was just like at my house. "You like doing dat?"

Mrs. Ka'ea patted my hand. "Of course. I get to help special children. It makes me feel good that, because of the work I do, they get taken out of bad family situations and put in a better home, with a loving mother and father who raise them as their own children." She smiled at me and stood up to check the timer. She called down the hallway to Toby, that dinner was ready. "You know, Landon," she said artfully, "one good thing about lawyers is that once you tell them something, they are not allowed, under any circumstances, to repeat it to anyone else. Did you know that?" I shook my head. Mrs. Ka'ea turned and ripped off foil from the steaming dish and rotated the mound of meat with forks. "And since I'm a paralegal, I'm in the same boat. Once someone tells me something, there's no way I'd repeat it."

Maybe lawyers weren't all that bad. They had to keep quiet, no matter what I told them. My ass would be introduced to new realms of hurt when Mom found out I aired all of our family's dirty laundry. But what about me and Luke? I looked back at Mrs. Ka'ea. "Do bruddas and sistas *sometimes* stay together?"

Mrs. Ka'ea nodded, a puzzled look on her face. "Oh, yes. Absolutely." She thought for a moment and then continued. "I'm sorry. Did I make it sound like that *never* happens?" I didn't know what to say, so I just shrugged. "Landon, siblings are sometimes split up, but most often, the courts try to keep them together, with at least one parent, because a divorce is difficult enough for kids to deal with."

My heart hammered away. Thank God.

Mrs. Ka'ea's kind voice gently coaxed me from my thoughts. "Landon?" She squatted next to me so that we were eye to eye. "You know my door is always open, right? You can come here anytime to talk, okay?"

I nodded as words swirled in my mind. Divorce. Custody. Adoption. Before Mrs. Ka'ea, those words were filthy. But now that I understood, I turned them over and over as though kneading through clumps of wet soil, amazed how they weren't so dirty anymore.

Mom took a handful of red roses to Mililani Mortuary. She stopped at Fujioka's in Waipahu before heading up Kamehameha Highway. This was only the second time she took me and Luke to see our grandparents. And on my birthday no less.

Trees blurred as we flew down the long, winding road to the cemetery. Mom parked near the same Mary statue as before. As we got out of the car, she reminded us not to step on anyone's grave. I was curious, but I knew better than to ask why Dad hadn't come with us.

When we reached Grandma and Grandpa's gravesite, Mom laid the roses on the grass in front of the headstone and ran her fingers across the smooth granite. She touched the lettering on her mother's name, then her father's, then the date. *Samuel and Mindy Bode. December 28, 1969.* The day they died. She knelt in front of her parents' grave with hands clasped together in front of her as though in prayer. Then she lowered her head. Sure enough, prayer, so I knelt too. I nudged Luke who wasn't even looking and yanked him down as well.

But instead of praying, Mom began talking. But not to me and Luke. "Hi, Mama. Hi, Papa. It's me, Minerva. No kidding, huh?" She chuckled stiffly. "I brought your favorite. Roses." Mom tilted her head and smiled thinly. She took a deep breath. "Well, these are my children. Last time I didn't introduce them. I know I said I wouldn't, but I don't know what to do anymore. So, here they are. The little one is Luke, and you should recognize the other one. That's Landon." She paused and swallowed something down. Long tears slid down her cheek. Luke put his arm around my waist and hid his face, burrowing deep into my side. "I know you're mad at me for keeping them from you. I'm sorry, Mama. Papa, please. I know you warned me. I know you said I would be on my own. But I need your help." On her knees, Mom held her body with both arms and curled over, the same way I did when I had food poisoning. "Oh, God. Mama, Papa, please forgive me. Give me a sign. Tell me what to do. Let me know I'm not alone in this." Mom's head hung low, and her eyes were on the grass in front of her.

Something caught my eye in the air above. Oh, my God. "Mom—"

Mom's voice was soft and shallow yet thick like mud. "Shhh, Landon. Not now."

I wanted to tell her that at very moment, right when she had asked for a sign, two birds flew over us, dancing in light, high circles above. And then they were gone.

The ride home on Fort Weaver Road was long. I had no clue why we had to go to Mililani Mortuary *today*. Luke probably thought the same thing. Or maybe he was just glad we didn't go back to Fujioka's. So, when we passed Renton Road in Ewa, I decided to ask why we had to go today, of all days, on my birthday. Shouldn't we have baked a cake or had a party?

Mom didn't speak right away. "Damn, selfish kid. Always something to complain about, huh?" She sounded mad, too far in to stop if she wanted to. After a moment, she shook her head. "Do you *really* want to know?"

What? I didn't expect there to actually be a reason. "Um, yeah?" I said brashly.

Mom looked at me when I answered. She had heard my sass. Another moment passed, but when she answered, she spoke simply. "I found out twelve years ago today, on January third, that my mother and father died. Okay? That's why we went today. I thought you'd at least appreciate I took you to see your grandparents."

Mom didn't know how many times I stayed awake at night, staring at the sky and wondering about the grandparents she kept from me. I wanted to know everything about them. What they liked, where they went, what they did. Everything. "How—"

But Mom cut me off in mid-sentence. And she was different now. Her words slapped with the sharp sting of mockery. "Let me guess . . . how did they die, right? And, oh, what a coincidence! Only a few days before your birthday too. Then there must be some connection, right?" I couldn't believe these were her words, coming from her mouth, on *my* birthday. Her sarcasm dripped away. "How come I can't even have my own sorrow? Why is it so important for you to pry into my past? Not today, Landon. One day, but definitely not today." Not letting go, holding on so tight that everything wilted around her, and she wondered why. Holding on so tight she pulled me under, caught beneath the weight of this day and what I did to bury my grandparents.

Needless to say, by the time we got home, I was pissed. I figured, what the heck? What was the worst that could happen? I might even get something I was looking for. So when Mom pulled into in the garage, I sprung the question. "So what, you and Dad going divorce?"

The question caught her off-guard, but she still answered quickly. Too quickly. "No, why would you ask that?" Her lips curled, and her voice was sassy. She gave a long rub down her nose with zero eye contact. After a moment, she side-eyed me, evidently wanting an answer.

I gave her what she wasn't able to give me: the truth. "Since I no can ask about da past, I might as well ask about da future."

That wasn't what Mom expected 'cause she made stink eye, half grunted/half hissed at me, got out of the car, and then slammed the door. I felt a little bad for saying it, but at the same time, no. Letting go was hard, I knew, but frick, it was still my birthday.

Mom said she was so stressed out she couldn't bake my birthday cake. That meant no singing either. She said next time not to stress her out with my wise-ass comments. But at night, I found a box on my bed wrapped in metallic blue and red wrapping paper. I smiled. There were party hats, streamers, and the words *Happy, Happy Birthday* floating everywhere on the paper. The gift was about the size of my pillow, but only a couple of inches thick. Luke had crashed on his bed already, his Lego house in the middle of the floor. I slid the house under our bunk so nobody tripped on it in the middle of the night.

I picked up my birthday present. The tag read: *To Landon. Love, Mom and Dad.* I held it, testing the weight. I shook it and recognized the sound. Lots of plastic pieces. I got really excited 'cause I knew for sure Mom got what I asked for. Good, I didn't have to open it.

I set the gift on our desk, and then ripped out a sheet from Luke's composition tablet. I gently pulled off the Scotch tape that held the tag to the present, trying not to tear any of the blue and red wrapping paper. I took a pen and scribbled a new tag:

Happy Birthday, Luke!!!

I know not your birthday yet, but dis your early birthday present. Hope you like 'em. Now maybe you can build da roof fo' your house. So open right away OK? Don't know how much more time get. Just promise me one ting. If we gotta let go in da future, no matter how hard going get, dat you and me going always stick together.

Your Brother, Landon

13

Dad said if someone didn't produce the *full* bottle of Jack Daniel's that should be in the kitchen cabinet, we were all going to get it. He had just bought a new one, but it was half-empty now. And he didn't drink it. Mom told Aunty Selma that ever since Christmas, he'd drifted further and further away. It wasn't long after coming home real late that Dad started drinking again. Nine or ten o'clock every night, he went straight to the bedroom, changed clothes, showered, and then grabbed the Jack Daniel's bottle and his short glass. He'd sit in the living room or the family room, sipping and clenching his teeth. If Luke or I came into the room, he snapped and asked why we weren't in bed already. And to turn off the light on our way out.

When the half-empty bottle still hadn't been replaced, Dad accused Mom. "What, Minerva? You like me be civil? You like me *try*? No trow away my stuff den." Mom claimed it wasn't her, but he drowned out her assertions. "I know was you, so no even try. I neva even complain once about dis pig-pen. Look da kitchen. Rubbish in da trash can. Dishes still in da sink. And dis table. Papers all ova da damn place. At ten o'clock at night? If you no like give me one reason fo' snap, one new bottle betta Harry Houdini in da cabinet by tomorrow."

Mom told Aunty Selma Dad had been nitpicking lately. He scrutinized every move she made as though under a microscope. The shower: she missed scum in the grout. The carpet: she left hairballs around the feet of the couch. The drapes: she must like stains on the fabric. Aunty Selma said it sounded like he was looking for a reason to be pissed-off. When it was all said and done, though, Mom still bought a new bottle of Jack Daniel's and put it in the kitchen cabinet.

Rosie's cage was in the kitchen now. Mom wanted Rosie near since she spent most of her day in the kitchen. She placed the stand and the cage behind the kitchen table, right next to the window so Rosie could look outside. During the day, Mom left the cage open so Rosie could climb out, grabbing and feeling her way around the metal bars.

Even after almost four months, Rosie still gave me the creeps. Besides the fact she was a mynah bird with milk-white albino feathers, her eyes were weird. Cloudy, pink, liquid . . . sacs. Whenever I sat at the kitchen table, Rosie jumped off her cage and scuttled close. It didn't matter if anything was on the table, she just scampered right over it. Then she stopped in front of me. She cocked her head and blinked her pink eyes in fascination.

What surprised me, though, was that Rosie gave up flying in the house. The first time she tried, she flew straight into the picture window in the living room. That was when Mom said she thought Rosie might be a true albino: blind as a bat. Since then Rosie stayed out of the air and only on her feet. It was kind of funny to watch her move about 'cause she almost always walked into something. She bumped into and then even tried to climb a cup that blocked her way. When Luke and I laughed, Mom scolded us. She said it wasn't the same as *Looney Tunes*, that when Rosie hit something, she actually hurt herself. How would we feel if we were blind?

Mom stuck out her finger as a perch for Rosie, and then took Rosie to the front door. When I asked why she would take a blind bird to the front door, Mom told me to watch my mouth. Mom stood there, Rosie on one finger, as she rubbed Rosie's head with another. Mom talked to Rosie too, but I couldn't make out what she said. Mom said that if I didn't have anything better to do, maybe I needed more chores. That was my cue to make myself as scarce as possible. In our room, I took in the sound of Mom's voice, so soft and gentle. So rare. I sighed deeply and then looked at Luke. He was listening, too.

But when Dad came home, Rosie somehow found her way back into the cage and stayed put. Once she heard Dad's voice, Rosie just sat behind bars, blinking two pink cloudy eyes.

I didn't look forward to going back to school 'cause I already knew what was coming: Afa Palaipale and his mouth. So when vacation was over, I had already expected the chicken noises from his side of the room. I guessed a two-week break was better than no break at all.

Mrs. Kato gave us a math test on the first day. Word problems. Everyone groaned when she explained we only had twenty-five minutes to complete the test. "And don't forget, in word problems, the answer is in the question. They're connected. Everything you need to solve the problem is there. You just have to know what you're looking for."

At the first problem, I thought I was going to flunk this test. By the third problem, I knew for sure 'cause that was all I could get to in twenty-five minutes. Mrs. Kato told us after lunch we all must've had *great* vacations

’cause nobody remembered a thing about word problems. She said we had to start all over again.

Mrs. Kato said when we started a problem, we needed to read it all the way through first. We had to make sure we understood what it was asking for. Then we needed to examine the information we had and how it all fit into the problem. Once we knew how the information fit, the answer revealed itself. She gave us formulas to memorize and several worksheets that needed to be done by tomorrow. Everyone groaned again. Mrs. Kato said we needed to eat, breathe, and sleep word problems.

That night at home, after everyone was asleep, I sat at the kitchen table with my math textbook and worksheets. I struggled with problem after problem. After an hour, my head hurt, and I wondered how to tell Mrs. Kato that I just didn’t understand. For a moment, I was afraid I might have to go for remedial help after school with all the slow and special ed students.

Also, for the second night in a row, I couldn’t sleep. I imagined chicken noises and the faces of the other kids, gratified by how my shame grew. I looked at the cabinet where Dad kept his Jack Daniel’s. Even though I could almost feel the answer in a hot whirlpool down my throat, I decided not to open the cabinet for the first time in two weeks.

Mom didn’t hear when I came into the kitchen ’cause her back was turned. She had Rosie on the kitchen counter and shook out a pill from a prescription bottle. She laid the pill on the counter and then slid the prescription bottle back into the spice cabinet. Her voice was strained, as she talked to Rosie. “I never thought I’d be taking pills again. My roses still won’t grow, my husband’s still drifting, and I don’t know what to do. Can *you* tell me what to do?” Mom lifted Rosie and kissed her. A couple of chirps. “But you knew I took *those*, didn’t you? You found out.” A moment passed. Mom still held Rosie close to her face and peered into the pink eyes. “I don’t blame you anymore. I don’t blame you for anything. Can you hear me?”

When Mom saw me at the kitchen table, she put Rosie back while she grilled me with twenty-questions: How long was I listening? Why wasn’t I doing chores? Why did I have to do my homework there? Boy, was she paranoid. She accused me of eavesdropping and then threatened me with more chores. After she calmed down, Mom decreed I just inherited all of the vacuuming for being nosy. Not just the weekly chore but the daily sweep around the house as well. Job number one: hairballs.

"Da *daily* vacuuming?" I asked. "Why gotta be ev'ry day? Not even dirty."

Mom snapped. "Don't talk back to me! You're really asking for it. I never talked back to my parents. You want another chili pepper? We'll see who'll be talking after that."

As Mom slammed dishes around, I looked down. What did I do? I just came to the kitchen to do my homework.

Mom's words came all at once. "And another thing," she ranted, "I'm tired of being blamed for the things you kids fail to do. Did you hear your father yelling at me? Start taking some pride in your chores."

Mom's words were in my head. They swirled and burned like a thick swig of Jack Daniel's. And as my eyes began to water, I felt them grit between my teeth.

Mom pressed on. "How does it feel to be yelled at? Not too good, huh? Then get your ass in gear, start the vacuuming, and stop looking at me like a dummy."

At this point, the hot streaks dripped down my face. "Why, Mom?" I blurted out. She turned and glared at me. "What I did?" I asked. But before she could say another word, I flew to me and Luke's room. I crawled into bed and curled into the sheets. I foolishly tried to hide in the folds, wishing I could sink into the fabric and just disappear. Then maybe Mom would finally see me. 'Cause right now her eyes were open, but she didn't see shit.

Every time Mrs. Kato saw my worksheets, she winced. They were usually only half done. But after a couple of hours at the kitchen table, my head got too sore to think. She asked me to stay in at recess. I knew it, she wanted to put me in remedial help after school. When the bell rang, everyone raced out except me. Mrs. Kato walked over and sat next to me.

"Landon, I notice you're having a hard time with word problems."

I hung my head so I didn't have to look at her. I didn't want to disappoint Mrs. Kato. I glanced out the window and saw Afa and some others stick their tongues out like the mentally-retarded kids in the special ed wing. I felt their eyes, crawling all over me.

"This is surprising to me, Landon. I didn't think I challenged you enough. You always seem to *get* every assignment, so it's surprising when a smart kid like you can't do something as easy as word problems."

What? Smart? I didn't know what to say. No one ever called me *smart* before. After that, I really couldn't look at her.

"I just wanted to tell you that it's perfectly fine to ask for help, okay?"

I lifted my eyes, my head still low. "I no can go remedial help afta school, 'cause I gotta walk my brudda home."

Mrs. Kato smiled and chuckled lightly. "Don't worry, I didn't mean you needed help from the Remedial Enrichment Program. They couldn't help you, anyway. You're way smarter than that. Just make sure you ask me, that's what I'm here for. I can give you pointers." Mrs. Kato said to try something tonight when I did my homework. She gave me a highlighter and told me to read each problem three, four, even five times through, and then highlight what I thought went into the formula. She said that for me, there was too much going on in the problem. Almost as if there were too many words, and I got lost in the information. She said to step back, look for the important parts, and then highlight them. Mrs. Kato said if I tried to solve a problem before even understanding it, I'd lose a lot of sleep in my lifetime.

Mrs. Kato didn't know the half of it. But before I left, I agreed to try her suggestion.

Half the time, I couldn't even hang out with Toby. I had so many chores I didn't even ask anymore. Otherwise, I risked another task getting added to the list. And even if chores and homework were done, and there was still time before dinner, Mom said no anyway. It seemed like she didn't even want me to leave the house anymore.

Every day, it was the same routine: go to school, get Luke after school, then walk straight home. No dilly-dallying 'cause there were things to do. Chores first, homework second, goofing off . . . maybe. Eat dinner, shower, go to sleep. Repeat daily.

Ever since Dad started drinking again, Mom had gotten more uptight. If we didn't do things in order, her order, we had better watch out. And worse, if we didn't do a good job on a chore, Mom laid it on heavy, saying we must want her to get in trouble with Dad 'cause we were satisfied with half-assed work. Occasionally, Mom hovered over us. She'd supervise and snap when we missed something. If we did shoddy work, as she called it, Luke and I had to do the chore over again, which better be perfect the second time.

I thought about flying again. Every time I scrubbed the toilet, wiped the baseboards, sorted clothes, or did any other brain-numbing exercise, my mind floated away. I imagined clouds, wind, and speed. I indulged myself. I could let go and be free. And just like that, I watched myself rise up among fumes of Pine-Sol, Windex, and Tide, drifting out of the bathroom, out the front door and into the sunshine, as my hands worked on.

My word problem worksheet was a mess of yellow streaks. But Mrs. Kato's idea seemed to be working. I had gotten my homework answers correct for the last couple of days. Mrs. Kato reaffirmed that I just needed to step back from the problem, to see how the smaller pieces fit into the big picture. When I offered back her highlighter, she said to keep it. It was mine.

Sitting at the kitchen table, I highlighted, then hashed out word problem after word problem. Since everyone was asleep, the house was quiet. So when Rosie suddenly hopped off her metal cage onto the table, I wanted to scream but held it in. Damn, freaky, pink-eyed bird.

I watched Rosie flit closer, scuffling over worksheets, stopping next to my hand. I started my homework again. After a couple of minutes, she hopped onto my arm and cocked her head so that only one eye showed. I side-eyed her and smiled. She just watched, as though appraising me with each neck tilt. I went back to my homework, but she hopped onto my worksheet.

"No can sleep either, huh, Rosie?" Her neck twisted, as if to see me better. I chuckled. The blind bird trying to get a better look. "You one funny bird." Her eyes blinked once, twice. "I no like do da last problem, but you gotta move so I can finish." Then, like Rosie could read my mind, she puffed up and took a stately shit on my homework. She shook and ruffled her feathers before deflating to normal size. "Not funny, Rosie." I put my finger under her, and she climbed on. I set her on the counter and got a Scott towel to clean my worksheet.

Rosie waited on the counter for me to come back. After I threw away her doo-doo Scott towel, I noticed Rosie stood right beneath the spice cabinet. I peeked into the living room to make sure Mom wasn't awake. Then I opened the spice cabinet and found Mom's prescription bottle. It was still half full with powder blue capsules. The label read: *For anxiety. Do not drink alcohol while taking Valium. Take only the prescribed amount. An overdose may be fatal. Keep Valium out of reach of children. Patient: Minerva DeSilva.*

I replaced the bottle in the cabinet and then slid Rosie into her cage. Why was Mom taking pills? I glanced at the highlighter on the table. I could figure this out. I considered for a moment. What information did I already have? Well, I knew that sometimes I took pills when I didn't feel well. That must be it! Mom must be sick too. So that was why she had been so uptight lately. I smiled and congratulated myself for having figured it out. I began to feel hopeful. When Mom felt better, she'd let me go to Toby's house, right? And that meant surfing.

Another problem solved. It really was easy to see when I knew what to look for.

Friday night after work, Dad showered, dressed up in church clothes, and then hunted all over his and Mom's room for his loose change bowl. Mom said she didn't know what he was talking about. He said he had a wooden bowl on his end table with a bunch of coins in it. Mom really looked as if she had no clue. "Where are you going, Leonard? It's Friday night," she said hopefully. "I thought maybe you could spend some time with us." Dad just searched on and muttered about how a koa bowl couldn't walk off on its own. Mom asked again.

Dad didn't make eye contact when he answered. And his lip curled. "I going out wit' da guys from work. We going drink, Dwayne's house."

Mom's face didn't change. She just watched Dad get ready, her eyes blank. No words. Nothing. Like she wasn't even there.

When I went to do laundry in the morning, Mom said she'd take care of it. No problem here, one less chore. She also said I could go to Toby's after breakfast. I knew it: Mom felt better. I smiled, proud that I had gotten it right. Her pills must be working.

After breakfast, I was about to brush my teeth, but I heard Mom in the bathroom. I peeked around the corner and saw her on her knees, her back facing me. I could see her face in the stand-up mirror on the wall. Her expression was hard and when she spoke, her voice was cold. "Think you're so sly. A real cool cat." Mom dug through the pile of whites to remove all the briefs. She kicked the rest of the socks and undershirts toward the work clothes mound. Then Mom held each of Dad's briefs up to her nose and inhaled the crotch area. She breathed deep and rubbed the fabric slowly between her fingers. When she was finished with one brief, she flung it at the pile of work clothes and hunted for another. The thick smell of VO5, sweat, and Brut wafted out of the bathroom. Her hands scurried over briefs, as she put them to her nose, sniffed, and then threw them aside. But when she came to one brief in particular, after inhaling and rubbing it, she stopped. Still clutching the brief, both hands dropped limply to her lap. Her jaw muscles went rigid as her teeth clenched, and everything seemed to slow to a stop, the inhaling, the rubbing, the discarding. It was as if she had stopped breathing altogether. For the first time, I noticed her eyes, how swollen they were, how puffy pink they were around the lids. How sick she looked. Mom sat there for a long time and just stared at herself in the mirror. At once, she slowly raised the brief to her mouth and sucked on the crotch part. It was so gross, but I couldn't stop watching. As soon as she put the brief in her mouth, she found what she was looking for. The brief sank back onto her lap, as she stared once again into the mirror, lost in her own reflection. "Son of a bitch," she whispered.

While I was vacuuming, I waited until Mom was in the yard to do their room. Mom's cardboard box was still on the floor in her closet. It was too good an opportunity to pass up. I left the vacuum on like last time and flipped open the cardboard box. I peeked over my shoulder while I dug around. Lots of papers, picture jackets, and even what felt like a photo album. I rummaged for something small enough to sneak away. When I felt a compact, plastic cylinder, I snatched it out of the box. It was a scratched-up, empty prescription bottle with a white cap still snapped on tight. The orange plastic was so old it had turned a murky brown. There was a faded, yellow label on the bottle that looked as if it used to be white. But as I inspected it, I realized it wasn't a prescription bottle at all. No patient name, no description what the drug was, no directions for use, and no warning about the drug. There was a date and only three other words on it: *May 1969. Estrogen and Progesterone.* I shook the bottle and realized something was in it. It wasn't a pill, but something was loose in it that had been stuffed in the bottom. I hid the bottle in my pocket, folded the box flaps, and finished vacuuming. When the chore was done, I headed straight to me and Luke's room.

When I popped the lid on the bottle, there was a funky smell: old, stale, rotten. Wrong. Wedged into the bottom of the bottle was a small, tightly-packed wad of paper. As I peeled open the wad, the paper felt greasy yet brittle, and it had crosshatched folds barely holding everything together like old scars on an old body. I could tell this paper had been folded and re-folded many times. When it was completely unfurled, I gasped. It was a letter from Grandma to Mom:

December 5, 1969

Dear Minerva,

Let me start by saying how disappointed your father and I are in you. We know about your escapades. Haven't we given you a wonderful childhood and a comfortable home? Haven't we given you everything you've ever needed or wanted? But yet you have always defied us. We tried to teach you, but you wouldn't learn. What you've been doing, make no mistake, is wrong, Minerva. We tried to reason with you, but you wouldn't listen. He stopped sneaking around here, so you snuck out. No more, Minerva. Never.

If not for your religion, then for the sense of morality that we tried to teach you! It's evil, Minerva. What you've been doing is evil and dirty. And we'll not let you get away with it any longer. God watches all of us, Minerva. He's always watching. He knows what you've been doing. You think you've gotten away with it? Think again.

I cringe to think how many you've had before. First it was the popolo, then the jap, then the pa-ke, then the flip. And now this beach bum. Were you their WHORE too? And I bet you fancy to think that you were the only one. Or at least that you were their FIRST, right? Well, think again. You were their WHORE because they like to WHORE, and they have WHORED, and they'll continue to WHORE after you. You are so naive.

You asked if you're invited on the trip your father and I are taking at the end of the year. No, you will not be coming on this trip because you are pregnant. You think you're hiding it? You are such a disgrace. Since you graduated, you've done nothing but dilly-dally your life away. It's high time you start taking your life seriously. You say he wants to marry you? I've changed my mind. Go ahead, let him take care of you. Make each other honest, if you can.

You have three options: move out and live with him, get married, or get un-pregnant. You know what your religion says about all three. I pray you choose wisely, or may God have mercy on your soul. Whichever way you choose, make sure you are out of our house by the time your father and I return home on January 10th. You have a little over a month to decide.

—Your Mother

P.S. Next time, make sure that the birth control pills you buy are from a doctor, with a prescription, and not from one of your friends. You probably got a year's supply of aspirin.

Birth control pills? I knew what *birth* and *control* meant separately, but there was a pill that helped control when someone made a baby? I didn't know that. I thought people only took pills when they were sick.

But then a few more words hit me when I glanced at the date. *Whore* and *naïve*. December 5, 1969. *Pregnant*. I wasn't sure what naïve meant, but I definitely heard whore before. I didn't know exactly what it meant either, but only women got called it and only in a bad way. It was a word Mom had heard a lot in her life, evidently even when she was younger. A strong enough word that it made her ask for birth control pills. A word that, even though it had nothing to do with illness, really meant sick. I glanced at the date and skimmed through the letter again. Then it hit me.

1969? *Get married, or get un-pregnant*? Holy shit. I was born less than a month later . . . and Mom and Dad weren't married yet? I felt a sinking feeling inside. This letter was about me. This was all my fault. But then something even worse occurred to me. I hunted through the letter line by line and then I saw it. *Birth control*. I didn't need to step back to see it was the right answer. I felt it in my bones:

Mom didn't want me born.

14

Why Luke was doing it, I didn't know. For the last few days, the first thing he did when we got home from school was head straight to the fridge. He grabbed leftover hot dogs, mashed potatoes, tuna and egg omelet, or whatever was packed away in Saran Wrap from the night before. I watched him shovel food down his throat, depositing it as fast as he could.

On our way home from school, I asked Luke if he had been eating school lunch. He got real quiet and began dragging his feet, not looking at me at all. My first thought was Darren Furtado and his punks. "Those kids still chasing you?"

Luke still didn't look at me. He shrugged weakly.

"What'chu mean you dunno?" Hold it. Something had just clicked. "You not eating lunch on purpose?"

Luke shrugged again. Then he looked away.

Oh, my God. I could already see it, Luke convulsing on the lanai again. "What da hell you tinking, dummy? You like get sick and wind up in da hospital again?"

Luke didn't look at me, but his eyebrows furrowed. "I not going get sick. And I not one dummy, Landon. I eat. Look." He pulled out a roll of Chinese Haw Flakes and peeled off a rubbery slice. He stuck it in his mouth with sassy precision, chewed the circular, brownish fruit-cardboard, then swallowed. "See? I eat," he said, strings of Haw fibers stretched across his tongue as though he had coughed up strands of blood.

I was confused. "Where you bought dat from? Woolworth's?" Luke nodded yes, made a face, and peeled off another slice. Luke told me how he snuck away when Mom took him to Foodland or Woolworth's and how he bought whatever he wanted from the candy section. And since Haw Flakes were cheaper than Life Savers, he got more bang for his buck. "But how? Wit' your lunch money?" Luke nodded again, slurping saliva as he deposited the fruit coin in his mouth. "So you buy only snacks instead of lunch?" I asked. "Mom going be pissed wen she find out." I didn't admit it to Luke, but it was actually a pretty good idea. If he saved his lunch money, he could eat when he got home *and* get snacks. Like getting two-for-one.

Luke side-eyed me. "I no only buy snacks, you know," he said slyly. Luke lifted his eyebrows confidently as though he had it all figured out.

I waited for him to continue, but he didn't. "So what you did wit' da rest of da money?"

Luke smiled deviously. "I saving 'em."

"Fo' what?"

Luke looked around as though to make sure no one was listening. "Lego," he whispered. "I get fifteen dollas and tirty-five cents. I going buy enough Lego fo' finish my house." He winked at me. I stopped walking, though, and just looked at my brother, a dirt cloud swirling around our feet. He was starving himself for Lego?

And for the first time in a long time, I noticed he still walked home barefoot.

Instantly, I thought about flying. I wanted to pull Luke high above ʻEwa Beach, higher than the clouds that hung higher on him than on me.

Rosie's bare feet gripped Mom's finger and curled. Out of the cage, she squirted her business on the kitchen table instead of the clean newspaper behind bars. Mom had a napkin ready to wipe up the blobs. She said Rosie must have saved that one all night. But every time it was the same. Mom pulled Rosie out and then she crapped, right on the kitchen table.

Mom sat and stroked Rosie's head. "Do you remember, Rosie, when I saved you from that mean, old cat? And look at you now, all grown up." Mom kept petting the bird. Rosie stayed on Mom's finger and craned her neck contentedly with each stroke. It was strange thinking about Zork. He had only been gone a few months, but it seemed a lot longer. Even stranger was a bird, no matter if she was blind, that didn't even try to fly anymore.

After school, Luke walked fast so he could get home to eat. When he was a few feet ahead of me, I told him to slow down 'cause I wasn't about to run. We had chores waiting for us at home. Luke started to whine, but I cut him off. I told him what he should be doing was eating school lunch. He kicked the gravel as we made our way down Pāpipi Road.

Just as I caught up to Luke, I heard a voice behind me. "Landon?" I turned around and saw Jason Jones, the haole boy from my class. "You got a minute?" he asked.

I thought about how Luke wanted to eat and decided to make him sweat. It would be good for him. Luke continued walking. "Yeah, Jason. Wassup? Try wait. Luke, you betta come back." He about-faced and stomped back to where Jason and I stood, dust clouds swirling about our legs. Jason handed me a small bag of peanut M&Ms. "What dis fo'?" I asked.

Jason smiled weakly. "I wanted to thank you for helping me with Afa." I shrugged it off like it was no big deal, but in the back of my mind, chicken noises rang out. Jason continued. "My mom goes crazy around the holidays and buys too much candy. We had some leftover M&Ms from Valentine's Day. So . . . thanks."

I looked at the package of M&Ms. "Um, no problem." Luke bumped into me and then leaned against my body, coveting the M&Ms from below. I glanced at Jason. "Dis my brudda Luke. I going share wit' him, okay?" Jason shrugged, so I handed Luke the package. We all started walking together. "Where you live, Jason?"

He pointed ahead. "Right on the corner of Ha-lee-po and Pa-pee-pee, in the two-story house." It was funny hearing him pronounce Hawaiian street names. I glanced at Luke. He chomped an M&M in half and held aloft the half-chewed fragment, as though inspecting the nut safely surrounded by a layer of chocolate. "My father works at Iroquois Point," Jason said, "and my mother stays home. I walk home this way every day." We turned off Pāpipi onto Hailipo and stood in front of a light blue two-story house with dark blue trim. Jason stood uncomfortably, as though trying to find the right words. Finally, he broke the silence. "I usually wait until you're walking home and have turned up Ha-lee-po before I leave the playground."

I looked at him for the first time, I mean, really looked at him. "How come?"

Jason smiled and shrugged. "I didn't want to make things worse by walking home with you. You're getting it bad enough as it is." As he turned to go in the wrought-iron gate, he stopped and looked over his shoulder. "Thanks again, Landon. And . . . sorry."

Jason tiptoed up the sidewalk to his front door. For some strange reason, I knew before he checked the handle that he was going to need a key. His house looked like the front door would be locked. Once Jason was inside, he waved, almost shutting the door on his hand.

I turned my attention back to Luke. He was busy swinging the bag of M&Ms around like a sling loaded with rocks. He had twisted one end of the bag so that there was a neck, testing the weight of whatever was left in the bag. "Luke, you save me any of my own M&Ms?" He smiled and stopped twirling the bag. He handed it to me. It felt almost empty. Fricken guy. I looked inside. "Only two red ones left?" I asked. "Ho, da pig, ah?"

Luke smiled wide. His smirk was a peanut-and-sweaty-chocolate paste, and his teeth were stained brown as though they were rotten. "I saving da best fo' last," he said.

The stains on Luke's socks looked like they were getting worse. This was the third pair. The stain was a dark brown rust, all over the toes and heels. Even after a second wash with Tide, and a third with Clorox, Luke's socks still didn't come clean. But in one sock, I also found a quarter. I showed it to Luke and asked what was going on.

He laid Han Solo and Princess Leia safely in a wooden bowl that sat next to his Lego house. Then he looked at me. "Dat's where I hide my money wen I go school, so nobody steal."

"In your socks?" He raised his eyebrows to indicate yes. "How much money you taking school?" When he said all of it, my eyes felt like they were going to squirt out of my head. "Fifteen bucks in coins?" I almost shouted. He nodded yes, his forehead creased. "You not afraid somebody going jack you fo' your money?" I asked. Luke shook his head no. "You not afraid? Den you more dumb dan I thought. I'd be scared if I was you. I not going be around in couple months fo' protect you. I going intermediate school next year, you know."

Luke's expression darkened as he pouted. "I no need you fo' protect me, Landon. And I not dumb, I know what I doing. I saving da best fo' last." He picked up his *Star Wars* figures and started playing again, ignoring me.

I stood in the doorway, unable to pull Luke higher. I knew that the harder I tried, the further he sank. He knew what he was doing? He was saving the best for last? He barely understood what was going on between Mom and Dad. I turned around and exhaled tiredly, gritting my teeth on the way to the bathroom.

I was so pissed that I didn't even remember to ask Luke how he got his socks so dirty in the first place. If he carried around all of his coins in his socks, Luke couldn't run away from Darren Furtado and his boys at lunch time. But Luke must still be having problems with them 'cause his socks were brown and dirty from running across the field. White and brown started to swirl in my head. I looked at Luke's socks. What the hell was going on?

Whenever I finished an assignment, Mrs. Kato asked me to take notes all over campus. She always asked if I minded doing an errand for her. And I always said no 'cause honestly, I didn't. I liked Mrs. Kato. Plus, she always *asked* and never told.

She said I saved her a lot of time and energy. "I don't know what I'm going to do next year when you go to intermediate school, Landon. Who will I depend on?"

"I can come back, Mrs. Kato, and run errands fo' you. I gotta walk my little brudda home afta school anyway."

Mrs. Kato chuckled good-naturedly. "I know, Landon. You have a big heart, that's why. I know you'd come back if you thought you could help." She smiled and thanked me.

Her words settled warmly as I walked back to my desk, so I locked them safely away like jewels in a vault. Her words nestled further into that quiet place, a deep refuge that no one knew about. It was a place that always made me smile inside.

Since talking with Jason, I always looked at his house when Luke and I walked past. But I still didn't talk to him in class or else the chicken noises would start again. The only time I talked with Jason was when we were grouped together for a class project or when we were on the same team for P.E. But every so often, I saw him look at me knowingly before he looked away.

As Luke and I passed the blue two-story house, I noticed Jason outside. He waved, jumped up from the porch steps, and jogged to the front gate. Luke tried to keep walking, so I grabbed him. Jason still wore P.E. clothes and was sweating. His chest heaved in and out as though he had been running. Just above his feet, he had something weird strapped to his legs. He smiled and asked what took us so long. He had already been home for an hour.

I held onto Luke while my jackass brother marched in place. "Luke's teacha made him stay afta school 'cause he neva like do his work," I said. Jason smiled and leaned against the gate. "What you get around your legs?" I pointed at Jason's feet.

"These are my father's ankle weights," he said simply. Jason explained how his father let him wear the ankle weights 'cause they helped him to run faster. When I asked *how* the weights made him run faster, Jason said they made him heavier, and that made his leg muscles stronger. So after he got used to the extra pounds, when he took off the ankle weights, he'd run faster.

"What fo' you like run faster?" I asked.

But before Jason answered, we both turned at the sound of glass smashing from inside Jason's house. Then two voices yelling. It had to be his mother and father. Jason leaned in close and whispered. "One day, I'm going to be the world's fastest runner." He glanced quickly toward the house.

"I have to go. See you tomorrow." He trotted up the sidewalk, opened the front door just wide enough to shuffle in sideways, and then peeked back.

We looked at each other for a moment, and at once, I saw everything, bolted safely within, trying to hide yet trying to escape. His eyes said it all, why he wanted to be the world's fastest runner. With a wave, the door shut, and the house swallowed him whole.

Above my bunk, I heard Luke eating in his bed. My guess was Haw Flakes. He unwrapped the paper, chewed with obnoxious slurps, and then swallowed. When he leaned over the edge of his bunk to check if I was asleep, I quickly shut my eyes and pretended I was down for the night. He rolled back on his bed and ate some more. After a while, I felt a shift of weight. Was he kneeling? Then Luke started praying. "Dear Jesus, please help me sleep. I having hard time now. Oh, and tank you fo' da good idea fo' Darren guys. Tree of dem, just li'dat. I know I suppose to be sorry, but I not. Felt good. Oh, yeah, so please help me sleep. I saving da best fo' last. Do dis in memory of me." I imagined him solemnly deposit another fruit-coin into his mouth, like in communion. He chewed a few times. "In Jesus name. Amen."

Luke rustled in bed, as he struggled to get comfortable. I heard him pound his head into the pillow, trying to sink into the night. After a few minutes, he leaned over the edge of the bed again to double-check if I was asleep. I let out a snore to make it more believable. He squinted, leaning closer for a moment, and then hoisted his hanging body back onto his bed.

It was well past three before Luke fell asleep, tucked in the fetal position. Standing on my bunk so I could see him, I smiled sadly as Luke drifted along in darkness, awash with all that he was starting to understand. I wanted to hug him and tell him not to worry, that everything would be all right. We'd always be together. But I also knew he needed to see it for himself.

Toby didn't like that I had started talking to Jason and warned me that Afa and his boys had been talking too. He said the more I talked with Jason, the more Afa puffed up, thinking I was too panty, too chicken to even protect myself. Toby said I had to be careful. "Why you gotta talk wit' da *haole* boy anyway?" Toby said, as he waxed down his surfboard.

Mrs. Ka'ea looked sharply at him. "Watch your mouth, Toby. I don't like *that* at all. It doesn't matter what color skin he has, we're all the same on the inside. He breathes, eats, feels, and hurts, just like the rest of us. In fact," she said craftily, "I bet he'd love surfing just as much as you do." Toby's face dropped, the disc of wax falling from in his hand. He was about to protest when his mom snapped. "Don't even start, Tobias. How about not going surfing anymore? *Ever.* I bought that board and the broken one from Chaz, saving your okole big time. Go get the school directory and call him up." Toby walked slowly away, puzzled as to what just happened. A half hour later, Toby, Jason, and I were in the water behind Toby's house.

For being so athletic at every other sport, Jason sucked royally at surfing. Toby and I treaded water by the rocky shore while Jason tried over and over to get up on the board. Every time he tried, he wobbled and splashed off the side. Toby swam over and coached Jason again on how to stand, on how to position his feet for stability.

We floated near the shore as Jason tried Toby's suggestions. Jason tried again and still fell. Big splashes with every slip. But what I noticed was that even though Jason made A, every time he slid off, he got right back on. I saw it in his face, set firmly in his eyes. Nothing was going to stop him from getting this.

Again and again, Jason plunged into the dark blue but surfaced among thousands of shiny coins of air, a determined rising out of the water and onto the board again. Right then, I didn't remember why I helped him with Afa in the first place, but I knew deep down I was glad I did.

Mom's voice was a deep whisper as she talked with Aunty Selma on the phone. She sat at the kitchen table and doodled away on the phone pad, the entire time staring absently out at Pupu Street. As Mom argued with Aunty Selma, she scribbled harder and harder with the blue ballpoint. "What am I supposed to do, Selma?" Mom waited, but the pen kept moving. After a moment, Mom scoffed. "I can't reach out to *them*. How can I pretend I'm one of the church ladies, after what I did? It was premarital, Selma! They'll want to know what the *problem* is. Have us come in for counseling." Mom shook her head resolutely. "Can you imagine? Airing our dirty laundry all over 'Ewa Beach, to people like . . . *that*. You said it yourself: a bunch of brownies, just like Leonard's family. And then every Sunday, I'd have to see them in church, sitting there judging me. No way." Mom glanced down at the phone pad and recoiled as if slapped. She ripped off the top sheet and crumpled it, all the while listening to Aunty Selma. "What choice did I have? I *had* to tell his mother. If I didn't, what would've happened to the kid and me? Yeah . . . sure. Selma, he was already pulling back!" Mom tossed her wadded-up scratch paper in the kitchen rubbish. "No, he would *not* have. And this is not being saved. He couldn't care less. He doesn't remember anything important like anniversaries or birthdays. That just tells me he was forced to. I mean, I see it now, all the way to the core. I treated him like he was my knight in shining armor, the king I gave my riches to. But what he sees is an investment, a live-in, tattletale whore. I'm somewhere he can insert his dick and keep it every once in a while, seeing as how he *had* to."

Mom stopped talking. She turned around abruptly and saw me on the couch. I looked back at her with a glass of water up to my lips, her stare locking with mine. For a moment, the silence was so loud it hurt. I wanted to ask my question, but before I could get it out, Mom swiveled in her chair and shrunk back into herself. She muffled her voice to cover up what she didn't want me to know.

But I already knew it. Mom didn't know I had read what Grandma wrote to her. I merely wondered why Mom let it happen in the first place.

Still, later that night, I dug through the trash and found the scratch paper Mom had scribbled on. When I smoothed it out, there was only one word, scrawled in angry blue ink, what Mom wanted to hide: *W-H-O-R-E.*

I wondered where Luke was when I got to Mrs. Shelley's room. Then I heard it: *Beef! Beef! Beef!* I didn't even realize my feet were pounding the ground, caught up in the flock of kids heading toward the cafeteria dumpsters. I knew deep down that Luke was there and he was in trouble. My legs pumped faster, my mind racing through questions and through even deeper promises of what I'd do to anyone who hurt Luke. Everything inside was still running as I skidded to a stop in the gravel. I plowed my way through the jeering throng of kids. Luke was there, a contestant amid a ring of faces. He had pinned Darren Furtado in the gravel. Luke sat on Darren's chest, and he unleashed everything he had, punch after punch, into Darren's face.

Before I even realized what I was doing, Luke was in my arms, still swinging away, hitting me with heavy fists that hurt. I held him close, so he couldn't swing at me anymore. His arms flailed all over the place. He struggled, as he yelled that Darren was never going to hurt him again. I told Luke to calm down, that it was me, Landon. Everything was okay. It was over. Still holding him, I felt his chest heave against mine, his breath shortening into quick puffs. I looked at his hands and realized that they were bandaged with some kind of bulging, brown fabric. I knew that color. Brown rust. My heart started racing. I let go of Luke and grabbed his hands, yanking at the material. The first thing I thought was that he was bleeding. But the moment I touched the fabric, I knew. Metal scraped against metal under wet, blood-soaked cotton. Those were his socks. Everything added up and sank horribly into place. I knew the real reason why he had been starving himself and why his socks were so badly stained. Luke tried to stop me from removing the fabric, but I held him in place and pulled.

As I wrenched the seeping fabric free, a handful of wet coins spilled onto the gravel and dirt. Luke fell to his knees and scooped them up. Darren Furtado staggered, being led away by a couple of friends. His face was swollen, and he dripped red from splits in his skin. He coughed and spat out a long strand of blood.

On his knees, Luke glanced at Darren, and then looked up at me. His body had begun to shake and tears were in his eyes. Suddenly, he flashed a miserable smile. "See? I told you, Landon. I saving da best fo' last." I felt his words, dark and pasty with dust, sweat, and blood, as they melted down a face that had begun to scare me. He wasn't one bit sorry.

And there, behind the dumpsters, I felt panic. Luke's own words grew around him like a . . . hunger. And I could see it all. In the coins that looked like bloody chocolate, in the palms of his own communion, in the dogged eyes watching dust settle on his triumph: Luke was getting real good with his hands. Just like Dad. Deep down, it was exactly what I was afraid of.

15

Luke was figuring things out between Mom and Dad, and he got more different by the day. Doing his homework, he stared at his composition notebook. His hands braced his head, unable to do anything except watch a blank page and glaze over with each breath. It was so different from when he drew a crayon Mom, Dad, me, and him all over his math homework. We had all held hands in front of our house on Pupu Street.

Luke watched me now. He thought I didn't see, but I did. When I made eye contact, he looked away, his lips still with the imprint of a question. It was so different from his off-the-wall ideas barely thought out before they left his lips.

He even started to grind his teeth during what little sleep he got. It was so different from when his chest rose and fell in a peaceful rhythm.

I tried to get Luke excited by asking him what he wanted for his birthday in a couple of weeks. He just shrugged and then said maybe Lego. I knew he wanted to finish the roof on his house, but he didn't have enough money to buy what he needed from Woolworth's yet. He said he had already considered breaking the house apart to build something else. I wanted to tell him it was okay to change his mind. Mom said everything changes, that we all did, so he shouldn't fight it. But how was an eight-going-on-nine-year-old supposed to see that as a good thing?

I wished I could stop how hot 'Ewa Beach was getting. Only a couple weeks until Spring Break and already the sun would not let up. Luke and I took turns gulping from the water hose in the shade, a ten-minute break from weed-pulling. Mom yelled at us from the front door. She said we'd better stop slacking off and to quit wasting water. She complained how we never did things her way, the right way, and how if she wanted something done, she had to do it herself. If we claimed we were only resting, we got head slaps, plus had to listen to more.

Mom lingered outside, like head luna of the plantation, identifying what and how and why we did everything wrong. Once she started, she didn't stop. She yelled about the smallest details, stuff we already knew, like not to pull from the top of the weed or not to put the dead weed back in the flower bed. After Mom got tired, thankfully, she went back in the house.

Luke and I dug in the mud again, looking for green growths. Luke looked toward the front door and then whispered. "Why Mom always snap now?"

I scoffed. "Why you tink? She all uptight 'cause Dad."

Luke pulled a handful of mud from the flower bed and just looked at it. "Why she gotta take 'em out on us now? She nitpick ev'ry liddle ting. She neva did li'dat before." He squeezed the clump, and wet soil oozed between fingers. He squinted, watching the mud bleed.

I made a face. "What'chu talking, Luke? You just neva notice before. She always grill us more wen her and Dad beef."

Luke didn't say anything. But his jaw muscles flexed, and his expression said it all: it wasn't fair. He frowned as twisted, green-and-brown mud-boulders fell from his fingers. Chunk after chunk plopped into a pile that he stuck his finger into, drawing eyes, a nose, and a mouth. A face he immediately sank both fists into, as deep as his body weight allowed him.

Dad marched to their bedroom, continuing the new routine for when he actually came home before the sun set: changed clothes, went to the kitchen, poured his first glass of Jack Daniel's, and sat in his workroom. The last couple of months, it was as if he had moved from room to room in an attempt to find the best place to relax. First, it was the family room, then outside to the backyard, now the workroom. Who knew where he'd end up next? He sat in front of the ham radio he never used anymore, staring at the map of the world on the wall above. His eyes glazed over red and bloodshot. On the map, he traced out some course over a faraway land. I heard him sip his scorching alcohol, each swig between clenched teeth. It sounded almost welcomed, like a last gasp from a drowning man. I knew and feared that sound.

Suddenly, Dad began a melody in a slurred cascade of tones:

"Wise men say, only fools rush in, but I can't help . . . " The word strained, and then the note broke as he exhaled. A long, hissing sip of whiskey. He inhaled again. "Shall I stay? Would it be a sin? If I can't help . . . " Dad hummed the rest of the line: (falling) (in) (love) (with) (you) But he didn't say it. Another hiss.

"Like a river flows, surely to the sea, (darling) so it goes, some things are meant to be . . . "

Dad swashed along, at home but on a wave he just couldn't break free of. One more long hiss, then the sound of an empty whiskey glass rang against the table.

Luke's eyes seemed empty. Tired, wet, and blank, all at the same time. I heard him crying late at night, and in the morning, his eyes were stained fire red. Recently, the only time his eyes weren't bloodshot was when he played with his *Star Wars* figures. He drifted off to a different world altogether. Han, Leia, and Luke Skywalker moved in and out of his Lego house, moving about their lives, except for when his newest resident was around: Darth Vader. Luke rarely played with Darth Vader, but when he did, Luke mixed up lines from the movie with some off-the-wall shit wandering inside his head.

When I did homework, I pretended to focus on math so I could listen. Part of me wanted to laugh, but if I did, I wouldn't get to hear this. Luke moved Han, Leia, and Luke Skywalker into one of the bedrooms. They sat all over the place, against the wall, on the bed, half in the closet. Darth Vader spoke in the doorway.

Deep, dark voice that echoed machine-breaths between sentences. "I have you now, Skywalker. You can't escape me. You are my prisoner."

A whining voice. "I'll never turn to the dark side, Vader."

"You don't know the power of the dark side. You can't resist. Join me, and we'll rule the galaxy as father and son."

"Never!"

"Then I will chop off your hand!" A hot, red lightsaber ignited as Luke Skywalker and Darth Vader started fighting. Luke Skywalker tried desperately to keep his hand from being sizzled to a stump. He kicked and scrapped and slammed his plastic body against Darth Vader in a battle to stay normal. It was a battle we both knew Luke couldn't possibly win.

Toby never lost when we played hangman, at least not yet. During Sunday school, Toby and I played on the sly in our workbooks while Mrs. Kepple mumbled about Bible stories:

"It's not Christmas anymore, but the three wise men are really important. Have you ever wondered what made them wise?" Was she talking about the wise men? It was almost Easter.

Me: *Bet you neva get dis one. Seven letters* _ _ _ _ _ _ _

Mrs. Kepple's eyes got real big—well, blank really—as she strolled around the classroom. "The wise men *understood.* They heard the messiah was coming, that He was born, and they acted. They didn't delay."

Foreheads around the room creased.

Toby: *Bet you I can. I undefeeted. T?*

"And was it a burden? No. Once they found out, they couldn't help but shout for joy with all the angels and saints and—"

Mouths were open, catching flies.

Me: _ _ _ *T* _ _ _ *What I get if I win?*

"Okay, try wait. What I said? Joy? Oh, yeah, okay. So they know now, ah? And they looked to Him, ready to follow, changed by Him."

The Santos twins winced, like they had to make doo-doo, not following a word.

Toby: *What you like? E?*

"They never hesitated once, because they felt different. They turned and headed straight for Him, ready to offer themselves, all to honor and to show their love for Him."

Everyone looked pretty uncomfortable listening to Mrs. Kepple.

Me: _ _ _ *T* _ _ _ *(Head hanging.) I like use your surfboard anytime even if you not home.*

"And what do you think the wise men said? Anyone? They said, 'Here we are, Lord.' And why did they say that? Because they were willing to be there. They wanted to be there."

Not like us.

Toby: *Shoots, what if I win? R?*

"The wise men were committed to God in a way that we all struggle to be. They focused on Him and were blessed."

Mrs. Kepple's stories were so off. I guessed it couldn't be helped.

Me: *I do all your homework dis quarter.* _ _ _ *T* _ *R* _ *(Head still hanging.)*

"And just like the wise men, Adam and Eve had their own commitment. But they broke it by eating the fruit. God gave them everything in Paradise but told them not to eat from the tree of knowledge. But did they listen?"

Nope, and from the looks of it, neither did we.

Toby: *Shoots, you going lose but. S?*

"No, they didn't. They couldn't help themselves, and they were punished. They were unfaithful to God and had to pay. Well, Eve had to pay more than Adam, if you ask me. He got off kind of easy, ah?"

Easy to put us to sleep. Geez.

Me: *No way, I going win.* _ _ _ *T* _ *R* _ *(Body hanging below the head.)*

"Okay, try wait. Adam, Eve. Try wait. Try pay, no . . . wait. They had to pay, for not doing what God wanted. That's right. So God punished them by making them different forever."

We really needed a different Sunday school teacher.

Toby: *N?*

"He changed them, never allowing them to return to Eden. Once they ate the fruit, once they tasted that knowledge, they were bound to be different."

Different from her! What a fruit.

Me: _ _ _ T _ R _ *(Legs hanging limp on a body under a head.)*

"This is a bad different compared to the wise men's good kind of different. The point is this. None of them, not the wise men or Adam and Eve, could ever go back because, whether through happiness or sin, they were still changed. The door was opened, and they went through it."

Good different and bad different? And a door? She was so off.

Toby: *A?*

"God gives us the choice to share in communion with Him. He won't force us, but He's made the choices pretty obvious in the Bible."

Obvious? Yeah, right.

Me: _ _ _ T _ R _ *(Arms hanging numb over legs on a body under a head.)*

"You can do what you want, and deal with whatever comes your way by yourself. Or you can participate in communion and have that sacrament of commitment to God too, just like all the rest of the church."

What did she say?

Toby: *H?*

"Because, after you receive communion just once, the body of Christ transforms inside you. Changing everything inside of you. It frees you from all your problems and all of your sins."

Free from everything? Not possible.

Me: _ _ _ T _ R _ *(Ex-ed out eyeballs above a dying body with two arms and two legs.)*

"That's what we're talking about today. Communion. Pretty soon, you all will join the church body in the celebration of communion."

Celebrate changing?

Toby: *B?*

"You have to realize how big of a step it is. It's a commitment to be different."

Me: _ _ _ T _ R _ *(Sad mouth, two ex-ed out eyeballs, dead body, two arms, and two legs. Hangman.)*

"Now, take out your workbooks, turn to page twenty-seven. Read the scripture and then answer the questions."

Toby and I had our workbooks out, so we just kept writing to each other.

Toby: *What da word was?*

I scribbled in the remaining letters.

Me: *v i c T o R y*

Toby shook his head, mad that he didn't get the word. Mrs. Kepple now walked around, so I head jerked toward her, indicating to Toby that we had to act like we were doing our work. When Mrs. Kepple glided by our table, glancing at our workbooks now turned to page twenty-seven, she smiled at how well we listened.

Sounds lapped against each other in the warm, evening air. I had started lying outside in the backyard on the lanai again. I stretched out after the lights went off in the house and felt the night all over me. I hadn't done this in a while. I listened to crickets sing, palm trees whisper against each other, and airplanes rumble overhead. I watched the blur of a twinkling sky and imagined myself up there. I listened to myself breathe. I inhaled and then exhaled among stars, weightless and floating far away. It would be nice if it were that quiet.

A light flickered on in the house. Through the glass door, I saw Luke peek out from the hallway. He was still having a hard time falling asleep. He tiptoed into the living room and then into the kitchen. He came to the family room and looked around. But then he turned back into the living room. He didn't see me on the lanai outside the glass sliding door.

Luke went to the hallway and glanced toward Mom and Dad's room. Then he tiptoed back to the front door. He gently grabbed the knob, unlocked it, and swung the door open. He rested the front door against the doorstop and then stood in the middle of the doorway. For a moment, I thought frantically that he might keep going, right on out of the screen door too. But he just stood there, staring out at Pupu Street.

His head leaned back with eyes closed, and the warm air filtered through the screen door. His body slouched, arms hanging limp at his side, then he wiped at his eyes. This was something new, something totally different. It was like he was stuck in the doorway, bound to those thoughts that kept him awake, realizing he was unable to change them. He breathed deeply, taking in the 'Ewa Beach air. I imagined him heating up with no way to release the pressure. He leaned open-palmed against the screen door, stuck there in the doorway. Somewhere between inside and out.

Mom now hit me and Luke when we didn't do chores properly. Or when we didn't come home from school fast enough. Or when we didn't act right away when she told us to do something. Or when we asked why we had to. Pretty much whenever anything went differently than she planned, we paid for it. Mom used the thick, wooden yardstick and whacked us across our butts and legs. She said we frustrated her. And since we couldn't remember how to do things properly, maybe lickens would remind us.

After the first few times, I got used to it and didn't cry anymore. Whether two or twenty whacks, it didn't hurt. Only the first one did, but after that, I went numb. But Luke was still fighting it. Mom had to hold his arm way up in the air, elongating his writhing body, just so she could get a good shot at his ass. I watched his eyes, burning red, wet, and full of questions. His expression twisted, each whack like a betrayal, the words written across his face: *Why, Mom?*

Luke sat gingerly in the family room as he watched Mom and Rosie at the kitchen table. His face hung hard after lickens from the yardstick. His eyes were sharp 'cause Mom was sweet-talking Rosie again. He shook his head while he listened to the airy sound that fluttered in from the kitchen. Rosie chirped back softly.

"My precious, you're such a good bird. You're always so sweet to me. What was that?" Another chirp. "Oh, I love you too."

Between sniffles, Luke sneered, his teeth grinding so loud I could hear everything wearing thin. He folded his arms and slouched, letting each one of Mom's words drive him further into the sofa. After a moment, he winced and adjusted himself so he was more lying on his side than sitting directly on his ass or legs. When Luke finally found a position he could tolerate, he whispered like Dirty Harry. "I hate dat bird. I like kill 'em." He turned to me, and the face I saw was Dad's. The eyes were Dad's. The words were Dad's, but they were coming from Luke. He was changing so fast that it might be too late to hold him. If I reached for him, he might just squish through my fingers. But he was going somewhere he shouldn't, somewhere far away, somewhere I knew I couldn't bring him back from. And he was going so fast I knew I had to do something.

"Brah, I feel sorry fo' you," I said to Luke, the words out of my mouth before I knew where they were headed.

His voice sounded like a wounded animal. "What?"

Suddenly, I understood what my mind had already. "You acking just like Dad. Wen you get all piss at somebody, you going just beat 'em up? Wise up. You like turn out like him?"

Luke's expression soured. He looked away and then to his lap. He cocked his head at me, the thoughts behind his eyes swelling into big, fat tears, the shame of it all dripping down and away. He glanced at Mom, then back at me, before folding his arms once again. I could tell I had just given him more words to think about, more words to keep him up at night. Hopefully, they might slow him down until he learned how to fly, like how I did with surfing. But at least one good thing happened. As he sat there letting it out, he started to look like Luke again.

So I stood and told him to follow me.

Luke sighed but reluctantly rose anyway. When he stood, I could see the welts already forming on the back of his legs. "What?" he said.

I put my finger to my lips and signaled for him to wait. Once we were in our bedroom, I told him to get out his backpack. I opened our closet and got out my old Humpty Dumpty stuffed animal. It was flat and oval shaped, pretty ratty. But squishy. I looked at Luke's turned backside. It was perfect.

When Luke turned around, he saw the stuffed animal in my hand and frowned. "What'chu doing wit' dat?" he asked. And then, his expression changed to fear, and he shook his head violently. "No way. I not taking 'em."

I smiled. "Luke, just put 'em in your bag—"

Luke zipped his backpack and slung it behind him. "Landon, I not taking 'em school."

I tossed Humpty Dumpty on my bed and then set my hands on Luke's shoulders. "Luke, trust me. You going be happy you had 'em." He looked at me funny. "You no need carry 'em around. Just pull 'em out and slide 'em unda your ass wen you need."

Luke's eyes narrowed. He seemed to consider it.

I retrieved the stuffed animal and handed it to him.

Luke accepted it and squeezed the cushion. He looked at me. "You wen' do dis before?" I smiled thinly and nodded. "Wen?"

"Long time ago. Kindergarten, first grade time. Was so sore, I just started taking 'em. But den, one day Mom just stop spanking me."

Luke waited for more, but then he realized there wasn't any. "How come?" he asked.

A wry smile crept across my lips. "Honestly? I dunno. But Mom took Humpty Dumpty away da same day she wen' stop. She wen' pack 'em deep in da closet." I looked at Luke and held his stare. "I dunno fo' sure, but I tink my teacha wen' call home."

For a moment, Luke just looked blankly at me. But then, he started smiling. Without another word, he turned around, unzipped his backpack, and stuffed Humpty Dumpty away.

It seemed like a great idea, so I called Toby to ask. He said he couldn't today, that he had to go to his mom's work. But he said he'd leave the surfboard outside for me to use. Why hadn't I thought of it before? It was the closest to flying that I had come. Watching Luke cry the other day gave me the idea. I could share surfing with Luke, so maybe he could fly too.

Behind Toby's house, on the rocks that extended over the Pacific Ocean, I told Luke about wave patterns, how they moved, how they changed, how each one was similar yet different. Why he had to keep his eyes in front of him, watching for any changes that were bound to come his way. Luke watched the ocean. His bare chest heaved as each wave crashed, an explosion that reached high into the sky. I inhaled, the rip and splash of water. And then I exhaled, the spray with a cool mist that soothed.

Luke was so excited; I could see it in his eyes. There was only one problem:

Luke couldn't swim. Mom used to take us to the pool at Palama Settlement when we lived in 'Ālewa Heights. She had been teaching Luke when we moved back to 'Ewa Beach. I was so excited to share surfing with him I didn't remember until Luke was screaming in the water.

I didn't realize Luke was so near the overhang, his feet curling like claws so that he could watch the power of the waves. I didn't realize as I set the board next to Luke, asking if he was ready to jump in. I didn't know how it happened, but somewhere between answering me and stepping away from the edge, Luke's foot got tangled in the leash and he tripped. I reached for him, but it was too late. All I could do was watch as if paralyzed: Luke's body spun, his knees struck rock, then his ass hit. And then he somersaulted backward over the edge. Next, the surfboard shot away like a missile and it fell too, still connected to Luke's foot. I instinctively jumped. I watched in horror as Luke plunged head first, his face swallowed by foam, then his arms, hands, butt, legs, feet. Then the surfboard speared in. And then, finally, me.

It felt like forever fighting against the downward pull of jumping in, lost in the shifting bubbles as my arms scrambled wildly in the explosion of blue and white. But when I surfaced, the surfboard was already up, bobbing between waves with Luke struggling to hold on. He had one hand over the top of the board, but it was a white-knuckled fist, tightly clutching and jerking on the leash base, screaming that he couldn't swim.

Drying off behind Toby's house, Luke's body shivered and goose-pimpled, while his teeth chattered. He said that when he hit the water, he thought *this was it*. He was about to die. "Felt like I was unda da water foreva," he said numbly.

I wrapped him in the towel. I didn't say anything 'cause I was lost on the threshold of what had opened in my mind: I could have lost him today. I could have killed him.

Luke's voice broke in. "Sorry, Landon."

What? "Luke, you no need be sorry, I da one sorry. I forgot you neva know how fo' swim." I smiled weakly. "I only wanted fo' teach you how fo' surf."

Luke shook his head. "Not your fault, Landon." There was a lightness in his voice I noticed right away. He sounded like Luke again, at least for now.

As we walked home, I cursed myself 'cause this could have turned out a *lot* different.

Dad was forever singing Elvis Presley now. He sat in his workroom with Jack Daniel's, drowning everything with each drunken word. "Take my hand, take my whole life too, for I can't help . . . " Then he hummed: (falling) (in) (love) (with) (you) He still didn't say it.

Mom eventually told Dad that she thought he had enough. After that, Luke went to our room. He tried to do homework. And when that didn't help, he played with his Lego house. But when Dad's voice changed, from singing to yelling, Luke could only stare. He rested his face in his palms for a moment, but then his head fell lower, as he grabbed at his hair in thick tufts. And it would be a long time before he could fall asleep.

After lying awake for a couple of hours, I watched from outside as Luke opened the front door again. Thinking that everyone was asleep, he took off his shirt and leaned his whole body up against the screen door. Arms extended from his sides, he offered himself to the dark, as though hoping for a cool breeze to give him some relief.

I watched Luke with a rising sense of panic. I didn't know what to do. I couldn't help him fly, but he was already at the door. I couldn't help him stay, 'cause everything was changing. Oh, God. He was so different.

Luke found me outside and lay down on his side, nestling into my body. He maneuvered so that the splotchy, purple welts on his legs wouldn't make contact with my knees. I reached over and wrapped him tight. His skin was cool, and it glowed in the moonlight of a dark 'Ewa Beach sky. And when his breath finally slowed to that steady, rhythmic melody of the unconscious, it was such a beautiful sound. Maybe he'd fly and maybe he wouldn't. Either way, that didn't matter so much right now. Somehow, it was enough that he could just get some sleep.

16

Being defensive was the best. Just like in football. Dad said the Pittsburgh Steelers and Dallas Cowboys got to the playoffs 'cause of their defense, not their offense. It was what they did to prevent the other team from scoring that won them Super Bowls. And if they were really good, they could even score points while on defense. Dad shook his head when his Steelers lost. "You can believe dat? Da Cowboys' defense and special teams wen' score twenny-one points dis game. Dey no even need one offense."

But Mom said there were two sides to every coin no matter what the game might be. It was another one of her sayings she busted out whenever she wanted us to do something. She said no matter how hard we fought it, there was no escape 'cause we couldn't have one without the other. "If you play now, the chores will still be there to do later. And if you do the chores now, playing will still be there, right? If I were you, I'd do the chores first." And we had better not talk back 'cause she didn't want to hear it.

While scrubbing the toilet with a toilet brush and Comet, Luke complained. "I hate chores. I wish I neva had fo' do 'em." I watched his arm go around in circles while I scrubbed the sink and wiped down the mirror. He barely touched the brush to the porcelain, just smooth passes around and around that didn't do much.

"Get use to it, Luke. And scrub dat toilet fo' real. You not even scratching da surface."

He made a face but then put his back into it, actually activating the turquoise crystals in the Comet with little splashes of water. "What if I ack sick?"

I shook my head soberly. "Tried dat already. Mom just going give you some chalky, pink, Bayer aspirin crap, den load you up on cough syrup. Take it from me, you going feel more sick. Worse dan just doing da chores in da first place."

Luke swished the toilet clean, the brush swamping water up the sides. "I still hate it. I going find one way."

"Tell you what, if you do, I give you five bucks I get saved from my birthday money. But you not going find one way. I should know 'cause I wen' try all da tricks in da book."

Luke stared into the foamy puddle, his eyes squinting with consideration. There might be no way around it, at least for now, but he looked like he was preparing to play the game.

So for now, better to just tackle chores head-on and be done with it. Luke would save himself a lot of frustration. He put his hand on the toilet lever and pushed. He watched the whirlpool of water suck itself down smooth, slippery-white walls, flushing everything away.

Luke loved to count his quarters. When I asked him why he did it so much, he said it was all part of the plan. He was close to what he needed for the Lego systems he wanted to buy. After that, he'd be able to finish his house. And if he didn't count the quarters to keep the idea fresh, he might get hungry at school and buy school lunch. What a bonehead. For a moment, I considered telling him that he missed one too many meals, and it made him stupid.

Sitting on his bunk, Luke put the quarters into piles of four. Then he grabbed a bunch and let them fall on each other. I listened to the coins splash into silver puddles. But somewhere in that metal cascade came a hollow, wooden rattle. The coins fell into something. When I looked, another handful of quarters glittered into a wooden bowl. And even though I had seen the bowl in our room before, it didn't click until now. Maybe it was seeing the coins with it.

My eyes narrowed. "Luke, where you wen' get dat bowl from?"

Luke glanced at me and then looked away guiltily. He shrugged his shoulders.

I couldn't believe it. "Luke, what'chu doing wit' Dad's loose change bowl? He looking for 'em, you know."

When I reached for the bowl, Luke snatched it away and wrapped it securely under his arm. "Who said dis Dad's one?" he asked weakly.

"You wen' take his change, too, ah?"

His eyes circled around, like a cornered animal searching for a way out. When he spoke, his voice was hurt. "No, I neva," he whined.

"What'chu tinking, Luke? You dumb, or what? And why you gotta steal fo'? You like be like Dad? Sneaking around—" I stopped in mid-sentence. Luke didn't need to hear that.

Luke looked at me funny. "What?"

"Nevamind. Just get rid of da bowl or put 'em back wit'out Dad seeing. Bum-bye he going broke both our asses." He couldn't argue with that. Game over. I lay back on my bed in bittersweet victory, wondering at what point Luke would stop pulling shit like this.

Luke piled his quarters, much slower now. From under his bunk, I listened to each quarter drop with purpose. And just when I thought he had zero defense, just when I thought he was beaten, he whispered darkly, "I not stupid. I know what I doing. Plus, I not da one like Dad. *You* da one like him. You da one still drinking his booze."

Luke's words crunched into me like well-executed tackles, one after the other, deeper and harder than the one before, landing everything right on the money. I wanted to tell him how wrong he got it, how badly he read it, but I couldn't. He had turned the tables on me and beaten me at my own game. And the worst part about it: he was right.

Right after the bell rang for recess, Mrs. Kato asked me to stay in. My classmates made noises like I was getting busted, oohing and hah-lahing as they scampered through the sliding door. Mrs. Kato motioned, calling me over to her desk. As I got closer, my gut suddenly tightened with fear. I probably was busted. What did I do? Mrs. Kato pointed to the chair, so I sat and braced for impact. "Landon, I wanted to let you know that I'm recommending you for G.T. testing and for the G.T. program when you go to 'Ilima Intermediate School next year."

All at once, my mind raced so fast it was hard to focus. "G.T.? Like . . . Gifted and Talented?" Mrs. Kato nodded yes. "Why me?" I asked nervously.

Mrs. Kato angled her head. After a moment, she leaned forward and inched her chair closer. "Well, your work has progressively improved. Also, you show excellent aptitude in creative projects. I think you would be a great candidate for the program."

The words wanted to come: yes. Yes. YES! But when I saw Afa strutting and clucking like a chicken outside the window, I felt something cut me off from what I wanted: No, Landon, you're too chicken, you're too dumb, you're too much of a hard-headed Portagee, you're never going to be able to. "I . . . I—" No words came. I didn't know what to say.

Mrs. Kato's eyebrows rose curiously. "Is the G.T. program something you'd like to participate in, Landon?"

As Mrs. Kato waited, my eyes sped back and forth along each thought. I heard Afa outside: "*Bawk-bawk-bawk-bawk*." Part of me wanted to, but the other part was too afraid. I wanted to find a way, but I still felt trapped. I didn't want to be so . . . different. Then again there were always two sides to every coin. Did I really care if I was different? Was it so bad?

Mrs. Kato extended both hands, as though it all were so simple. "All you have to say is yes or no, Landon."

I felt my answer getting pushed and pulled. I thought about Mom and Dad, how they fought a lot lately. What if they got divorced? What would happen to me and Luke? Everything Mrs. Kato offered me suddenly seemed so far away. And the more I thought about it, the more I craved it and became afraid. Not now, I had to protect, had to hold everything together. Better to just play defense.

Mrs. Kato then raised a palm in surrender. "Tell you what, Landon. You think about it. Talk to your mom and dad. Then you let me know what they say, okay?"

All I could do was nod my head yes. Then Mrs. Kato dismissed me to recess. Everything finally slowed, but I still felt the pressure inside me, like when I got close to false-cracking Afa. I felt jittery but was glad it was over, even if my stomach was still flexed tight.

At the door, Mrs. Kato reached out her hand. "Are you feeling all right, Landon? You're flushed red." But before she could check my temperature, I was gone.

Mom had a new habit: leaving the house in the afternoon. And it was getting more frequent too. She'd wait until Luke and I got home from school and then tell me it was my job to watch Luke for a couple of hours. I didn't know where else she went besides Fujioka's in Waipahu. And the only reason I knew that was all the potted, miniature rose bushes that kept piling up, as if waiting to be planted. Otherwise, she said not one word about where she'd been.

After she got home, Mom put her newly-purchased plant on the kitchen table by Rosie. She also went outside and snipped a fresh bud from her ailing rose bushes. She stuck the cutting in a vase with water and set it on the end table in the living room for Dad to notice. Which he never did. And when Mom brought it up, Dad got mad and tried to avoid the entire situation.

Mom explained to him how they had to try if they were going to make this marriage work, how he had to see things from her side and she from his. She bombarded him with arguments: how their relationship could go either way; how she and he were one flesh, and how no man should put that asunder; how they just had to work together. There were many words, so many angles, so many possibilities. Dad maneuvered around Mom so he could go to bed. He said his one option right now was to sleep so he could get up tomorrow and go to work. Somebody had to make money so that the rent got paid and food got bought. Period.

But Mom didn't learn. She always pressed forward when she should retreat. If she got in his way, Dad sometimes got good with his hands. Other times, he dodged her and headed for some kind of safety in the bedroom. Either way, game over.

All this over a stupid rose in a vase, shriveled red petals on the end table like dried blood on a playing field. And I still didn't know where else Mom went in the afternoon.

The afternoon light bled through the window into Toby's house. I loved to watch the waves as they came in. White lines seemed to hang horizontal across the blue. Suddenly, waves would crush against rocks outside, dazzling liquid explosions that reached up through the fading light like metallic fingers into the sky. Then they fell.

Mrs. Ka'ea sat at the table with soft sunlight spilling over her paperwork. She said she was working on a child custody case. One problem was the mother was in drug rehab, while the father had a criminal record. Another problem was the paternal grandmother wanted to hanai the kids, but she was already on welfare. The courts were skeptical whether she really wanted the children or if she was using their custody as a way to get more money. Plus, the mother didn't want to give up her children completely. Mrs. Ka'ea said it looked as if the courts weren't going to award custody to any of them. It sounded like a lose-lose situation to me.

But Mrs. Ka'ea shook her head with a smile. "It's actually a win-win situation for them. Just think, if someone didn't force these people to prove they could handle raising the children, those poor kids would probably end up worse off after the family split up. But this way, the children won't have to grow up in a bad situation and, after getting adopted, will be with a family that really wants to love and take care of them."

I winced thinking about me and Luke. "But what if da kids no like? I mean, what if dey like stay wit' at least one from da family?"

Mrs. Ka'ea shrugged her shoulders. "Well, the children don't really have a say. The courts don't typically think children are capable of deciding what's best for themselves until age thirteen or fourteen."

My mind sped up, not liking what I had begun to realize. On one side, everything could remain the same: not wanting to be different but unable to stop that. On the other, there was the possibility of something new: wanting the chance for something better, but not being able to do a damn thing about it either. There were two sides to every coin. And both of them sucked.

I must have made a face 'cause Mrs. Ka'ea asked me what was wrong. "Not fair da courts tell kids dey gotta live wit' somebody else," I said. "What if da odda people lousy too?"

Mrs. Ka'ea smiled kindly. "Then the courts move the children again. Hopefully to a better home the second time."

When Mrs. Ka'ea said the kids *move again* and *second time*, that was when it struck.

Move. Move away. Move, again.

Move from 'Ewa Beach.

Move from Toby.

I felt another wave coming, and with it, an idea worse than what I had already understood. When it crashed, it felt like whitewash across my mind:

Without Toby, there'd be no surfing.

Luke needed a swift crack upside the head. He had to get his eggs in gear and get rid of that stinking koa bowl before Dad figured it out. When Dad asked Mom about it again, their voices punching through the house from their bedroom, I snatched the bowl from inside our desk drawer and shoved it into Luke's chest. Quarters spilled over the edge, and Luke reached out instinctively, as though to help someone who had fallen.

"Get rid of dis now," I told him. Only one option. No more playing around.

"But—"

I cut him off. "But nothin'. I wen' cover fo' you already, but if Dad come in here, we both going get pounded." I had to play it safe already. "If you not going give it back, get rid of it. Quit futting around. You taking one big chance wit' *both* our asses."

Luke looked at me as he considered. Eventually, he tucked the brown bowl under his arm and scurried out. After a moment, I heard the screen door hiss shut.

Twenty minutes later, when Luke came back, he dragged his feet as though defeated. He went straight to the desk and counted his quarters. His face was long and hard, and he gritted his teeth. He stared blankly and parceled out each coin. There were so many things going on, but not a word to me. So much he wanted his way, but not sure how to get it. He probably didn't even know why he wanted to keep the bowl in the first place.

"Where you wen' go, Waipahu?" I asked.

There was no hesitation, just indignation. "You *said* get rid of 'em."

I couldn't believe Luke was giving me attitude. Without thinking, I wound up and slapped Luke upside his head. He turned, rubbing the back of his skull, and gave me a nasty look. "Why you sassing me fo', Luke? You and me, we bruddas. We gotta stick together."

Luke stared long and hard before he answered. "If dat *so* important, why you hit me fo' den? It's 'cause you still drinking, and now you even more like Dad." He turned sulkily away.

My first impulse was to crank Luke again. But as I wound up, the feeling suddenly slipped away. Why had I hit him in the first place? I knew I had thought it moments before. But did I really mean it? I was angry and frustrated and just . . . reacted. Just like Dad. Drunk, out-of-control, good-with-his-hands Dad. I felt a sinking feeling inside. What the hell was I thinking?

Dad got an early start this afternoon with his Jack Daniel's. From his workroom, he called out accusations whenever Mom walked by. Why did she keep dumping liquor from his bottle? He knew what she was up to, what her game was. He *knew* she was throwing away a little every day so he'd drink less. She couldn't hide anything from him. Mom stood in the doorway, claiming she had no idea what he was talking about. "So what, Minerva? You trying fo' tell me da kids been dumping 'em and not you? Fess up, no sneak behind dem. C'mon, I mean, da kid did *ruin* tings, but—"

Mom's voice broke in loudly. "Leonard, don't!" Her voice rang into silence. "You're drunk. Stop, before you say something you regret." They stared at each other, Mom at the doorway, Dad ready in his chair. A standoff. Two teams with nothing to actually win.

Mom was the first to attack. "Besides, Leonard, I'm not the one . . . *sneaking*. You are. You haven't been at work afternoons and nights. I drove by."

I got lost in the crush of noise that followed. In that confusion of yelling, of advancing and retreating, of pushing forward while trying to contain, somewhere between it all, a glass explosion punctuated the fight. I ran to the living room, in time to see Dad striding toward their bedroom. Mom stood in the kitchen and held Dad's third or fourth glassful of Jack Daniel's to her breast, staring into the brown liquid. On the floor behind her, water was everywhere. But then I saw it. Against the wall, a wilted rose lay among shards from the shattered vase.

Mom didn't say anything as I inched closer. Her hands gripped Dad's short glass of Jack Daniel's as her knuckles turned white. Suddenly, she began to shake. The whiskey bobbled around the lip of the glass, in danger of lurching free. I could tell she wanted to throw the glass, but at the same time, she wouldn't let it go. For her, there were always two sides.

When I bent down and picked up slivers of glass, Mom finally recognized me. She set the Jack Daniel's on the floor and her hands fell to work as well, fumbling with the broken pieces. There were no words, just quick movements to pick up and restore, trying to get things as they had been. I watched Mom's face crease like hard lines in leather, and I saw it in her eyes. After cleaning this, she would wait a few days, cut another rose, and set it in another vase.

She just didn't get it. Why did she keep pushing the issue?

All at once, I became so scared I had to ask. "Mom, if you and Dad divorce, you going put us up fo' adoption?"

It was quiet for a long time. Mom just looked at me. Finally, she spoke. "No, Landon." Her voice was weak and her head low. She couldn't make eye contact. She breathed deeply a couple of times. And when she spoke again, she smiled thinly. "Your father and I are not going to get divorced. Don't even worry about that." In other words, she was so clueless she was lost.

But not me. I saw exactly where she was and exactly where this was headed.

Mom and I scooped shards of glass in silence. Dad's Jack Daniel's was right beside us. The whiskey jiggled whenever one of us accidentally bumped the glass. Deep in the brown sloshing liquid I saw myself swirling about, as though underwater and unable to rise out of it. I had to force myself to look away. What I wouldn't do for just a sip.

I inched backward and with two hands on the floor, lowered myself to check if I got all the broken glass. I peeked at the whiskey again. But this time I saw Mom's hand through it. As she wiped the floor, her twisted hand looked trapped in brown, as if it was the only part of her near the surface. And in that moment, I was scared 'cause I saw us both in the same glass.

When Mrs. Kato asked me to stay in after school, I was no longer afraid. I already knew what was coming. So when she said she needed an answer about testing for the G.T. program at 'Ilima Intermediate, I blurted out the answer that had become easy: No.

Mrs. Kato was surprised. "Why not, Landon? You have great potential. Have you talked with your mom and dad?"

I nodded yes. She didn't need to know I hadn't spoken with either of them. But I was sure *I* didn't want to participate. I was convinced it was only a matter of time until Mom and Dad had a *final* fight. Like a Super Bowl. What I needed to focus on was protecting myself and watching out for Luke when it did happen.

I didn't tell Mrs. Kato how there were always two sides to everything. I didn't tell her I was caught, stuck between what I wanted and what I needed. Mrs. Kato said okay and dismissed me. I could tell she was disappointed, and that was the last thing I wanted to do. As I was about to scurry toward freedom, I stopped at the door. I wanted to tell her thank you for thinking I could do the G.T. program, even though I didn't deserve it. I also wanted to tell her why.

But I didn't. I didn't dare tell her about Jack Daniel's or divorce or adoption, or that I was sure Luke and I would have to move soon. I didn't tell her that was the reason I wouldn't even attempt the G.T. testing. Why start something when I would just have to leave? I was sure I wouldn't be going to 'Ilima Intermediate next year. I would have to live with whoever my foster parents were, 'cause even if Mom was too blind, I still knew the score. Mrs. Kato waited for me to say something, but I swallowed it all down. I turned and plowed head first into the swirling, thick 'Ewa Beach afternoon. And that day, it burned all the way home.

17

By April the air fell in heavy, hot blankets over 'Ewa Beach. As Luke and I walked home from school, the street blurred ahead of us as though under boiling water. Heat from above and heat from below. Just couldn't escape it. Not that Luke wanted to anymore.

Luke had warmed to 'Ewa Beach now that his problems were gone. He talked about how he wasn't chased to lunch anymore, how the other kids wanted him on their team for P.E., even how he was now one of the most popular kids in his class. He said nobody even teased him once about his Humpty Dumpty pillow. And to top it all, since he stood up to them, Darren and his boys had somehow become Luke's friends. Maybe not *friends*, but at least they didn't hassle him anymore. Instead, they focused on Sonny Chikazawa whose horn-rimmed glasses were so thick he looked constantly surprised. Luke said he actually liked school now. *And* 'Ewa Beach.

I smiled tightly. I wished I could say the same for me. Every chance Afa got, he tried to stir things up between us. He just wouldn't let it go. During P.E., we did the shuttle run, carrying chalkboard erasers across the sizzling basketball court. Mr. Waterhouse timed us individually. Every time

I came back with an eraser, Afa made a comment. "Look, da chicken run fast . . . He look like one tree-piece KFC." Everyone laughed. On our way to lunch, the same thing, Afa's mouth just wouldn't quit. "Chickens no eat. Dey get *eaten*." More laughter.

Even in our classroom, Mrs. Kato grilled us for disrupting the lesson. We had to sit with our heads on the table, full-on third-grade style. I sank deeper into the cool plastic as Mrs. Kato lectured us about being disrespectful. But it was all Afa. Every time. When I answered one of Mrs. Kato's questions, Afa furtively peeped *bawk-bawk-bawk-bawk*, making everyone giggle. He even had some followers that joined in, echoing chicken noises all around the room. Mrs. Kato said if we acted like babies, she'd treat us like babies. I closed my eyes, drifting deeper into the silence of the room. But the cluck was still there, pushing at me even when it was quiet.

As we neared Pupu Street, Luke looked at me as if he had something very serious on his mind. He wiped sweat from his face. "You not one chicken, ah, Landon?" I felt Luke's eyes on me, wave after wave of the same question, pressing into my chest, my ribcage, my gut. I didn't say anything. I just shook my head no. After a moment, Luke went on. "'Cause I almost wen' beef wit' one fourth grader 'cause he said you one panty. You not, ah, Landon?"

Once again, Luke's eyes were all over me. How could I explain that even though he might have solved his problems with his hands, there was a better way? "Sticks and stones, Luke." But when I glanced at him, I realized I wouldn't be getting away from this. His pained eyes said it all. *You not, ah, Landon?*

Ms. Shimizu got an empty, two-liter Coke bottle to show us the Cartesian Diver experiment. First, she filled the bottle with water and then submerged the plastic diver. When she released the diver, we all watched what looked like a miniature, fluorescent orange army man hover about an inch from the top. For some reason, I thought about surfing, like when I got tumbled in whitewash after wiping out. I'd be lost somewhere under my board, glassy air coins exploding free and rising high above me toward the light. Ms. Shimizu burped the air from the bottle and capped it. She asked us to hypothesize what would happen when she squeezed the bottle from the outside. Faint chicken noises came when I said the diver would float higher. She said that was a good guess. But when she squeezed the bottle, the diver sank. Everybody oohed, 'cause it defied logic. Drifting back to the ocean, I remembered when my lungs would finally give up the last of my breath. I began to sink yet watched as shiny discs rose faster, seeming to jiggle more violently the higher they went. Then it hit me. They weren't getting *faster*, they were getting *farther*. And so was I! Without air, I had become dead weight in the water. When Ms. Shimizu handed me a Cartesian Diver, I whispered. "Da ting wen' down 'cause get less bubbles inside fo' hold 'em up, yeah?"

Ms. Shimizu smiled, her eyebrows raised in surprise. "Yep, and with less air, more water presses against the diver and pushes it down."

What Ms. Shimizu said made sense. I had tried to figure all this out in the water behind Toby's house. Now I knew. After I expelled my air, I plummeted as if being squeezed from the outside. And then, when I couldn't take the burn in my chest anymore, I kicked off the sand toward the fractured sky. But a peculiar thing happened trying to figure this out in the last couple of weeks. As I challenged myself to stay under longer, to take the pain, I started to like it.

The homily in church really reached Mom today. For the umpteenth time, Dad didn't come with us to Our Lady of Perpetual Help. This time he said he had too many things on his mind, so Mom needed to stop pestering him.

Sitting in the pew, Luke and I on opposite sides of Mom, we listened to Father Thomas talk about the gospel. He said it was a comforting passage from Matthew. "'Come to me all of you who are weary and heavy-burdened, and I will give you rest.' Think about that. No matter what you've done, where you've been, or what you've become. Jesus says to just come to *me*. He'll remove all pressures, all restrictions, all impediments, if you just *come to me*. No matter what shadows linger over you, Jesus will make them disappear so you can rest easy once again."

As Father Thomas plugged away at the homily, Mom suddenly grabbed my hand. At first, I was surprised, but when she wrapped both of her hands around mine, I was completely stunned. Mom held my hand close to her body as tears streamed down and splattered onto her lap. Sometimes on our hands. I searched her face for an answer, a clue, maybe even just a hint of why, but there was nothing. Her eyes stared at the altar, but she was somewhere far, far away.

Mom didn't let go, and I didn't try to pull away. After everything that had happened, it felt good to be this close. She was so upset her hands shook while she lightly stroked the top of my hand. And with the same miserable expression on her face, she started pressing her index finger into my skin. She drew her finger harder and harder across my knuckles, over each angle of bone. The more pressure she applied, the more painful it got.

But without warning, Mom's finger began moving in a different direction across my hand. At first, I couldn't tell what she was doing, but I kept watching. All at once, I recognized she was repeating a pattern. Then I saw she was scribbling letters, the same five over and over again. Instantly, it came to me, and the air in the church became so thick it was oppressive. I felt as though I couldn't breathe when I finally put the letters together: *W-H-O-R-E.*

Just like in Grandma's letter to Mom.

Just like when Dad yelled at her. Whore.

All over my hand.

When Luke came around, asking questions, I already knew he wanted something. He flashed that charming smile, offered to fold clothes, and then worked without complaint. Before long, though, he got down to business. He wanted to know how much time we could spare after school before Mom would start snapping. Oh, yeah, and if I would take him to Woolworth's. I wanted to laugh 'cause he thought he was so smooth. I was about to say it wasn't a good idea. Mom expected us home right away. But when he said he saved enough quarters to buy what he needed for his Lego house, I smiled and told him okay. He hadn't touched his Lego in weeks.

Woolworth's was right behind 'Ewa Beach Elementary School, so Luke and I made our way to the toy section quickly. We chose two construction sets and three smaller packs of Lego and hauled everything to the register. The cashier, a Portuguese lady with red lipstick, smiled and appraised us impressively. "Wow, Christmas in April, ah?" Both Luke and I smiled back. "So, what? Cash or charge today?" We both laughed a little this time, but not as loud as the lady when Luke said cash. When she got control of herself, she tilted her head at us. "Coupla characters, ah? Put the toys back and den run along and play, okay?" But when Luke placed two gallon-sized bags of quarters on the counter, the lady almost choked for air. "What's dis? Your lunch money?" After she laughed at her own joke, she made sure we were serious and started counting. Coin after silver coin clinked on the counter. The sound was so crisp and clean that Luke's face seemed to lighten with each sweep of the lady's hand. It was like watching him re-emerge. The more she counted, the more free he seemed. And when the two bags of heavy quarters were no longer his, Luke's smile finally came through.

As Luke and I walked home with Woolworth's bags, we passed by Jason's house. I could hear his parents yelling inside. Jason sat in the window with his forehead pressed against the glass like a sad, lonely fish looking out of his tank. Jason slowly lifted his hand, and even though it looked painful, he softly pasted it against the window to say hi. I raised my hand, not waving it back and forth, just an open palm toward him. Jason's hand slid down the window, but his face didn't change. It said everything. How he was stuck there, trapped in some crazy experiment gone wrong. I said a silent prayer for him. *Run, Jason, run!*

Toby and I were held captive in the kitchen by all the free smells his mom cooked up: miso soup, pork stir-fry, fried gyoza. Sweet, sugar-glazed meat mixed with salty shoyu on the sample plates she prepared. Sitting at the table, I watched Mrs. Ka'ea command everything to life: lifting, pulling, chopping, scouring. The entire kitchen breathed as she slid back and forth, from stirring the pot of noodles, to storing leftover vegetables in the fridge, to scrubbing dishes in the sink. Nothing stayed put, as even she was always in motion.

As Mrs. Ka'ea washed dishes, she stood on what looked like a book to help her reach into the sink. It wasn't like Dad's footstool at home, so I asked her what it was. When she said a Bible, I almost choked on a noodle. "Why you standing on one Bible?" I asked uneasily.

Mrs. Ka'ea answered matter-of-factly. "Well, it's one of those old, illustrated copies, so it's thick. Puts me just at the right level. Besides, isn't the Bible my foundation?" She tapped the cover with her foot and chuckled at her own joke.

If Mom knew Mrs. Ka'ea used the Bible as a footstool, she'd never let me come back here. Right then, I decided what Mom didn't know wouldn't hurt her. Besides, was it really *that* big of a deal? I chuckled. "My mom would slap my head if she ever seen me do dat." But then I thought of something else. "She been crying a lot in church lately. How come, you tink?"

Mrs. Ka'ea joined me and Toby at the table and shook her head with a smile. "You always have the most interesting questions, Landon." She sucked in a twist of noodles and then chewed. "I think people cry at church for different reasons. For some people, it's happiness. Like the Holy Spirit's in them, so they can't help but cry for joy. But for others, it's because they're sad. It's like they're trying to get rid of some burden they carry around, so they can't stop crying until they believe God has forgiven them."

For a moment, I was quiet. "But if Mom ask, He going forgive, right? So, why ev'rytime she gotta cry fo'?"

Toby glanced at me curiously and then looked to his mom.

Mrs. Ka'ea's head tilted to the side. "I don't know, Landon. Maybe she feels bad for something she did in the past. Maybe she's trying to say sorry. Maybe she feels like God isn't listening. There are thousands of reasons why, Landon. But rest assured, whatever it is, she wants it off her back." Mrs. Ka'ea smiled reassuringly.

Then everything stopped 'cause we forgot to bless the food. We all lowered our heads as Mrs. Ka'ea said grace. Her words lingered in the air, like a holy mist. Outside, waves fell, crushing against the rocks. Right then, I decided I didn't give a damn if Mrs. Ka'ea used a Bible as a footstool. *This* was heaven, right here in Toby's house, not some silly book, and it had somehow come to me.

Jason met me at Toby's house to go surfing. He found me and Toby out back, watching the waves. The swells were pumping, white-foamed lips that crushed with lots of pull from underneath. We shouldn't go out today. Jason stood behind in his track sweats, and after two or three sets pounded the rocks right in front of us, he asked if we were really going out in *that.*

"Nah," Toby said, "no good dis. Da buggah cranking. Prob'ly crunch my board in half." Jason looked relieved. Toby turned to me. "Landon, we go show Jason da storm drain. But try wait, let me get one flashlight." Toby hurried off into the house.

I wondered how to tell Toby there was no way in hell I wanted to go back in the storm drain. I was sure someone lived there. And I didn't want to go into the *Help Me* man's turf 'cause he had been staying out of me and Luke's room. I met Toby at the door to tell him we should just really stay away. But Toby whispered that we weren't going in the storm drain. Then he winked at me. At once, I knew he had something up his sleeve. Toby led the way, and we all climbed the rocks away from his house.

In the mouth of the storm drain, the three of us stared into black, the flashlight casting a beam far into the dark. Stuck at the opening, none of us made any move to go farther in. Jason asked what was so special about this. It was just a drain. There were plenty of these on the mainland.

Toby raised his chin so that he was looking downward at Jason. "Yeah, da mainland get dis kine storm drain, but dis one different. Dis one *haunted*." Toby made his eyes big, nodding slowly.

Jason took a step back and looked down, realizing he was inches from the opening. And when he spoke, his voice shook. "What do you mean . . . haunted? Like with a ghost?"

I wanted to laugh, but I didn't 'cause Toby didn't know how close he really was. Besides, it was a good thing Toby was teasing Jason. He wouldn't do it if he didn't like Jason.

Toby peered into the storm drain, aiming the beam deep. "Get one mean ghost in there."

Jason looked at me, then back to Toby. "How do you know?"

"I seen 'em wit' my own eyes. Da buggah come out night time. I was sitting ova there," Toby said, pointing toward the rocky overhang. "I was just fishing wen I seen dis misty cloud, coming out da opening. Da buggah keep coming steady at me, but den she start changing shape. Me, I all scared, ah? But I neva know what fo' do. Was like I was stuck there, no can do nothin' but watch." Toby strained to see as he took a step farther into the storm drain.

Jason's expression was still, somewhere between waiting and wanting. The pressure continued to build. "What happened?" Jason asked, his voice breaking, totally into the story.

"Da buggah came all solid, right there in front my eyes. And you know what I seen? One *woman*. Da buggah change shape into one lady, and she start walking toward me. But her face, oh my God, her face was so . . . " Toby said, trailing off, still staring into the darkness.

Jason waited for Toby to say more, but when he realized Toby had drifted off, he spoke in a whisper. "What did she look like?" Jason's words hung in the air.

Toby waited a couple of seconds then spun around fast with the flashlight below his jaw, shining light into his mouth and up his nostrils, his face a twisted, fiery mask as he roared like a monster. Jason was so into the story that he yelped, stumbled out of the storm drain, and ended up splashing ass-first onto the wet rocks. Toby stepped down from the mouth of the drain, half-laughing, half-asking Jason if he was all right. He offered his hand to Jason, and at first, Jason paused, kind of salty. But between chuckles, Toby said he was sorry, that he couldn't resist, and pretty soon, Jason was laughing too. Toby helped Jason, hands locked, pulling him up. When Jason stood, he drew his sweatpants back down his legs and then covered his ankle weights.

I pointed to Jason's feet. "How come you brought those?"

"I bring my weights everywhere," Jason said. "I've brought them before when we've gone surfing. I just take them off before we go in the water."

Toby chimed in. "You wear 'em ev'ry day?"

"Not at school, but once I get home, I put them on so I can run faster. The ankle weights make me heavier." A large wave slammed into the rocks below, causing Jason to look toward the ocean. A spray of glittering water sprinkled over us as the wind pushed against it.

Toby cocked his head. "Why you like be heavier?"

Jason answered simply. "Because if I weigh more when I train, I'll be stronger when I take the ankle weights off." Toby still looked like he didn't get it.

I started talking before I even realized what I was saying. And, of course, my thoughts had already dived into water. "Toby, if you only surf small waves, you only going be liddle bit good. You not going be able fo' handle big waves, ah? But if you take all da big waves and get good, den wen you go back to da small waves, you going rip 'em up big time."

Understanding broke on Toby's face and a smile crept over his lips. Jason nodded as another wave exploded, shooting high above us before raining back down in a gleaming drizzle.

This was the first time I felt it: we were all together. We were all the same. Not just me and Toby, with Jason stuck on the outside. Not me and Toby, *local*, and Jason, *haole*. It felt like we were finally in the same . . . space. Comfortable and warm like a salt-sprayed 'Ewa Beach afternoon. And there was no more pressure 'cause the three of us were finally friends.

Right around two in the morning, I moseyed to the kitchen 'cause I couldn't sleep. The house was quiet, just the flutter of the drapes from the ocean breeze. So when I flicked on the kitchen light, I almost yelled 'cause Dad sat at the table. He scared the crap out of me. He squinted and told me to flip that damn switch off. As the light fell, I watched Dad disappear into black, only his short glass sparkling as he lifted it to his mouth. I listened to the swig, the grit between teeth, then the swallow. I imagined the splashing heat, and I knew the fumes from here.

"What, you know what you did, boy?" Dad asked, his words slurring.

"I neva know you was out here—"

Dad cut me off. He leaned forward. "You like talk back? You like get wise?"

I didn't know what he meant. What did I do? His eyes glinted in the darkness, two shiny, angry coins of light. I guessed he had been drinking for a while so I stood right where I was. I didn't dare move, and I didn't say anything.

Dad snapped again. "I said, you know what *you* did?"

I felt trapped, wanting to breathe, wanting to run. But I could do neither. I just knew I wanted him to stop. I chanced a glance at him. He was still sitting there as though waiting for an answer. "Sorry, Dad," I said tonelessly, hoping that would be enough.

Even though it was dark, I could see him looking at me the way he always did. Something just beneath the surface. Dad gulped more Jack Daniel's and swallowed it down. "You no even know what you saying sorry fo'. Why you not in bed, anyway?"

I thought fast. "'Cause I like somethin' fo' drink." I wasn't lying too badly.

Dad faced the window, sipping from his glass. "Get your water and go sleep, boy." Dad inhaled deep, and then growled while he exhaled, as though all of this had been too much to bear. As I tanked a cup of water, I listened to the ocean in the distance. How calm it was. How relaxing. What I wouldn't do to be out there, drifting along in that cool place right now. That was why I came to the kitchen in the first place. Dad's voice suddenly broke in. "Hurry up, damn kid. Get to bed." He took another sip, chased by another swallow. But somehow I felt the burn. I looked for an answer in the shadow of his turned back but found none. *What did I do?*

I could hold my breath underwater for almost two minutes now. Jason's ankle weights gave me the idea. I didn't tell anyone, but I would sneak by Toby's house to the jagged shore and dive in. Underwater, I looked for a shelf of sand, one with rocks nestled on the shifting ground. I inhaled hard before diving deep, grabbing some rocks, and holding them on my lap. The first few times, I counted *one-Mississippi*'s to see how long I stayed under. But now, I just sat there on the sand. I sat and just . . . *felt* everything as it all thrust into me at the same time.

I felt the weight press me into the sand and hold me down. I felt the heavy cold water completely swallow me. I felt the sway of everything, rocking me back and forth. I felt how quiet it was. I smiled at how my body still wanted to float, how it still wanted to rise.

There was no breath for words, just the soft, tickling grains of sand below, and churning, ever-sinking layers of water above. I watched shadowed fish fly across a glowing, liquid sky. It was a totally different world. One I was really wanting to stay in.

And every time I felt *that*, every time I considered just letting go, that was when it would happen: pressure on my lungs. Coins of air slipped, jellyfishing up and away. The water around me got warmer and warmer. In short bursts, pouches of air escaped, dazzling higher and higher in spurting silver clouds. I watched the air bubble toward the surface as my chest sizzled. I no longer felt my body trying to rise. Only the increasing weight of water holding me down.

The less air I had, the heavier I felt. At this point, between the crunch in my chest and the sway of my body, I could stay put. Between the cool ocean and the heat within me, I could finally get some rest. Between soft sand and relentless water, it could be quiet. All at once, with everything crushing down, with the last of my air flitting away, I always had to choose.

And so far, as I punched off the ocean floor, streaking out of a billowing sand cloud, I always headed toward the air. I raced my own breath toward the sky. For a moment, in mid-flight, I imagined I was a bird, spearing through a blur that dripped away with every upward inch I soared. It was always the longest rising of my life.

So when I stretched for the surface and finally pierced through, nothing ever felt as good as inhaling a deep breath of blue sky. In my chest, cool searing needles stung and soothed all at once. No pressure from above, and my legs were so numb there was nothing below. I felt light. Free. And as

I floated along, each whip of air was clear and pure. Clean and forgiving. But it always happened, my legs remembered where they were, and like the squeeze of a bottle, water started tugging at my feet. That was when I always felt the weight of everyone's words:

Gifted and Talented. All you have to say is yes or no.

Chicken. Panty. You not, ah, Landon?

W-H-O-R-E. You know what you *did, boy?*

And just like that, instead of asking why, I inhaled deep and dove for quiet once again, knowing the answer would come to me.

18

As I came into the kitchen, Mom told me to stop doing that if I knew what was good for me. I had a sore molar in the back of my mouth I was constantly touching. Mom said to let it go, it would come when it was ready. When I asked how long it would take, Mom only shrugged. "Who knows? It's the last of your baby teeth. Your adult one's coming in, but the more you play with that one, the more likely it will get infected, and then you'll really be sorry. It'll be all *your* fault. So stop messing with it."

For the last couple of nights, I hardly got any sleep. My jaw thudded like a heartbeat, a pulsing, circular rhythm around my face. When I did finally fall asleep, I was so tired I should have crashed for the rest of the night. But half an hour later, I woke up to bloody dreams of my teeth falling out. In these dreams, I actually felt my teeth grind together, and then it happened. First, a molar came out, then a canine, then another tooth, and another, until eventually, my front teeth started to loosen. I wanted to scream as each one came free, but I could barely breathe. When I started to gag on the iron-red taste steadily oozing down my throat, I woke up.

Sitting up in my bed, I tasted real blood in the back of my mouth. Like metal, but worse. Rotting, like rust. Even if it was only a couple of drops, my pulsating headache always made me feel like pulling that damn tooth out. I slipped my finger into my mouth as I considered it. Sure, it would be my fault, but at least it wouldn't hurt anymore.

In the last few days, Luke managed to piss off both Mom and Dad. I tried to warn him, but he just wouldn't listen. A true, stubborn Portagee: hard head. He asked Mom *why* we had to do chores. I watched open-mouthed as Luke's words floated through the air and lingered in front of Mom. And for such disrespect, he got head cracks and ass slaps. Plus, when he asked again, his *discipline* got doubled in the appropriate combination of head cracks and ass slaps every time, as if Mom had suddenly become a math genius. Mom said Luke should know better by now. Yesterday, Luke was up to eight. What a hard head. But he didn't cry once.

Dad sometimes brought home a crossword, or a word find, or even a jigsaw puzzle, and on the rare occasion he forgot it on the family room table, Luke and I knew we could get away with figuring out some of it on the sly, just not the whole thing. Otherwise, Dad got pissed. It was his crossword, his word find, his puzzle. *He* should be the one to finish it, to put the last piece into place. Mom told Aunty Selma that it was typical of *him*. Just like a kid that had to be in control. If he couldn't have things his way, then no one could play at all. So when Dad found his Super Word Find completed courtesy of Luke, Dad rolled the book into a makeshift baton and smacked Luke over and over with it, as if punctuating his frustrated words: "Damn. Stupid. Jackass. Kid." Fricken hard head.

But when Luke suddenly snapped at Mom, reckless words splattering out of his mouth, saying he didn't see *her* doing any chores, asking why we had to do so many, my jaw fell open. This passed all other stupid things he had ever done. I imagined the fallout: Luke's head swollen, his legs criss-crossed with red welts so bad that he couldn't sit. For a second, I scrambled, thinking how to fix this. But I couldn't. I knew there was no way to take back something like that once he opened his mouth. There was nothing to do but wait.

But instead of yelling, Mom bit her lip and looked at Luke sadly. She dropped a couple of long, wet tears that burned the side of her face. Her chest fluttered as she struggled for words. I could see it. She wanted to lash out but held it in for some reason, as though molding the verbal ass-whipping that begged to be free. When she spoke, her voice swelled with disappointment. "Who do you think I am?" She breathed deeply, as though trying to find the strength. "I'm your mother, not some punk friend from school." Luke's eyes fell. He could feel it coming on too: guilt.

"Is that any way to treat your mother? The person who sacrificed her body for *you*. I had to take all the pain, everything. For *you*. And this is how you repay me?" She turned away from Luke and wiped at her eyes. "Go, get out of here. Don't help me out. But when it comes time, I'll remember you. Go ahead, beat it." She walked away, the words already deep inside Luke.

I watched in amazement. This was better than any head crack or ass slap. Luke was frozen, stuck somewhere between his dignity and her guilt. I didn't know what made him think he could get away with talking back to Mom. His expression was so pained I could almost hear the heavy, throbbing beat that must now be inside his head too.

Even if it was quiet underwater, there were still some things I just couldn't stop hearing. Things so quiet I knew they were there, yet so loud I wished they weren't. Still submerged, I tried to drift into the sway of everything around me, into the cleansing wash of water, into each mouthful of air. For a while, this had worked, but now it seemed I couldn't get away.

I couldn't avoid the thoughts: separation, divorce, adoption, Dad, Mom, whore. All inside me. Thoughts floated then spread out so thin they felt taut. I looked around, trying to sink into a world that was a constant, swashing blur. Fingers of limu reached upward from rocks lodged deep under sand. I tugged on the seaweed, stroked it, but didn't pull it out.

I couldn't get away from my heartbeat: continuous splashes, one after another that needled across my face. Swell after swell, splintered sets continued to pound. The vibration pumped through the back of my head, a current that slid long and hard against my eyes and nose, then surfaced with a heavy thud in my mouth. Down here, I could really feel the upward thrust, the eruption waiting to happen under a tooth-plugged cap.

I couldn't escape the ocean: a quiet filled with so much noise. It was the sound of everything that had always been there. A sound I just didn't notice before. I closed my eyes and listened. Since everything was muffled, I always thought the crashing waves would be the loudest sound underwater, but it wasn't. There was something a lot closer, a lot louder. It was a tickling in the ear, almost words, like a hushed, unmistakable warning. Like salty whispers, each wave, each current came closer yet said nothing.

But it was there. And I understood it. Something was coming for me, something I couldn't get away from. And it really felt like I shouldn't be down here, at least not yet.

Luke should be getting his homework done, but instead he played with his Lego house. It was like a puzzle he wanted to finish. Piece after piece already locked into place, he pulled each one off, fingered the plastic block, then re-set it. And somehow, between this back and forth of choices, his house started to grow a roof. But at the same time, his composition notebook sat open on our desk. I peeked at his language arts assignment. A journal response to Mrs. Shelley's question: *What do you want to be when you grow up?* It seemed easy enough. I glanced at Luke. He joylessly snapped another piece into place.

"Luke, why you no just do your homework? Just answer da question. Easy dat." No response. "Why you no just do 'em, bum-bye Mrs. Shelley going call home—"

He cut me off, his voice real salty. "Why *you* no do nothin'? You only listen." He glared at me and then looked down. He went back to his Lego.

"Why I no do what? Listen what?"

This time, he didn't look up. "Nothin'. Nevamind." His words were heavy with blame. I asked him again but only got the hollow echo of Lego construction in response.

I didn't know what Luke was becoming. The frame defined the space, the walls went up, the roof covered, but the rooms were for hiding. I felt it all in my mouth: a pointed, focused pressure. His words lodged deep inside and started to pound upward. I wanted to tell him not to act like this, that right now, we should be sticking together. I wanted to grip him tightly and make him tell me what he meant. I wanted to explode, but as I tried to speak, no words came. Nothing.

Then, as his silence grew, like a quiet finger pointing at me, and the sound of interlocking plastic pieces fitting into place, Luke's words made sense. I knew exactly what he meant. Now that he understood, he blamed me for Mom and Dad. But what did he really think *I* could do?

Dad shut the screen door behind him, home early today after work. Luke vacuumed the family room while I sat on the floor in the living room, spot-treating food stains on everyone's shirts before putting them for wash. Dad stood there, blocking the afternoon light from the doorway. He looked from me to Luke, then back at me. He glanced toward the kitchen as his expression soured. "You guys do dis ev'ry day, Landon?" It couldn't be the first time he ever noticed us doing chores. I nodded with minimal eye contact. "Who she tink her? One fucking luna?" I looked back up. Dad's chest rose and fell sharply.

And then we both heard the scattering rattle and clacking of plastic. Dad shook his head 'cause he knew that sound too. Mom had quickly hung up the phone and was scrambling to get dinner started. When she peeked into the living room, Dad flashed the meanest stink eye I ever saw. He turned away and strode to the hallway. Around the corner, he stopped, just out of sight from where Mom was, and faced me. It was a look I would always remember: a heavy forehead, red, swollen, watery eyes. Everything pressed down so hard his nose stretched for air and his lips creased. It seemed as though he wanted to say something right then, to squeeze something through those clenched teeth, but he held it in. Thoughts, words, tears. Everything was held suspended across his face, spoken in a way I didn't understand yet. Everything was there, lurking just beneath the surface, all while he looked at me.

There were a lot of things I wasn't supposed to do that I did anyway. With my second glass of Jack Daniel's, I sprawled out on the lanai in the backyard. Under a dark sky hanging heavy over me, thoughts surfaced in a slow, tight rise from somewhere deep within. I imagined them flap in a frantic upward swim, half-fluttering, only to be yanked back down with another gulp of whiskey. I didn't know why, but this started to seem funny. Each thought strained to reach higher in my mind only to get rammed back into the hole it came from. I wanted to giggle, the ripple of blurry thoughts spreading in black waves over me. And just as everything settled, even across the smooth, jellied surface of my thinking, other thoughts struggled to fly.

Rosie: I shouldn't let her out of her cage anymore. Rosie had finally started to flutter around the house. At first, 'cause she was so blind, she would fly into everything. But she seemed to have found a perch she liked. Dad's recliner. The problem was that every time she landed on his favorite chair, she always took a shit on it. Not just one or two green-and-white blobs that were easy to clean up, it was more like seven or eight good-sized splatters, wet and dripping in white streaks down the cushion. The first time, Dad was so tired he didn't even notice the bird crap he smeared all over his shirt and hair. After that, Mom didn't want to take any chances. Only Mom could let Rosie out now.

Surfing: I shouldn't worry so much about it. What was the big deal? That I might drown? I washed clothes. I took baths. I did stuff with water every day, and nothing happened. But that was quite all right . . . Mom could just keep talking on the phone. I wasn't that worried.

Drinking: I shouldn't touch Dad's Jack Daniel's. I felt bad that Dad accused Mom for dumping it, but that couldn't be helped. I knew better, but Jack Daniel's helped my tooth feel better. It numbed everything so I could fall asleep. And, really, why would Mom drain only *some* of Dad's liquor? She wouldn't empty it little by little. Mom would dump the whole bottle one time. And it never failed, they started beefing about missing Jack Daniel's and then—

Calling the cops: I shouldn't have done that. Now Dad pointed the finger at me, Luke, and Mom. But mostly me. He didn't like the police coming over, blue lights flashing in front of *his* house, waking up all of *his* neighbors, just so they could see *him* plucked outside and escorted to the police car, driven away to Grandma's house to cool off for the night. But I only called that one time. Didn't he consider that maybe he and Mom woke up the neighbors? Dad said if he caught any of us calling the cops, our fingers were going to wish they hadn't dialed.

I felt the liquor swirl in my stomach as everything got hazy. It wasn't funny anymore. My stomach swirled hotly, around and around. I wondered again why Dad was always looking at me. It was getting foggy. Maybe he knew it was me. Thoughts twisted. But still, I only did it that one time. Spinning. The cops came over at least twice a month. Getting heavy. Dizzy.

Staring into the dark, black blur of sky, I saw thousands of stars stretched with each blink into long, murky, crisscrossing rays of light. And, as my body got lighter, as I rose higher and higher, something shifted, and I realized I was no longer looking up, but rather down into the sky. Man, was I drunk. I stared into the depths of what now looked like the ocean, into a dark, speckled churning, trying to swallow me whole. I swam at the surface, gliding across the sky, dipping between two worlds. I felt myself wanting to sink deeper into the dull black, into the heavy upward pull. As I drifted between water and air, between staying awake and falling asleep, between flying downward and drowning upward, I felt caught. Suspended. Stuck.

I wanted to give in to the black but I felt the reason wedge itself deeper, holding me in place like a life jacket buoying me up. Luke. I still felt bad for slapping him that time and didn't ever want to slip up by hitting him again. But at the same time, other thoughts rippled and surfaced. If all that was so important, why was I still doing this? Why couldn't I just . . . stop drinking? Or better yet, why *wouldn't* I?

Dad's note on the box of his jigsaw puzzle was clear. *DO NOT TOUCH! DIS MEANS YOU LUKE.* I slid the note aside so I could see the picture. Luke Skywalker's X-Wing, with R2-D2 inserted snugly behind the cockpit, speeding through space, chased by a Tie Fighter with lasers in mid-blast. So far, only the frame was complete on Dad's puzzle, straight edges all the way around a big hole in the middle, and scattered pieces inside. I fought the urge to test some pieces. I shouldn't even start. I knew I'd want to keep going until I saw the whole picture.

I left the box in the center of the unfinished puzzle. I inspected the pieces already in place along the frame, how it formed a great negative space. It was funny how, with so few of them in place, I had a hard time believing it could turn into the same image on the box. Almost as if I couldn't see beyond the cavity. Like I needed the whole picture to slap me in the face.

Mrs. Ka'ea got in Toby's face. Right after I came over, Toby mentioned something about his cousin's truck, and his mom lost it. This was the first time I saw her so mad. Toby sat on a chair, saying he was sorry over and over while his mom grilled him from above. "Don't lie to me, Tobias. I can see it in your eyes. I can hear it in your voice. You were riding in the back of Chaz's truck *again*. I've told you before: you are not allowed anywhere but in the front seat. Do you want to end up like the surfboard that flew out of the truck? Smashed into a thousand bits of fiberglass? One bounce. That's it. That's all it takes." Mrs. Ka'ea leaned in close and yelled savagely. "Is that what you *want*?" She turned her back as Toby's face beat out hot, messy tears. She whispered to me, realizing I was still there. "Landon, please go home. You can play with Toby tomorrow." She wiped her eyes and nodded toward the door.

Outside, I leaned against the front door and shook all over. I slid all the way down the door as though submerging underwater. I felt the fear in my stomach, and even though Mrs. Ka'ea's words were for Toby, I heard them as though they were for me. How Toby should remember what God said, to honor his mother and father. How he shouldn't go against his mother's wishes. Did he want to live with his father? Well, then, he needed to learn that until he was all grown up, she was responsible for him. And it was her way or the highway. I could hear Mrs. Ka'ea move closer to him. Her voice muffled for a moment as she must be hugging Toby.

She spoke in spurts, starting and stopping like a leaky faucet. "You're my one and only, Toby. I can't lose you." I imagined her wiping the hair from his face, his wet eyes emerging. "You shouldn't be doing those things."

Toby still cried. "I know, Mom. I'm sorry—"

Mrs. Ka'ea cut in. Her voice had softened. "Toby, I only want you to be safe."

"I know, Mom—"

"Promise you'll never do that again. Please, Toby. Please. You worry me."

"I know, I'm sorry, Mom. I'm sorry. I promise I won't."

Then there were only muffled voices. I closed my eyes and could see Mrs. Ka'ea holding Toby again. Holding him close, right where she wanted him. Holding them both until she stopped the drowning inside. I opened my eyes and sat there, wishing I could trade places with Toby. Mrs. Ka'ea loved her son so much she cried over him and begged him for *his* own good. What did my mom do? She yelled and hit us. She took pills and bought plants to get back at Dad. She scribbled all over my hand at church: *WHORE.* I pinched my eyes shut, realizing just what had bothered me. Grandma's letter to Mom.

What did Mom do? She took birth control 'cause she didn't want me to begin with.

"Both Mom and Luke wen' Foodland," I answered Dad as he stepped outside, watching him slide the glass family room door shut. It was weird. His eyes were so bloodshot they looked yellow. But then I saw what was in his hand. Great. I plucked another white BVD from the clothesline. Dad sat down in his lawn chair, cradling his short glass of Jack Daniel's. He leaned back heavily, orange sunlight glowing off his skin, and let out a long, tired breath.

"Eh, boy, stop fo' now," Dad said, his words a bit slurred. "Come sit down ova here."

I looked at him, not understanding. I still had chores to do. I couldn't relax yet. I snatched a pair of dry, stiff socks off the line. I kept working as if Dad's words hadn't happened, letting them fade into nothing but afternoon heat.

But Dad's voice rang out again, louder this time. "Boy, I said drop it. I like talk to you."

Suddenly, thoughts shot through my head. My heart pounded. He knew I had called the cops. Dad knew about the Jack Daniel's. He knew I kept quiet while he and Mom fought about it. Oh shit, oh shit, oh shit. I turned around slowly and set down the laundry basket. I walked breathlessly to where Dad was reclining and sat on the concrete in front of him. There was no way out of it. I glanced up as he sipped from his glass. Dad's face twisted when the liquor hit the back of his throat. He gritted his teeth into a grimace and chased the heat with cool air.

We sat in silence as a plane rumbled overhead. I peeked at Dad, trying to read his expression. Something was definitely on his mind, but for some reason, I got the feeling it wasn't about calling the cops. Or about his missing Jack Daniel's. Clearly tipsy, Dad fumbled for words between swigs of whiskey. Something was pushing its way forward. It was all over his face: how he wouldn't look at me, how he held his mouth tight, how he flexed his jaw muscles. I wanted to ask him what was going on.

But when he looked at me, he wore the same look I had seen so many times before—in church, at home, everywhere between Mom and Dad. All aimed at me. And only at that moment did I recognize what it was. It was an accusation that had been there all along. I suddenly knew I didn't want to hear what he had to say.

"Not always like dis, boy," Dad said, indicating the house, the property, perhaps Pupu Street and 'Ewa Beach too. "Wen me and your modda was young, was some good times. Da bess. I rememba da first time I seen her. Was down John's Beach, Barbers Point side. I dunno why she there, she one townie, dat's why. But her and some girlfriends come down and was watching us guys surf. She just lay on da beach, getting one mean tan. Was her senior year high school, Christmas vacation time. Me, I already pau school, just working Matsuda's gas station, 'cause I good wit' my hands, ah?

"Your modda was un-real. All dark from going beach, ehu color hair, long, slinky legs. Real attrack-tive. Wen I seen her dat first time, I come all funny inside. I dunno what fo' say. I tink her out of my league. But her girlfriend come tell me your modda like my numba. At first, I was all jazz. I was blown away 'cause dis fine wahine like me. At da same time, I neva like jump in right away, but I figga, nah, only one phone numba, ah? And den I really wen' tink about it. Wen one *girl* ask fo' your numba, dat mean she no get time fo' games. She no like *play* around. You know what I mean? I neva knew dis back den, but she one tip-ick-o woman. Wen she know what she like, she going fo' 'em. And she not going stop till she get 'em.

"So wen your modda call me up, we plan fo' go cruz down Waikīkī side. But afta I hang up da phone, I tinking, how lucky me? Dis fine local wahine like me. But same time, somethin' stay bugging me, trying fo' tell me somethin', but I no could figga 'em out. Da next day, we wen' cruz Waikīkī, den up Tantalus. We was up Tantalus, looking down at da Honolulu city lights, you know, getting close, talking stories. And den I figga out what was irking me: it was da way your modda *talk*. She sound so fricken haole, make me sick. She make me feel stupid. Like she betta dan me, like ev'ry odda haole I eva met. By da time we reach Tantalus, she wen' correck da way I talk seven times. Right den, I was going take her home, 'cause I no like deal wit' dat, but was too late. Afta she correck me, I turn away, all disguss, ah? But wen I turn fo' start up my car, right at da same time, she wen' go where she neva should of. Till dis day I wish she neva. And wit' her mouth too. Wit' da damn ting about her dat irk me most: her mouth."

No, no, no. I looked away. I didn't want to hear any more.

"But was da most un-real feeling in da world. Shit, she make me feel betta dan surfing. Was like . . . flying. You tell me, how I going get rid of one feeling li'dat?" Dad fell silent. I heard him take another swig of whiskey.

This was like a bad dream. Why was he telling me this? Despite how icky I felt, I snuck a glance at him, hoping he was no longer there. That *this* would somehow mercifully be over. But Dad just stared off toward the fence.

Finally, he spoke again. "Afta while, I getting all use to how haole her, but most 'cause we seen each odda ev'ry day. She make me *fly* ev'ry time. I use to sneak inside her house up 'Ālewa Heights night time. Your modda was wild. She date anykine guys before and tell her modda and fadda straight. She no like da kine guys dey like her date. Plus, she like football back den too. How's dat? I tinking, dis da closess to Heaven on Earth I eva going get. Dat was before—" Dad trailed off and looked at me. His eyes were the same. Sharp and focused. "Dat was before *you*, Landon."

Please, I begged him in my mind, please stop.

"Your modda wen' change big time wen she was going have you. Wen we found out summa time, she was okay, 'cause we still hiding 'em from her folks. But wen came close, she wen' freak out. She tell, 'We gotta get marry, no can have one child out of wedlock, no can have one abor-shen.' I tell her fo' try wait, we not ready fo' get marry. But she get all funny kine, crying fo' hours, getting real quiet wen I no could see her ev'ry day. She accuse me I not going take care her afta I wen' use her up. She say I going find somebody else. But I neva was going leave her. I know my responsibility. But den, behind my back . . . she wen' talk to my modda.

"Now, you gotta undastand, since I was small, was only me, my modda, and my brudda and sista. Wen my fadda wen' maké, I became da man of da house 'cause I da oldest, ah? My modda ask me fo' fix somethin', I figga a way fo' do 'em. She ask me fo' help my brudda with his homework, I find da time. She ask me fo' give up my Saturday surfing fo' go take my little sista doctor, I sacrifice. Like I said before, I was da man of da house. I wen' buss my ass, but my modda know she always could lean on me. Whateva she ask, I no could say no.

"So wen your modda wen' talk to my modda, you know what she did? She say I no like marry her now I got her pregnant. Bullshit. I woulda marry her, but I wanted fo' choose. I no like be force. Your modda knew how close I was wit' my modda. And she wen' use dat against me. So wen my modda hear dat crap from your modda's lying lips, she buss my ass and make me marry your modda da very next week. She say she no can believe she raise such a lousy son. You can believe dat? Afta all da shit I wen' do fo' her growing up? Your modda wen' come between us. Landon, no cry. You woulda been took care of. I promise. But I neva want *dis*. Not like dis. Not like one stinking animal, all cage-up wit' no choice in da whole damn ting.

"Now, wen I seen you and Luke bussing your asses, while your modda only talk on da damn phone, I get sick. You guys remind me of wen I was small. I no can handle already. I no feel like doing shit fo' her. Dat's why I stay out late plenny now. 'Cause wen I see both of you working so damn hard, it's me on my hands and knees all ova again, breaking my ass, and I no feel like helping either of dem anymore." He downed the last of the Jack Daniel's in his glass. But I felt the burn in my stomach. And it was starting to grow.

"I neva choose fo' be one fadda to my brudda and sista. But how I going turn my back on my blood? Hah? Tell me? You ask me what happen, Landon? *You* wen' happen." Dad looked away fast when he saw it all rise behind my eyes and stood up quickly. As he walked around me, he set his hand gently on my head, like a priest would in church. "I telling you dis

’cause you should know before tings change. Your modda no like you know dis. She no like you know who you *are.* I neva like hurt you, Landon. Dis not your fault, but I like you know ’cause you getting older. So wen you make your own decision in da future, you can live by ’em. I like you know so you no fuck up like me.” Then he let go of my head.

Dad scurried into the house with the glass door sliding shut behind him, but his words were still on top of me. I sat there swollen with knowledge, with something inside that wanted to burst. Already running in wet streaks, my face burned with pressure screaming to escape. I wanted to explode, but there was nowhere to go. I wanted to hide but couldn’t get away. I wanted silence, but Dad’s words would still be there, like a hand over me, like his finger pointing. The truth pressed painfully through skin, keeping me right where I sat. Dad didn’t say it, but he didn’t need to. His message was clear. *I* was what happened. All of this was my fault. And just like Mom, he wished I had never been born.

Another plane flew overhead. I watched the silhouette rip across the salmon-purple sky toward home, across the speckled light of a thousand stars winking at me. I closed my eyelids tightly like a shutter, trying to imagine myself in that snapshot high above Pupu Street. I kept my eyes pinched tight against the drowning I felt. In between was the rusty, iron taste of blood in my mouth from a tooth that needed to come out.

I knew I shouldn’t, but I opened my eyes. It was a picture that had been there the entire time. I just couldn’t see until it was right in front of me.

19

At least *this* wasn’t my fault. Like that mattered. After the police left, Dad’s words had exploded at Mom, Luke, and me. Loud words that sloshed around heavily, made thick on waves of Jack Daniel’s. Even as upset as he was, Dad realized Mom couldn’t have called ’cause they had been fighting the whole time. And since Luke was so young, Dad targeted me as prime suspect number one. “What I told you about calling da cops, hah? You like me broke your fucking fingas?” Over and over I swore it wasn’t me. “Who was den? Da liddle one? No way. You da one doing ’em. You no tink you wen’ do enuff? You tink you pretty *big* now, hah?” Suddenly, he grabbed my index finger and bent it back until I fell to my knees. Mom yelled at Dad to leave me alone, but he just stood over me, too far in to stop.

My voice squeaked between sobs. "Wasn't me, Dad. I promise, I neva call." Dad forced my finger back so hard I screamed. "Da neighbors, Dad! Dey hear ev'ryting!"

Then Dad stopped. He looked at the front door and then through it for the first time, his eyes swelling with suspicion. How could he have not thought of that before? The neighbors flicked on their lights, they looked from their windows, they cracked their front doors, all 'cause of the rude noise coming from our house. Dad let go of my finger and slowly faced the front door, the swirling glass of liquor still in his hand. Then he started yelling from inside the house. "Da neighbors get big ears, ah?" His voice boomed as he punched the screen door open. Then he tripped drunkenly out toward Pupu Street. In the front yard, Dad continued his rant. "You tink I too loud? Hah? Say 'em to my face." Words slurped from his mouth as I watched in horror from the window. Jack Daniel's spilled over the lip of the glass. "Anybody, I no care. Any of you fuckas." His cheeks were as red as his eyes, wearing an expression so pissed he looked like he was smiling. All while spinning around like in the *Sound of Music*. "I neva move back 'Ewa Beach fo' people mind *my* business. You heard me?"

Mom stood just inside the front door, face down, head shaking. Luke ran to our bedroom. Up and down Pupu Street, lights flickered on.

I decided to take Luke to 'Ewa Beach Park. Even if it was blazing hot, he merrily swung his sand castle set the entire way there. We sat in the sand so the water would creep over our toes and then slide away. On this side of 'Ewa Beach, the waves broke farther out 'cause of the coral shelf that reached into the ocean. Not like behind Toby's house where the waves smashed right there against the rocky shore, spraying high into the sky and even onto his house. Loud thundering booms. Over and over again.

It was quiet and calm here.

Luke filled his bucket with sand and then dumped it into a big pile. He said he was going to build the best sand castle ever. One after another, he loaded bucketfuls of sand onto the same spot. I wanted to ask him if he was also going for the *biggest* sand castle ever made. But since he was so into it, I decided not to bug him, not even for fun. I knew he was still having a hard time sleeping. And being at the beach had to be better than him staying at home. He'd just space out at our desk, unable to do homework or even play with his Lego. So tired and lethargic, he wouldn't do anything. He'd end up just sitting there . . . listening.

The water washed up the shore, cooling off my legs, then back down. Luke squatted to the side, already building a wall so the waves didn't ruin his castle. It was nice here, nestled in the warm sand, the waves crawling up my legs like gentle thoughts, then back down easy. At first, it felt good. But then I started to drift along with the hum of the ocean, each thought intensifying as if adding more static to an electric charge. My tooth still hadn't fallen out, and it throbbed with pain. It was already May, which meant next year was intermediate school. Afa's chicken noises hadn't stopped. Would they by the time next school year began? But then again, who cared? I might not be in 'Ewa Beach, so that wouldn't even matter. I thought about separation, divorce, adoption. What I *was* and how it was all my fault. Dammit.

I asked Luke if he wanted to swim 'cause it was too hot on the sand. I offered to stay with him in the shallow part if he wanted. He said he'd rather keep building his sand castle, so I headed for the water. As liquid curled around my legs in warm, crystal clear eddies, I called back to Luke, telling him not to wander anywhere 'cause I'd be watching from the water.

There was something about the ocean, about the rhythm of waves, that just made me feel better. Something clean and cool. Something quiet. With my head still above water, I inhaled a chestful of air and held it. When I did this, I could float my entire body on the surface. And as I lay back, with white wisps of clouds dotting the sky and with the rising and falling motion beneath me, I dipped my ears under the water to listen. It was a sound I wished Luke could know. Soothing. Peaceful. I knew it could help him. I floated along, eyes lost in aimless air and ears filled with the tinkling Pacific Ocean, the calm so dreamlike, so blue, so careless and free, that I imagined myself up in the sky.

As I released air, I tried to stay afloat. I felt the downward pull on my body. I knew no matter how hard I struggled or how much I relaxed, I was starting to sink.

It was funny, though. Sinking and never coming up didn't scare me anymore. I almost *wanted* to drop beneath. I wanted the water to swallow me, to absorb, to wash. To . . . bathe me. I wanted to plunge deep into that muffled world. But I knew I had to fight the urge to slip below. I looked back at the shore. Luke was still building his castle. I breathed deeply a few times. Not yet, I told myself. I still had to keep an eye on him.

Luke begged to let Rosie out of her cage, so I made him promise to clean up all the bird crap she would make. And, of course, we didn't dare do this while Mom was home. Rosie could fly much better now. It was like she could see. She knew exactly where she was going and exactly what she wanted to do. So when I released her sliding door, Rosie bounced to the opening of her cage. She leaned forward, head stretching left then right, nails scratching against metal. Then she stepped off and flapped hard one, two, three times, and she was away. In the air, Rosie was simply elegant, pumping her wings easily, banking out of the kitchen, through the living room and toward the family room. I watched how smooth and fluid her wings were, cutting through air. She wasn't as clumsy as before, a frantic fluttering of slapping sounds, spraying feathers everywhere. Now it was just an almost soundless flight.

After easing into the landing on her new perch, Rosie touched down, swelled up, and shit-plopped right there on Dad's recliner. Luke and I laughed as she ruffled, shaking all over with relief. Then she plopped one more time. She stretched her wings, squawked as if laughing with us, then folded them back against herself. Plop, number three. It was incredible a bird had that much crap. Luke laughed so hard he was on the floor. Number four. Four times, even after a short flight? Then a thought crept in: what if flying made her so excited that she couldn't help it, no matter how far she flew? Number five. Rosie was so lucky.

Luke was so distracted he had a hard time doing homework. Whenever he wasn't playing with his Lego house, he sat at the desk, his composition notebook opened. He could sit for hours, but no homework got done. For some reason, he concentrated while snapping plastic pieces together, but when it was quiet, when both of us were supposed to be doing our homework, he spaced out. Mom and Dad's voices seemed to seep through the walls and into our bedroom, soft at first, but growing louder. I watched Luke at the desk, slouching in the chair, hands around his head. He grabbed at his hair, yanking on it as if it were seaweed anchoring him to the bottom of the ocean. The louder Mom and Dad got, the deeper into the chair he sank.

Deep underwater, I could hold my breath for over two and a half minutes now. And it seemed as though the longer I held my breath, the more I could escape the words. So instead of just sitting, rocking back and forth in the cool, quiet ebb and flow of the world around me, I began to dig in the sand. I inspected limu, touching the rooted branches of seaweed, the ones that grew out of coral, that rose in a slow, constant billow, making the rocks look like they had healthy, purple, living hair. I swam around, my arms pumping hard to keep me under, looking for new places to explore. As much as possible, I darted in swift, gliding flights, arms spread wide, soaring as far as I could before having to work again to keep myself beneath the surface.

When I decided on a new spot, I always sifted through the sand to see what treasures I could find. It was incredible how much trash there was: empty beer cans, broken Styrofoam coolers filled with sand, smashed bottles. At first, I would shoot to the surface to check every little thing, to see if I found something valuable. Most of the time, it was rubbish, worn smooth by the flowing sheets of sand below. There were only two things I kept so far. The first was a dull, worn-down quarter, still silver but almost completely bald. I could barely make out George Washington or the 1970 below. Maybe it was the surprise of stumbling across *anything* of value in an ocean, or maybe it was the shock of discovering my birth year on it when I did. Either way, the quarter struck me as . . . significant. So I got in the habit of carrying it on me, tucked away in the small pouch inside my shorts. One night, though, I used it as a paperweight for my homework and I saw Luke *coveting* it. The first chance I got, I used Dad's Black and Decker to drill a hole in the quarter. After that, I wore it like a pendant hung from a twine lanyard.

The other object I found underwater and kept was a broken piece of glass. There were a lot of glass fragments on the ocean floor, but this one was blue. A deep, transparent sapphire when I held it up to the sun. Plus it was almost a completely circular disc. From the squiggly, cursive *L* on one side and the grooves around the sand-polished edge, I guessed it was from the bottom of a beer or liquor bottle. I had seen enough of those to know.

But after removing something green from the sand, I shot to the surface to get a better look at it. It felt hard and odd-shaped. Inspecting it as

I treaded water, the object turned out to be a miniature jade frog. From the funny writing on the front, I figured it was a Chinese good luck frog. Victor Ah Fook in my class had one. He always put it on his desk when we took a test. "Can neva have too much luck," he said. In the glistening afternoon sun, the jade burned, glowing a deep, emerald color.

But underwater, the green was even warmer, especially when the diffused rays of sun hit it. In fact, there was something almost magical that happened. A burst of light, needles of every color stabbed out from the frog, like a glowing piece of the sun, right in my hands. Without warning, a mean thrust of water swept the frog out of my hand, and before I could grab it, the frog hit the ocean floor in a cloud of sand. It was amazing how fast it got buried under layer after layer of murky, ever-shifting sand. In those few moments, between me scrambling, shooting my hand at the sinking frog, and then ramming my hand into the sand where it hit, I watched as the sand completely swallowed the jade.

So fast, yet so quiet. It was a good thing I thrust my hand into the sand when I did. I felt the frog tumble along as though hopping on the ocean floor. I didn't want to lose my good luck. I snatched the frog from the sand, and I realized how different this world was from the one above. Swift, yet everything moved in peaceful slow motion, spreading out so I could see and navigate safely. Soft, yet with enough force the water let me absorb any impact and keep on going. And quiet. So many sounds in the ocean—like the washing of the waves above—but to me, it was just . . . peace. No more words, no yelling, no accusations. No more breath for any of that. Lucky indeed.

Toby didn't want to talk about his father. He got real quiet and wouldn't go any further, just continued waxing his surfboard. Behind his house, the ocean bellowed against the rocks. Water shot up, branching out into a colorful spray that rained down over us. I wanted to ask him about what his mom said, to find out just how similar we were. At the same time, I wanted to say sorry, that I didn't mean to pry. When I apologized, Toby waved it off. "Nah, no worry, Landon. I just neva tink about dat fo' long time." Sorry, Toby, but I thought about it every day.

When Toby was ready, he stood at the edge of the rocky overhang, waves smashing below, and prepared to jump. He looked over the edge, feet curling over rock, inhaling the whipping air that flowed off the water.

Suddenly, Toby pumped his legs, and then, in one fluid motion, sprung from the rocks, tucking head-first into a downward bullet. His mom had warned him not to dive like that, how he couldn't possibly know the depth at any given time 'cause of the shifting waves, how he needed to start listening to what she said. I wanted to say something, but Toby was already in mid-flight. I watched as he approached the water, how his arms stabbed forward, elongating his body. I watched how sleek he was, gliding through the air like a quiet slipping thought. I held my breath just before impact. Then the water accepted him, as easy as slurping a noodle: arms, head, body, legs, then feet. It felt like minutes since he went under. All I could see was the swirling foam, layer after crushing layer of water piling on top of him. So at last, when his head finally broke the surface, I felt myself breathe again. Toby called for his surfboard. As he bobbed up and then down over each glassy wave, he looked right at home. Comfortable. Content, knowing everything would always work out.

Luke tried to do his homework but ended up crashing on the desk, with his head lying on one side of his opened composition notebook. I inspected his homework. Scribbled in Luke's handwriting, the journal assignment read: *What is your most favorite thing and why?* I wondered for a moment what it was. Lego? Funny, I didn't really know.

I looked at the peaceful rise and fall of his body, all while he slumped over the desk. I was glad he was at least able to get some sleep. But when Mom and Dad's voices crashed in the living room, Luke's body jerked to the sound. He twitched but remained asleep. Words flooded the room, spilling everywhere and then quickly slithering back. His mouth puckered into a tight frown, and his eyes quivered. Then I saw it. His eyelashes were moist and tangled together like wet seaweed, flitting as though reaching out for help.

Dad was outside, yelling at the neighbors again. And Mom held the screen door open, calling out to Dad in a teeth-clenched whisper. "Leonard, get in. It's late already."

Dad halted his cyclone in the middle of the yard and faced the house. "What, Minerva, you shame? *You* should be, but I not! I no give a shit what dey tink." Dad waved around to indicate the neighbors. "Why you even go church, hah, fucking Catholic hippo-crite? You all high-and-mighty, 'Ālewa

Heights girl, but you da one got pregnant." Mom set her jaw against Dad's words. "Who you tink you, damn whore? You not da luna of me and you sure as hell not my modda either." Dad cocked his head to the side, real sassy. Jack Daniel's leapt, diving from the glass, splattering all over the ground.

Mom's breathing was shallow. "Why don't I down all my Valium, then, just like you said? Is that what you want, Leonard? So you can be done with me once and for all?" Mom shook her head and turned away, letting the screen door hiss shut on him.

Dad just sucked on his whiskey glass and glared at Mom as she left.

The 'Ewa Beach air came through our bedroom windows in long breaths, salty gusts that filtered through the rusty screen and splashed on the bedroom floor. I listened to the ocean in the distance. Lying on my bed, I imagined I was out there under the waves.

Mom and Dad were still going at it. Luke was asleep at the desk again. I lay in my bed and fingered the blue beer bottle disc, rotating it as it caught the light in our room. I put it up to one eye and closed the other. The world turned instantly blue. I was so amazed I switched it to the other eye. It was like being in the sky and underwater, flying and swimming, all at the same time. The room got cool, the walls receded into nothing but blue, and I began floating. Not up or away, but floating *along*, drifting on a wonderful, lulling tide. I didn't realize when it happened, but I started to feel heavy, going deeper and deeper. But this time, I let myself sink . . .

Until I lay underwater in the sand. Outside, the parked cars melted into fish, the yellow streetlight blurred into a fractured sun, the wind swayed into currents that washed back and forth over me. The world was so familiar I instinctively held my breath. I wanted this blue to last.

I glanced at Luke crashed out on top of his homework. I wanted to teach him how to swim, show him how to sink, hold his hand and bring him down here with me. Down here where it was quiet. For a moment, I believed it was possible. But for only a moment. I removed the glass from my eye. I wanted so bad to share this with Luke, to tell him everything I knew about the air, the ocean, the waves. About how peaceful it could be. But he wouldn't hear me. He didn't even know how to hold his breath like I could.

I hopped off my bed and stood over Luke. His head rested on one side of his open notebook. On the other side, Mrs. Shelley's writing, in big, red, screaming letters all over his undone language arts assignment:

INCOMPLETE. YOU DID NOT EVEN WRITE ONE WORD ABOUT YOUR MOST FAVORITE THING. DO NOT TURN THIS IN UNTIL YOU HAVE AT LEAST ATTEMPTED THE ASSIGNMENT!!!

Right there, I picked up the pencil and scribbled in Luke's handwriting, my wish for him next to his shallow breathing:

MY NUMBA ONE TING

—by Luke DeSilva

Da ocean is my most favoritest ting in da hole world.

I luv da ocean 'cause no can hear nothin but da waves.

20

There was always a breaking point.

On the water, a wave always spread thin, dragging on reef and curling over. It folded, looped, twisted, and eventually flattened out, making way for the next one. With a really big wave, the water barreled, forming a long tube, squinting smaller and smaller. I imagined it was a jaw closing in on me, and if I didn't aim for the sunlight, I knew I'd get crunched.

On the football field, when things were really close, there was always one play that decided the game. Neither team wanted to give up the play that meant defeat. But never fail, it came down to either good *offense*, like a perfectly-executed play, maybe a nasty stiff-arm, or good *defense*, like a tough goal line stand, a fumble recovery, or a timely interception.

There was always a threshold for people too. Like Mom when we talked back or whined about doing something she told us to do. Or like when Dad mellowed out after work and Mom tried to talk to him. Or Luke when he wanted to play with his Lego, but he had to do chores.

And me, when my head throbbed from my sore tooth. I started moaning at night 'cause it was so sore. When I lay down, it hurt even more, pounding so hard across my face I felt it in the back of my head. I wanted it out already. Mom came in to check on me and Luke and found me sitting up in my bed, pillow wrapped around my head.

Mom said she'd help me get my tooth out. She said she didn't realize I was in so much pain. Plus, she didn't want me waking up Dad or the neighbors. She said I didn't need to go to the dentist, though, just for a baby tooth. So she went and got things together: sewing thread, hydrogen peroxide, and lots of Scott towels. For the *blood*, she said. I didn't like the sound of that, but at this point, I didn't care. With the supplies ready, Mom told me to open my mouth. She asked if I had a bad headache. I nodded yes. She said that was typical, to get migraines. She said my tooth looked small 'cause my gums were so swollen.

This was Mom's plan. She would tie a long piece of thread around my tooth and tie the other end to the knob on the bedroom door. She'd be on the outside, and on the count of three, she'd yank the door shut. The tooth *should* pop right out. I asked Mom if she did this before, but she only mumbled something about her folks doing this a long time ago. She didn't quite answer the question, but I figured, what the heck? It couldn't get much worse, right?

Ready? On the count of three: *One. Two. Three!*

Mom yanked on the knob from outside, whipping the door shut. One problem, the tooth didn't come. But even worse, the thread didn't break, so when Mom jerked the handle, my whole head flew too, slamming me square into the door.

Mom slowly opened the door, looking at me sprawled out on the bedroom floor, a long line of sewing thread connecting my mouth to the door like a caught fish. She said maybe the tooth wasn't ready to come out just yet, maybe the roots were still too thick or the gums were too swollen. As I undid the thread, Mom brought me a couple of aspirins. She told me to try not to let the headache bother me. Only a few more days and it should be gone. *Should?*

Before the school bell released us for Memorial Day weekend, Toby said he couldn't hang out for the next few days 'cause he was going camping with his father's side of the family. He and his cousins were all going to ride down to Mokulēʻia before the grown-ups so that they could check out the surf and set up camp. The family would be there from Saturday to Monday, so he and his cousins had to kapu a campsite, set up tents, drape tarps over the tables, that sort of thing. They had to do all the hard labor so when the grown-ups came, it was easy.

Toby was so excited 'cause he loved to hang out with his cousin Chaz. But when I asked Toby if he'd be going down with Chaz in his *truck*, Toby's expression soured. He knew what I meant. "No worry, *Dad*. I going be safe." He said it the way Luke would say it.

"Nah, Toby, no make," I said. "Rememba what your mom told you—"

He cut me off. "I said no worry. Only minor dat. You listen ev'ryting *your* modda say?"

Then the bell rang. We stood and stared at each other. We both accused each other without uttering a word: Toby, you know you shouldn't. Landon, you know *you* shouldn't.

When the bell died away, we said good-bye. Toby made off toward 'Ewa Beach Shopping Center, and I turned to the third grade wing. But I stopped and looked back at Toby. I watched him walk through the playground, the just-spoken words that linked him and me together getting thinner and thinner the farther he walked. I wanted to say something else but knew it wasn't my place. I had said enough. Toby made his way through the fence and headed up Pāpipi Road, everything stretched as far as it could. But once he was out of sight, the image snapped, like a broken rubber band. Then he was gone, and it was time to go get Luke.

On Saturday, Mom wanted us gone for a few hours, so I took Luke and his sand castle set back to 'Ewa Beach Park. After we made ourselves comfortable in the sand, I took off my shirt, and Luke saw the twine lanyard for the first time. He made a face and pointed at the quarter. "How come you wearing 'em like one Olympic medal?"

I fingered the quarter as I considered what to say. Finally, I opted for the truth. "I found dis in da ocean, under da sand like buried treasure, and I neva like lose 'em. Plus, I neva like you find da buggah lying around and *accidentally* spend 'em. I neva woulda seen 'em again."

Luke's brow furrowed. "What you saving 'em fo'? What you like buy?"

I smiled and shrugged. "I dunno yet. But had to be I found 'em fo' one reason, ah?"

When we got home, Aunty Selma's Volvo was in the driveway. Walking through the garage, I could hear her talking to Mom. "You thought about it before, Minerva. So why pretend like this is new? All along you knew it might come to this." I stopped by the window to listen. I peeked through, seeing Mom with her arms folded, something black draped over them. "What did you think? I tried to tell you years ago. Before you had the other one. But you wouldn't listen. You thought things couldn't get any worse—" Aunty Selma stopped, as Luke opened the screen door and walked in. I hurried to catch up to him. Aunty Selma snapped at Luke. "Can't you stay outside and play, or . . . something?" I curled my arm around Luke and pulled him back toward the door. Mom placed a pair of Dad's black work slacks and a spool of thread on the table. She covered her eyes and then wiped them with the pants leg.

"We just came from there," I said, real sassy, not caring nor waiting for Aunty Selma's response. I forced Luke out the door before me.

Aunty Selma ranted about us and then about Dad. Luke sprinted to the back of the house. I sat down below the kitchen window, out of sight. "Typical. A damn, typical, low-class bum. Just like his father. Did you see that? That's what happens when you mess around with something you shouldn't, Minerva. Those are your kids. No class, just like their brownie father's side of the family. What the hell were you thinking?" Aunty Selma's words squeezed through the screen window and oozed all over me. Thick, suffocating words that coiled around my body. Words I now knew all about. After all, wasn't their marriage my fault? I peeked through the kitchen window as Aunty Selma took the slacks and began hand-stitching the puka. "Minerva, wake up and smell the coffee. You guys haven't since the beginning of the year, right? You told me how he was before: *every* night. And now he's working late, *every* night. Grow up. That's the one thing the man's good at." Aunty Selma worked the needle in and out of the black fabric. "Sorry, Minerva, but somebody has to tell you straight. Start thinking about how to protect yourself. Nobody's coming to your rescue. Remember what Mama said? She made me promise I wouldn't. I mean, sure, I'll help you. But I have a tenant downstairs now. You can't stay there. So you better figure out what you're going to do *if* it gets to that point."

Mom's expression was pained. Her chest heaved as she sniffled. Aunty Selma knotted the stitch, snapped the thread, and then examined her work, holding the slacks out in front of her. Satisfied, Aunty Selma handed the pants back to Mom. "There, all fixed."

Ms. Shimizu said the last science project of the year would be Styrofoam cup phones. All we needed were two Styrofoam cups, a small hole in the bottom of each, and as much string to connect them together, depending how long-distance we wanted to talk. Ms. Shimizu warned that the phones wouldn't work unless the string was taut. So for that reason, she said maybe we shouldn't try to communicate with someone in downtown.

Pretty soon, we all looked mental, Styrofoam cups to our ears, shouting into a cup for the other person to stop coming closer. Ms. Shimizu and Mrs. Kato watched us and laughed in the back of the room. After our phones were done, Ms. Shimizu partnered us up to test them. I instinctively looked around for Toby but then remembered he wasn't in school today. And if that wasn't bad enough, I got paired with Afa Palaipale. Mr. Chicken Noises himself.

Ms. Shimizu told us to take turns. One person spoke while the other listened. She even gave us the phrase to say: *Hello, my name is* _______. And if that didn't come out clear, the phone needed to be worked on. On my phone, I talked first. Afa held his end a foot away from his ear, rolling his eyes. "Hello, my name is Landon." I then held the cup to my ear.

He put the cup to his mouth. "Hello, your name is *bawk-bawk-bawk-bawk*."

I yanked the cup away, his voice still ringing in my ear. The cord stretched taut between us, each end pulling on Styrofoam. Neither of us let go. I breathed deeply, trying to stay calm. I gritted my teeth and sneered at Afa. He smiled real cocky, laughing at me, just loud enough to hear. He lipped *what* to me, crunched the Styrofoam cup in his hand, half of *my* science project, and flung it to the ground. I wanted to hit. I wanted to . . . hurt. But it took a bigger man to walk away from a fight. I drew another deep breath. I could tell the end was coming. And soon.

Afa laughed again, picked up his two cups and coiled string, and took them to where his boys were in class. I glanced down at the cup on the ground and noticed that my hands were flexed into fists. Also, flecks of white Styrofoam littered the ground. Now, all that was left of two parts of my science project were white chunks of Styrofoam, trickling to the ground like falling teeth. I let the string fall through my fingers. Not yet, Afa. Not yet.

Toby wasn't at school the rest of the week. For the first couple of days, I actually didn't really even think about it. But when Mrs. Kato asked me on Friday if I had heard from Toby, I realized I hadn't seen him at all.

That afternoon, thoughts shot through my mind. I wondered if he was okay or if he was still mad at me or if he had a family emergency or if he had to go live with his dad. Thoughts looped around, winding tighter as Luke and I walked home. I decided to sneak out and go to Toby's house after my chores were done. What if that lucky bum was still surfing in Mokulē'ia? A wave of comfort broke inside, and I smiled with that thought. His family was still at the beach. That was why he wasn't at school. I wished I had listened closer to what he said about Memorial Day weekend. I was sure he said something about missing school this week.

When I got to Toby's house, I stopped before I rang the doorbell 'cause the sound of the waves startled me. It was really loud today. Behind his house, every explosion of water seemed to hit twice, each echoing crunch louder than the one before, smashing into rock in rhythmic breaths. Then I noticed the house was dark and quiet. No cooking. No lights on.

Everything slowed as I pressed the doorbell. One, two, three times. No answer. Then I knocked. No answer. I checked the knob. Locked? Toby's front door was always open.

Panic raced through me fast and hard, winding tighter until it knotted my stomach. I ran to the back of Toby's house and stood on the rocks overlooking the ocean. Where was he?

Then I realized something else. Where was Mrs. Ka'ea? Toby went camping with his *father's* side of the family. I felt the whipping sting of salt air. Through my feet, I felt the heavy thud of each wave detonate below. I felt the shower of water, like needles across my body. Each wave came in so fast there was no break, just constant swells plowing angrily like cuss words against the rocks. I closed my eyes and inhaled deeply. Each wave was connected to a strange pulse. I exhaled, then breathed again. Each wave rose and fell, as though whispering a message into the air. I just couldn't make out the words yet.

Sitting in our backyard, I saw my second shooting star. It blazed across the night sky with a glowing tail that looked like a long, suffocating leash. As if the tail was holding the star from going as fast as it could and wouldn't let go. I imagined the star trying to dive, like a caught fish thrashing, but it couldn't 'cause it was still connected. Finally, the star fizzled, breaking free and disappearing into the night.

I closed my eyes to make a wish. I had to keep them closed, or else the wish wouldn't come true. I took a deep breath and set my jaw to think of a good wish. But then a stinging jolt shot down my tooth and ricocheted through my face, causing me to yelp, making me forget about the wish. And making me open my eyes.

Outside, I sat on our classroom lanai at recess with my elbows propped on my knees, covering my eyes as if holding them in. The voices around me blended into one loud, vicious hum. I hadn't gotten much sleep 'cause my tooth still pounded. My head felt huge, like it pressed out from every angle.

Someone sat down next to me. It was Jason Jones. He started talking, so I looked at him. I had a hard time concentrating, but I tried. "We're leaving the day after tomorrow. I know we only have three more days of school, but she says she can't take it anymore. We're going to go back to Mississippi to live with her great-aunt, or somebody."

Wait a second. "Who going?" I asked.

Jason looked at me funny. "My mom and I."

I took a deep breath. "Going . . . where?"

"Back to Mississippi."

I rubbed the top of my head with my hand. "Why?"

"Because my folks are getting a divorce." Jason leaned closer. "Are you okay, Landon?"

Everything stopped around that word. Between the pulse in my head and the torment in my mouth, the word echoed louder and louder: divorce. Divorce. DIVORCE. I nodded, having just heard what Jason asked. "Yeah, I alright. My tooth bugging me. I sorry about your modda and fadda, Jason. Dat sucks."

He smiled and shrugged. "It's actually okay. At least I get to go back home." I knew what he meant. I had heard enough of it from Luke. "I get to see my old friends and go to the same school as before. I just wanted to tell you because you've been cool. You and Toby. Do you know where he is? I wanted to tell him good-bye too."

I took a deep, nervous breath. I had been trying to contain my panic. "I dunno where Toby stay. Nobody been his house fo' da last few days. Memorial Day weekend, his whole family wen' camping. I neva seen him since den."

Jason nodded as though that didn't seem strange to him. "Well, when you see him, please tell him I said thank you. For everything. I'll always remember surfing, like that time—" The bell started ringing, signaling recess was over. Jason stood, turning to go into the classroom, but stopped. "I almost forgot. I have something for you, Landon. I won't be in school tomorrow because the movers are coming. I'll ask my mom to stop by your house, or something, okay? I'll get it to you somehow." My head hurt so badly I only heard his feet scuttle away.

As I looped thoughts of Toby around me in neat circles, I tried to reel in everything above the sound of feet shuffling past into the classroom. Where *was* Toby? And now this, Jason was leaving? No! I flexed my hands into fists and breathed deeply. A blur of shoes and slippers sped past. I squeezed my fists so tightly my thumbnails turned white. But it didn't matter. I still felt everything slipping through my fingers.

I dialed Toby's house. No answer.

I rang Toby's doorbell repeatedly. The bells chimed inside. No answer.

I knocked wildly. A hollow thud over and over. No answer.

What was I supposed to think when I saw Dad's koa bowl, the one I told Luke to get rid of, come sliding out of the storm drain? I first heard it rattle in the darkness as though something was coming closer. Then I watched the bowl spin slowly on a current of brown sludge and finally fall from the mouth of the storm drain with a splash. I picked up the bowl and knew it was Dad's by the *L.D.* burned into the back.

What was going on? Luke threw away the bowl, and it ended up here? Did Luke drop it in the rain gutter, and it just made its way out now? But then I gasped. Maybe the *Help Me* man took it from our rubbish. Maybe he was still watching us. I hadn't thought about him in months. I looked deep into the darkness. Maybe the guy was right around the corner, fucking with me.

Thoughts swirled around each other, tangled in every possible direction of maybes. My gut strained as my body shook with anxiety. That was when I decided I wasn't about to stick around to find out what the deal was. I wound up and flew the bowl as hard as I could into the darkness. And then I stood and screamed into the black. "Leave us alone!" I turned quickly and just like a chicken, scurried over rocks back toward Toby's house.

It was a clear June night. No clouds around, just thousands of blinking lights against a screen of black. I thought about shooting stars. They were actually stars that died. Mrs. Ka'ea told me almost a year ago. But what killed them in the first place?

How did a star die? Was it old age? Did it fight for its life, only to lose at the end? Was it just making way for a younger star? Or did it *want* to go, tired and worn out after all it had been through? And then, as if right on cue, long and white across the sky: my third shooting star.

I watched the tail and saw it as something holding on but wanting to be free. As if it just rode along with the forward thrust. If that were true, then I knew how the star felt. I felt it with my tooth every day. I felt it with surfing, when thinking about Mom and Dad. With Toby and Jason. And even when I thought about Luke. I watched the dying star spiral away into nothing.

I closed my eyes, ready to do this right. I reminded myself not to crunch down on my jaw this time. I breathed deeply, wanting this wish to be good. I didn't know when I'd get the chance again. I let my thoughts spread out long before me: Luke, Mom, Dad, Toby, Jason. No separation, we'd stay close. No adoption, we'd stay here. No divorce, we'd stay together—

Something bumped into my chest. It scared me so badly I opened my eyes. Again. Luke curled into my body, his back against me. His voice was groggy. "I no could sleep."

I draped my arm around my brother and held him close, thinking about another wish I'd never get back. I wondered if it was bad luck. Like a pebble into water, that thought disappeared, leaving only dark ripples. I thought about it again: I got to hold onto Luke. It couldn't be all bad. At least I was still connected. I glanced back up into a sky that sparkled. I smiled. There were at least a thousand wishes up there that hadn't happened yet.

It was the second to the last day of school, and my head pounded 'cause of my tooth. I didn't even get one full hour of sleep the night before. It was like my tooth had somehow come to life to make things more and more unbearable. At recess, I sat outside on the classroom lanai again. Toby still wasn't at school. Also, Jason had been gone for the second day now. I sat there and concentrated on breathing, on just making it through today and the short day tomorrow. But in the back of my mind, the grim thought was still there. Then what?

Out of the blend of sounds around me, I heard it, like a siren coming closer:

Bawk-bawk-bawk-bawk

I didn't look but I knew Afa was approaching. As his voice got louder, I felt the surge within me, the rising pressure. Afa talked to the other boys I knew had crowded around, telling them to look at how scared I was, how I had to cover my face, hiding my eyes and crying like a girl. How he'd kick my ass any day. How chicken I was 'cause I wouldn't say anything and would only walk away from him. "Landon, you so panty. Fricken girl, you so weak." He didn't know how strong I was being. But he kept his mouth going, pressing further with each word, pushing me harder and harder. "Why you no stand up like one man, hah, chicken ass?"

The break happened so fast I barely even felt it. I gritted my teeth hard, popping my tooth loose, feeling blood swell in the back of my mouth. With every upward spurt, I let go. With the last few months of pressure behind me, I snapped. My eyes swelled white as I jumped up to rush Afa. He must have seen my bloody face 'cause he ran. With my headache gone, I chased Afa. With nothing holding me back anymore, I felt free. And with every pump of my legs, there was release. The boys were behind, yelling, "Beef! Beef!"

Afa ran like a panty, screaming like a girl. When I caught up to him, I tackled Afa, slamming his head into the ground. Then I sat on his chest, pinning his arms under my knees so he couldn't move. My forehead creased and I sneered as blood seeped through my teeth. I let red splatter all over his face and felt his body shake under me. I ground my teeth with each heaving breath I took, staring Afa square in the eye. I wanted to plug his mouth so bad. I wanted him to *feel* everything. Every noise. Every cluck. Every word.

But his eyes. It was all there, and that was when I remembered.

I remembered why I helped Jason with Afa in the first place. I remembered why I chose to become the sixth-grade chicken. I remembered why I swallowed it all down. Jason's eyes were like Afa's right now: scared. Like Luke, when he fell into the ocean. Like me, when I thought about divorce. Like Mom, when Dad got good with his hands.

Instead of cranking Afa, I blew my tooth out so it smacked him on the head. With long strands of blood hanging from my face, and with everybody watching, I coiled back all my anger, all my frustration, winding everything up. I decided to really let him have it. I leaned close, still staring him in the eye, and then clucked like a chicken. "*Bawk-bawk-bawk-bawk.*"

21

Mrs. Kato said if we were given a chance, we should take it. She said we never knew if we'd have the opportunity again. After the bell rang on our last day as sixth graders, Mrs. Kato asked me to stay. She said even though I didn't want to participate in the Gifted and Talented program at ʻIlima Intermediate School, she still submitted my name for testing next year.

"I'm sorry, Landon, I just couldn't let you slip through the cracks. With your potential, the G.T. program is an excellent opportunity. It'll give you a lot of options." Mrs. Kato extended both of her hands, palms up. "Options are like doors, Landon. In this hand," she said, showing me her right, "is one option, one door. And in this one is another. After choosing one, the other closes forever. You need to choose wisely because you can never go back." Still sensing my hesitation, Mrs. Kato indicated for me to sit. "Landon, I didn't always *want* to be in ʻEwa Beach, or to even be a teacher. When I was in college, I got an opportunity to travel across Europe. I went from England to France to Germany and Poland. I walked the beaches of Normandy. I sat in the ashy dirt of Auschwitz and just . . . cried." Mrs. Kato stopped and gazed outside, adrift in some memory. "There was so much sadness, Landon. So much that needed to be made better." Mrs. Kato exhaled quietly and then looked back at me. "I sat there, under a gloomy sky where so many were held and eventually killed, and realized what I needed to do. My parents and grandparents and countless other families were held in a camps against their will. In America, no less! That should never have happened. So I came back here, to where it all *began* for me."

I thought about the story Mrs. Kato told the class about World War II and the Japanese in Hawaiʻi and how her parents met. "You teach here 'cause of Honouliuli?" I asked.

Mrs. Kato nodded. "Hawaiʻi had five internment camps, Landon. Most people don't even remember where the one at Honouliuli was. I needed to do my part, helping children to learn as much as they could, to remember the past. So, hopefully, we wouldn't make the same mistakes in the future.

But I never would have chosen *this* unless I took the opportunity to go to Europe in the first place."

I thought about the past ten months in 'Ewa Beach, as dark clouds crossed my face. "What if I like live someplace else da rest of my life?"

Mrs. Kato chuckled. "I'm not saying you have to stay in 'Ewa Beach, Landon. Although you do have a big heart and you would stay if you thought you could help. But that's not the choice in front of you today." Mrs. Kato smiled and took a deep breath. "You have such potential. Your job, though, right now is to learn as much as you can from as many people right here in 'Ewa Beach as you can. So you can go as far as you need to." Mrs. Kato leaned in, obviously excited. But instead of raising her voice to make a point, she lowered it. "If you decide to come back to 'Ewa Beach like I did, then, great. Maybe one day you'll be someone who I refer students to. Maybe you'll tell the stories of this place and this time to help future children, so they won't forget. Whatever the case, I know you'll help make things better no matter where you go."

With words like those, it was hard to argue. But what about Luke? What about Mom and Dad? I fumbled for the right thing to say. "I dunno . . . I mean—"

Mrs. Kato interrupted. "I'm not saying the G.T. program is going to be easy, Landon. But this is a chance to change *everything.* You never know if that chance will come again. So please consider it. Will you do your best on the G.T. test next year?" She looked at me, and I simply nodded yes. How could I say no? "You'll probably still have to walk your brother home, so will you stop by and visit me next year? Let me know how you're doing?" I agreed eagerly, thanking Mrs. Kato as she gave me a hug. I hugged her back, and it felt good.

Running toward the third grade wing, late to pick up Luke, I could think of only one thing. What if Mrs. Kato was right? This might be my only chance. To change everything.

Luke was happy to be going to McDonald's after school. I promised him we'd get Big Macs to celebrate the end of the school year. He never had an entire Big Mac by himself. Mom always told him he was too small for a whole sandwich. Besides, what did he think, money grew on trees? So, naturally, when I said I'd buy a whole one just for him, he jumped at the opportunity. That was so Luke, thinking with his stomach.

Luke found us a table while I waited in line to order. I looked out the glass walk-through to 'Ewa Beach Bowl. I watched as old men and women stood poised, considering where to attack. Then, in slow motion, they walked, getting faster, then striding, getting closer and closer to the line until they twisted their bodies and released the ball. Some people were real smooth, the ball barely touching the wood, gliding in a graceful, spinning curve down the lane. But other people released the ball too high, letting it go airborne, allowing it to slam onto the polished surface. I imagined a huge crack where the ball landed. These balls bumped and skipped in a strange twitch before clipping a couple of pins or wobbling down the gutter. I wondered if people realized what they did to the floor, or how clumsy they looked, or if they even cared. I wondered if they'd change if they had the chance. They *should* want to bowl better, right?

I got two Big Macs, but we shared one large fries and one large drink. Luke alternated between burger and fries. He took turns between the two, savoring each bite, making each mouthful of Big Mac last. When we got to the bottom of the fries, Luke dumped the rest, sorting out the crispy bird-legged kind, piling them in front of him. "What'chu doing, Luke? No need eat da burn ones. I know you no like 'em. Just throw 'em away."

He picked one up and then looked at me with a smile. "Watch," he said. Before I could tell him not to, Luke flung the crispy fry into the air above him. Mom would kill him if she saw him doing this. The fry looped over itself, hanging for a moment, then sped back down. Luke adjusted his open mouth under the falling French fry. It slid into his mouth smooth and easy. A couple of crunches, then it was gone.

"Luke, you know Mom going broke your ass she eva see you do dat, ah?"

He picked up another fry and pitched it higher in the air than last time. "What she dunno not going hurt her," he said, mischievously employing one of Mom's favorite excuse-phrases. He caught the fry again and chomped it into bits.

"She not telling you fo' not do 'em fo' *her*, Luke. She telling you fo' *you*."

Luke picked up another fry and tossed this one higher yet. "Why, so I one *good* boy, no disgrace her, ah?" This time, though, he must have thrown the fry too high and lined himself up too perfect 'cause the fry came down so fast it flew deep into his throat, causing him to choke.

I pounded his back a couple of times with my open palm. Finally, a slimy shard of potato came launching out of his mouth and skidded across the table. He breathed hard, his chest rising and falling. Once the danger passed, I realized I was so frustrated I had to fight the urge to smack Luke. My idiot brother. I took a deep breath, mustering all the patience I could. "So what, dummy, you tink you know why Mom told you dat now?" Luke nodded, his eyes watery. It was about all he could do. "No take chances li'dat."

I cleaned up while Luke caught his breath. He flicked one of the empty Styrofoam Big Mac containers I hadn't thrown away. "Why you saving da cup and da Big Mac boxes?" I smiled 'cause the Styrofoam containers were a big reason I wanted to come to McDonald's.

I picked up the cup and shook it at him. "Da cup is fo' soda while we walking home. It's noon already and we get one long way fo' go in da sun." I smiled and felt all my frustration drip away. I grabbed the two Big Mac boxes. "And these is 'cause I like show you somethin'."

Luke raised his eyebrows. "What?"

I winked. "I going show you how fo' fly."

Rosie flew crazy now. When she was done hanging out on Dad's recliner, I normally picked her up and put her back in her cage. But now, when Luke and I let her out, she not only went for a healthy shit on Dad's chair, she took flight again and flew in circles around the living room. Pink, blind eyes zoomed around, somehow finding their way back to her cage. She never flew the same path either. Sometimes she looped deep into the living room. Sometimes she flew real low. It was like she couldn't make up her mind about what she wanted to do.

When Rosie first did this, she zipped into the wall or the window or into the screen door. But now she rarely crashed into stuff on her journey through the house. Needless to say, Luke got a kick out of this. He said it was better than *Looney Tunes*.

What was funny to me, though, was that Rosie never tried to fly *away*. She always went back to her cage. Crazy bird.

Jack Daniel's burned even more after I lost my tooth. Now the sting shot through my mouth, long before it hit the back of my throat. It sizzled the cavity where my tooth had been as I sat outside with a glassful, looking at the night sky. I took another sip and started to feel buoyant. I noticed that my headache had been gone for a few days now. I drifted along, rising.

After a couple of glasses, I was so light I thought about how it must feel to really be free, to have arms like wings and to just glide. I closed my eyes and felt it. This was the part I liked the most about Jack Daniel's: floating weightless and warm.

Eventually, the sky began to blur. It always happened. Stars got murky, and I started slipping back toward Earth. Nothing could keep me up there for long. This I knew.

My feet touched down first, then my ass, then my back, then my head. And as the sky splashed dark over me, I realized I was sinking into the ground. My breathing got shallow, and I gasped like I was already under, drowning in concrete. My thoughts got thinner, except for one, and as I looked at my reflected image in the glass, it was so distorted I appeared monstrous. And the more I stared at myself, the more the image was like a finger pointing back at me. I thought about how impatient I had felt toward Luke lately. I wondered if it was 'cause of my drinking, 'cause I was losing control. I felt the numbness spreading so I closed my eyes once again, inhaled deeply, and knew the answer to my own question. Luke was right. This was no longer just Dad. This was me too. I knew I should stop, but I'd do it every time. I knew I needed self-control so I wouldn't hit Luke again, but I also needed the few moments of flight.

The next thing I knew, there was a sound coming out of the darkness, like a hammer to my temples. At first, I didn't recognize it, but then it repeated again, with greater urgency this time. Sluggishly, I recognized it as my name. "Landon!" I tried to open my eyes, but it was too bright. Through a fog of drowsiness, I wondered why my bed was so cold. And why was I shivering? Where was my blanket? "What the hell are you doing out there?" That was Mom. Suddenly, everything stopped as I remembered where I was. Oh, shit. I had fallen asleep outside, and it was already morning. I forced myself into a sitting position and opened my eyes groggily. Mom stood just inside the sliding door to the family room. I instinctively reached for the whiskey glass and slid it behind me. But Mom had already seen it. "What are you doing with your father's glass?"

I rubbed my eyes and yawned to buy time. I had to think fast. "I was thirsty last night and I neva like wake nobody up by turning on lights.

Was on da counter, so I just used 'em." I peeked at the glass. Thankfully, it was empty.

Mom seemed to consider. "You slept out here all night?"

I got stiffly to my feet and then nodded. "Was so hot," I offered as I stretched. I picked up the glass, hoping Mom couldn't make out the lie.

At the door, Mom took the glass from me and sniffed it. Maybe she could smell something, and maybe she couldn't. She just stared at me for a moment. "Why are your eyes bloodshot, Landon?" she asked sternly.

Crap. I hadn't even thought about that. On mornings after drinking, I usually got to the bathroom to wash my face before having to deal with anyone. Looking blankly back at Mom, I knew that if I didn't say something soon, I was busted. And then I realized the answer was staring me in the face. "Why your eyes bloodshot . . . *Mom*?"

Mom appraised me and then finally shook her head. She shoved the glass back at me. "Eat your breakfast and then brush your teeth," she snapped. "You got chores to do."

In the kitchen, I set the glass in the sink, trying to catch my breath. My heart hammered away as I counted my lucky stars. I knew Dad still blamed Mom for dumping his whiskey. And truth be told, I had been drinking a lot more lately. I thought about how that all could've just turned out, how busted I could've gotten. It was bad enough that Dad drank, but if Mom caught me too? I didn't want to think about the record-setting lickens I'd be sure to get. I was so jittery my feet were almost numb. I tried to breathe evenly as I leaned against the kitchen counter. I knew I had to stop drinking, that was for sure. But how? If getting scared shitless wasn't a good enough reason to quit, I didn't know what was.

I showed Luke how to build a Styrofoam spaceship. First, he had to get any Styrofoam box container, like the ones from our Big Macs. Then, he had to wash it out with soap and water, or else he would have sticky leftovers and bugs. Mom would kill him if that happened. Last, he had to take the scissors and slice square holes into the upper part, the lid of the container. I suggested two holes in the front and two holes in the back, for the front *and* the rear of the cockpit. So the pilot and co-pilot could see both ways. Also, I told him to cut out a hole on each side just in case somebody attacked from the right or left.

Luke sliced his container, building his very own spaceship, and I had to admit, it was pretty good. The first time Toby showed me this, mine came out all hamajang, more like a spaceship *wreck* than a spaceship. But in no time, Luke's was fired-up and ready to go. Before I could tell Luke what to do, he already had Luke Skywalker sitting inside his very own spaceship, flying around our bedroom. I smiled. Luke was already in his own world. He was flying for the first time, and he was grinning. Oh, God, he was grinning!

Then I thought about Toby again. I didn't think I ever thanked him for showing me how to do this. I promised I wouldn't miss that opportunity when I saw him again. I glanced back at Luke, still thinking about Toby. Luke was going into hyperspace now. I imagined the star needles stretching long before he slingshotted away.

Luke and I had been letting Rosie fly around the house, but Luke always forgot to clean up the bird shit on Dad's recliner. That was the deal, I told him. He accepted it. I opened the cage, let Rosie out, and caught her if she got away. He cleaned up the goop she left behind. But Luke rarely remembered to keep his end of the deal. It got so bad that whenever I heard Dad come home, I flung everything aside to check if his chair was clean.

So what happened when I failed to double-check?

Dad lowered himself into his chair, and his hair smeared white-green globs across the sweaty vinyl. Then he thrust his head back, punching deeper into the chair, pasting not only his oily VO5 hair but his undershirt as well. He didn't see the speckled and sticky cotton yet. Even when he turned his face, rubbing his cheek deep into a wet, gooey mess of feathers and shit, and then swiped with his hand and yanked it forward to see, he still stared dumbly at his hand for a moment. But then everything brutally snapped into place.

Luke and I listened from our bedroom. Mom pleaded, crying to Dad that she didn't let Rosie out of the cage, for him to please let her keep the bird. Dad yelled that this was it. He was tired of finding little spots of bird shit around the house. And he didn't give a damn if the bird was blind. One more time, and that bird would be sorry. One more time, he promised, and Mom would be even more so.

I looked at Luke on the floor with his *Star Wars* figures. His face was frozen, eyes boring straight down into his hands on his lap. I could tell he was stuck between his intergalactic adventure and the argument going on in the kitchen. He clutched Luke Skywalker and Darth Vader, one in each hand. Han Solo sat in Luke's Lego house, watching.

I whispered. "Luke, why you neva clean up da mess? You know *you* suppose to. Dat's your job. You wen' choose it." Luke looked at me, his eyes glazed over as his forehead creased. He didn't answer. He knew it was his fault.

But when we heard glass breaking, without even so much as a thought, Luke dropped his toys and stood quickly. He hurried to the door and looked back. His nose was turning red. "At least I do somethin', Landon. You no do nothin' but listen. And drink." Luke ran down the hallway to Mom and Dad's bedroom. What the hell was he doing? I got up and chased after him. Luke knew better than to leave our bedroom when Mom and Dad fought. He might as well paint a target on his back. But even more than that, Luke's crap had to stop. Every day, Luke drifted further away from me. It felt like I was losing him. He wised off, he didn't listen anymore, and he definitely had gotten brave with his mouth. As I ran down the hallway, it felt like the last chance, like he was heading down a path I wouldn't be able to.

I rounded the corner to Mom and Dad's bedroom, ready to physically yank Luke back to our bedroom, by the ear if I had to. I was ready to *make* him to see that he needed to change, that he couldn't take chances anymore. I was so frustrated I was ready to hit him and count myself justified. What did Luke want, to lose his only brother? To break us apart? We had to stick together. But when I came through the door, I saw Luke on the other side of the bed, eyes wet and mad, both hands gripping the telephone receiver. And then I heard it, in fearful, quivering English, as if his pidgin was suddenly dead. "Hello. Give me the police. Yes. It's an emergency." It hit me like a punch in the jaw. Not only was Luke the one who had been calling the police, he was right. At least he did something. I only *listened.*

Ever noticed the sound a plant made when the wind blew through it? Even though each plant's sound was different, it was a calm and soothing whisper, like knowing, gentle words. I watched Mom's rose bushes sway, speaking softly with each gust, colorful buds rocking heavily in waves that flowed from an invisible tongue. I closed my eyes and listened:

Were they happy to be here? Growing, bending, stretching, with no choice but to twist higher in a vivid, colorful swirl. With no choice except to reach up toward the sky.

Or were they sad? Rooted, stuck, alone, forced back and forth beyond their control, with no choice whether they were pulled from the ground or not. With no choice except to display themselves to the world. Only to have their reds, pinks, and whites severed from the only veins that could *free* them. And then left fallen on the living room end table, like a victim of a crime.

I felt the wind pick up. The buds squirmed violently with each gust. I wondered what they'd say if a storm came ripping through. Once again, I listened. Happy or sad?

Luke knew he shouldn't throw his toys around. But he did so anyway. Mom had just given him lickens for doing a half-assed job in the bathroom. So he lay sullenly face up on the carpet next to his Lego house and kept tossing his Han Solo action figure in the air. I was somewhat thankful. At least he wasn't trying to catch it with his mouth.

I didn't like how angry he looked, so I decided to try to distract him. "So what, Luke? You neva tell me. How was, using Humpty Dumpty?"

Luke glanced at me and shrugged. "Okay. Afta while, da odda kids like use 'em too. Dey thought was fo' da rock-hard chairs." He looked at me funny. "Why, you like 'em back?"

I shook my head. "Nah, keep 'em. Use 'em next school year if you like."

Luke turned back and stared at the ceiling. He launched Han Solo again. He was quiet for a moment, but then he suddenly blurted out as though he couldn't hold it back. "I wen' use 'em almost ev'ry day. Sometimes I wait fo' Mrs. Shelley stand by my desk fo' pull 'em out. But she neva ask me once why I using 'em." He fell silent again. Luke eventually snorted and made a face.

"Sorry, Luke."

He shrugged again. After a long silence, he shook his head. "Not your fault."

"Yeah, but . . . " I said, trailing off. Luke eyed me, as though waiting for me to finish my sentence. But I was thinking about how Mom hit him way too much now. Angry, frustrated, disappointed, it didn't matter. Half the time I wondered if she was really that mad at Luke or if she just needed a target. And with that thought came another, heavy with shame. "Luke, I shoulda said 'em long time ago. But I sorry I wen' slap you dat one time. No good dat."

For a moment, Luke seemed confused. But then his eyes focused as he considered.

"I promise, Luke, not going happen again. Bruddas no should do dat to each odda."

Luke nodded and smiled tightly. "Okay," he said and then lay back on the carpet.

And that was it. I wanted to talk to him some more, to distract him. But I didn't know what to say or how to make it better. So instead, I just kept quiet and gave Luke the space he needed. I watched Han Solo fly up and down a few times, how he floated, rotated, spun. Then I glanced at Luke's house. The removable roof lay on the ground next to Luke. It looked as if he had finally finished the house, now that the roof was done. Inside the house, Luke Skywalker, Princess Leia, and Darth Vader were scattered in different rooms. And even though their bodies were twisted, arms and legs in strange positions, each head was turned upward as if they all watched Han Solo levitate, lingering above them.

I skipped rocks above shallow waves at 'Ewa Beach Park. Flat, smooth river rocks worked best. I wound up, flicked my wrist, and let them fly. If I leaned over and got really close to the water, releasing just above the surface, there was a better chance the rock would catch two, three, even four times before sinking.

I thought about the promise I made to Luke. I knew I really meant it when I said it. I didn't want to hit him, but I wondered if Luke believed me. It was the look on his face, the doubt sputtering forth a question he ultimately let fade into oblivion. What about my drinking? Maybe Luke was just waiting for me to do it again, like Mom or Dad. I shook my head and exhaled as much shame as I could. No luck. It was still there. I wound up again.

The rock smacked against the water a few times before falling in. It looked strong just after I let go, but after a few feet, it got weak. I never noticed that before. The rock only flew for a little bit. And even though the rock was solid, the water always won. The water allowed the rock to have its way at first. But it was as if the water knew the rock would eventually give up. The rock had no choice. It couldn't change.

But water was constantly shifting, swelling, churning. It was always changing. That was when it hit me. Rocks had to go . . . down. I thought about what I had been doing with Jack Daniel's, how impatient I had been with my brother, and I realized Luke was right. As much as I didn't want to hear it, the two were connected. I fingered a rock in my hand. I had been as thick-headed as this stone was dense. The rock could fly, but not for long. And, hell, I didn't want to sink. I wanted to rise. For more than just moments. And for more than just myself. Right then, I knew what I had to do. I had to stop drinking so I could fly too.

When I got home, Luke was outside playing with his *Star Wars* figures. I saw the dogfight from the driveway. He had two Styrofoam Big Mac containers-turned-spaceships shooting across the yard. He made Luke Skywalker zip all around, zooming high and low, as Darth Vader chased. No matter what Darth Vader did, he couldn't catch Luke Skywalker.

Inside the house, Dad was yelling at Mom again.

But Luke just kept playing, stuck in some distant universe, far, far away from here. Luke Skywalker was the best pilot in the galaxy. He flew around the tree, over the flowerbed, through the rose bushes. Luke Skywalker scorched across the yard, thinking he lost Darth Vader, but then lasers shot at him. He swerved, back and forth, to dodge the blasts.

Mom was yelling at Dad now. Pleading with him to put *it* back.

Instead of running away, Luke Skywalker turned around and flew straight into Darth Vader's ship. Glass broke inside the house as Luke flinched, crunching Darth Vader's Styrofoam ship between his fingers.

Suddenly, Dad punched the screen door open, took three steps out the door, and flung Rosie on the sidewalk. She skipped on the concrete, like a pebble on water. I looked at Dad, and he at me, our eyes forced into a lingering stare as the screen door hissed shut behind him. Mom was crying inside. Dad glanced to his left at Luke who stood in front of the house with one smashed Styrofoam spaceship in one hand and Luke Skywalker's undamaged one in the other. Luke's head was down, and he was unable to move.

Dad focused on me again. His eyes narrowed into slivers. "Dat fuckah neva going fly around my house again. Shit on ev'ryting. Fricken bird." He stared at me without blinking, his tongue digging the inside of his mouth. Mom cussed at him from the doorway. Dad yanked the screen door open and bolted back inside, ready to continue the battle.

I walked down the sidewalk to look at Rosie. She was a contorted mess: wings yawning every which way, head and neck crooked to the left, feet still twitching. My stomach lurched as I turned to Luke. He was looking at me now, eyes glazing wet. "I sorry," he said. "I neva mean—" He stopped.

I felt my breath catch. "You wen' let her out again?" I asked apprehensively. Luke nodded, his expression pained. He knew this was his fault. He didn't move, but tears dripped down both sides of his face. I watched as Luke clenched his hands into fists, popping both Styrofoam spaceships. His arms shook violently, and then he threw both spaceships across the yard. They got caught in Mom's rose bushes. He sobbed now, head low. He didn't move, just stood there, crying.

I looked back at Rosie on the sidewalk. Her lifeless body lay over a jagged crack in the walkway. Her feet had curled stiff. There were feather skid marks and blood on the concrete. I stroked her wings and whispered. "At least *you* had da chance fo' fly."

THREE

22

Dead meant dead, like Rosie. Gone, left, never coming back.

Mom was crying. She knelt in front of her rose bushes all day. Eyes blinked out fat tears that rolled down her face. Hands worked slowly in the mud, staining fingers and clothes red. From the screen door, it looked as if she was streaked with blood.

I could tell her mind was somewhere else. Between working and wiping her eyes on her shirtsleeve, Mom reached for the slightly open buds, gently touching the firm petals. She spaced out, one hand stroking the living color, the other hand limp at her side. And then she leaned in close, whispering to them. She wiped her face again. It must be so hard to see.

While scraping Rosie off the ground, Mom cried. When she wrapped Rosie in Scott towels and slid Rosie's body into a gallon-sized Ziploc, Mom cried. After shutting the freezer—Rosie's stiff body inside getting stiffer—her hand lingered on the handle, and Mom cried.

When Luke saw Mom put Rosie in the freezer, he wanted to make a funeral for the bird. He didn't like the idea of Rosie not getting to rest in peace. "What Mom keeping her fo'?" He glanced outside to make sure Mom wasn't coming and then opened the freezer.

"You betta not, Luke," I warned. He looked at me as cold air exhaled from above, hovering about him like frozen breaths. "You seen how sad Mom? She still holding on. If she no see Rosie in da freezer, and she find out you wen' bury her, she going broke your ass big time first, ask questions later. Dat's *her* bird, not yours. You gotta let her say good-bye wen she ready." Luke's eyes darted back and forth. I could see it already, Luke stealing Rosie. When Mom realized it, I'd be the first to get it. Mom would say I should know better. I should somehow stop these asinine exploits from my off-the-wall brother before they happened.

Luke's brow furrowed. "You no tink dat we should make funeral?" Luke whispered. Chilly clouds spewed from the freezer, engulfing him in a strange mist.

"Nah, we should. Weird, freezing 'em li'dat. Rosie no can be free. But Mom gotta see dat fo' herself. She not ready fo' let go. So no do nothin' dumb, okay?"

Luke's expression hardened. "I not going do nothin' dumb. I know what I doing." Luke shut the freezer door and then stood at the window, watching Mom. The imprint of his sweaty thumb lingered on the handle before fading.

Mom said I was a Doubting Thomas. Actually, whenever Luke or I disagreed with her, she called both of us that. "Ye of little faith. Fine, don't believe me. You're such a Doubting Thomas." It was another one of her favorite phrases. Probably 'cause it came from church.

Then we had to listen to the story about how Thomas was one of the original twelve apostles. How after Jesus died and rose again, Jesus appeared to the apostles before going to Heaven. How they were all happy to see Jesus, happy to know that He was alive. Mom said the apostles *all* believed, just by seeing Him again. But not Thomas. He wouldn't believe it actually was Jesus until he got to touch the holes in Jesus's hands and sides. "All of the apostles had *blind* faith, except Thomas," Mom said authoritatively, as if that explanation was all the proof she needed. That I should let it go and believe her now.

Even if I still didn't completely agree, it did make *some* sense. Mom was pretty blind.

When I fell asleep long enough, I dreamed about Toby:

Everything was in slow-motion. We both surfed behind his house and the waves were cranking. Water crashed into mist that we speared through for fun. But before either of us could do anything, the water melted into air. I kept surfing, flying now, skimming through a light blue sky, no land in sight, happy I was finally doing it.

But when I looked back, about to tell Toby to look at me, my wish was finally coming true, I saw Toby falling. For a moment he was suspended, but when I reached my hand for him, he dropped. I couldn't stop my board from gliding forward. I couldn't do anything but watch. My eyes were glued to his hand as it plummeted, fingers open, falling. And thrashing.

That was how I woke up, wildly reaching for Toby, so close I could almost touch him.

Even though Mom was pissed at Dad, she was still trying. She would snip off a rose and set it in a vase on the end table in the living room, hoping he'd notice. Each one died, however, shriveling a few days later, twisting into a brittle hint of what it was. Yellow, white, or pink rose petals always bruised in light-brown splotches as they faded and withered into gnarled chips. But red rose petals bled a dark brown, choking into a deep purple that eventually rotted black.

Mom talked on the phone with Aunty Selma, wiping her nose with a soggy Scott towel. "I know, Selma, you've said that before." She didn't want to hear it anymore, didn't want to believe it was true. "You can't prove it's only a matter of time. What? *I* should file? How am I supposed to do that? I've got two kids." Mom's voice got louder, swelling into a shout. "I know I don't cook and clean how he wants me to, but he shouldn't have killed my goddamn bird!" She covered her eyes with the wadded-up sheet.

In the living room, crispy petals flaked off a dying rose, scattering all over the end table. Mom didn't ask me to, but I took the rose, cleaned up, and then hid it with all of the other ones I took. I didn't want Mom finding crumbly rose carcasses in the trash. Mom's eyes were still too full and too blurry to see. No matter how many roses she set out, her marriage was dying.

When we died, did our eyes close automatically?

Or did they stay open, holding on long after we'd gone, as if we weren't ready?

Rosie's eyes were open. Big, wet, empty eyes. I doubted she was ready.

Luke figured Mom was ready to let go after a couple of weeks 'cause she had been crying a lot less. Whenever he got an idea in his head, he couldn't see anything but that. I tried to tell him not to rush Mom. I tried to tell him he needed to wait. But did he listen? Nope.

Even if I just explained to him twice why he shouldn't bug Mom, Luke went and asked her if we could make a funeral for Rosie. I stood in the kitchen, my eyes boring a hole into Luke's back. He was so damn blind and selfish, selfish, selfish. Mom's eyes got moist as she breathed deeply. The sound of the ocean came in through the window. Her chest fluttered. For a moment, while Mom seemed to consider, everything calmed. Everything stilled, slowing almost to a stop. I waited, bracing for the eruption.

But instead of yelling at me and slapping Luke across his thick skull, Mom wiped at her eyes. She swallowed her emotion down, nodded slowly to Luke, and smiled. "That's very sweet, Luke. I think it's a great idea. Rosie would like if we said good-bye to her. She was a part of this family for a while too, right?" Luke raised his eyebrows at me, as if to say, *See?*

Luke and I dug Rosie's grave in the flower bed. Mom thought that was a good place for Rosie to be laid to rest, with all the pretty colors above and lots of branches to climb. When we were ready to place Rosie in, Mom told me to get Rosie from the freezer. Damn.

Her wrapped-up body was so cold it felt weird. As my hands tingled, from the kitchen to the flower bed, I couldn't help thinking that this used to *be* Rosie. This solid wad of paper and plastic used to flap her wings and fly around the house.

Outside, Luke held the sweaty Ziploc in both hands. He closed both eyes. "Dear Jesus. Please watch ova Rosie. She was one good bird. We going rememba her fo' all da good stuffs she did. Like . . . um . . . eating, and chirping, and, and . . . " He squirmed, as though searching for the right thing to say. "Oh yeah, we going rememba her fo' making us laugh wen she fly into stuff and wen she take craps—" Luke stopped. Both Mom and I looked at Luke. Mom wanted to ask, 'cause her eyebrows raised. But she also knew she shouldn't in the middle of a funeral. She closed her eyes again. But across my face, my open mouth, my flaring nose, my exploding eyes, everything screamed at Luke to *shut up*. We never told Mom we used to let Rosie out of her cage. Luke continued praying. "But, Jesus, Rosie stay blind, so please help her find her way to Heaven. For yours is da kingdom, da power, and da glory. Foreva and eva. Amen."

By the time Luke finished, Mom was crying, but a thin smile crept across her lips. She patted her eyes with a crinkled Scott towel. Luke lowered Rosie in, and we both covered her with sad, wet dirt. After we packed the mud over Rosie, Luke leaned close and whispered so that Mom couldn't hear. "Good-bye, Rosie. I sorry. Was my fault." He glanced at me and smiled weakly. Then he stood up, making room for Mom to kneel.

This was the first time I felt it, and even though it was a little blurry, I was almost certain. Luke saw more than I thought he could.

As I looked through the blue glass disc I found in the ocean, I daydreamed. I squinted one eye shut, holding the glass to the other eye, looking into a cooler world. I started to drift, feeling the pull. It was so blue I felt thin, like I was in two places at once: underwater and above the clouds. I smiled. This was Heaven.

I let myself go. I sank into and then soared deeper into water I hadn't swum yet, diving higher into air I had yet to touch. And right now nothing mattered 'cause I was free and light.

But when Dad came home, I rocked back and forth on ripples I knew were coming, watching from the backyard as he walked toward the kitchen. Mom was on the phone with Aunty Selma while she cooked dinner. Her voice hung, like an unpleasant vapor. After sniffing it out, Dad immediately turned around and made for their bedroom. A few minutes later, he came back into the living room, having changed into shorts and a nice polo shirt. But instead of grabbing his drink from the kitchen, Dad went straight for the front door. He glanced toward the kitchen, shook his head, and slid out. He gunned the Chevy's engine and peeled out down Pupu Street. I watched all of this in blue.

Mom made it to the window only to see the tail end of the Chevy as dark pouches of smoke dissipated over the asphalt. Her head hung low.

Even from here, through the mesh of screen windows and the glass of a blue disc, I could see what was coming. Why couldn't Mom? Or better yet, why *wouldn't* Mom?

I could see it already. When Mom picked up the phone, the first thing I thought was that she would be on it for hours. As I vacuumed, I imagined what was being said. Hello? Oh, hi. How are you? But then, she let out a gasp, as she covered her mouth and looked at me. Probably Aunty Selma, telling Mom she needed to face it: sooner or later Mom was going to get divorced. Mom's eyes swelled with tears. Why didn't Mom just accept it already? Not that I wanted them to get divorced, but I was tired of fighting it. I was tired of worrying about custody and adoption. I was tired of not sleeping, feeling empty and drained all day, every day. I just wanted to know what would happen already. Who Luke and I were going to be with.

And who I should let go of. I looked at Mom crying in the kitchen. She still wasn't ready to see.

After a few minutes, Mom hung up the phone and called me to the kitchen. She asked if I'd like a glass of water. I noticed she wasn't only sniffling, but her fingers bored into the soft part of her hands, like piercing thoughts across her palm. She said to sit down 'cause this wasn't going to be easy. What? She was acting weird. Then it hit me. Dad must have called her from work to say that he wanted the divorce.

But when Mom opened her mouth, what she said was so crisp, so sharp, so in focus I couldn't make it out. It was too direct. Too pointed. Too painful to see. Toby was . . . wait.

"What?" I asked in disbelief. Mom's words had finally gelled together into an idea as Mom said it again. And even before Mom finished, I knew I didn't want to hear any more. I turned around and went back to the living room. I switched on the vacuum and yanked it back and forth. No, no, no, it couldn't be.

Mom grabbed the vacuum from me and turned it off. "Toby's dead, Landon."

I stood there frozen. Dead? Toby couldn't be dead.

Mom sighed. "That was Celeste Ka'ea, his mom. She wanted to tell you because you two were so close."

I shook my head back and forth. Toby can't be dead. Dead meant *dead*, like Rosie.

"The funeral is on Friday at Mililani Mortuary."

Friday? What funeral? Everything sped up as thoughts of Mom and Dad exploded into thoughts of Toby and surfing. I speared through it all, through a fog of denial: Toby was still at the beach, his family went camping, for Memorial Day weekend, he went down early, with his cousin, to surf. Everything stopped. Oh, no . . . his cousin. The surge of fear was so strong I stumbled backward. Then the wave smashed down on me in two painful words: Chaz's truck.

As it crashed, I felt myself go under. Caught beneath it all, I gasped and struggled for breath. Under here, I flailed for something to pull me out of this fluid haze. Still unable to see, still not wanting to see, I barely heard the part about Toby in the morgue, alone and freezing, not yet put to rest 'cause his mother and father fought for weeks over what kind of funeral Toby should have. I didn't hear 'cause I was drowning, slipping further from fear into guilt. Why didn't I tell Mrs. Ka'ea? Toby was going to ride with Chaz, and I didn't say anything.

As a flood of regret streamed down my face in hot streaks, I heard Mom say she was sorry but it was true. Toby was dead. I suddenly yelled at her. "What'chu doing? Stop it! Dis not funny!" And then I ran. I hit the screen door and kept on running. I suddenly needed to go somewhere. Away from the living room, away from the phone, away from Mom. Everything burned as I ran blindly down Pupu Street. I didn't know where I was going. And I didn't care.

By the time I walked in the door, it was already late. I didn't care if I was busted. Mom sat on the couch, waiting. Both Luke and Dad must be asleep. As the screen door shut, Mom just looked at me. She didn't scream, she didn't yell, just looked and watched. I could still feel the ocean all over me, sad, stinging mists. We watched each other, unsure of what to say. Once I figured I wasn't in trouble, I turned to go to me and Luke's room. Mom finally spoke up.

She was calm, subdued. "Where were you, Landon? I drove around looking for you."

I stopped and looked back through the hallway door. "I wen' to da shore. I just sat and listen to da waves." I didn't wait for Mom's response. I went and lay down on my bed, dirty and all. I didn't care if I soiled the bed sheets. I rolled over to face the wall, pulling my knees up to my chest. As I pressed my head deep into the pillow and pulled the sheets up over me, I felt a strange urge to do laundry. But for the life of me, I couldn't seem to let go of the fabric.

I heard Mom come in a few minutes later. She set a plate and cup by the side of the bed, and then sat down next to me. She whispered, gently, like before. "I'm sorry I had to be the one to tell you, Landon. I brought you some dinner." There was a long silence, the kind that rang in circles and wouldn't stop. She made her voice as cheerful as it could get. "It's a tuna sandwich, your favorite." I knew what she was trying to do, and it wasn't working. As the quiet strained between us, Mom stood. "Good night, Landon. Just know that you can talk to me, okay?"

I rolled over to look at her. "Toby's *not* dead, Mom."

Mom took a deep breath and smiled weakly. She looked me square in the eye when she spoke. "Landon, you know he is. I told you. He flew out of his cousin's truck. I'm not trying to hurt you, but you have to accept that he's gone."

How would she know? She never knew what Toby meant to me. All she cared about were her damn rose bushes. I suddenly didn't give a damn. "Easy fo' you fo' say, ah?"

Mom's brow furrowed. "What's that supposed to mean?" she asked quietly.

At this point, I didn't even care how it sounded. I didn't care how it hurt her. "How come you no see dat *our* family dying? How come you no accept dat?"

Mom recoiled, looking as if she had just been slapped. She stood quickly and placed her hand over her mouth. She hurried out the door as she shook her head.

I looked at the tuna sandwich. Chunks of meat were glued together by grayish-white mayonnaise globs that drooled off the bread. I stared blankly at one murky, dangling blob, until looking at a tuna sandwich somehow made sense. The glob finally came free and splattered on the plate below. Oh, God. Toby.

I didn't know why I did half the things I did anymore.

On the day before Toby's funeral, I took the dried rose cuttings behind the garage and built a pile. I drenched the brittle sticks and petal chips with Dad's lighter fluid. I soaked them until wisps of white fumes lingered over the mound. I inhaled the stinging sweet. I struck a match and dropped it onto the heap.

And then I watched the burn. I watched as the dead flowers came alive in a splash of flames. I watched as every fight every flower ever was melted into crispy smoke. I watched as each charred, bony twig crackled with strange words and dissolved into whispers. I should have told Mrs. Ka'ea. I should have called. I should have said . . . something. As the fire intensified, waves of guilt crawled up my body. *Why, Landon? Why didn't you tell me?* I felt the hole in my stomach burn, swelling with each scorching word. And as it hit my eyes, as the dancing fire swirled eddies of heat higher and higher, I exhaled all of my breath just so I could stand here drowning in this swirling, choking blur.

I couldn't breathe as I entered the chapel at Mililani Mortuary. With every step, I thought about Toby. Not ready, so not ready. As Mom and I moved farther in, I heard the soft, sad music of a piano. Toby wasn't *here*. He couldn't be. A line of people shuffled down the middle of the assembly hall. There was no way Toby was here. The thick air stunk with the vulgar, sweet scent of flowers. Violets, lilies, roses. Chrysanthemums, orchids, carnations. Some flowers hung, some were potted, some were in arrangements, and woven between them all were gnarled, twisted branches. Blossoms stung the room with bleeding color. Purple, red, yellow, and pink everywhere, as though spattered across the white walls and wood panels. A bird of paradise stood proudly at the front. And that was when I saw it, a coffin. But that was *not* Toby's.

For a moment, I wished Luke was here, not at Aunty Selma's for the afternoon.

Before I realized what was happening, I discovered myself in a line of people that moved steadily forward, as though something pulled at me with each step I took toward the front. I rocked back and forth, concentrating on one foot in front of the other. I tried to keep my breaths even as I clung to what had gotten me through. There *had* to be a mistake. That coffin wasn't him. There was just no way. And then, farther along, I saw Mrs. Ka'ea through a fog of people to the left. She was crying, blowing her nose. Hugging people, trying her best to smile. Each person approached, full of kind words. She was holding on as tightly as she could.

In front of me, the crowd suddenly faded, and I saw the coffin. I felt something inside me snap. It was faint, and I couldn't tell exactly what it was. But I could feel it, the flooding that wanted to rise. But I held it in. I stepped forward. My legs got cold, weak, and then numb. I felt hot and cold at the same time. I took another step. I couldn't breathe, couldn't see. Another step and I recognized the face, and then—

Everything happened so fast I didn't realize what I was doing. There were streaks of color, a dizzying blur of faces and flowers, and a burn in my legs. Was I running? I plowed through the line of people, up the aisle and out of the chapel, running away as fast as I could. Mom called to me over and over. And that was when I realized what had broken free inside. I had wanted to cry. But, no. If I cried, that meant I had to accept it. Right now, I just had to run.

When Mom found me, I was at Grandma and Grandpa's grave, thinking about Toby's face in the dream I had. It was the same face that was in the coffin. Solid, cold, frozen. Like he was still refrigerated in the morgue. But it was his skin that did it. Tight, pale skin with a slight, powdery tint of green just beneath the surface. Not enough to scream it, but enough to know: Dead meant *dead*. It didn't even look like Toby, but I shook that off 'cause I *knew*.

Mom put her hand on my shoulder. I flinched under her touch. "Why Toby had fo' die?" I looked up at her, hoping she actually had an answer. The wind whispered through the trees.

Mom looked at Grandma and Grandpa's grave. "I don't know, Landon. I don't know why people die like *that*." Our eyes met as flashes of Toby shot through my mind. I saw him surfing, sun glittering off the water. Mom reached to touch the headstone. For a moment, she looked as though she was going to cry. But she didn't. She knelt and then settled onto the soft ocean of green grass surrounding us. Mom began speaking, still looking at the headstone, still staring into the names of her parents. "I'm going to tell you something, Landon. This is the only time I will ever say it." She paused and then glanced at me. "I don't know why I'm telling you this. Maybe I *have* to. Maybe it's because I know you'll understand now." She looked back toward the grave and took a deep breath. And when she spoke, her voice was loaded down with memory but also somehow soft and warm and magical, like an afternoon mist rising off the ocean. "My folks were huge football fans, Landon. Well, Mama really wasn't, but Daddy was. He would go to as many games as he could. So Mama and Daddy would get dressed up with their favorite team's colors, waving pennants, buying hot dogs, cheering like crazy people. Daddy loved it. Mama went because she knew it would make him happy.

"Well, not only that. She liked the vacations Daddy took her on. They not only went to games here in Hawai'i but they also went to games on the mainland. You see, Daddy was a pilot. He had friends coming in and out of Hawai'i all the time, from places like New York, Los Angeles, Atlanta. He had pilot friends in almost every state. When I was young, he would fly from one end of the country to the other. As I got older, though, Daddy flew mostly between here and the West Coast. And when he was gone, it was only Aunty Selma, Mama, and me.

"Some of the best times were when it was just the three of us, outside in Mama's garden. There was every color of rose you could imagine: red, white, yellow, pink, orange. Mama even grew daisies, chrysanthemums, sunflowers. We would stroll through the garden in the afternoon, talking about how our day at school was. Sometimes Mama made teatime right in the middle of all the flowers. She set the table with a white tablecloth, and we had iced tea, milk, and cookies. I remember once carrying a white basket on my forearm. I must have been about eight. It was mid-morning and the grass was still a little damp. The sun was still low, so it was just warm enough. We all walked through, Aunty Selma and I were laughing, picking the best blooms to make a haku lei with. Later that week, they turned into a head dress for my first communion." Mom looked at me and patted the grass gently beside her. I swallowed hard and then sat.

"Mama loved roses, Landon. She had a gift for making them grow. I always told myself that I would have a garden like hers when I grew up. But that was before—" Mom stopped and looked at me. She glanced up. Clouds trickled by. She inhaled deeply, nodding her head, and then kept going. "Those damn football games always lured Mama and Daddy away from Hawai'i. Daddy would get a ticket for a Southern Cal football game, and the next thing you know, he'd fly off to California. Mama typically went with him, and most of the time when I was young, I did, too. I loved going on trips. So did Mama. I mean, back then, I thought I loved football, too. But that's only because we were getting on an airplane and going somewhere far away." She looked to the sky and closed her eyes as though enjoying the warmth of the sun.

"I loved flying. We got to sit in first class. Daddy said *that* was the only way to fly, not crammed together like all those poor schmucks who had to fly in coach. The common folk *back there*, he'd call them. We, on the other hand, got to sit in the front section of the plane, order anything we wanted, as much soda and treats as we could fit in our stomachs. And the stewardesses back then were these tall, blonde women who were always so nice and polite to us. As a kid, I remember I wanted to be a stewardess. Whenever I told Daddy, he would say I needed to hurry and finish elementary school so I could apply at the airlines. That way, I would *always* be able to fly for free." Mom laughed weakly at the memory, her eyes finally drifting back to the headstone. Her voice hardened.

"I didn't go with them on their last trip. They went to California to watch football. And it never failed, Daddy always got tickets for this one particular game on New Year's Day. I loved going because we'd go to Disneyland or Knott's Berry Farm afterwards. Sometimes Daddy would charter a plane and take all of us flying. But this New Year's Day game, even Mama loved going to it. Do you know what it was called? The Rose Bowl.

"It was like Mama was in *Heaven*. So many different kinds of roses. She was truly happy to go to that football game. While Daddy was at the visitor's center, Mama and I walked the fairgrounds and explored the expo, getting lost in the overwhelming haze of colors and fragrances. She even did some shopping, picking up new cuttings. Most of the time, they got confiscated when we got back to Hawai'i, but she did manage to slip a few plants through. In fact, I still have one of those that Mama snuck through in the flower bed at home." Mom held back a sob. This was getting harder for her to say.

"But this one time, this one trip, I didn't go with them. I *had* to stay home. It was just before you were born, Landon. In fact, I went into labor only a few hours after Aunty Selma told me what happened to Mama and Daddy. You see, Daddy had chartered a private plane a few days before the game. No one really knows for sure what happened, but the investigators said there was an engine problem, probably a stall, and then they just . . . fell out of the sky.

"It wasn't until a few days after the wreck that Aunty Selma and I found out. Once the investigators learned who owned the plane and who it was chartered to, they called the number Daddy left on the rental contract. That was January third. Your birthday. I couldn't even fly up. Aunty Selma went while I was in the hospital having you. She brought what was left of Mama and Daddy back home in a small, wooden box." Mom squinted, drifting back through time.

"I was so mad at them, Landon. I was pregnant with you, yet they left me. Right when I needed them most. But worse, they left me with nothing. I was being kicked out of the only home I had ever known. Forced out because I got pregnant. Because I was a disgrace. That's how my Mama left it with me." Mom's eyes were still closed, but tears bled mascara down her face. "Mama was angry. She had Daddy put everything, the entire will, in Aunty Selma's name, making my sister responsible for the bank accounts, the cars, the house. Everything. And to top it off, she left without leaving me a damn clue about *this*. How was I supposed to raise a family? I was pregnant, alone, scared. I needed them. I needed *her* to show me how to be a mommy." She looked at the grave once more. A sharp inhale, and her voice got hard again.

"But since they cut me off, I decided to cut *them* off. I refused to bring you here. For what they did to me, they didn't deserve to be a part of your life either. But not only that, I kept Luke from them too. I kept you both from your grandparents. But mostly . . . I kept you from *her*. From your grandmother. She forced me to make a life I wasn't even sure I wanted. And then she left me without saying if I was doing it right." Mom's hands shook as she wiped at her face. She was so far back and so far away she couldn't find her way home anymore.

It was the only thing I could say and it was the only time it ever came. I touched Mom's hand and called to her. "Momma." It took a moment but it brought her back.

Mom looked at me with the warmest smile I ever got from her. "There wasn't enough of your grandparents to make an open casket funeral, Landon. So Aunty Selma and I buried them here, got a nice headstone memorial and had a small funeral for them. When we laid them in, I put in a small, potted rose bush too. Look here," Mom said, as she pointed to the grass over my grandparents' grave. There were a couple of small twigs that grew up through the turf. She touched them lightly. "I noticed these last year. These are rose bushes trying to grow up through the ground. From the same pot I placed on top of Mama and Daddy's casket. The groundskeeper must mow right over them every week. That's why I didn't see them before.

"But when I finally saw these growing, I knew Mama and Daddy were still alive. They were reaching out to me in those roses at home, in every single rose I touched since they died, and I didn't even notice. They tried to talk to me, but I wasn't listening. So when I saw this one, it hit me like a lightning bolt. Mama and Daddy were still watching over me. I figured things couldn't be much worse so I brought you and Luke as soon as I could. Like a peace offering.

"If I let them in, maybe they'd help me. Maybe they'd send some advice my way." Mom's words trailed off as she glanced toward the sky. It was completely overcast now. She looked back at me. "But the worst, I mean the absolute worst part, is that I didn't get to say good-bye. All I had left was my mother telling me to get out, that I was a disgrace, and that they didn't want me anymore because I was dirty." She held her stare in mine and I could see it, a shadow deep, down in her eyes. It was a regret that had eaten away at her for years. I read it in Grandma's letter to Mom. Like a ghost, it settled once again over her: *WHORE*.

"What am I trying to say, Landon? Since I don't have my parents in front of me, since I can't . . . touch them anymore, I have to say good-bye a little each time I come here. And it's taking a long, long time." She breathed deep. "People come into your life and people go. We don't know why. Some people are special, and they leave colorful marks on you. Like imprints on your soul that never fade. Once they touch you, you're never the same. You have to forgive them for that, for making you love them that much." She paused and tried to smile, a tear puddling between lips. "But *when* you do that is up to you."

For the first time, I realized Mom wasn't so blind after all. In fact, her words showed me what I had to do. In the chapel, the service was just about over by the time Mom and I walked back in. After the final prayers, I asked Mrs. Ka'ea if I could see Toby one last time. And as the lid was opened, I felt the rush in my body once again: hot, chilled, numb, and sweating.

I forced myself to look at Toby's face. A small part of me still didn't want to believe he was gone. From my pocket, I pulled out the blue glass disc I found in the ocean. I placed it on Toby's chest, resting my palm on Toby's cold, solid body. Toby was so stiff he felt like a sheet of thick, icy metal, incapable of anything but sinking. The cold rose up through my fingers.

Standing there, I realized there was only one thing left to do. I had to touch his face. I had to touch Toby's skin to be able to do it. I knew I would never be ready, but as I reached out, I could feel the welling inside. But I had to touch him to believe. And as I did, I felt skin so cold, I almost choked on the rising inside. I leaned in and whispered, knowing I wouldn't be able to in a moment. "Now you can be two places at once, Toby. And now you can fly safe too. Just hold da glass up to your eye, and you going be underwater or way up in da sky. Just hold 'em there, and you going be in Heaven. I promise."

With that, everything came free. I knew it beyond a shadow of a doubt: Toby was in there. For the first time, I truly believed it. My legs gave into the numbness bolting upward. My knees buckled, and there was nothing left to hold me up. And then I was falling. There was a commotion of voices behind me as hands tried to hold me up. But I had finally let everything go, good-bye pounding in hot, continuous streaks down my face, 'cause I knew for sure. Dead meant dead. Gone, left, never coming back. Like Toby.

23

There was so much space now. Except for chores and church, I didn't have to get out of bed until school started. The whole summer, I just lay in the same place, staring at white ceiling panels that stretched from one side of the room to the other. I thought about Mom and Dad, about how I believed they would be divorced by now, about how I thought Luke and I would already be adopted, living somewhere far away. I thought about the G.T. test I promised Mrs. Kato I would take. I thought about how small everything felt in me and Luke's room, and yet from way down here on my bed, how much space there was above me. I noticed a baby roach scurrying across the ceiling, brittle legs that scuttled with purpose like fingers on a typewriter. Luke walked in, saw me spacing out, and then tiptoed back toward the living room. It had been a while since I gave a damn about what was going on in his head. I watched the roach as it crossed the room and then turned around. Back and forth, it traveled the length of the panel, going around in circles. Funny, even if it wasn't getting anywhere, it didn't slow down one bit.

Way in the back of Our Lady of Perpetual Help, I saw Mrs. Ka'ea. It was the first time since Toby's funeral that she came to church. She sat in the back of the parish, saying the prayers, wiping her eyes with a handkerchief. Mom smacked my arm, telling me to turn around and stop staring, to quit fidgeting and act my age. As Father Thomas explored the scriptures, explaining how Jesus would love us no matter where we went in this world, I glanced back at Mrs. Ka'ea. She looked up at the rafters for a moment and sighed. Father Thomas kept on about how Jesus's arms were spread wide, protecting us. I wondered what Mrs. Ka'ea was thinking.

After church, Mrs. Ka'ea came over to our pew. Mom asked how she was getting along. Mrs. Ka'ea couldn't look back, shrugging as she lied. It was hard, but she said she was okay, as well as could be, all things considered. "I'm glad I came today, though. I guess I forgot the answers will only come in God's own time. I've got to stop trying to figure this out or I'm going to go crazy. So I thought I'd come to church. Baby steps, right?" She turned and looked at me. "But I'm more concerned about Landon." Mrs. Ka'ea smiled. "I haven't seen you in . . . what, a couple of months, Landon? How are you doing?" She reached down and gave me a hug.

Even though it felt good, I saw Mom watching sharply. "I okay, Mrs. Ka'ea."

She patted me on the head. "You know my door is always open, Landon. Whenever your mom says it's okay for you to come over, it's all right with me." I saw Mom smile thinly. I didn't know exactly what Mom was thinking, but something was there. Mrs. Ka'ea turned to Mom. "Minerva, would it be all right if Landon came over for an early dinner sometime this week? There are a couple of things I'm sure Toby would want him to have."

Mom answered Mrs. Ka'ea while looking at me. "*Of course,* Celeste. Is tomorrow at five o'clock all right?" Her voice was so fake. Why was she acting like that?

Mrs. Ka'ea ruffled my hair again. "Great. See you then, Landon." She shuffled out the door behind other parishioners.

On the way home, Mom finally said what was on her mind. "That's the last time you're going over there, Landon. After dinner, that's it." The car bumped over potholes.

Something stirred within, and I didn't want it creeping any higher. "Why? What did—"

Mom cut me off. "Don't you take that whining tone with me, Landon. And don't you ask me if you can go over anymore either. It's so obvious. I'll bet she wants you to come over every other day now." I didn't say it, but what was so wrong with that? "Did you see how many times she touched you? It's quite pathetic, actually. She loses her son, and now she wants to hold onto mine? No way. She needs to deal with this on her own."

My breathing became shallow. How to describe what I felt rising inside? I couldn't believe Mom just said that. I thought back to the graveyard, to Grandma and Grandpa, to Mom and me talking on an overcast day. All of that was now gone. I glared at Mom in the driver's seat. We were in the same car, but she might as well have been on the other side of the universe.

All of the space was back. The car rattled again, plowing over another pothole as Mom focused silently ahead. I followed the path of her eyes to the windshield. Beyond the glass, the sky was a blue expansive map over 'Ewa Beach. So clean, so vast, and so high above this place. I side-eyed Mom as we turned onto Pupu Street. A smile crept across my lips. Mom shouldn't worry. I wouldn't dream of asking if I could go over.

When school started, I was not ready. Not ready for how noisy 'Ilima Intermediate School was, the flood of laughter and yelling that started the moment recess did. Not ready for the back and forth between six classes, shuffling through dusty hallways and wincing at the tardy bell when it screamed to hurry up and get to class. Not ready for eighth grade boys that gave all the seventh graders stink eye, sizing us up, boys with eyes I made sure I didn't look into, knowing before anyone ever told me I shouldn't, knowing that was just the way things were.

I was not ready for how different intermediate school was. Almost all the girls were bigger than me and had somehow grown big chests. I couldn't believe when I saw Vicky Lau, the same girl from Mrs. Kato's class last year. She was half-Chinese and half-Hawaiian, and last year, she was still short. But now, she was taller than me and had almost the same size boobs as Mom. She kind of slouched and didn't say much anymore. After a couple of weeks of school, I tried to say hi, but she just waved and ran off to her next class. I watched as she scuttled toward the other side of campus, shrinking with each step she took. But somehow I still felt small.

Social Studies was one of the few classes I liked. Every day, our teacher Mrs. Palacios stood in front of a map of the world. Mrs. Palacios told us to clear our desks 'cause she wanted to see how well we memorized our homework. She said we needed to study geography first, *before* we got into history, so we could fully understand the world we lived in. Mrs. Palacios thought that before we learned about the truths and changes we were a part of, we should first understand the landscape we all lived and died in. When she said that, I cringed.

The world map Mrs. Palacios showed us today didn't have any borders. The picture looked three-dimensional. There were weird, squiggly circles around the mountains with numbers in the middle of the lines. Mrs. Palacios said the lines showed how high the mountains were. So, the smaller the circle, the higher up we were.

"What do you find at the top of a mountain?" she asked, pointing to one, waiting for someone to answer. I knew the vocab word was called *vista,* but even though I liked the class, I didn't say anything. No one did. We all floated along in silence, somehow aware that in intermediate school, we shouldn't volunteer the answer. We just needed to keep our heads up and stay above the teasing wash of voices that would come if we opened our mouths. At the same time, we all knew that when the teacher called on us, we needed to have some kind of response. I looked around. It was quiet; everyone was just trying to survive.

But if Mrs. Palacios asked me, I knew what I'd say:

A vista was a high place, good for looking down on everyone.

Just being in Toby's house soothed me. From the moment I walked through the door, I felt the day slip off me: school, homework, Mom and Dad. Everything washed away, like I was high up on one of Mrs. Palacios's vistas, looking down as my anxiety evened out into calm ripples all around me. I quietly set the front door in place and realized it wasn't locked anymore.

As I sniffed the free smells coming from the kitchen, I almost expected Toby to come bounding down the hallway. It felt like he was still here. I could see the kitchen table from the hallway, and on it, propped upright in a frame, was Toby's eight-by-ten school photo. Taped to the picture window above were old crayon drawings I assumed were from when he was a kid. I gingerly stepped forward, feeling as though I were intruding. As I got closer, I realized Mrs. Ka'ea had set out a plate of chocolate chip cookies and two glasses of milk. For me? But why two glasses? There was also a mess of ripped-open envelopes and cards on the table, and a box of new ones that said *Thank You For Your Sympathy* on the covers. I stepped from the hallway and was about to greet Mrs. Ka'ea, but something told me not to. Mrs. Ka'ea stood at the sink on her Bible-footstool and just stared sadly outside. I had never seen her like that in the kitchen. She was usually a whirlwind of activity, commanding everything to life. I watched her turned back a moment longer and felt I knew exactly what she was thinking about. When her head hung and her whole body trembled as though cold, I hurried back to the front door. I waited a moment before I opened it again and then slammed it loud enough for Mrs. Ka'ea to hear. Then I called out to her. She said to come on in.

By the time I sat down at the table, Mrs. Ka'ea was sailing from one end of the kitchen to the other, from sink to stove, cleaning, stirring, and cooking, all on cruise control. When she had a free moment, she sat down as well. I knew better than to ask her how she was feeling. So instead, I pointed to the two glasses of milk on the table and asked who the other one was for. She smiled, gave me a wink, and then quickly wiped at her cheek as though it were itchy. "For me. Think I'm going to let you enjoy all these cookies by yourself?" She glanced down at the cards. An open one began by expressing sorrow for Toby's death, addressing Mrs. Ka'ea familiarly as Celeste. Mrs. Ka'ea quickly piled the cards into a neat stack, sliding them to one side of the table and covering them with an envelope. Then it fell awkwardly silent.

Crap. I hadn't meant to intrude. So, since I had wanted to ask for a while, I figured, why not now? "Your name mean anything, Mrs. Ka'ea?"

Mrs. Ka'ea shook her head as she swallowed down a bite of cookie. "You do keep me on my toes, Landon. *Which* name?"

My brow furrowed. "Dey both mean somethin'?"

Mrs. Ka'ea nodded. "My first name is Celeste. Like *celestial*, or heavenly body. My mother told me when I was a little girl I was her gift from God, sent straight from Heaven. She figured, what better name than Celeste?" My mind drifted along with her words: dark sky, full of stars, a bright moon searching after a sun long gone. "And my last name is from my husband. Funny you should ask, Landon. I always thought it was fate I had married my ex-husband, because of his name. His mother told me Ka'ea means 'The air' or 'The rising.' I like that. I have two names that deal with the sky. I guess you could say I'm pretty airy." She laughed, looking at her arms. "Or you could say I'm pretty *hairy*. Either way. I guess I should thank my Okinawan mother for these furry arms, huh?" She smiled as the ringer on her stove went off.

After dinner, Mrs. Ka'ea had me sit in the living room 'cause there were a couple of things she wanted me to have. The first was Jason Jones's ankle weights. Mrs. Ka'ea explained that Jason happened to catch her at home right before he left for Mississippi. He had wanted me and Toby to split his ankle weights, to each have one strap, so we'd always remember him. Mrs. Ka'ea put the ankle weights next to me and pulled out a folded piece of paper from her pocket. "And when Jason realized that you'd be alone, he wrote you this letter." She gave me the paper. It felt as heavy as a boulder.

"Read it later, Landon. It's for you only." I couldn't read it right now if I wanted to. This was happening way too fast. Thoughts came one after the other, in circles, like the waves rolling and crashing outside.

From the hallway, Mrs. Ka'ea then dragged out Toby's surfboard. When I saw it, something deep in my stomach lurched, a cold that scrambled up my body. An image of Toby shot through me: wind, water, him and me, sliding through a spray of liquid sunshine. Mrs. Ka'ea set the board down, and when she spoke, her voice broke. "I know Toby would want you to have this. You were the best friend he could've possibly had, Landon. Thank you, for your kindness to my son." The cold was still racing upward. What was I supposed to do with the surfboard? I didn't know what to say. Toby had straddled the board. I could still see him rising and falling. I didn't want to say yes, and at the same time, I couldn't say no. Mom didn't know I had even tried surfing. If I took it home, I'd never be able to use it. And then there was what Mom said in the car after church. She'd have me throw the board away, and I would *never* do that. I had to think fast. What could I say?

And then, the answer hit me. "Tank you, Mrs. Ka'ea, but I can keep da board and da ankle weights ova here? More easy if I use 'em from here instead of dragging 'em from my house." I was never going to tell Mom I came here anyway. Mrs. Ka'ea nodded and said the surfboard would be outside so I could use it whenever I wanted. As Mrs. Ka'ea hoisted it, the shiny surface glinted from the ceiling light, flashing like a lightning bolt. I forgot how long the board was. At times, I thought it made Toby look so small in the water.

I was glad I didn't have to take the board. Really glad. The truth was I never wanted to use the board again. I watched as Mrs. Ka'ea dragged Toby's surfboard out the sliding door in the family room. It was a large, heavy burden still connected to her, a white shadow of guilt still hanging over me. I should've called and told her what Toby had said. He might still be here.

With all the windows shut, everything was black in our classroom. Mrs. Ellory said since we had the basics down for lab work in physical science, we could go ahead and start the next unit. She flipped on a projector, and a hot, white block of light appeared. She clicked a button twice, and then we all saw it: outer space. And stars.

Mrs. Ellory began her lecture by talking about space, about the reasons to study science. Groans came from different parts of the room, but honestly I didn't mind. Mrs. Ellory talked about the value of science, why it was so important and what it could do for us. I tried to listen, but I was already weightless, lost among the pictures flitting across the screen. The sun, the moon, the Milky Way, a dance of a thousand stars, all somehow revolving around each other. Mrs. Ellory's voice and her images came so fast, one after the other, that sound and thought began to blend. Somewhere between blasting off in a space rocket and silently slipping away from Earth on the Voyager probe, I heard Mrs. Ellory clearly, as she stopped on one slide in particular. "With so much space out there, we have to reach out no matter what the cost. As human beings, we *have* to explore. It's in our nature. The Voyager probe here," she said, pointing at the screen, "is on a journey out of our solar system. It's going to be a long, cold, lonely trip. But that's no different than what we're on. We're stuck here on Earth, completely alone, going around and around. But imagine if we made contact with just one other species. We'd find out we weren't alone in the universe. But even better, we'd know that *we* did it. We'd thank no one but ourselves, proving we can do anything we put our minds to. Making our wildest dreams come true. That, my friends, is why we study science."

As Mrs. Ellory opened the windows, sunlight flooded the room. I could barely see the transparent outline of the projected image anymore, like a ghost of the Voyager probe. I squinted to see the stars beyond but could only hear the fan from the projector spinning.

Over and over, it was the same thing recently: Mom stood over Dad, her face red, trying to get him to talk. Begging him, really. Dad slouched deeper into the recliner, still gripping his Jack Daniel's, eyes glossed over. No way he was going to talk.

From the living room, Mom seemed huge as she loomed over Dad. Or maybe Dad had sunk so far into his chair he looked small. Either way, Mom didn't see it, but I knew Dad did. There was too much distance between them.

Mrs. Ellory said the oldest surviving species on Earth was a cockroach. In some ways, they were just like humans. They ate, slept, ran, mated, and pooped. Cockroaches could even carry diseases, just like humans. But cockroaches could do one thing human beings couldn't. Mrs. Ellory said this one thing had helped cockroaches survive for millions of years. Cockroaches could fly. And what she said made sense.

Way up in the sky, above everyone and everything. So much space, but safe and finally free. It was something I had known for a long time. I just hadn't been able to do it yet.

Mrs. Ka'ea wasn't home when I went over. In the back, I sat on the moss rock wall overlooking the ocean. The waves pounded the rocky shore a few feet away, spraying high into the air. I looked out over the swelling blue, the rising and falling. It all reminded me of Toby. I took in how vast the ocean was. From Diamond Head in the distance on my left, to the edge of a lonely, blue world on my right. I imagined Toby paddling out. Eddies of wind whipped off the water, spiraling around me for a moment, then slipping past. I saw Toby thrashing his arms, showing me how to catch a wave. I stared into the water as crests continued to glide, one after the other, white, glossy tips that rode to a peak. I remembered Toby standing, then dropping in from that shimmering vista. Nothing bothered him. He could let it all go and just . . . surf.

I shook my head. I was never able to do that. Even now, I *still* felt like the chicken of the sea. I cycled through thoughts, lost in a whitewash of my own anxiety:

The envelope I held right now. It was from the G.T. test I took today. I wasn't sure if I made it into the program or not. The lady said to give the envelope to my parents. Yeah, right.

Jason's letter, the one I carried everywhere, stuffed in my pocket. I still hadn't read it yet. Mrs. Ka'ea said it was private, that I should read it when I was alone. It felt good right where it was. I wasn't sure I wanted to read it at all.

The ankle weights and Toby's surfboard, over there against the house. Two reminders from friends long gone, friends on different journeys than I was, friends that left me with so much and yet so little.

The waves crashed in a pattern I understood, as though the same words were whispered again and again. I imagined it all in Toby's voice, a murmur spoken directly to me. *Come to me, Landon.* Another wave crunched against rock, and the mist spread high, settling in a gentle whisper that called me by name once again. *Come to me, Landon.*

"Landon?"

The voice almost made me shit my pants. I turned around to see Mrs. Ka'ea walking toward me. She gave me a hug, asking why I was staring off into space.

"Just tinking. Sorry I neva call before I come, I just—"

"Don't apologize, Landon. You can come whenever you want. You know my door is always open for you." Mrs. Ka'ea looked out at the ocean and inhaled a deep pouch of thick and salty air. Still looking out over the water, she spoke quietly. "You still see him too, huh?" I said I did. "I come out here myself, Landon. I guess it shouldn't surprise me that you're here too. You did spend a lot of time with Toby, especially out there on the water. Sometimes I still imagine him coming in on the next wave." Mrs. Ka'ea chuckled sadly, still gazing toward the ocean. She glanced down at me and indicated the envelope on my lap. "What's that, Landon?"

I sighed, tucking the envelope under my leg. "I took da G.T. test today. Dis da results."

She smiled. "That doesn't surprise me, I always knew you were smart. Did you open it?" I shook my head no. "Don't you want to know the results?" I shrugged my shoulders 'cause honestly, I wasn't sure. I was having a hard enough time as it was. I didn't know if I wanted to add anything to it. "How about if I read it and tell you what it says instead of you having to do it? Would that be easier?" I didn't want to say yes . . . or no. Instead, I just handed her the envelope, feeling the best way was to stay quiet. Maybe I was still just trying to survive.

Mrs. Ka'ea opened the envelope and examined the letter. I watched her face for any indication, and that was when it hit me. I really did want to know if I made it. I was just too scared to do it alone. Mrs. Ka'ea suddenly folded the letter and slid it back into the envelope. She didn't say anything for what seemed like forever. Then she shook her head. At first, I thought it was a bad thing, but then she smiled and rustled my hair. "You made it big time, Landon. Not only did you qualify for the program, but your IQ tested at one hundred thirty-eight. Ninety-eighth percentile. They'll be modifying your schedule so you'll have all G.T. sections. It also says you'll keep a couple of the same teachers. Palacios and Ellory, I think."

I fumbled for the letter, wanting to read it for myself. "What does IQ mean?" I asked, scanning the paper.

"It means you're *smart*, Landon. One hundred thirty-eight is a really high score. It means you can do anything you set your mind to. Remember when I told you if you reach for the stars, your dreams can come true? Well, this means that you, Landon, need to dream *big*." I smiled for a moment and then looked out toward the ocean. I couldn't look Mrs. Ka'ea in the eye. I felt something coming, something that had been chasing me, making me feel small and hunted. She squinted at me. "Landon, you are going to accept this offer into the G.T. program, aren't you?" I shrugged my shoulders again. "What do you mean you don't know?" I couldn't look at Mrs. Ka'ea. The last thing I wanted to do was disappoint her, but I could hear it in her voice. If she only knew how badly I had already let her down.

I didn't expect it, but Mrs. Ka'ea sat next to me on the moss rock wall and draped her arm across my shoulders. As she touched me, my eyes swelled with what had been wanting to come. And then, like a torrent, it came. "I dunno if I should start da G.T. class. My modda and fadda always beef. My brudda always doing stupid stuff. Jason gone, and now my best friend too—" I stopped, meeting Mrs. Ka'ea's gaze. The guilt was too much. My bottom lip pulled tight. I had to tell her about Toby. I just had to. "I not who you tink. I no deserve good stuff."

Mrs. Ka'ea wiped my face. "Landon, don't say that. You're such a good kid—"

"But it's my fault!" I said, as my face twisted under what I had yet to speak aloud.

Mrs. Ka'ea shifted and rubbed my back. "What is, Landon? Go ahead. Let it out."

I struggled for air. I thought back to Memorial Day weekend. I heard Toby say it all over again: No worry, *Dad*. What else could he have meant? And then it all came out in a rush of words. "I sorry, Mrs. Ka'ea. It's my fault Toby wen' die."

Mrs. Ka'ea slowly removed her arm from my shoulder and leaned slightly away. "What do you mean?"

I tried to control my breathing. "Da last time I seen Toby, he said he was going down Mokulē'ia side wit' his cousin fo' set up camp early." I looked up at Mrs. Ka'ea eagerly. "I tried fo' remind him what you said. Fo' him only ride inside. But he . . . " I dropped my head in shame.

Mrs. Ka'ea lifted my head so that I looked at her. "Landon," she said sternly, "this is *very* important. What did Toby say?"

My lip pulled long again. I breathed deeply, trying to calm down. "He said: No worry, *Dad*. Dat he going be safe. But da way he said 'em, I got one funny feeling. I thought maybe he going down wit' Chaz guys, and dat you neva know."

Mrs. Ka'ea smiled weakly. "Landon, you—"

I felt the panic surge. "I not who you tink! I coulda said somethin' but I neva. If I said somethin', you coulda stop him. I neva like rat him out. But I neva like hurt you either."

Mrs. Ka'ea gestured for me to slow down. "Landon?"

I was sobbing now. "I sorry, Mrs. Ka'ea. I so sorry."

Mrs. Ka'ea lifted my chin so that I looked at her once again. Then she placed her hand over my lips so I'd stop talking. "Landon, shhh. This isn't your fault." I tried to protest, but she patted my lips with her hand again. "Shhh. Listen. I knew Toby rode down with Chaz that weekend." My face wrinkled under the confusion. She . . . *knew*? "Toby asked, and I gave him permission. We had a long talk about it. He knew he wasn't supposed to ride in the back of the truck. He just chose poorly when he was with his cousin."

I shook my head. "But da way he said 'em, he meant—"

Mrs. Ka'ea cut me off this time. "Did he say he was going to ride in the *back* of the truck?" I thought about it. I shook my head. "He told you not to worry, Landon, that he would be safe. He didn't mean he was going to damn well do whatever he wanted to anyway. He said what he did because he had already gotten the third degree from me. He knew what I expected, and he didn't need to hear it from you, his friend."

I searched her face for disappointment and couldn't believe there wasn't any. "But, Mrs. Ka'ea, if I told you I thought Toby might, you neva woulda let him go."

Mrs. Ka'ea draped her arm around my shoulder again. "So sure, are you?" she said warmly. "Landon, if you had told me your fear, I would have spoken with Toby again and he would've promised he wouldn't. What it came down to was that I had to trust Toby to make the right decision."

I heard what Mrs. Ka'ea meant, and it surprised me. "You still woulda let him go?"

Mrs. Ka'ea nodded solemnly. "As a parent, I would've had to." Then Mrs. Ka'ea spoke in a soothing voice, a voice I had always wished to hear from Mom. "Was this the reason you haven't gone surfing yet? Because you felt guilty? Landon?" Mrs. Ka'ea got blurry as my eyes pumped out against what I still felt responsible for. She stroked my hair. "I could tell you hadn't gone yet. The board is clean and exactly where I left it. Landon, the absolute worst thing we can do is hold on too tight to Toby. We'll just get stuck in a rut and not move forward. God knows some things remind us of him so much it feels like he's still here. Probably everything, huh? But even if those hurt the most, you have to embrace them. For example, like surfing—"

I cut Mrs. Ka'ea off as something even deeper than guilt found its way out of my mouth. The panic was back. "Why? I no like surf. Why I gotta surf?" After I asked it, I wasn't sure I wanted to hear the answer. It was a truth so painful there was no vista high enough to escape it.

"You have to let go," Mrs. Ka'ea said simply.

There it was: let go. I had to say good-bye. I had to be alone, be small, be afraid. I had to go on a long, cold, lonely trip with so much space I couldn't possibly do it by myself.

"Landon, I'm not saying you should forget. Not at all. Definitely remember. But you need to push forward because that's what Toby would have wanted." I looked up at Mrs. Ka'ea. "Do you think Toby wants you to get so depressed you can't do anything? Toby would *want* you to go surfing. And you need to."

I was crying again. "Why?"

Mrs. Ka'ea wiped my face again. "You two connected on the water with a surfboard, Landon. Toby reached you with surfing. And now, in the same way, you need to reach him." Mrs. Ka'ea leaned forward, trying to make eye contact. "It's okay to go surfing again, Landon. Just as it's okay to say good-bye. It doesn't mean you love him any less. But you need to let go, so both of you can get some rest." Mrs. Ka'ea rubbed my back again as I heaved and struggled to breathe. When she spoke, her voice broke a little. "Toby wouldn't want you suffering, Landon. He'd want you to remember, but he'd also want you to move on." As Mrs. Ka'ea removed her arm from my shoulder, things began to make sense. Mrs. Ka'ea turned toward the house. I wondered how she did it, how she found the strength. No matter how far I went, she always knew how to pull me back.

Mrs. Ka'ea shuffled to the surfboard, picked it up, and carried it over. She set it on the wall next to me. Mrs. Ka'ea stood behind me and bent over, her arm reaching past my face, pointing at the ocean. She sniffled and then whispered in my ear. "There's a big ocean out there, Landon. Lots of space for just you and my Toby. Take your time. Go say good-bye. For you and for my son." By the time she finished speaking, I found I had already turned and snuggled close to Mrs. Ka'ea, finally letting go but also holding on.

To feel is to know, and feeling this, I knew Mrs. Ka'ea was right.

With every stroke in the water, she was right. With every dive beneath and with every wave I carved on Toby's surfboard, she was right. There was nothing but space. Space to feel, and space to remember. And I did remember. Like never before, I did, ripping through water, pumping across wave faces, across thoughts, across memories. Listening to the splash of voices and the crush of laughter, I glided over wave after wave, feeling Toby with each stinging needle of water that clung to me. And then, between tireless waves and balancing on them, it happened. Between facing what I didn't want to and plowing over it, I finally realized I was alone. Between riding in and always paddling back out, I actually felt that I'd be okay.

Straddling Toby's surfboard, the ocean rising and falling beneath me, I knew I was no longer shackled to Toby. He was a part of me, always would be. Toby was connected to surfing, the closest yet I'd come to flying. I looked at the endless horizon. The shimmering pathway made by the setting sun. From my pocket, I removed Jason's letter, knowing I finally wanted to read it. I was going to leave it on the shore, but Mrs. Ka'ea got me a Ziploc to put it in. She said I needed to take it with me. I rolled over and lay back on the surfboard, legs dangling into the ocean. I smoothed the Ziploc to see better, wiping at beads of water. I could make out thick, dark, pencil marks.

Dear Landon,

I'm sorry to hear about Toby. I know you're going to be really sad when you find out. You can call me in Mississippi. I'll write the number on the bottom of the letter. My mom said it's okay to call collect. Sorry about Toby again, Landon. And thank you. For everything.

Friends Always,
Jason

I laid Jason's letter on my chest, letting the plastic suck against my skin, and then I inhaled deeply. I stared into the blue sky above, into the blue that reminded, into the blue I named Ka'ea. The ocean swelled up and down through a board that shimmered. I glanced once again at the letter, at how Jason signed it. He was right. We would always be friends, the three of us.

And even if there was so much space and I was still alone, I no longer felt small. No more going in circles for me, unless it was on Toby's surfboard here in the water, paddling out and streaking back in. I looked toward the shore at Toby's house, back through glistening sprays that reached high into the air. Even though it was close to evening, Mrs. Ka'ea still sat there, watching from the wall. Seeing me look back, she waved. Mrs. Ka'ea said I had to let go. I waved back, knowing *now* just what to hold on to.

24

Even though every problem had a solution, things didn't always come out the way I wanted them to. In Mr. Lee's G.T. math class, we were doing functions. We had to take a few numbers, plug them into some crazy formula, and once we understood the answer, we could then solve the equation. Mr. Lee said our job was to figure out how the function worked, to really know what made it tick. He reminded us that numbers always added up. There was no magic involved in the process, no fairy tales. No . . . happily ever after. If the numbers didn't come out, we had to go back and check our work 'cause the problem wasn't flawed, we were. He said to follow these helpful hints:

1) Check our variables. Mr. Lee said variables changed and were usually different values for different functions. And to also remember that variables were only *substitutes* for numbers, substitutes for the real thing. If we gave the wrong values to our variables, then no matter what we did, nothing would go our way.

2) Check our computation. Mr. Lee said to remember the key to any solution was precision. We couldn't expect to solve anything if we hadn't gone through the proper steps. Nothing would ever make sense if we went about it wrong.

3) And, last but not least, check ourselves. Mr. Lee stressed that everyone made mistakes. Everyone. Maybe we copied down the function incorrectly from the text. We couldn't let ourselves get lost in translation, in how we moved from one medium to another. That was unacceptable in a G.T. class. We needed to stay focused or we shouldn't be here.

At school, I spent hours in class hurting myself with an opened math book on my desk, trying to make sense of functions. Like a machine, I plugged in numbers. Adding, subtracting, scribbling, and ultimately, erasing. And every time, when I checked the back of the book if I had the correct solution, I was wrong. I leaned hard into the chair, staring at my paper. I was frustrated with the pencil marks, how greasy-black they looked, how they burned through pink eraser streaks. It didn't make sense. What was I not doing right? I knew things didn't always come out the way I wanted them to, but this should add up. Maybe Mr. Lee was right. Maybe I was flawed. I shouldn't be here.

I should've been watching Luke more the last couple of months. In the time between Toby's death and finally dealing with it, I realized Luke had gone from mental to mad. While sitting at our bedroom desk doing my science homework, I noticed Luke making his *Star Wars* action figures fight. Not just the I'm-gonna-get-you-now kind of fighting between Darth Vader and Luke Skywalker like he'd done before. Luke's eyebrows hung low and his forehead creased angrily. He took turns with all of them, including Han Solo and Princess Leia, punching, kicking, and swearing in spit-flying cuss words students at 'Ilima Intermediate would be proud of. Eventually, Luke got tired, so he loaded all four figures, two in one hand and two in the other, and smashed them together between his palms. When two of them fell into the Lego house, the figures landed, motionless. What made me afraid was Luke had the other figures stand over them while crying, saying how sorry they were, that they *had* to. They had no choice. But if that wasn't bad enough, one of the figures said, "Problem solved." What problem? Where was he getting this from? He had done mental things before, but he never rammed things together, making them . . . die. Today's recently deceased: Darth Vader and Princess Leia.

Honestly, this was something totally new from him, and it scared the shit out of me. I cursed myself for not keeping a better watch over Luke. His face remained hard and twisted as he manipulated the action figures' arms and legs. He set each one back into the house, his jaw flexing. I had been so preoccupied the last few months it was like seeing him for the first time. Like *he* was the one who had just come back, changed from some crazy adventure.

I realized that I had no answers and that I had to start over. I needed to understand how he operated now. I just hoped I wasn't too late.

Too late, just like in *Romeo and Juliet.* We just finished the play in Mrs. Sakuoka's G.T. English class, and Dad was right. The ending sucked. The kids had to hide everything 'cause their families couldn't get along. What was worse was they didn't get to be together anyway. I remembered how Dad said he always hoped the ending would come out differently, but it never did. No matter what, all Romeo could do was squirm from the poison just as Juliet woke up. All she could do was watch as her love died right before her eyes.

But something didn't make sense.

Why would two people, from two totally opposite families, want to be together if they knew it was a problem? The solution seemed pretty clear to me. When I asked Mrs. Sakuoka, she said that was a good question, but to consider Friar Laurence. "Why did he agree to help Romeo and Juliet get married in the first place?" The class was silent for a moment. Then Amy Sasaki raised her hand, mere moments before a bunch of others did. Mrs. Sakuoka was about to call on Amy when an office monitor appeared. She asked Amy to hold that thought. And as we waited, I couldn't help but feel glad I was in the G.T. program, even if I didn't think I *truly* belonged. But what was so good about G.T. classes was they operated the way school should. The teacher asked a question, and students responded. That was how it worked. None of this pretending we were dumb, acting as though nothing computed, like students in the regular classes. Mrs. Sakuoka apologized to Amy and asked again why Friar Laurence would help Romeo and Juliet get married in the first place.

Amy's hands were folded confidently on her desk. "Because of love," Amy said.

Mrs. Sakuoka tapped her chin thoughtfully. "You're right, Amy. But there's something more. What did Friar Laurence hope to change?" This time, nothing. No hands went up, but as I looked around, eyes focused in books as fingers dazzled pages back and forth. It sounded like wings flapping. And as I flipped pages too, thoughts fluttered loose inside me. I raised my hand slowly, realizing it was just like Mom and Dad. Mom went against her parents while Dad went against what he thought of haoles. Mrs. Sakuoka raised her eyebrows in surprise. "Landon?"

"Friar Laurence wanted fo' help change da hate. Try bring 'em together." The class moaned quietly, knowing it was true and frustrated that I got it first.

"Right you are, Landon. Friar Laurence hoped to change hate to love by marrying the lovebirds. He hoped to unite the families and bridge their differences, like helping them to move past the confusion of a feud, for example." Mrs. Sakuoka tilted her head, smiled artfully, and pointed at me. "Whether or not he made a wise decision is another question entirely. And that's the subject of your upcoming assignment." Mrs. Sakuoka chuckled. "Um, thank you, Landon, you can sit now." I looked around. Everyone was seated. The class chuckled as well. Why was I standing? I must've stood when I gave my answer. I slid back down, slumping into my chair. So shame. I imagined the faces all turning to me, pairs of eyes that multiplied, examining me, totaling, taking notes, and remembering. They were adding everything up, I knew it.

Just when I thought I had it down, I messed it all up. I should've known I would. Nothing ever came out the way I wanted it to. I should just quit. Even if I liked G.T. classes, I should just go back to the regular ones. Easy. Problem solved.

When we complained about how hard Newton's second law was, Mrs. Ellory told us to stop whining. To show us, she had Bronson Simeon come to the front of the class and asked him to push her hands as hard as he could. Bronson looked from side to side, in a panic. He didn't want to hit a teacher. So at first, he softly tapped her hands. Mrs. Ellory encouraged him, saying to really put his back into it. This time, he pushed harder. Then Mrs. Ellory raised her voice, telling him to just *push* her already. She said it over and over: push me. Push Me. PUSH ME!

Mrs. Ellory pressed forward with word after word until Bronson snapped. He lashed out at Mrs. Ellory's hands, and she stumbled back a couple of feet. Mrs. Ellory turned to the class, completely excited, as we all sat shocked, still wondering what just happened. Bronson inhaled hard. He was upset. Mrs. Ellory put the question to us. "Did you see that? When Bronson pushed me, he created an *action*. And with the force from the push, I went flying back into a *reaction*. The end result of an action is a reaction. Get it?" And the class did. Well, at least I did. I had seen a lot of Newton's second law at home. Mrs. Ellory thanked Bronson and indicated for him to take his seat. Bronson's eyebrows, however, sank with each breath, as he swallowed down whatever he was feeling. Mrs. Ellory told us to get out our notebooks.

But as I watched Bronson sulk back to his seat, something hit me. I could tell Bronson wanted to say something. He wanted to dive deeper into a problem instead of figuring how to solve it. He wanted to hit until he felt better. I had seen that look many times before. On Dad.

And with the thought of Dad came another: Mom. She always tried to talk to him, got in his way, forced him to listen to word after word, thinking that helped him to figure things out. She didn't realize she only created another problem. I glanced at Bronson and felt bad. He wouldn't have done that if Mrs. Ellory hadn't pushed him to begin with. But then, wouldn't that make Mrs. Ellory's words the *action*, and pushing her the *reaction?*

I wanted to ask but I already knew that Newton had gotten it right. No matter what the action, something was bound to happen. But Mrs. Ellory was lucky. Things didn't always come out the way we wanted them to.

I wanted to see what Luke was doing, so I started raking leaves into a pile near him. Then I plucked out snagged leaves from the aloe vera plant. I watched as he knelt on the sidewalk in the front yard. He leaned forward, on his knees like in church, looking close at a couple of praying mantises. One green body lay motionless on the concrete while the other one bobbed up and down over it, claws raised at Luke.

"What'chu did, Luke?"

The praying mantis snapped at Luke's finger as he tried to touch the dead one. "I neva did nothin'. Dis preying man-tiss wen' kill da odda one. Chop da head off. Now she no like me touch 'em. How come she wen' kill 'em, Landon?" The praying mantis lunged both claws at Luke, holding them high. It looked as if it was swelling up, making itself as big as possible.

The green legs squatted and bounced like a boxer, ready to lash out. "I dunno, Luke."

"Try look, Landon. Da ting really one preying man-tiss. She wen' kill dis buggah dead. Preying Man, dis. Get it?" He smiled at his own joke.

"You mental, ah? It's not *preying* like you hunt and kill somethin'. It's *praying*, p-r-A-y. Like you pray to God?" I watched as he thought about what I said, as words seemed to grow and multiply. I knew something was coming, a solution, a reaction, and I saw it in his eyes. I saw it just before he slammed his open palm hard over the two praying mantises. Thin, green arms and legs splayed out flat beneath the weight of his hand. A few limbs twitched slightly.

Leaning his entire weight on the insects, he made a sassy face at me. "Either way, problem solved." What the fuck? I watched as Luke lifted his hand and inspected the leftover praying mantis jelly on his palm. He winced, and his lips pulled into a frown. His eyes squinted slowly shut, a dark equation of eyelashes sealed tight, as tears squeezed their way through.

There were so many words that wanted to come, so many questions, everything frantic like thrashing through the pages of a book. "Luke, what's happening to you?"

Luke inhaled a bulk of air. Covering his face with his hands, he whispered two chilling words, hissed through clenched teeth, "Help me."

Everything stopped. That sounded so . . . familiar. But before I remembered why, the thought was gone, replaced by more important ones.

Help him? I didn't know how.

I saw math problems in front of me:

Numbers like bodies, twisting and curling on paper, dying to be solved.

Answers, like words I didn't understand. Words that came out all wrong.

Homework continued to pile. And no matter what I did, there was no end in sight.

There had been nothing from Dad for weeks. He just sat in his recliner, drinking and spacing out, letting Mom's words slap him in the face. He sank deep into vinyl, under questions he didn't want to listen to, confronted by thoughts he already *knew*, retreating behind eyes Mom had yet to figure out. At this point, Mom just wanted him to say something. She stood over Dad, pleading for a response. I guessed that anything, even if it wasn't what she wanted to hear, was better than nothing. She should just leave him alone.

Dad looked tiredly at Mom. He inhaled with bitter slowness. I could see it in Dad's eyes before it even happened, knowing this wasn't going to come out the way Mom wanted it to. Dad stood and pointed in Mom's face, his voice slurring. "You like know da problem? I tired of you ruining my fucking life." Dad tried to move past her, but Mom stepped in his path, placing her hands against his shoulders. She wanted him to say more. He grabbed her wrists and physically moved her body to the side. Mom's fingers spread out helplessly, pink palms that faded white above Dad's tightening grip. "You ain't eva going block me again. You hear me?" He flicked her out of the way and walked toward the kitchen.

Mom was crying. "What's happening to you, Leonard?" Dad turned and looked hard at Mom, years passing in the long, cold stare between them. He stood there, shrouded in thoughts and Jack Daniel's, wanting to say more, wanting to show her the answer only he knew, the only way he knew how. Instead of leaving it at that, Mom added to the problem. "How did *I* ruin your life? You're a big boy. You chose *this* just as much as I did."

I saw it before Mom did. All of the quiet and all of the thinking and all of the answers surged in Dad's frustrated breathing. From his tight, round, explosive eyes to his mouth that didn't care anymore, all of it splattered out in a frenzy of words and actions that somehow made sense to him. "You fucking bitch," Dad growled. He rushed Mom and grabbed her face with one hand, scrunching her cheeks together so that she looked like a caught fish gasping for breath. And with the other hand, he held her head in place by the neck. "You like know what I tinking? Hah? I sick and tired of all dis!" Dad sneered so wildly he looked like the devil himself. "I tink you need fo' shut your mouth and open your fucking eyes. *I* wen' choose dis? One fucking housewife dat no listen and only cook and clean wen she like? Hah? You no can have my dinna ready wen I come home, but you can stay on da phone all day wit' your sista, talking shit about me. Hah? You always ack like one stinking child, playing tit fo' tat wit' *my* money. Ev'ry week you buy plants. Who da fuck need so many roses? Hah? Only you." Mom squirmed under his clutch, but Dad only clamped tighter, letting her have it, word after word after word. "What's your *purpose* in dis house, hah? Too fucked-up in da head fo' even know what your function is." Dad leaned close and barked in Mom's face. "You no can just leave me alone, hah? I fed up already. I just like mellow liddle bit, figga some stuffs out, but you no can just shut up! Know your role, woman. And rememba, I neva choose *dis*. You did." Dad flung Mom at his recliner, and she bounced hard off the vinyl, tumbling over the armrest to the floor.

Mom screamed at Dad, and then it really started.

It was a clutter of words strewn across the family room and the living room, then from the living room to the kitchen. I watched it all as I pressed my back into the screen door, wondering when it was ever going to end. I wanted to crumple the words up and throw them away. I wanted to take a match and burn them. I wanted to close my eyes and never hear them again. But the words would still be there, wouldn't they? Like pencil lead scarred onto paper.

When I opened my eyes, Luke stood outside the front door, watching from behind the screen. He had probably been there the whole time. With a pained face, he whispered to me. "Landon, why *you* no help?" What? He didn't know I was trying to help, that I hurt myself thinking up ways to fix this. I slid down the length of the screen door and kept going, feeling the additional weight of Luke's guilt push me further into that dark place I didn't want to be.

Luke opened the screen door and stepped over me. "Why I always gotta do somethin'? How come you no can *help me*?" He ran toward Mom and Dad's room. The screen door slammed, but it was Luke's words that echoed: Help me. Help me! HELP ME!

I thought I was.

Sitting in Our Lady of Perpetual Help, I tried to figure out how to stop my head from pounding. Ever since Mom and Dad had their last beef, there had been a crisp jolt in the back of my skull, vibrating in circles to the front. It came and went all day long. If I thought about Mom and Dad, or Luke, or about all the homework I hadn't done 'cause I couldn't concentrate, it shot through my head. It felt like catching a fist to my temple. How did I make this stop?

I needed to fly, high above this place. No more Mom and Dad, no more Luke, no more school. Quiet and free.

Father Thomas began lecturing, and honestly, I was glad. His voice drifted so close I didn't have to think anymore. "We see man's folly in *Kings* today. God gives us that which separates us from the animals: free will. *Choice.* But what we often forget is that along with choice comes consequence. We're foolish enough to think we can do as we please without affecting someone else. We see that when the Israelites made poor decisions, there was a fire-and-brimstone reaction from God. The Israelites thought they solved their problems, but in fact, they only made more for themselves." Father Thomas moved behind the altar.

"In the gospel of *Matthew*, we see betrayal, sure. But that's not the point. Judas Iscariot, one of the original twelve disciples, betrays Jesus for a few pieces of silver. And once he realizes the significance of what he's done, he is so guilt-ridden that he commits *suicide*. He hangs himself. What a bad choice. Judas probably thought killing himself would be some sort of redemption. Wrong answer. Judas only made things worse for himself. He chose his will over God's. Judas basically told God there was no way God could save him. God is very clear with how He feels about suicide. We see the Bible full of explanations of how God deals with problems that arise because of the choices we make. His consequences are swift and precise. Where do you suppose Judas is right now, hmmm? Remember that with free will comes consequence. So remember the Israelites and Judas, and choose wisely. Let us pray."

As Father Thomas sat to meditate, the church was silent. Heat settled in waves, causing my thoughts to rise and pulling my eyes to the rafters. I thought about the word he just gave me. Suicide. It was an ending. One I could control, one I could see, one I could understand. And I knew how the answer worked. It would be cool and quiet. And . . . final. I would exhale as I looked up, silver coins of air slipping to a watery surface. The only difference now was I had the name for it.

The name I gave the ocean: Ka'ea. The air. The rising. It was both Toby and surfing.

I thought about how I could hold my breath underwater.

All I had to do was exhale. It could come out the way I wanted it to.

I watched swells line up, one after the other, stretching in long equations I understood.

I heard Toby's call. *Landon, come to me.* I knew where he was. It would be easy.

I knew the function, the variable, and what to plug in. Problem solved.

Mr. Lee saw me stay in after school. My legs got weak as I approached the front, hearing all of Mr. Lee's reminders echo. I knew how hard he tried to get me to understand functions and now I was about to disappoint him. But honestly, at this point, I didn't care. This was it. I had to solve *something*. Either I got rid of one problem, or I'd get rid of another. But when I told him I didn't want to be in the G.T. program anymore, he said he already knew.

"Mrs. Sakuoka and Mrs. Ellory spoke with me at lunch, Landon." I dropped my gaze, unable to look him in the eye. They had talked about me? I felt the weight of shame, as my head wilted by the neck. "Honestly, I'm surprised, Landon. I didn't think you'd quit this easily." I flinched from the sting of guilt. "I mean, after all your hard work, why quit now? You're selling yourself short by taking the easy way out, don't you think?" The longer I listened to that, the harder I became inside. I let the words prick against my body, words that finally faded as I started tuning them out. Mr. Lee waited for a long time, but I refused to say anything. "I bet right now, you want me to just shut up and let you out of the G.T. program, right? No. I'm not going to let you go, Landon." I looked up at him. "Not until you show me the problems you were working on last."

I didn't understand what he could possibly want, but I pulled out my notebook anyway. I flipped through pages to the most recent pencil slashes and eraser burns. Functions lay scattered half-dead across the page, problems partially solved. I handed him the notebook and waited. After skimming through several problems, Mr. Lee grabbed his red pen and began circling. When he spun the book around, I saw tight rings of blood, wringing the middle of each set of numbers. Looking closer, he had indicated the same step in each equation. "Look, Landon," Mr. Lee said, pointing to each halo of red, "in each function, at the same point in your solution, you're *adding* when you should be *multiplying*. Think of it this way: everything inside the parentheses is like a family. What happens to one variable happens to all of them. If you multiply the first variable, you can't just add the second one without multiplying it by the same number. Otherwise, you're cutting the function off from itself. You're killing it before it even has a chance. Apart from that, you're following all other proper rules. Here, try to multiply all the variables and *then* add." He handed me a pencil, and I started scribbling. And just like that, functions operated as they should. One by one, answers came out. One by one, problems went my way. I looked up at Mr. Lee, and he smiled. "Landon, if you add when you should multiply, you'll always be only half way there. You'll never get the answer you were looking for."

As I finished the last problem, functions finally made sense.

"Landon, it was just a mistake, a . . . bad choice, to add instead of multiply. That's easy to fix. Just make sure you don't make another one." I smiled and nodded, knowing exactly what he meant. "Good. I'll tell your other teachers the problem's solved, that you're sticking it out."

As I walked to 'Ewa Beach Elementary School, I thought about Mom, Dad, and Luke. Then I thought about Mr. Lee, how he was mostly right. I was sticking it out, even though not everything was solved. I heard Luke's words again: How come you no can *help me*?

But at least the problem was clear:

Mom and Dad. Division. It was a result I already saw. So had Dad. But not Mom.

Luke. Not just addition. Multiplication. Or else I was only half way there.

The solution: Mrs. Ka'ea. The variable. My substitute for the real thing.

'Cause without her, things wouldn't come out the way I wanted them to.

25

I wanted them to stop, but they wouldn't. Today it was about money. Mom said Dad didn't know how to save while Dad claimed Mom was the spendthrift. Back and forth they argued, never getting anywhere. In the kitchen, they wasted hours. Dad took refuge in his Jack Daniel's while Mom dragged it out. She wanted Dad to say more and swallow less, rapping the counter with her gardening gloves in rhythm as she spoke. Dad bought too much liquor. Mom bought too many plants. Dad went out too often. So did Mom. I went to our bedroom in the middle of this whirlwind of words. How could so little between them amount to so much?

It was already half way through October, and things hadn't changed a bit. But honestly, I wasn't surprised. When I had asked Mrs. Ka'ea what it took to get divorced, she said it all depended on what two people decided. There were so many factors that sometimes it was hard for people to even *realize* it would be better to go their separate ways. And then suddenly it hit me. Dad already saw it, but Mom? Before anything could change, Mom needed to simply . . . see. That was when I knew what I needed to do.

In our room, I watched Luke as he played with his Lego house and *Star Wars* figures. His accusation still weighed heavily on me. He asked how come I didn't help *him*? I lay back on my bed, both arms out at the side like an airplane. I thought again about what Mrs. Ka'ea had said and smiled. It felt good that I had finally made a choice, that I was about to do something to help. I thought about how Luke had no problem calling the police on Dad. I looked back at him, wondering how he did it. And how did he save over thirty-five dollars in lunch money to buy Lego? I wished Mom and Dad could see it. They just had to put something aside and eventually they'd have a lot to work with. Plus, they could have everything they wanted. Mrs. Ka'ea said we should all put money away for a rainy day 'cause when it rained, it poured.

I thought about the storm that would come once everything happened. At first, I wasn't sure who to approach, but after listening to Mrs. Ka'ea, the answer was clear. Mrs. Ka'ea said in her experience with family law, she saw all kinds of situations: wives cheating on husbands, husbands hurting daughters, wives abusing elderly in-laws. But most often, it was husbands beating on wives. She said it was like society hadn't learned anything in the last thirty years. It drove her absolutely nuts. She said she hated to see wives ignore all the signs. Tolerating the physical abuse, making excuses and delaying the inevitable, all for husbands that were either unpredictable, drunk, or already one foot out the door. My heart had almost stopped. It was like she was talking about my family. Mrs. Ka'ea said that in this situation, she would encourage wives to file first, every time. Husbands were typically the breadwinners and could therefore take care of themselves. And in practice, the law wasn't always a hundred percent impartial. When wives initiated the proceedings, the situation was viewed as bad enough, and only then were they taken more seriously. Going about it that way, wives had less to fear and more to gain to help themselves afterward. If it was the other way around and wives beat on their husbands, Mrs. Ka'ea said she'd feel differently. But she also said she had yet to see it, even once.

I closed my eyes and imagined the clouds already swirling around Mom. I really hoped she'd buy it. I felt the wind whisper her response through the windows, less an answer than an accusation from somebody who clung desperately to nothing. *Why would you do this, Landon?*

'Cause you weren't getting anywhere, Mom.

As we walked home from school, Luke told me he had to collect some sand and small pebbles for the Open House Door Decorating Contest at school. He said his class's theme was *Paving A Path To The Future*. They planned to have a bunch of different vehicles, as many as possible: bikes, cars, trucks, buses, and even spaceships (his idea). First, they were going to make the vehicles out of construction paper and empty milk cartons. They wanted each one to almost drive right off the door, real 3-D style. And under the vehicles, a path would stretch forth, full of gravel just like the roads here in 'Ewa Beach. Luke said his job was to collect road supplies. They planned to glue sand and pebbles onto the path, helping the door come to life.

As we walked, heaps of thick, scorching air seemed to burn upward from the asphalt. In addition to talking, Luke had been kicking a rock since we turned onto Hailipo Street. Each time we caught up to the rock, he whacked it again. But when he did, he also booted gravel and dirt into a cloud around his feet, making a sweaty, muddy film all over his legs. I was going to tease him about how he'd never again complain about being too white for 'Ewa Beach, but I didn't. It had been a while since he had simply . . . talked. Free and easy. I knew enough to just shut up and savor the sound of his voice. I glanced at his dirty legs. That wasn't a problem. We had lots of soap and water. I was just glad he was opening up again.

Listening to Luke, I remembered last year, how the door contest was right before Halloween, how our class worked so hard, and how we won the pizza party. This year, it was the same thing. Luke's Open House was right before Halloween again. It didn't matter that Halloween was on a Sunday. The contest was on the Friday before, just like last year.

At 'Ilima Intermediate, we didn't have anything babyish like that. Our teachers said we could dress up if we wanted. But to celebrate Halloween, there would be a dance in the cafeteria instead. Pretty much everyone went to the dance, except the few who always chose to stay with Mr. Okasaki in his B.O. locker room. They would watch old, eight-millimeter films or play cards, checkers, or chess. But we could do whatever we wanted. It was our choice.

We were almost half way down Hailipo Street when someone called out, "Landon, try wait." Both Luke and I turned around. Imagine my surprise when I saw Vicky Lau hustling toward us. Luke looked at me at once, his eyes narrowing. "Dis must be your liddle brudda," Vicky said as she slowed down. She smiled nervously, her arms folded across a three-ring binder, holding it snug against her chest.

I was still at a loss for words. The last time I tried to talk to Vicky she just ran off to class. "Um . . . hi, Vicky. Dis Luke," I said. And then I turned to him. "Luke, dis Vicky from my class last year." Vicky said hi, but Luke just made googly eyes at her. I sighed and tried to explain. "Sorry, Vicky, my brudda small-kine weird." We all started walking together. I made eye contact with Luke and gave him major stink eye, which meant he better knock it off.

As we got farther down the street, Vicky combed her fingers through her hair as the wind ripped at it. She finally pulled it behind her ears, brushing it back as she talked. "I neva seen you in any of my classes dis year, Landon. How come?"

I didn't think anything of it, so I opted for the truth. "'Cause I in da G.T. program dis year." As the words left my lips, something inside told me that maybe a lie would have been better. My gut locked up 'cause Vicky looked quickly at me. Dammit, I shouldn't have said that. I must've made her feel stupid. I stared ahead and could feel her eyes probing the side of my face. I didn't want her thinking that I thought I was smarter than her. On the other hand, I didn't know what else to say. I just looked down.

Vicky didn't say anything, but her eyes continued to burn a hole in the side of my face. Finally, Vicky broke the silence. "Wow, Landon. I neva know you dat smart," she said, her face still aimed at me. I listened to the gravel crunch as we walked along. Then Vicky suddenly spoke up, as though she had forgotten something. "I tink dat's cool, Landon." The way she said it was so soft, her voice lifted my chin, compelling me look at her. That was when I felt her eyes: how still, how explosive, how deep. They dug into me, trying to get closer. She stopped walking, pointing down a cross street, off Hailipo. "Well, dis my stop, Pohakupuna. I live right down there. I glad I got to talk wit' you." She flipped her hair and then twirled it, holding it with one hand. "By da way, Landon, you going da Halloween dance?"

"Yeah, I tink so, 'cause I no like smell da locka room any more than gotta. P.E. time nuff." We both laughed. I looked at Luke who had both hands on his hips, giving *me* stink eye now. He didn't see what was so funny.

Vicky shifted the three-ring binder but still held it snugly to her chest. "Uh . . . save one dance fo' me, 'kay? See you at school, Landon. Bye, Luke." Vicky turned down Pohakupuna Road, heading toward the fire station. I stood there as she got smaller the farther she walked. I glanced down at Luke who smooched his lips up at me. I shook my head at him.

As we continued walking, Luke sang. "Landon and Vick-*eee*, sitting in one tree, K-I-S-S-I-N-G. First come love, den come marriage, den come Landon wit' one baby carriage." Over and over Luke teased, all the way until we reached Pupu Street. As we turned the corner, I told Luke if he knew what was good for him, he better shut up 'cause I got something for him too. I showed him my fist. He got the picture. The singing stopped.

As we walked home, I thought about Luke's song. First came love? I wanted to tell Luke he got it all wrong. Love didn't always come first. It should, but it didn't. If it *always* did, I was pretty sure Luke and I wouldn't even be here.

In Our Lady of Perpetual Help, we sat near the upright fans in the back, relishing the cool air every few moments, needing to be rescued from the 'Ewa Beach heat. For the last ten minutes, Father Thomas had been delivering his sermon, talking about how people were so desperate to be saved from their sins that they'd do anything, even if it went against God's will.

"Protestants *protest*. They go against the oldest, most direct path to God: Catholicism. Protestants feel we all have to choose to be baptized. They call that being *born again*. Protestants don't understand there's only one birth, and it's through sin that we're born. They fail to see it's the responsibility of parents to cleanse a baby, to baptize it as soon as it's born. As Catholics, we know what would happen if that child were to die, where it would go. Therefore, we baptize immediately. Just as Ernesto and Grace Salvador are doing this morning for their child Rebecca. The family wants to thank the parish for our prayers for their late mother Christina. But as death comes, so does life. The family also wants to invite us all to a reception following mass under the tent in the parking lot. So, if you can, please remain after service today to welcome Rebecca into the family of God, into the joy of everlasting life. Let us pray."

We didn't stay for the baptism 'cause Mom was in a shitty mood. On our way out to the parking lot, Luke realized we weren't hanging around for the reception and began whining. "I hungry. How come we no can stay?" Mom cranked his ass and dragged him to the car, grumbling about how she couldn't believe she was raising two clueless kids. Damn, greedy pigs who just wanted more, more, more. She asked Luke if he even listened during church.

As Mom drove home, she didn't say a single word, all the way down Pohakupuna Road. The car rocked back and forth over potholes. Mom finally looked at Luke in the rear view mirror. "Hey, dummy, are you *that* blind? The reception wasn't for *you*. Damn, rotten kid can't even behave in church." Mom exhaled in disgust. "Don't you know what's going on, or are you just doing this for attention? I'm sick and tired of this, Luke. You're always pulling stunts like today." Luke sank deep into the car seat, sliding safely under Mom's words. But Mom kept pressing, her voice getting louder. "Well, why don't you open your mouth now, huh? Why do you always wait for the worst possible moment to make a scene? Answer me!"

"Why you yelling at him fo'?" I asked. "You da one made da scene, whacking him."

The silence grew as Mom side-eyed me. I could tell she was getting ready to let me have it, but I didn't care. Suddenly, Mom hit the brakes so that we didn't ram into a slower car. Then she tailed the guy in front and shook her head. "Perfect, just perfect. Thanks, Landon, you just reminded me. Not only do I have two clueless kids, I have two *low-class* kids. How many times have I told you about speaking pidgin? The way you two kids *talk* is exactly why Luke doesn't understand why I'm so upset. How about behaving properly and doing what you're supposed to? You two remind me of your brownie father. Absolutely clueless." She pointed to the car in front of us. On the faded chrome, the bumper sticker read: *JESUS SAVES. COME TO THE CHURCH OF CHRIST.* "Landon, I bet you don't even know what that first part means."

I wanted to tell Mom neither did she, that even though everyone at church was Catholic like us, the reason we didn't stay was that she still thought of them as nothing more than just low-class people from ʻEwa Beach. But instead, I gave her what she asked for, in the sassiest, most standard English I could muster. "It means God loved us so much He sent His only son to *save* us, so that we could have eternal life."

Mom side-eyed me again and then looked forward. Her jaw muscles flexed so hard she sneered. I knew Mom didn't like it, but she asked the question. She shook her head, still tailing the slow car with the bumper sticker. Out of nowhere, she scoffed, "Protestants."

When I asked what paperwork was needed to get divorced, Mrs. Kaʻea looked at me funny for a moment. But then she organized her papers from work, slid them to the side of the kitchen table, and removed a couple of loose sheets from her satchel on the floor.

She placed the first one before me and was about to speak when she stopped. She set her hand over the paper. "Landon, why do you want to know?"

I shrugged my shoulders as if I didn't really care. "I just curious," I lied.

Mrs. Ka'ea paused and then slid the paper closer to me. "This is the first paper that would need to be filled out. *Complaint for Divorce*. This is for the husband or wife who wants to initiate the process. This second one," Mrs. Ka'ea said, sliding the other paper over the first, "*Summons to Answer Complaint*, is sent to the spouse to respond to the initial *Complaint*."

I looked at the papers as if they were the wafers used during communion at church. It's all I would need to change everything. To *do* something. But then I caught myself. "You wen' fill out these wen you got divorce?"

Mrs. Ka'ea smiled and nodded. "The very same."

I considered for a moment. I didn't know too many other kids from school besides Toby, and then Jason, whose parents had gotten divorced. Luke and I would be so . . . different. "You no was shame?" I asked.

Mrs. Ka'ea slipped both papers out from beneath my hands and tucked them under the stack of papers from work. "Yeah, I guess I was. But it was the best decision I ever made."

"How come?"

Mrs. Ka'ea stopped for a moment, glanced out the window toward the ocean, and took a deep breath. "Don't get me wrong, Landon, I was scared like hell. No one in my family had ever been divorced. The church says, 'What God has put together, let no man put asunder.' Until death do us part, right? But I didn't care. My ex-husband's physical abuse was enough to motivate me. And there came a point when I had to choose. Either do something right then, or stay in a bad situation forever."

I glanced at the papers Mrs. Ka'ea had tucked away. I listened to the waves outside and felt the same happen to thoughts within. Not only was it Mom against Dad at home, but now it had become Mom against me and Luke. And the more I thought about it, the worse it got. If I gave those papers to Mom, it could also be Mom against me, Mom and Dad against me, and even God against me. Holy shit.

Mrs. Ka'ea asked me what was wrong, drawing my attention back to the kitchen. I must have been frowning. I backtracked through thoughts quickly. Mrs. Ka'ea had said there came a point when she had to choose. "What made you finally do 'em?"

Mrs. Ka'ea smiled tightly and then looked back outside. Her voice softened, as she opened a door that must've been closed for years. "I got married while still trying to finish my associate's degree. My husband tried to make me stop. You know, he wanted the typical housewife to cook and clean and pick up after him. But my degree was important to me, so I continued to take classes. And then came the fights. A lot of them. I knew pretty early in the marriage I had made a big mistake, once he started hitting me. But I always figured I had to stay. After all, I did have a child to think about." Mrs. Ka'ea breathed deeply, lost somewhere in the past. "I would have stayed for Toby. But I knew eventually it would kill me, or worse.

"Ironically, it was Toby that finally made me do it. In a sense, my son saved me. When Toby was about five, I took a criminal law class. One case we discussed scared me more than anything else ever did." She looked at me. "This woman in Michigan had been abused the same way I was. After years of staying in the situation, giving her ex-husband chance after chance, she killed him. She waited until he passed out, too drunk to do anything about it. Then she poured gasoline around the house and lit a match." Mrs. Ka'ea's hand shook. "I knew that same . . . rage. I wondered if I was capable of doing something that drastic. It scared me, for so many reasons. This woman was lucky because she got to keep her children. I didn't know if I would be that lucky with Toby. I would've had to go to jail, for sure, then stand trial. What would've happened to Toby then?" Mrs. Ka'ea took a deep breath, as though coming back to the present. "So, to answer your question, Landon, I did it for Toby. But as I said before, it was the best decision I ever made. It was like being . . . born again." She wiped at her eyes and then shook her head. She chuckled humorlessly. "Besides, there was no way I was going to let C.P.S. get involved. So I took control of the situation, legally."

My brow furrowed. "What's C.P.S.?"

Mrs. Ka'ea smiled tightly, perhaps anticipating my question. "It's a government agency. Child Protective Services. Case workers come in and check up on parents to see if they're doing the absolute best for their children."

I thought about the welts Luke and I had on our legs, the fighting, the drinking. "Dat's not a good ting?"

Mrs. Ka'ea thought before answering. "C.P.S. has a *lot* of power, Landon. It's great when they put a stop to child abuse. But if I had gone to jail, C.P.S. would've said I was an unfit mother. Toby would've been taken away and placed with one of our relatives. Or maybe even put in a foster home." Mrs. Ka'ea shook her head at the memory. "Can you imagine that? Toby having no choice in the matter, and through no fault of his own, all of a sudden uprooted from the only sense of a *normal* life he ever knew? I could never do that to my son, Landon."

I thought about Mom and Dad, how they fought and how desperate Mom might get. I knew it was shitty to think, but I wasn't sure that would be so bad. Maybe I didn't need the paperwork after all. I didn't want anything bad to happen to Dad, but without him *and* Mom, at least Luke and I could be adopted. The question left my lips as immediately as the thought hit. "If C.P.S. say we gotta go fo' adoption, would you adopt me and Luke?"

Mrs. Ka'ea's eyes narrowed. "Wait, what? Why? Has C.P.S. already contacted your parents?"

Oh, shit. I shook my head earnestly. "No."

Mrs. Ka'ea's voice was stern. "Then why would you ask something like that, Landon?" I didn't know how to respond, so I just looked down. Mrs. Ka'ea's voice softened. "Landon?" I still wouldn't look up. She lifted my chin with her hand. Her touch was so soft. "Landon, have you told me everything that goes on at home?" I nodded, but the truth was that I hadn't told her about Mom and Dad hitting us. I was too ashamed. "I know it must feel horrible at home, Landon. But you have to understand. Before you and your brother would *ever* be put up for adoption, C.P.S. would intervene on your behalf. Something drastic would have to happen for them to take you away from your parents. They would encourage your parents to work out their problems, or to consider divorce or some other alternative. But you and your brother would stay with at least one of your parents, or possibly even a relative." Mrs. Ka'ea smiled kindly. "Now, I don't want to hurt you, Landon, but I think you deserve to know the truth." She waited until I met her gaze. "It sucks that the system works this way, but from what you told me, C.P.S. doesn't really have grounds to get involved. I mean, it's bad for you at home. But C.P.S. is the last resort after all else fails." Mrs. Ka'ea grimaced. "Do you understand what I mean by that?"

I glanced down, trying to process what Mrs. Ka'ea said. Of course I understood. It was bad at home, just not . . . bad enough. Which meant my parents were shitty, but they weren't *shitty enough*. Unfortunately, something really bad would have to happen. I nodded, having then understood: I was stuck. Was there a worse place to be? I looked Mrs. Ka'ea square in the eye. "But *would* you adopt us?" It was all I really wanted to know.

Mrs. Ka'ea's expression softened. "Landon, given the chance, I would gladly." She reached out and rested her palm on my cheek. "But realistically, that would *never* happen." She then sat back and took a deep breath. "I know it's not what you want to hear, but you're just going to have to be strong. Be there for your little brother. Continue to be a good son to your mom and dad. Help them to realize what's more important. But whatever happens between them, *they* have to come to it. Okay?"

I nodded sadly, knowing Mrs. Ka'ea was right. I had to be strong. For a moment, I imagined how nice it would be to live here, but then I caught myself. Who was I kidding? There was no easy way out. Nothing huge was going to come along and fix this.

Mrs. Ka'ea continued, sounding upbeat. "Maybe you're going to be able save them, Landon, like Toby saved me. For your mom, it would be the second time."

I thought for a moment. "*Second* time?"

"Your mom would've died with your grandparents in that airplane crash you told me about if it wasn't for you, Landon. You saved her then, giving her a second chance at life. It's like when you were born, so was she. That's what you need to do for both of your parents now."

I never thought of it that way before. Just like from church. Born again.

Just then, the buzzer on the washing machine went off in the hallway. Mrs. Ka'ea smiled kindly and excused herself.

I took a deep breath as I dipped deep into thoughts. When I exhaled, it was as if I had come up clean. I didn't need something drastic to happen. I needed to approach Mom with the papers. Yes, that was *exactly* what I should do. I quickly retrieved the *Complaint for Divorce* and the *Summons to Answer Complaint* from beneath Mrs. Ka'ea's stack of papers. I folded up both and slipped them into my pocket. Mom needed to see, and this was how she would come to it. Funny, I felt oddly relaxed. Maybe 'cause it no longer felt like God was against me, even if I could still hear Mom muttering about Protestants. I wanted to give her that second chance.

And that was why I would always love Mrs. Ka'ea. She was the ocean that saved, the air that washed in salty breaths. She was the rising, helping me to go in the right direction.

Heading toward home, Luke was still complaining. He hadn't let up since we left 'Ewa Beach Elementary School. It was like he had saved it all day, and if he didn't let it out now, he would explode. But I didn't mind. I was lost somewhere between what he was saying and the papers I snuck away from Mrs. Ka'ea's house. In the back of my mind, I knew I needed to talk with Mom. I needed to give her that chance. I just didn't know how to do it. Luke talked about how the girls always wanted to play kick and catch with the boys. So when the boys finally let the girls play, the ball always flew off to the side, never going high enough in the air. And that wasn't the worst. The girls in his class were ruining their door decoration. Once the vehicles were made, the girls tried to decorate them with too many colors. He got sent to the office for snapping at Esmerelda Augustin. He told her not everybody had book-book cars like her family.

Luke looked up at me. "Girls mess ev'ryting up, ah, Landon?" He wanted me to agree.

I thought about Mom and then Mrs. Ka'ea. "Some do, but not all girls mess tings up."

Luke squinted his eyes. "Who no mess stuff up? Vick-*eee* . . . your *girlfriend*?" He stuck out his tongue like he wanted to throw up.

I cocked my head at him. "Vicky not my girlfriend."

Luke giggled. "Yeah, right. You guys was making eyes at each odda. I seen 'em." He started rolling his eyes, the same mental way as before.

"Whatevas," I said, shaking my head as we walked. Luke dry-heaved as if he were about to throw up. In between Luke's hurling noises, I thought about Vicky Lau. Eyes like the sun, exploding with light. Hair like seaweed, flowing underwater. I looked back down at Luke, knowing I had to approach Mom soon, for all of us.

Vicky was pretty, and she was nice. But I wasn't about to let her mess anything up. I didn't want to do what Dad did. I didn't want to fuck up like him.

I straddled Toby's surfboard, rising and falling while I looked up at the sky. I lived in pockets of clouds that floated by in silence. I breathed in every set of waves as they burst in glowing color. Like little treasures, the liquid gems settled in a soothing, crystal mist.

Air and water, together in one word, spraying and washing me clean: Ka'ea.

I inhaled both, tucking them away, knowing it was only a matter of time.

When I finally came back in, Mrs. Ka'ea sat on the wall, waiting. I knew something wasn't quite right 'cause when I greeted her, she just offered me my towel. I wasn't sure why, but it felt like I was busted. Oh, crap. Maybe she realized she was missing the divorce paperwork. I dried myself off in silence.

Mrs. Ka'ea patted the wall. "Have a seat, Landon." Once I was beside her, Mrs. Ka'ea took a deep breath. "I want you to be honest with me, Landon. Okay? Will you?"

I nodded, knowing where this was headed. The last thing I wanted to do was to lie to Mrs. Ka'ea, so if she asked whether I took the divorce papers, I swore I'd tell her the truth.

Mrs. Ka'ea cleared her throat. "When you jumped off the rocks this afternoon, I saw the welts on your legs. And just now, the marks on your upper arm, from being grabbed. That's when I realized I had seen them before. I just didn't put it all together until today. You asking the other day about divorce, C.P.S, adoption." She paused and then picked up my hand, holding it in both of hers. "Tell me how you got those bruises, Landon."

I had to think fast. I didn't want Mrs. Ka'ea contacting Mom 'cause I didn't want Mom knowing I still came to Toby's house. What could make marks on my arms *and* legs? "I . . . I fell," I lied. Mrs. Ka'ea stared at me blankly. "Down the stairs," I added.

Mrs. Ka'ea smiled, lips drawn tight. "You live in a one-story house, Landon."

I stared back, stuck. It only took me a moment to recover. "No, no. At . . . at school." I hoped she didn't notice my hesitation.

Mrs. Ka'ea seemed concerned. "What happened?"

I swallowed hard and made it up as I went along. "Was recess time, and I was walking down da stairs wen I wen' slip and hit butt first on da top step. But den I kept slipping down da steps like I riding one bumpy slide." I motioned with my hand to demonstrate the proper angle of my arms', legs', and, apparently, ass's peril.

Mrs. Ka'ea let go of my hand and folded her arms. She was quiet for a long time. "You want me to believe . . . that?" I nodded and shrugged. "You sure there's nothing you want to tell me?" I looked down and shook my head. After a moment, Mrs. Ka'ea sighed and then stood. "Okay," she said weakly.

I sat on the wall and watched Mrs. Ka'ea close the sliding door behind her. I felt like shit. I had sworn I'd tell her the truth, but instead I lied my ass off. And the worst part was that I was pretty sure Mrs. Ka'ea knew it.

During lunch, the dance committee scurried around the cafeteria, sticking decorations on the walls. Orange and black streamers, balloons of the same colors, and posters that read: *TRICK OR TREAT.* I thought back to Luke last year with his underwear stunt and chuckled to myself. The teachers wanted us to be in the locker room or in the cafeteria when the bell rang. Toward the end of lunch, the janitors closed all of the windows while the cafeteria ladies came out with brooms to sweep up loose trash. It only took a few minutes, but after the windows were closed, everyone in the cafeteria began sweating. Add that musty scent to about six hundred half-finished paper lunch trays in heaping trash cans and at least the same number of warm, half-drunk milk cartons, and what we had was a curdling, creamy-vegetable sweetness that would linger in the air during the dance. A horde of students swarmed into the cafeteria, spreading throughout the room. The bell rang, trapping me in with most of 'Ilima Intermediate. For a moment, I thought that maybe Mr. Okasaki's locker room might have been a better choice.

Before the dance started, the cafeteria ladies asked us to help move the tables against the walls. Once that was done, Trisha Murakami, our student government president as well as M.C., told us not to panic, that the lights were about to be dimmed. I heard people making fun of her, saying we weren't babies who were afraid of the dark. I looked around and noticed most of the boys sat at lunch tables on one side of the room while most of the girls sat way on the other side. But when the music began, some boys automatically got up and made their way to the girls' side. Like they had no problem asking a girl to dance. I watched as some girls reached their hands out, real soft and gentle, touching the boy's hand. They stood and walked to the middle of the floor where a mass of people had formed. But I also saw some boys get turned down. So shame. I sat back and looked up at the spinning silver ball the dance committee had attached to the ceiling. Needles of light dazzled in pinpoints against the wall. For a moment, I began to drift, getting lost in the sounds around me. There were muffled voices and billowing music like a theme song from a movie. And then the silver ball looked like the Death Star from *Star Wars*. I felt myself floating above everyone.

Until I heard my name, yanking me back down to Earth. "Hi, Landon." It was what I was afraid of: Vicky Lau. And her eyes.

God, she was so pretty. "Uh . . . hi, Vicky." That was all I could say before looking down.

Vicky sat next to me, leaning back on two arms, her legs crossed and swinging nervously, scratching the surface of the concrete below. "The dance pretty cool, yeah?" she asked. I could feel her eyes staring at me again. I nodded, not sure what else to do. "I notice you neva ask nobody fo' dance. How come?" I shrugged my shoulders. A couple seconds passed. "No need be shame, you know. Just go and ask. Da worse dey can say is no." By the way she said the last part, I could tell she was smiling now. And still looking.

Thoughts of Mom and Dad dove in and out of my mind, images that splashed into a tangle of feelings and words, images that warned, images that told me I had to keep me and Luke together. I heard the words echo: Divorce. Separation. Adoption. I finally worked up the courage to look into Vicky's explosive eyes. I didn't want to be mean, 'cause honestly, I liked her. But I wasn't going to let Vicky mess anything up. I looked back down. "Nah, Vicky, I no feel like dance right now. Dat's why I neva ask nobody," I lied.

"Oh." Vicky looked away, out toward the dance floor, legs still swinging beneath us as a new song started playing. I knew she really wanted to dance, and with me.

Between trying to convince myself I didn't want to dance and making excuses for why I shouldn't, Vicky turned to me. "I just remember I wanted fo' tell you somethin', Landon." I glanced at her. She was biting her lower lip, unsure how to say it. Vicky struggled, mustering the words. "I . . . heard about . . . Toby. I really sorry, Landon. I know you guys was close." And just like that, with those few, kind words, I felt the warmth, like a smile. It grew, coming from deep inside, like reaching into a purse and removing a warm, sparkling gem. And as it rose, unlocked but still safe, I saw it, glittering brighter than any light on any wall. The higher it went, the more light it gave off, and the cleaner I felt. And the braver and the stronger I felt.

It was enough to help me find the guts to open my mouth, enough to help me understand that one dance wasn't going to change what I had to do or mess anything up. It was enough to make me want to help Vicky, to put it all aside so that she could have what she wanted, too. So for the first time that day, I took a chance. I stood up and noticed how Vicky's forehead furrowed with disappointment, probably assuming she either upset me by what she said or that I was about to ask someone else to dance. But I turned to Vicky, extending a hand toward her as though offering her the shimmering words she had just given me. "Vicky, you like dance?"

Vicky's eyes glinted in a way I had never seen as a smile stretched across her lips. And as she reached for my hand, everything slowed. The silver ball rotated, gleaming like the spotlight at Barbers Point, as it spun in long streaks that barely moved now. The music dropped away. Words and sounds faded into heat, and then into nothing. Thinking and breathing halted as I anticipated the moment I knew was coming. I watched and waited for her hand to melt into mine. And when it did, everything blurred in slow motion.

Hand in hand, we swirled into music, swashing back and forth on some strange wave I had never felt before. We sank deeper into a slow dance, deeper into the rhythm of each other, and somehow I realized I didn't want it to end. In this ocean of movement, Vicky and I became weightless, as though we were both rising off the ground. The cafeteria dripped away as we pulled free and soared high over everyone, higher even than the silver ball on the ceiling. And somehow we were completely alone. The spinning light flashed in Vicky's eyes like snapshots, images I secretly tucked away as if each one were a sparkling treasure. And as a new song played, faces of other students blended into one long streak of color below, like seeing it from a carnival ride. Around and around, Vicky and I held each other, lost in the motion between us. I closed my eyes when I recognized the song. Carpenters. I knew it 'cause Mom used to sing it.

Sharing horizons that are new to us
Watching the signs along the way
Talkin' it over, just the two of us
Workin' together day to day
Together

I tried to block out thoughts of Mom and Dad. Not now, please, not now. But the words whispered anyway. Mom and Dad didn't get anywhere new. They didn't talk. They only yelled. And they didn't do anything *together* anymore. Oh, God, please make it stop. I didn't want to think about them now.

And when the evening comes, we smile
So much of life ahead
We'll find a place where there's room to grow
And yes, we've just begun

I couldn't get away, like each word was said straight to me. I thought about what was about to begin with my family. Would it be divorce, separation, adoption? I felt Vicky wash comfortably against the inside of my arms, back and forth. I suddenly hoped the place Luke and I found was still in ʻEwa Beach. But then I thought about the divorce papers I took from Mrs. Kaʻea's house. I should approach Mom tonight. I had to give her that second chance. As the music began to fade, I suddenly remembered an earlier part of the song that I didn't recall hearing. I felt Vicky in my arms and realized why. Just thinking the words, though, filled me with so much excitement I could barely breathe.

Before the risin' sun, we fly
So many roads to choose
We'll start out walkin' and learn to run
And yes, we've just begun

After Carpenters, the next song played, and then the next, and the next. And Vicky and I kept swaying. We drifted on the same wave, on the same cloud, in the same ocean and sky. I inhaled, knowing that changes were coming and that our paths probably wouldn't be the same. So I tried to hold on to this moment, savoring it for as long as I could. 'Cause even if Vicky and I had danced now for fifteen minutes, I knew there still was so much of life ahead.

Just before we went to Luke's Open House at ʻEwa Beach Elementary School, Dad came home with a paper sack and what looked like a bottle stuffed in it. He walked straight to his and Mom's bedroom, and about a minute later, Mom's voice could be heard. "Leonard, why are you buying all this liquor? And why do you smell like a . . . *rose*?" Mom's voice rose to almost a shout, like heavy thunder that rolled through the house.

Luke's face dropped. We both knew what swelled in their bedroom. I looked at Luke who could only stare into his lap. I knew he was really hoping to show off his class's door. I grabbed Luke's hand and yanked him outside.

"Where we going, Landon?" Luke asked, as we headed down Pupu Street.

I stopped, crunching gravel beneath my feet. "We going your Open House. And Luke, I know I neva say 'em long time, but we gotta stick together, 'kay? You and me." Luke considered, and then smiled and nodded. And just like that, Luke began talking like we were walking home after school. Just like that, it didn't matter if Mom wasn't coming anymore.

Before going to Luke's classroom, I wanted to stop by to see Mrs. Kato, my teacher from last school year. Even though there were some parents milling about her room, when she saw me, Mrs. Kato still gave me a big hug. "And how are your G.T. classes, Landon?" she asked, squinting with playful suspicion. "You better have good news for me." She winked.

I laughed. "I doing good, Mrs. Kato. I promise. I had hard time wit' functions, but Mr. Lee wen' help me."

Mrs. Kato murmured her approval. "Mr. Lee's a very good teacher. I was just joking, though, Landon. I already knew you were doing well. Mrs. Sakuoka, your English teacher, is also the G.T. coordinator at 'Ilima Intermediate. She told me how pleased she is with your progress." I shrugged uncomfortably, surprised that my teachers, from two different schools no less, had been keeping tabs on me. But then again, I really shouldn't be that surprised. I knew how much my success meant to Mrs. Kato. "I'm so proud of you, Landon. Make sure you listen and learn lots from all your teachers, okay?" After I said I would, Mrs. Kato turned to Luke. "Is this your *little* brother?" I glanced at Luke and realized that Mrs. Kato hadn't seen him since last year's Open House. "My goodness, look how big you've gotten." Luke waved sheepishly. Mrs. Kato looked around. "Where's your mom?"

I smiled tightly and shrugged. "She no could come, so just us tonight."

Mrs. Kato nodded as though she understood. Then she glanced at Luke as if she had just thought of something. She turned to me. "What grade is he?" she asked, pointing to Luke.

"Fourth," I said, uncertain what she was getting at.

Mrs. Kato inhaled deeply, contemplating. "Has he been tested for G.T. yet?"

I almost choked. Gifted and Talented? I wanted to tell her the only thing Luke was gifted and talented at was being a bone-head. Instead, I merely shook my head.

"Well, I'm the G.T. coordinator for 'Ewa Beach Elementary. Since you qualified, Landon, I wouldn't be surprised if Luke did as well. Siblings often do."

I looked at my brother who was gazing off toward an art display. He had already lost interest in the conversation. G.T.? I wasn't buying it. "I dunno," I said skeptically.

"Landon, I'll talk with his teacher. There's no harm in that, right? And if she gives me a recommendation, I can test him as early as December." Still seeing the dubious look on my face, she lowered her voice. "What's the matter?"

I fumbled for the words. First, who knew where we'd end up once things happened between Mom and Dad. Second, Luke was so . . . off. "Sometimes he not all there. He dunno wen—" I stopped, exhaling in frustration. Luke was, at the moment, staring open-mouthed at the ceiling. I pointed at him as though in explanation.

Mrs. Kato suppressed a laugh and shook her head. "Landon," she said, "I wouldn't be surprised if he's even more G.T. than you."

I thought I had misheard. "Fo' real?"

Mrs. Kato nodded. "A lot of times, G.T. students have so much going on in their heads they space out or act up. But their brains are going all the time, helping them to see things and make connections most people wouldn't."

I glanced at Luke as I considered. Luke *was* often in his own universe, doing something off-the-wall.

Mrs. Kato broke in. "Remember, Landon, it's a chance to change *everything*. Why not take it?"

For a moment, I just stood there. The more I thought about it, the more I knew Mrs. Kato was right. Divorce, separation, even adoption loomed over us, but until they happened, what were we supposed to do? Stop living? This was a chance, just like the one I got. Why *shouldn't* Luke take his? "Okay," I agreed simply.

Mrs. Kato smiled. "If Luke's recommended for testing, I'll call him out of class and send the permission form home with him." She stopped and considered something. "It shouldn't be a problem for your mom or dad to sign it and get it back to me, right?"

I smiled wryly, remembering who had signed *my* permission form. "No worry, Mrs. Kato. I make sure you get 'em back."

Outside Luke's classroom, I looked once again at his door: *Paving A Path To The Future*. The first word that came to me was *colorful*. But before I could say something about it, Luke brought up Mrs. Kato. "What she like test me fo'?" he asked suspiciously.

I looked down at him, taken aback. Had he really been listening in Mrs. Kato's room? I thought at most he had only been catching flies. Either way, it must have really been on his mind. "She tink you might be good fo' Gifted and Talented classes, like da ones I get." His lips scrunched. "She tink you smart," I said mischievously. "I told her lose money, dat, but she like test you anyway."

Luke made a face at the ribbing, but then he looked down, lost in thought. Finally, he peeked at me. "What'chu tink, Landon? I should do 'em, or what?"

I shrugged. "Up to you, Luke. I mean, G.T. classes is more hard dan regular ones, but . . . betta. More interesting."

Luke thought about it, and then his face wrinkled. "Dat's right. You get plenty homework."

"Yeah, but you going get plenty homework either way."

Luke studied his classroom door, picking at the gravel pathway. "You like your classes?"

I nodded solemnly. "Way betta."

Luke looked me square in the eye. "How come?"

I thought for a moment and then smiled at what surfaced. "Dey make me feel less . . . different." I watched, as Luke's face lit up. "You know what I mean by dat?"

It was Luke's turn to nod solemnly. Then he bit at his lower lip, weighing the possibility placed before him. Finally, he made eye contact. "If can, I going do G.T. classes too."

On our way home, Luke prattled on about his class's door, how he was sure they were going to win the pizza party this year. But when I asked Luke why the vehicles were so colorful with flowers and spots like they all wore muʻumuʻu, Luke made a face. He whispered it was 'cause of the *girls*. I chuckled as I remembered how he said girls messed everything up. "You seen da road under da trucks and airplanes?" he asked. "Came out nice, ah? Rememba? I wen' bring all da sand and gravel. At least da girls no could work on our road, ah?"

Girls. I smiled, thinking back to the dance today. Back to Vicky. "Hey, Luke. I like ask you somethin'." He looked up at me. "It's okay if Vicky walk home wit' us on Monday?"

Luke's expression soured. He looked at his feet as we walked along. "I thought you said *we* gotta stick together?" Luke kicked a rock in front of him and sent it skidding.

I smiled, knowing exactly what he meant. "Luke, *nobody* going come between us or keep us apart. Whereva I go, you go, and whereva you go, I go. We going stick together, I promise." I stressed the last part, and although it seemed to pull Luke back, he was still frowning. So I reached into my shirt and slid the twine lanyard from my neck. I showed Luke my 1970 quarter hanging from the woven thread. I finally knew what I wanted to use it for. "Luke, even wen we come older, if you eva need me, you call me wit' dis, and I going come flying." With both hands, I draped the lanyard around his neck. I pointed to him and then me. "Dis, Luke . . . you and me? We bruddas. Not just right now. We bruddas *foreva*."

Luke looked straight into my eyes, checking to see if I really meant what I said. I kept my eyes focused intently on him. I wanted him to know that *he* was my priority. After finding what he was looking for, Luke glanced down and then back at me. He nodded and said it was okay with him. Then Luke started singing. "Landon and Vick-*eee* sitting in one tree—"

But before he could get to the K-I-S-S-I-N-G part, I cut him off by showing him my fist again. "Luke, you betta knock it off. And no do dat wen she walk wit' us." He giggled as we made our way closer to home. All I could do was shake my head.

Dad's car wasn't in the garage when Luke and I got home. We opened the front door and walked in to find Mom sitting at the kitchen table. Her swollen eyes stared off into nothing. She looked at us for a moment, confused. Her nose was red and ran so much she had to keep wiping it with a Scott towel. Mom stared at us as though expecting some kind of explanation. I pushed Luke toward our bedroom. One glance at Mom, and Luke went with quick steps. But I stayed. "I thought both of you were in your room, Landon. Where were you this late?" Her voice came out thick and heavy. She sounded more curious than angry.

The fact she wasn't angry was a good sign. I needed to talk with her about the divorce papers. "We wen' Luke's Open House."

Mom looked down at the table. "Oh." She squinted, trying to hold back about missing yet another thing, but hot tears already streamed down her cheeks. Mom buried her face in her hands. I hurried to me and Luke's bedroom, grabbed the papers, and took them to the kitchen. Mom looked at me and then at the two sheets I handed her. Her forehead creased as she glanced over them. "What's this, Landon?" She paused a moment. "*Complaint for Divorce*?"

I was proud of myself 'cause I was finally helping. "It's one chance fo' be born again," I said. Mom turned sharply to me, her eyes narrowing into murderous slivers. But it was too late. I already started so I kept going. "It's one second chance fo' you, Mom. And fo' Dad."

Mom cocked her head to the side and frowned. As Mom glanced over the second sheet, I watched her face, hoping for a clue, a sign, something that showed what she was thinking. Moments passed. Nothing. Mom scanned one paper and then the other, gripping both tightly to keep them steady. And for some reason, the longer I waited for Mom to speak, the more hopeful I got. Mom had to see I was right. It must be hard to swallow, just like it was for me, but it was the only choice that made sense. By the time Mom looked up, I had convinced myself she would open her arms to me. I was so confident in what I had done and why, I was sure she was about to thank me. But when Mom opened her mouth, I realized I couldn't have been more wrong.

She inhaled deeply, and when she spoke, her words came out dangerously slow. "Where did you get these?"

I didn't know what to say, so I opted for the truth. "Mrs. Ka'ea. But I neva tell—"

Mom's face twisted angrily. "Who the hell told you to air our dirty laundry, Landon?"

I staggered back into the living room as Mom stood. "What?" I asked. "I just thought—"

She waved the papers at me. "What did you think? That this house is open, for everyone to see inside?"

"I was just—"

Mom cut me off, yelling in my face. "You just *what*? You thought you could wipe *my* mistakes clean, just like that?" She snapped her fingers at the end of the sentence. "You think it's just that easy, don't you, Landon? What about a job? I have no work experience for over fifteen years. No employer in his right mind would hire me at my age. Do you think I can magically put food on the table without a job? And what do I do when alimony and child support run out, huh? There's no way in hell I'm going on welfare. You think you're so damn smart, tell me what I need to do." Mom flung herself into a chair at the kitchen table and huffed impatiently.

"I dunno. You could go school like Mrs. Ka'ea—"

Mom exploded from the chair and stormed at me, yelling again. "With *what* money, Landon? And that's another thing. Why are you still going over there? I forbade you from going to her house. Do you know what that means? *Do you?*" She screamed, splattering saliva dots across my face. "It means you're not allowed to do something. Just like divorce, goddamn it! Do you know what your faith says about divorce? It's forbidden!" Mom turned and took a few slow steps across the living room. She stopped and breathed heavily, her back facing me. "Don't you think this just might have crossed my mind before, Landon? Give me a little credit. But what about my vows? 'For better or for worse.' I take my vows seriously because I made them before God. How can I break a promise to God, Landon?" She swung all the way around, an idea surfacing as her arms spread wide at her sides. "Oh, Christ. That's where that *born again* comment came from. You think you can save me, Landon? You think you're my own personal messiah?" She snickered as she made a face at me. "Sorry, I already have one."

Mom's words hit so hard I felt the numbness creep down my spine and into my legs. Mom sat down tiredly at the kitchen table, propped her elbows, and supported her head with both hands. From behind, Luke pressed his head into my back. He curled into my body, hiding in the safety of my shadow. And I knew exactly what he was saying when he grabbed a wad of my shirt and tugged me toward our bedroom. Nobody was going to come between us.

Mom pressed against her temples with her thumb and middle finger. "I can't believe you did this, Landon. How am I supposed to look Celeste in the eye at church now?" I was about to tell her that I didn't tell Mrs. Ka'ea everything, but then Mom picked up the divorce papers, holding one end in each hand. Mom looked at me and gritted her teeth. Without a moment's hesitation more, she yanked, tearing paper. I felt it slow at first, the raw, fraying fibers of my help as they were exposed. That was what Mom thought of me. Mom ripped all the way down the sheets, looking at me the whole time. The farther she tore, the further I went. I still felt Luke pulling me toward our room. I wanted to go, but not yet. I had to see Mom make her choice.

Mom crumpled each half, wadded them up, and then threw them across the room at me. The two wads landed at my feet. I bent down to pick up the mangled clumps of paper and glanced at Mom, knowing things were going to change. I already knew things wouldn't come out the way Mom wanted.

I looked across the living room at how far away Mom was. I tried to feel something, but right now, I didn't care. She made her choice. And, truthfully, this was better. It really was. I knew it wouldn't be right away, but something drastic was bound to happen. Mom had her chance, and as far as I was concerned, she blew it. Plus, once the C.P.S. people heard what I had to say, this would all have to end in one word for me and Luke: adoption. For a moment, I imagined how nice it would be to get away from this house. I wondered if there was some way Luke and I could live with Mrs. Ka'ea. I felt a door closing within, a door I shut hard upon Mom and willingly locked.

Mom headed to the kitchen cabinet and started digging through pill bottles, so I finally let Luke direct me to our bedroom. With every step away from Mom, I knew from now on, it truly was only me and Luke.

Long after Luke was asleep, I lay awake in the dark, watching amber streetlight cast shadows on the carpet below. I crept over to where it was brightest and then lay on the glowing carpet. I inhaled, holding my breath in the golden light . . . holding on tight. As I exhaled, I thought back over today, back to dancing, back to Vicky. Back to a floating, spinning world I never wanted to leave. It was a place where it was okay to take a chance 'cause I could still have everything I wanted. I sat up, my skin bathed in streetlight, and looked at Luke sleeping on his bunk. After a moment, I lay back on the carpet and smiled. I did have everything I wanted, and more. I now knew that not all girls messed things up. Some did. But not all.

26

We had just begun a weather unit in Mrs. Ellory's G.T. physical science class. But I didn't need anybody to tell me a storm was coming. For the past couple of days, 'Ewa Beach wasn't hot. Low-hanging clouds hovered all day as chilly air moaned painfully through the hallways. A lot of students actually brought sweaters to school.

Mrs. Ellory told us we were at the tail end of hurricane season. She explained hurricanes formed when pressure systems collided. When lows and highs rammed into each other, the air had to go somewhere. So it swirled, spinning around and around like water in a toilet. Mrs. Ellory asked us if we ever watched the way toilet water whirlpooled, the way it went faster and faster until it completely flushed away. She said it was similar for a *cyclone*, or a hurricane. The force and wind sucked around in a cyclone became violent 'cause there was so much spiraling energy, searching for areas of less pressure.

Hurricanes didn't care who we were, what we desired, or what we cared about. They'd surge forward, destroying anything in their way. Hurricanes had no minds, so there was nothing to reason with. All we could do was to watch for signs in the weather so we could avoid any disaster. That was why we studied weather, to keep us safe.

The bell rang as Mrs. Ellory told us what to watch for. She mentioned the calm before the storm while everyone just packed their bags. They were more interested in the freedom of recess. But I stayed back to ask Mrs. Ellory what she meant.

"The calm before the storm, Landon, is a period when everything settles down. The wind stops moving, and the waves smooth into nothing but ripples. Everything gets very still and very quiet. When that happens, it's only a matter of time. So if you see it get like this, get ready. Because something big is coming."

It was something I already knew, more than in the chilly air and strange clouds lingering above 'Ewa Beach. Mom and Dad hadn't spoken for almost three weeks. And now it was *real* quiet at home. Mrs. Ellory didn't know how right she got it. Something big was coming.

Luke's questions came at the worst time. Like when we were walking home with Vicky. He was always saying stuff like: *You and Vicky boyfriend-girlfriend? Why you not holding hands? You in love? Why, you guys fighting? So, you wen' kiss yet, or what*? Since Luke started doing this, Vicky talked about love and relationships, how curious she was to know what it was like to kiss, and when we walked, her pinky finger whacked into mine all the time now. It was like the pressure built even more each time Luke opened his mouth.

Luke sat on the floor of our bedroom and played with his Lego house and *Star Wars* figures. "Landon, how come you no kiss Vicky?"

I looked up from my homework and shrugged. "I dunno, I guess I not ready fo' do dat. But you know what, Luke?" He looked up at me. "You gotta stop asking boyfriend-girlfriend kine questions, 'cause you making 'em hard fo' me."

Luke's brow furrowed. "What'chu mean?"

"You wen' make Vicky tink dat stuff wit' your questions and now she like me do 'em. I no like do 'em if I not ready. Why you ask me dat kine questions anyway?"

A thin smile broke slowly across Luke's face. He was quiet for a moment, rearranging Lego furniture, moving the pieces about in his house. "'Cause funny, dat's why," he finally said. "Ev'ry time I ask in front Vicky, you get all antsy, like you gotta make doo-doo."

Luke giggled, but I didn't. "So you doing 'em on purpose?"

"Yeah, just like da time—" He stopped and looked at me.

I didn't like the sound of that. "Like *what* time?" I snapped.

Luke's face softened as he smiled broadly. He was about to say something but stopped. He chuckled, snorting under his breath. Luke finally took a deep breath and then exhaled only two words in a long, painful whisper. It was a plea I had definitely heard before: "*Help me . . .* "

For a moment, Luke and I just looked at each other. His words echoed: Help me. Help me! HELP ME! Suddenly, I was back running out of the storm drain as fast as I could with Toby. I felt the splash of dirty water all over again, feet carrying us out of the darkness and away from somewhere we shouldn't have been.

"Dat was you?" I asked, trying to stop the rush of memories. Luke smiled and nodded. "No way. You neva know we was in da storm drain." Luke was so mental he wasn't capable.

Luke made a face. "Could hear you guys from da front yard. Afta you pass da gutter by our house, I wen' whisper real loud what Toby said. But instead of 'can I help you,' I wen' change 'em to 'help me.' More scary li'dat, ah?"

No way. Luke couldn't pull off a joke like that. "What about da flashlight?"

"I seen you guys drop 'em. Get light from da manhole and da gutter, ah? Later, I snuck inside da storm drain and found 'em. Shoulda seen your face wen you seen 'em on your bed."

Luke and I stared into each other's eyes. He wanted to laugh but held it in, waiting to see what I was going to do. I thought back over the last year, realizing my assumptions about Luke had been all wrong. A smile finally broke as I shook my head. I always thought Luke couldn't see that much. Right then, we both busted out laughing.

Without any warning, I jumped on Luke and started tickling him. Since he was still a lot smaller than me, I circled my hands around his entire body and pinned him down. It was only a couple of minutes before we were both gasping from laughing so hard, but it was more than enough. Luke and I lay on the carpet, trying to catch our breath. And as the room swirled above us in waves of laughter, I couldn't help but wonder what else Luke could see.

When I went to see Mrs. Ka'ea, I asked about the Michigan woman who burned her husband alive. Mrs. Ka'ea explained how the woman tried to let things simmer down between her and the guy who was technically her ex-husband, how she appeared normal on the outside but was actually losing it on the inside, stewing and plotting out her only chance at freedom. We sat at the kitchen table as the ocean crashed angrily outside.

Mrs. Ka'ea smiled. "Why are you asking about this, Landon?"

"Just curious," I lied, not wanting to tell the truth. It had been three weeks since Mom ripped up the *Complaint for Divorce* and the *Summons to Answer Complaint*. I hadn't told Mrs. Ka'ea, though. How was I supposed to tell her that not only did I steal the divorce papers from her, but Mom had shit all over the very idea?

"Well, I don't think the Michigan woman was thinking clearly, Landon." Mrs. Ka'ea checked the time and then stood. "Besides, given the chance, I'm pretty sure she'd choose to do things differently." She arched her eyebrows and smiled again as she headed to the oven.

Mrs. Ka'ea wouldn't be smiling if she knew what I was thinking. I just *knew* something was coming at home, something big. The pressure was building. Mom had been so quiet she must be on edge . . . stewing and plotting, just like the Michigan woman. I thought about what that would mean for me and Luke. I didn't want anything bad to happen to Dad, but Mom made her choice when she crumpled the papers in my face. Why should I help her now? Why should anyone?

Another wave thundered outside and echoed through the house. I looked out as the spray reached toward the sky. The rainbow shimmer was so vibrant it seemed almost palpable. And then it all just faded and fell.

Mrs. Ellory said some storms faded, but others got more intense. She drew a cyclone swirling in red ink on a transparency of the Hawaiian Islands. She said there was a storm out in the Pacific Ocean at this very moment called 'Iwa. It was still a long way off and pretty weak. If it got stronger, swelled into a hurricane, and headed north a little, there might not be any school in a couple of days. Some kids in class began cheering, but Mrs. Ellory scolded them.

Her eyes were calm and steady. "How can you be excited about a hurricane?"

"'Cause there might not be school tomorrow," Bronson Simeon responded simply.

"When I said there might not be any school in a couple of days, I meant there might not be any school *left*." And that was when it hit. Everyone got quiet. "Hurricanes are extremely dangerous with nothing to cheer about. They have no regard for human life. Some people may even die because they didn't prepare properly. Everyone here should go home and stress to your parents to stock up on canned goods, tape your windows, and call relatives who live at higher elevations because you might need a place to stay."

The class was silent, still thinking about Mrs. Ellory's words. I glanced around. Everyone looked frantic and lost, eyes wandering with nowhere to go. It must be the first time they ever thought something like that. But now they knew it, too. Something big was coming.

It was something I should be thankful for. Luke didn't ask any questions while we walked home with Vicky. He wanted to when he saw me and Vicky holding hands. Every few steps, he peeked on the sly, glancing at our fingers snugly interlocked, and the whole time, I could tell he wanted to say something. But he didn't. And I was glad for that.

Later, sprawled out on our bedroom floor, Luke played with his Lego house and *Star Wars* figures. I listened to him move things about as he unsnapped and re-snapped plastic. I let the sound fade into the background. I stared into the jade frog between my fingers, the one I found in the ocean a few months ago. I twirled my good luck slowly so that I could see all the angles. I held it up to the light as shafts of rainbows shot out like arrows.

I squinted my eyes, and the colors stretched into thicker bands. "Hey, Luke, thanks fo' not asking nothin' today wen we was walking home."

"Nah, no worry. But why you no just kiss her already?" Luke looked at me.

Why was he so focused on kissing? I put the jade frog in my pocket. "I dunno. I mean, I like, but I no like rush either. Nah, pretty soon." But I'd be lying if I said I hadn't been wondering about it lately. It was something both Vicky and I wanted to do. Vicky's eyes often held me stock-still, exploring the skin between my eyes and my lips. I always looked away, though, not wanting to get swept up into it. Her eyes were so powerful. I wanted to be ready. I wanted to choose when. I didn't want to fuck up like Dad. And Mom.

"Earth to Landon," Luke said, drawing my attention back to him. He had picked up Princess Leia and Darth Vader and held them face to face. "Not dat hard, Landon, just put your guys' lips like dis—" Luke pressed the two action figures together, making juicy, slurping, smooching noises between them.

I watched my brother and wondered if he really was this off. Just when I thought he had things figured out, he did something weird. Proof positive: he already knew Han Solo and Princess Leia were together. They should be the ones kissing. "You mental, or what? Look who you making kiss. You know who Princess Leia and Darth Vader, or what?"

Luke smirked at such a silly question. "Yeah, dat's Mom and Dad."

Everything stopped. "What?" I sat up in bed, facing Luke.

Luke side-eyed me. "I not one dummy, I know what go on in dis house. Dat's why I make Princess Leia and Darth Vader fight now, 'cause dat's Mom and Dad."

"Dad not Han Solo?" I asked.

Luke scoffed as if I was the mental one. "No. *You* Han Solo. Dad's da . . . *bad* guy."

This was the second time in the last few days Luke had surprised me, so I decided to test it further. "Hold it. Why you do dumb tings den, like playing *Star Wars* figures in church, or like da Halloween-underwear ting last year, or like playing Lego in da living room wen you know not suppose to? Dat's pretty dumb to me."

Luke furrowed his brow in thick ripples of skin. "'Cause funny, dat's why. Ev'rytime, ev'rybody just get more and more mad. But not me, I just laugh. But if I do somethin' li'dat, den ev'rybody forget why dey was mad in da first place. And just li'dat, problem solved. I no care if I get yell at. But I not one dummy and I not mental, so no call me dat no more."

And just like that, as simple as asking the question, my brother emerged right before my eyes. It was something I hoped for so long to see, something I hoped for so long to be a part of. And as Luke revealed himself, I watched the shreds of his deceit unwind in slow circles, the pieces he spun high into a wall and then into a house he could understand and hide in. I looked at the swirling scraps that now floated calmly around the room, knowing Luke wouldn't need them for long. I stared at my brother and felt a smile creep across my lips. It was like seeing Luke for the first time, and I liked what I saw.

"I promise, Luke. I neva call you dat again." 'Cause now I knew. Mrs. Kato was right. Luke probably was G.T. He saw just as much as I did but had been doing more for a long time now. But he wouldn't have to do anything like call the cops anymore. It wouldn't be long until the storm hit.

I saw it first. Luke and I were almost home from school when I noticed a strange car in front of our house. A Chevy Monte Carlo? Like the ones cops use. As we made our way down Pupu Street, a million thoughts raced through my mind. But the one in the forefront: did *it* happen? Did Mom finally do something to Dad? And even if I was still pissed at Mom, the first thing I felt was . . . sad. I didn't get it. Shouldn't I be glad? That was when I knew I needed to talk with Mrs. Ka'ea. Oh, God. What did I do? Whatever Mom did to Dad was my fault.

When we got to the front door, I held Luke back. I didn't want him seeing anything so I peeked my head through the screen door first. I didn't know what to expect, maybe blood or guts, Dad lying on the linoleum in the kitchen like Rosie was outside. But all I could make out was a man in a suit, sitting at the kitchen table. He was talking to Mom who also sat.

"It was an anonymous phone call, Mrs. DeSilva," the man said. "But the caller said your son described skidding down the steps at school like he was," the man paused as he referred to his tablet, "'riding a bumpy slide.' It was enough to raise a red flag for her. And, frankly, it was enough for me too."

Suddenly, I knew who this man was and why he was here. I had only told that thing about the *bumpy slide* to Mrs. Ka'ea. I quickly yanked Luke inside and let the screen door hiss shut. Still sitting, the man turned around and eyed me and Luke frozen by the front door. He was Japanese and dressed really nice, with a tie even. He took a sip of coffee. Mom slowly stood. I tried to get a read on her, but her expression gave nothing away. When she spoke, her voice was hollow. "Landon, take your brother to your room . . . please."

I ushered Luke forward, but before I turned the corner, I saw the man's eyes as he inspected my legs. He knew.

In our room, Luke flung his backpack at the foot of the bed and then climbed onto his bunk. "Who dat, Landon?"

It was hard for me to hide my smile. However, by the time I closed our bedroom door, I had it under control. The man was a good thing. Mom would have to stop hitting us now. But I also didn't want to push it by making it worse for her, considering how bad things were between Mom and Dad. Mom could just as easily lose it and take it out on us anyway. I stood on my bed and looked intently at my brother. "Luke, just keep quiet, 'kay? If he come in here, only answer wen he ask you somethin'." I waited for Luke to respond. "Okay?"

Luke had no clue what was going on, but he finally nodded.

I sat down at the desk and waited.

After a few minutes, the door opened. The man came in and set the door in place behind him. Luke sat up in bed, his legs dangling over the edge. The man stepped forward and offered his hand. "You must be Landon," he said. I stood slowly and met him in the middle of the room. After we shook, he handed me a card. "My name is Glen Nakasone. I'm a caseworker with Child Protective Services. Do you know what that is?" I nodded, not sure what else to say. "Can you do me a favor, Landon? Can you turn around so I can see the back of your legs?" I rotated and saw Luke's confused expression. "You can face me again, Landon, thanks." Mr. Nakasone scribbled in his tablet and spoke as he wrote. "Eight inch welts, prolonged, both legs." Then he asked Luke to do the same. When Mr. Nakasone was done, he indicated the card in my hand. "Things should get better. But if this happens again, you make sure you call me, okay?" I nodded and thanked him. I nudged Luke, and then he did too. Mr. Nakasone smiled and left.

But he evidently stayed and talked to Mom for almost an hour. Luke and I watched from our room when he got into his Monte Carlo and drove away. And then we waited. I wondered what kind of mood Mom was going to be in and how long we had to wait to find out. Mercifully, it was only a few minutes later when Mom opened our bedroom door. Luke and I both sat upright in bed. She stood in the doorway appraising us. Without a word, she went to our closet and removed all of our shorts, making a pile on the floor. Then she grabbed a pair of jeans from my side of the closet and one from Luke's. She slung them over the desk and then stood over us. She spoke curtly through clenched teeth. "I don't give a damn how hot it is in this godforsaken town. For the next couple of weeks, you will both wear long pants to school. Do you understand me?" I nodded and assumed that Luke did the same. Mom turned around, scooped up our pile of shorts, and then stormed down the hallway.

When she was gone, Luke started to whine. "I no like wear jeans—"

I stood quickly. "Shut up, Luke. Don't you get it?" He shook his head, surprised by my tone. "Mom and Dad just got busted. She like us use jeans so da bruises heal."

Luke still looked confused. "So?"

I exhaled in frustration. "Luke, how long take fo' bruises go away?"

Luke made a face. "I dunno. Couple weeks. But why she wen' . . . " he trailed off, the idea finally dawning on him.

"You know why she like us use jeans now?"

Luke smiled. "'Cause she not going hit us no more. She no like nobody from school rat her out while da buggahs disappear."

I finally allowed the smile to break on my face. "Dat's right. And you know what da best part?" Luke shook his head. "Mom tinks was somebody from school wen' report her."

"What?" Luke asked, his forehead creased. "You mean wasn't somebody from school?"

I shook my head and backpedaled a bit. "Nah, I guess fo' you da best part is you no need use Humpty Dumpty no more. But fo' me, it's Mom tinking was one of my teachas."

Luke looked at me funny. "Why is *dat* da best?"

Not only did Mom have no clue Mrs. Ka'ea reported her, but nothing had happened to Dad either. "It just is."

Mrs. Ka'ea was surprised to see me since it was already after dark. When Dad had come home, Mom told him about Glen Nakasone from C.P.S., and another fight erupted. I knew I'd be able to sneak out for a short time without being missed. Mrs. Ka'ea asked me if everything was all right. I said everything was fine but that I needed to talk with her.

Sitting on Mrs. Ka'ea's couch in her living room, I wanted to come clean, but it was hard to say. I didn't want Mrs. Ka'ea to think less of me. My insides strained so tightly 'cause I knew I had to say something. Mrs. Ka'ea sat down, letting me fumble for the words.

"I dunno, I mean, I wanted fo' tell you right away, but—" I couldn't say it. I felt the guilt as it smeared across my stomach.

Mrs. Ka'ea's voice was calm and patient. "But what, Landon?"

I looked down into my lap as the tears began to come. "But I was shame."

Mrs. Ka'ea slid closer on the sofa, curling her arm over my shoulder. "Landon, what on earth do you have to be ashamed about?"

I looked at her miserably. "I stole da divorce papers from you, Mrs. Ka'ea. And den I wen' lie wen you was only trying fo' help me."

Mrs. Ka'ea sat there and let me cry. After a while, she rubbed my back. "Landon?"

Amazingly, Mrs. Ka'ea didn't sound angry. How? I sheepishly glanced up.

Mrs. Ka'ea just looked back sympathetically. "I knew you took those papers, Landon. After you left, I checked under the stack first thing."

I wiped at my eyes. "You knew, and you neva scold me?"

Mrs. Ka'ea chuckled good-naturedly. "Why would I? If you had asked for them, I would've had to give them to you. They're official, public documents. They're not mine." She brushed away hair from my face. "But more importantly, Landon, I knew *why* you took them. And why you lied to me."

I couldn't believe it. "You not mad at me?"

Mrs. Ka'ea smiled and waved it away as if it was nothing. "Heavens, no. You want to tell me what happened to those papers, though?"

My expression soured. It all came screaming back. "My modda wen' rip 'em up."

Mrs. Ka'ea sighed. "Sounds about right." She took a deep breath. "Landon, I think what you tried to do was a fine and wonderful thing. You tried to get your mom to realize there was a better way." She waited until I looked at her again. "Remember what I said before, though? Whatever happens between your parents, *they* have to come to it on their own." Mrs. Ka'ea winked. "But sometimes, you know, something drastic happens, and it helps people to start thinking about things."

And with that, I felt all the shame and all the guilt flood out so fast and hard my eyes stung. I would've let Mom do something bad to Dad. And yet Mrs. Ka'ea still thought I was worth the trouble of contacting C.P.S. I covered my face with both hands.

"What's the matter, Landon?"

Everything had fallen into place. I tried to control my breathing. "Why you so nice to me? I not a good person, Mrs. Ka'ea."

Mrs. Ka'ea took my face in both her palms. "Landon, don't say that—"

"I not! I came mad wen Mom wen' rip up da papers and threw 'em in my face. Felt like she no care about me and Luke, so if she not going care, I not." I frowned and sniffled. Mrs. Ka'ea rubbed my back again as my body heaved. "I neva like live wit' Mom no more, so I neva said nothin' to nobody. I figured just leave her be, pretty soon she going snap." I searched Mrs. Ka'ea's eyes to see if she understood. "What kind person would do dat? I woulda let her do somethin' bad to Dad, just like dat Michigan woman did." I wiped my eyes with the back of my hand. "Why call C.P.S. fo' help somebody like me? I no deserve good stuffs li'dat."

Mrs. Ka'ea squinted as she began to piece it together. "So you were hoping something would happen. And if so, then you and your brother would have to be put up for adoption?" I couldn't look at Mrs. Ka'ea, but I nodded. My eyes were dripping again. I already knew Mrs. Ka'ea was disappointed in me and honestly, I couldn't blame her. I wasn't who she thought I was. I couldn't possibly be the same boy who was friends with her Toby. I was so disgusting 'cause I would have stood by and let Dad get hurt. I could feel the words already. *Get out of this house. Now. And never come back.* But when she spoke, her voice was gentle. "Landon?"

I looked up at a blurry Mrs. Ka'ea and blurted my question before she could ask hers. "Bad fo' feel li'dat, yeah?" I stared at her, waiting for her wrath.

But instead, she smiled. "Actually, Landon, I think it's pretty normal to feel that way. It's not your fault you feel mad."

I couldn't believe what I was hearing.

"But would you really want your dad to die?" she asked. I shook my head no. "Would you really want your mom to go to jail?" I shook my head again. "Good. Then I'm glad I called C.P.S. At least now you don't have to worry anymore."

I wiped my nose with the sleeve of my shirt. "Why?"

Mrs. Ka'ea smiled wryly. "Don't you think it's pretty *drastic* for parents to have C.P.S. come into their home and check up on them?" She raised her eyebrows meaningfully.

It took me a moment, but then I got it. Mrs. Ka'ea was so smart. "Dey going make Mom and Dad tink about what's best fo' us."

Mrs. Ka'ea nodded. "Your caseworker will at least make them consider the possibility of divorce as a better alternative to what's going on now. And since they know they're under a microscope, not only will you and your brother be safe, but they'll think twice about the way they *interact* with each other." She grinned and arched her eyebrows in self-satisfaction.

With moist eyes, I stared in disbelief. "So you not mad, or . . . or disappointed wit' me?"

Mrs. Ka'ea shook her head. "Well, I won't be, if you tell me one thing. And you have to promise to tell me the truth." I nodded eagerly, wiped my eyes again, and then waited. Mrs. Ka'ea grinned artfully. "I had been wondering about this for a while now. Does your name mean anything? I told you about my names, but you never told me about yours."

I choked on snot as Mrs. Ka'ea chuckled. She must have known she caught me off guard. I wiped my nose. "Um, I dunno about my last name, but my modda was da one who name me Landon. Mom said she always like da name Landon 'cause Michael Landon. She use to watch one old TV show wit' her mom and dad, and one of da actors was Michael Landon. And wen *Little House on the Prairie* came out, she would watch all da time. And wen I was still real small and Luke was only one baby, Mom whisper in my ear while we watching *Little House on the Prairie.* She tell me she love Michael Landon, 'cause dat's how one fadda should be, strong and kind, so watch him close. I neva know what she mean back den, but I tink I do now."

Mrs. Ka'ea nodded slowly and sighed. "You know, Landon, I can't think of anyone better you should be named after." Mrs. Ka'ea smiled as the buzzer went off on the stove. She stood and made for the kitchen. But instead, she stopped, bent low, and gave me a long hug. It didn't matter if there was a drowning buzz in the kitchen. Mrs. Ka'ea leaned back so that she could look into my eyes. "Remember, my door is always open for you, Landon. And, in the future, if you have to live far from Pupu Street, I'm still just a phone call away. Okay?"

The air over 'Ewa Beach was hot, thick, and damp. No rain yet, but our teachers released us early from school 'cause it was going to pour. They said the hurricane was coming, so for us to hurry home and stay safe. As Luke, Vicky, and I walked home, I noticed there was no breeze whistling about anymore. In fact, there hadn't been any wind at all since yesterday. This must be what Mrs. Ellory meant by the calm before the storm. Just as we got to Pohakupuna Road, everything dimmed as if a light switch had been flipped. The three of us looked at the sky. Dark gray clouds rolled over each other, full of potential. We all stared upward in silence, knowing this wasn't normal. Vicky's fingers curled into mine, grasping tighter.

A voice ripped through the quiet. It was Mom. "Landon, what are you two doing, looking into the sky like a couple of dummies?" She had pulled up in her car and was yelling out the window at us. Then Mom saw Vicky. And then our hands. Her eyes narrowed as she shook her head. "And who's *this*, Landon?" Mom raised her hand as if to stop me from speaking. "You know what? Never mind. Just get in the car, we're going home."

Vicky's fingers loosened, but I held on tight as I looked in the car windows. "You going throw away some plants?" I asked. "No more place fo' sit." There were potted rose bushes on the front seat and a hapu'u fern and potted ti leaf plants in the back. Branches hung out the windows. "And Mom, dis Vicky. My . . . girlfriend. And I walking her home."

Mom inhaled deeply and sneered. The car revved loud. "Luke, get in, we're going—"

But I cut her off. "Luke coming wit' me. It's my job fo' walk him home safe. We both going walk wit' Vicky, and den we coming home." Luke slid behind me as if to hide.

Mom's expression smoothed out but it wasn't hard to see what lingered just beneath. "Don't worry, I'll be home when you *both* get there." Mom jerked the car into gear as she muttered something about how I was whoring already. She stepped on the gas and peeled out, tires spitting gravel and sand at our feet. We all watched as Mom turned onto Pupu Street, not even slowing at the stop sign. Luke looked up at me and smiled. I nodded at him, knowing exactly what he meant. We needed to stick together. Nobody would come between us.

When we got to Vicky's house, Luke said he'd just wait on the wall by the mailbox. Just don't take too long. And then he winked at me.

At Vicky's door, she turned and faced me. Everything started to slow. Even though the afternoon was getting dark, Vicky's face glowed orange, caught momentarily in a pocket of light. And her eyes! A fiery auburn, like twin stars streaked with yellow. I already knew what was coming. Vicky twirled her hair around and around until it was thick enough to hold all at once. Then she gripped it against her chest. She looked down nervously and then back up at me with those wide, light brown eyes that were still ablaze with the color of sunset. "You really meant I your girlfriend? You neva said 'em before." I nodded, feeling right now as the moment of jumping in, like hovering over an eight-foot drop into the ocean. It was a moment of finally letting everything go. I felt a smile that had been wanting to surface for a long time now. Vicky reached out and wrapped her arms around me, her hands fitting into the grooves of my back. As we hugged, I was amazed at how snugly we fit together. I inhaled and was suddenly back in the cafeteria dancing with Vicky, lost in the sway of our bodies.

As Vicky leaned back to look at me, arms still holding us together, I remembered that I wanted to give her something. I reached into my pocket, removed my jade frog, and placed it in my palm. I wanted Vicky to have it. "Dis my lucky frog. If you hold 'em up to da light, I promise you going see somethin' magical."

Vicky gazed at the cloudy, green jade, gently touching the frog with her index finger. She said for me to wait, that she just thought of something and she'd be right back. Vicky ran into the house. After a couple of minutes, she sidled out the front door and reached for my hand. She turned it over, palm up. Vicky placed a small, crystal heart in it. Then she covered both of my hands with hers, our fingers locking and our gifts between. "Dis my lucky charm. My heart. On da back is da Chinese symbol fo' *Remember.* So I always rememba what I love. I like you have 'em now, so you always rememba too."

With words like that, it was easy to choose. So I let it happen.

With Vicky's words swirling above us, with words that made me smile instead of cry, I couldn't help but lean close. I felt her exhale a ripple of breath that washed clean against my skin. And as our lips touched for the very first time, as I felt just how soft she really was, as I closed my eyes, I wondered why this had been such a hard choice to make. Kissing Vicky felt . . . right. Like surfing. Like an answered prayer. Like . . . Heaven. And through spinning thoughts, through this new world opened before me, I heard a whisper as I remembered:

I don't want to fuck up like Dad. And Mom.

But as Vicky and I continued to kiss, I realized I didn't have to worry. She had put her heart into my hand. She trusted me, and I knew enough from listening to Mom and Dad to know that was a rare and precious thing. But I also knew I would do whatever it took so that she'd *always* trust me. Right then, I smiled 'cause I knew it would never be like Mom and Dad. I would always have love first.

Before Luke and I even got near the house, we already knew what was coming. Dad was home early from work. His Chevy was in the garage, the keys were on the seat, and the car was still warm. Mom's voice suddenly boomed, roaring like thunder. Sounded like they just started.

The street was so quiet it was easy to hear everything in the kitchen. I listened to both of their voices, going around in circles. Luke looked through the window, and he frowned.

"Tell me the truth, Leonard. You think I don't see the matchbooks from all the different hotels? Work conventions? Right. What an alibi. And the company's paying for it? That many times with *overnight* accommodations? No way. At expensive hotels like the Ilikai and the Royal Hawaiian? And now the Hilton Hawaiian Village too? Sorry, it's too perfect. Huge, classy, *romantic* hotels, and how convenient, they all have ballrooms for your . . . *conventions.* I'm not stupid, Leonard. They also have *bedrooms.*

"All this time I was hoping you were just buying more of your toys with all the money. Did you know I went by your workplace *again?* That's right, today, and you weren't there *again.* Even after asking your co-workers and seeing the truth written on their faces, I still didn't want to believe. I still had hope in us. In spite of all the signs telling me otherwise, I thought you still gave a damn. How naïve. I prayed to God you weren't doing me that way, Leonard, the whole time never questioning where all our money went. But now I know."

Dad's arms spread out at the sides, high above his shoulders. "What'chu like hear, Minerva? Hah?" Luke's jaw clamped down hard, his teeth grinding loudly.

Mom's words came slow and thick. "Tell . . . me . . . the . . . *truth* . . . Leonard."

Dad shook his head. "And what if it's ova? Hah? What if we been ova fo' long time?"

Mom yelled so loud her voice broke. "*What*?" It was the cry of a wounded animal. Mom's voice echoed, dragging down the street the carcass of the only word she could utter.

At this point, I pulled Luke by the arm and snuck through the front door to our bedroom. I told him to forget his homework. Luke put down his bag, still looking toward the kitchen at the sounds punching through the house. His face was different. I could tell he was holding on and coiling tighter. I wanted it to stop, and fast. First, I grabbed the crumpled wads of divorce paperwork, the same ones Mom threw at me. Next, I pulled out the matchbook I took from Dad's nightstand and told Luke to grab his composition notebook. When he removed it from his bag, I noticed it was the same one from last year. Perfect. Last, I selected two of Luke's *Star Wars* action figures. Princess Leia and Darth Vader. Then I told Luke to follow me.

Behind the garage, I told Luke to tear out whatever assignments he no longer wanted in his notebook. He went straight for the ones from last year that were soaked with Mrs. Shelley's screaming red handwriting. We shredded and crumpled those first few assignments as well as the divorce papers, making a pile in the dirt. Luke asked what we were doing, but I just said this was how I made myself feel better after Toby died. It helped me to say good-bye, and since he understood pretty much everything, he should know how to say it too. Luke continued to rip out sheets of paper while I grabbed Dad's lighter fluid. When I came back, I told Luke to step back. I placed Princess Leia and Darth Vader on the crinkly mound and then squirted lighter fluid over everything. Clear liquid gushed out, soaking paper and drying in milky streaks over the plastic people. I watched fumes rise like white fingers, swirling about us. I inhaled the burn.

I handed Luke the can of lighter fluid and then tore a match from the matchbook. When I struck the match, it sizzled alive like a yellow-orange teardrop dancing across my fingertips. I looked at Luke. He stood there waiting with wide, glowing eyes. I told him to say good-bye.

Then I dropped the match. Once I let go, it was something I couldn't stop.

When the match hit, fumes were swallowed by flames, like a blossom of light reaching up toward us. The flower of heat bathed warm against our faces. Luke leaned in to watch.

Through a veil of fire, white paper faded black and crinkled like old, sun-burnt skin, finally crumbling away. Princess Leia started to sweat black beads down her face, her hair dripping off like make-up and eyeliner smeared by crying. And Darth Vader, flattening out, started to expand as he melted, getting thinner the longer he lay in one place.

I kept adding more paper, so the fire didn't stop.

It was a glowing blanket for two people who would soon vanish. Flames licked easily through each sheet of paper until not only were Mrs. Shelley's words gone but so were the *Complaint for Divorce* and *Summons to Answer Complaint*, curling into crispy flakes that broke off and tumbled into the heat. Underneath, Princess Leia and Darth Vader spread out in two soft puddles. One white, one black. And as the fire kept burning, the plastic from each figure bled closer to the other. The two puddles finally came together in a thick, painful embrace, white stabbing into black, black grabbing onto white.

Dad's car roared out front, drawing my attention from the fire. I glanced around the back of the garage only to see Dad's car reverse out of the driveway, then speed down Pupu Street. I heard the screen door hissing shut and then just glimpsed Mom as she turned back into the house. I knew that something big just happened.

When I went back behind the garage, I almost didn't understand what I saw. Luke held the can of lighter fluid and was squeezing more onto the fire. Why was he doing that? Luke knew he should never to do that, right? That he should never squirt lighter fluid onto an open flame . . . right? And then everything suddenly sped up. Oh, shit. I never warned him not to.

It all happened so fast I couldn't do anything. I couldn't even yell to warn him. I could only watch as leafy, writhing flames shot upward, as though climbing out of the fire and up the stream of liquid to the can he still held. I didn't know if he saw it or felt it first, but just before the flames reached his hands, Luke flung the can away and began to turn.

But it wasn't fast enough or far enough.

The can exploded, a dazzling blast that splashed Luke with liquid fire. The force of the explosion knocked Luke off his feet and sent him tumbling in the dirt. The blast sounded like a gunshot, rolling over itself across a dark, 'Ewa Beach sky. When I got to Luke, he squirmed in the dirt, rubbing his arm and one side of his body with his hands, screaming for me to get it off of him. All over his side, dots of glowing, metallic embers, red and hot, melted into juicy, raw flesh. I grabbed the water hose and turned it on full blast, dousing Luke while trying to flick the specks off as fast as I could. Some were so deep I couldn't get them out.

Mom came running and when she saw the fire, she yanked the water hose from me and put the blaze out. Luke moaned loudly now. I was trying to pick him up when Mom shoved me, yelling to get the hell out of the way, that I had done enough for one day. She hoisted Luke's limp body with quick upward jerks and then carried him inside. I lingered there on my knees, watching her disappear into the house. And as the screen door hissed shut, I felt it start. Thick, heavy plops of rain pocked the dirt around me. A few at first, but without warning, the sky fell as thousands of crystal drops pummeled me. I felt the sting of each, like painful reminders that I could've just killed Luke. I stared into the needles of water coming down. I imagined going into hyperspace, hoping this was all just a bad dream. But instead of flying away, I found myself out in the rain, afraid of what I was hearing. The storm was far from over. A hurricane was coming.

By the time I even thought of going back in the house, it was black dark outside. None of our neighbors had any lights on. What was even stranger, though, was that no streetlights came on either. It was like Pupu

Street was deserted. I could only hear the hum of rain and the wheezing gusts of wind that had come to life again. Even our house was dark. Why weren't the lights on? It felt weird, strange. So peaceful. Maybe too peaceful. I got off my knees and sloshed through the rain, out of the mud behind the garage and toward a dark house. When I opened the screen door, I realized I was soaked. Yet one more reason to get yelled at. But at this point, I didn't care. I just wanted to know how Luke was doing.

As the screen door shut, I flicked the light switch but nothing happened. That's when I saw Mom bending over the couch in the living room, shining a flashlight on Luke. Only her chest and face glowed. Everything else faded into shadows. She was taping Scott towels over Luke's burns. Mom didn't look at me. In the dark, I couldn't tell if Luke was moving or not. My stomach lurched, and my fear found its way out of my mouth. "Mom?" Nothing, no response. Her hands kept moving over Luke's body. "Mom?"

She swung her head. "What?" Mom snapped.

I fumbled for the words. "Is . . . Luke . . . okay?"

Mom turned back to Luke, ripping off another piece of Scotch tape. "No, does it look like he's okay? He's burned and he's got Scott towels for bandages. I can't even go to the fucking store because it's closed."

"Is Luke *going* be okay?" It was what I really wanted to know.

Mom looked at me again, this time straightening up. The flashlight made a spotlight on the floor, illuminating her at the same time. "No, he won't be okay. He'll have scars for the rest of his life because of you. I expect this kind of crap from him, but not you, Landon."

"I was only trying fo' help—"

Mom yelled, cutting me off. "Help? How in the world is *this* helping?" She pointed at Luke and then ranted on sarcastically. "You want to help, Landon? How about you convince the electric company to turn the power back on during the hurricane so I can at least see what the hell I'm doing? Or better yet, convince your father to take time out from his little tryst, so he can drive home and give me back my car keys, so I can then take Luke to the fucking doctor your father's not even going to want to pay for."

I didn't understand. "Dad took your keys?" Mom smirked and nodded. "Why?"

"I told him I'd find him and his little hussy. Even if it meant driving around Waikīkī all night in this storm."

I couldn't believe it. So if Luke needed to see a doctor tonight, he might not be able to? 'Cause of Mom and Dad's fighting? The idea of the C.P.S. suddenly seemed so pointless it was almost funny. "What about one ambulance?"

Mom scoffed at me. "Look around, genius. No lights, no electricity, no phones. The lines are down already. We're stuck here tonight."

Why was it all so impossible to Mom? "How about da neighbors? Dey can drive us."

Mom seethed. "Go look up and down Pupu Street, brainiac. Nobody's home."

"Why we no can start walking den? We can carry Luke, take him doctor."

Mom laughed viciously. "Start walking? As shitty as it is, it's still safer if we stay put. But if you think you can *outrun* a hurricane, by all means, be my guest." She indicated the door. "Let me know how that turns out."

My anger and frustration grew into words. "Why *you* wen' let Dad take your keys den?"

Mom's expression soured. "Oh, sorry, I'm sure your father would have left my keys if he knew what you had planned for this evening. What the hell were you thinking, Landon?"

I couldn't believe this. Mom was blaming *me*. I looked at Luke and knew what I wanted to say. I looked at Luke and felt it rising. Mom had so many opportunities to change, so many chances to avoid this, and she blamed me? I looked at Luke and felt the pressure within. I looked at Luke and knew it had to be now. "At least *I* did somethin'. I tried fo' help Luke feel betta. You only fight wit' Dad. You no care about us. If you did, *you* would do somethin'. You would listen to da C.P.S. guy. You would ask people at church fo' help. At least do somethin'! But you no do nothin'. You blind to ev'ryting." My words echoed through a silent house.

For a moment, Mom didn't say anything. She just looked at me and tried to breathe evenly. "Fuck you. You hear me, damn, jerk kid? Fuck . . . you. Just like your goddamn father, blaming me for everything. Get out. Go and whore, just like him." Mom suddenly walked toward me, the beam from the flashlight slicing in front of her. "I said get out. Get out of this house now!" Mom screamed at me as she pushed me repeatedly against the screen door. I backed up, my hands flailing, trying to get her to stop. "How dare you raise your hands to me, you brat!" Then she started slapping me with an open hand, across any part of my head and face she could reach. "I said get out! Get out of here! Now!"

Then Mom really began hitting me, striking with both hands. Her right was a fist, and her left was a flashlight. Blow after blow connected: right, left, right, left. I screamed, saying sorry over and over. The only thing I could do was cover my face with my hands. With every impact, I saw more red, my head jolting each time with a flash across my eyes. But Mom just continued to punch. The entire time, I got dizzier and dizzier while Mom screeched like an animal, yelling for me to get out. And through it all, I heard Luke's voice crying out. "Please stop, Mom! You hurting him! Please stop!"

That was when I fell. Mom hit me so hard I ripped through the screen door, breaking the metal frame in the middle. I tumbled over backwards, tangled in a mesh of screen and metal like a caught fish writhing to be free. As I fell toward the porch, I felt the metal frame scratch down the length my back, then down my leg. And just before impact, I realized strangely that my feet were above me, somehow in the air, and that I was falling head first toward concrete. Something in me raced, some kind of impulse that shot my arms above my head so that I might soften the blow. But it was too late. Nothing could stop this once it started. My fingers touched first, only a fraction of a moment before my skull crunched into concrete.

Everything was fuzzy. A heavy thud pulsed forward from back of my head in stinging waves across my face. I could hear muffled noise but couldn't make out any words, only vibrations. I felt myself sit up, reach back, and touch at the base of my skull. Wet hair. Was that rain? When I looked at my hand, the tips of my fingers were smeared red. Blood? I felt myself trying to figure it out like I would homework, with the same dullness of thought. Was that really blood? How? Through the throb in my head, I heard the hook-and-eye on the screen door and Mom's voice say something. And then it connected. Screen door, Mom's voice, Mom coming: toward me. At me! FOR me! Something basic took over, my arms and legs scurrying backward into the rain, fearfully away from Mom. She reached down, asking if I was all right. But I kept scuttling over concrete, slipping but still trying to get to my feet. The more Mom tried to touch me, the more I thrashed, understanding only that I needed to run. And then, before I even realized it, I was already on my feet, already past the mailbox, already sprinting down Pupu Street.

Mom yelled my name over and over. For me to come back, the hurricane was coming.

Then Luke was calling my name. But at this point, I didn't care. Something inside told me to just keep running, so I did. And I didn't look back, not once.

Looking out the mouth of the storm drain, I watched sheets of rain dive to an angry ocean. Waves exploded into a constant drizzle that blew into the storm drain like a fog. In the dark and through this veil of mist, it was hard to tell where the sky ended and the ocean began.

I leaned against the concrete and let a heavy flow of water rush over my feet toward the opening. In the last half hour, the amount of drain water had risen at least four inches. I knew I wouldn't be able to stay here for long. Images flashed across my mind. I leaned my head back and closed my eyes. It was still so vivid: get out. Get out! GET OUT! Then . . . falling. I opened my eyes and felt it all down my face, from Mom's words to Luke's burns, scars that would never heal. This was all my fault. I never meant to hurt Luke.

I wanted so badly to talk to Mrs. Ka'ea, but her house was dark. She must be with relatives, waiting out the hurricane. She would know just what to say to help me see everything would be okay. But then again, would she? Would Mrs. Ka'ea be able to make *this* better? No matter what she suggested, no matter what I tried, nothing worked and things only got worse. Mom would never change. And if Mom got too good with her hands, like Dad . . .

My fear and panic rose so violently I started to shake. I didn't want me and Luke to be stuck with Mom. And if I reported Mom to Mr. Nakasone at C.P.S., he might make us stay with Dad. I shook my head. Mrs. Ka'ea was wrong. Mom and Dad didn't need the second chance. And after what I just did to Luke, neither did I. But Luke did.

Mrs. Ka'ea said something drastic would have to happen.

What could I do to make sure Luke wouldn't have to live with Mom or Dad anymore?

The wind whipped off the ocean and pulled my eyes out of the storm drain, over the edge of the rocky shore and into the thrashing surf below. The wind howled over the ocean, as though screaming the answer at me. I inched toward the opening to look down at the churning water. I suddenly understood. I imagined pouches of air jellyfishing toward the glassy surface. The calming sway. The water in my ears. It would finally be quiet. The more I thought about it, the more I knew I could do it for Luke. It was certainly . . . *drastic* enough. And with one kid instead of two, it should be easy for him to get adopted. I wondered if there was a way for Mrs. Kaʻea to get Luke. She said given the chance, she'd gladly adopt us. So that was what I'd give Luke: the chance.

I thought about Mom, how Mrs. Kaʻea said wives usually got the kids in a custody dispute. Then I thought about how badly Mom had hit me, how the warning from the C.P.S. didn't even matter, and how one day she would turn her sights on Luke. When that last thought hit, it was enough to convince me. Mom needed something drastic? Things weren't *bad enough* at home? Then I'd make them bad enough.

I instinctively dug in my pocket and removed Glen Nakasone's card. Seeing it now for what it was, just a soggy scrap of paper, the whole idea of the C.P.S. seemed like such a joke. No adult could help me. Without another thought, I shredded the card, letting the pieces fall into the rushing drain water like so much debris. I alone could make this right.

In my pocket was also Vicky's crystal heart. A gift from the girl with eyes the color of sunset. This afternoon, it meant love. But right now, the crystal felt cold and hard between my fingers, like a strange . . . betrayal. Like a dead promise. Was that the way it was supposed to be? Boys and girls paired up, convinced themselves they were in love, and then made boys and girls of their own, only to end up beating the shit out of their children later on? I slid the crystal heart into the small pouch inside my shorts and folded the flap securely shut. Let it die with me.

A heavy blast of wind came screaming off the ocean. It knocked me into the wall and sent me stumbling deeper into the storm drain, splashing onto all fours. I faced the mouth of the drain and rose slowly. Just outside, the air surged heavy with rain, swirling and slapping, no longer coming down from sky to ocean, but falling from side to side. There was now one long, blurry, convulsing wall of water across the opening. It seemed that God Himself was thrashing and howling 'cause of what I was about to do.

Then I heard the explosions of water below, a rising beat. It was the ocean, calling me, like so many times before. I closed my eyes and listened to the pulse of the ocean. It would be quiet down there. I could finally get some rest. My breathing became shallow. I knew it was a sin, but I didn't care. This was for Luke. This was the only way. I took a deep breath.

And, finally, I opened my eyes and started running. I ran toward the opening. I ran from what together Luke and I couldn't escape. I ran . . . so that Luke might get free. I ran as fast as I could out of the opening and into the storm.

And then I jumped.

27

Out of the storm drain, I took two last strides on wet lava rock and then leapt off one foot, springing as hard as I could into a thrashing blizzard of rain. I expected to plummet eight feet straight down into the roaring surf below. Instead, I felt something crunch into me.

Another screaming blast of air.

It was a solid punch from an invisible fist, and my body curled around the impact of wind. I flailed about, the world smearing before me, spraying fast like water from a nozzle. Everything was black and wet. Wind and rain stung my eyes, as questions whirled about me. Where was the splash? Where was the sinking? Hell, where was the ocean? I closed my eyes and just *felt.* Inside, everything rose and fell at the same time.

And just like that, I opened my eyes 'cause I knew what was happening.

I was flying.

Like shredding on Toby's surfboard.

Like looking up, lost in blue.

Like closing my eyes and making a wish.

It was a moment I would never forget. I was completely . . . *free.*

But as the moment passed, it gave way to another, and I was surprised by the fear it brought. Luke. He wouldn't be stuck with Mom or Dad anymore, but now, from way up here, that somehow wasn't enough. He'd be all alone, as untethered as I was now.

And that was when I wanted down. I didn't need to *save* Luke. I just needed to *be* with Luke. I could hear his voice accusing me, how my promises were nothing but lies. That was what my death would do to him. And in the very words I had said so many times before, that we'd always stick together,

I heard the truth. I needed my little brother just as much as he needed me. I might have wished for this flight more than anything, but I no longer wanted it. I wanted life. I wanted Luke.

That was when I felt the downward pull. I fell, spinning full speed in a tight spiral toward a black mass I figured must be the ocean. The surface came fast, and just before impact, I had just enough time to take a deep breath, knowing there was nothing left to do but land.

Being underwater in that way was so . . . final. It was completely black. I didn't try to fight the current. I just pinched my nose to make sure I didn't lose any air or let in any water. My body tumbled, somersaulting end over end. To keep calm, I began counting off how many seconds I had been under. I knew I had about two minutes. The pressure built with each revolution my body made, as if white-hot needles in my chest were burning outward.

It was almost thirty seconds later when I felt my back hit sand. At least that made it easy to know which way I had to go. I stood and sprang upward, but the force of water cycling was so strong it pushed me back down, splaying me all over the ocean floor. I squatted and tried with everything I had to launch off the ocean floor again. But once more, I was hurled back down, this time into a large coral boulder lodged in the sand. My chest started to burn as I clung to the rock, realizing just how powerful the current was. Oh, God. What have I done?

For a moment, I stopped, defeated. It all seemed so unfair. Now that I wanted to get back to Luke, I couldn't. Now that I finally understood how alone he'd be, I couldn't do anything about it.

But then I realized it wouldn't only be Luke. Mrs. Ka'ea would be alone . . . *again.* So would Vicky and Jason. Even Mrs. Kato and my G.T. teachers. How could I have not realized it before? There were so many people who believed in me, cared about me, reasoned with me. People who showed, helped, taught. And this was how I repaid them? By giving up?

I felt my body lurch.

No! I was not defeated. I was sick and tired of feeling that . . . low.

Tired of wishing on falling stars.

Tired of being pushed every which way.

And that was when I realized the answer was right in front of me. I was still clinging to a coral boulder. Up meant less water, less pressure than down here. By this point, my chest sizzled. I struggled as I mounted the coral, fighting against a current that wanted to rip me free and send me sailing deeper into the ocean. I gripped the jagged rock and didn't dare let go. Perched up here, I felt lighter already. Oh, God. Air. I needed air.

I crouched low on my coral boulder vista, knowing I'd only get one chance at this.

And when I felt the water cycle back once again, I punched off the coral as hard as I could, riding an upward current toward the surface. I knew I had to hold onto as much air as I could. I needed to remain as buoyant as possible. So when the same current bent back down, I broke free and soared upward through black to what I knew was the sky. Higher and higher I went, precious coins of air slipping out the closer I got to the surface. The water churned like wet fingers slipping over my body, unable to hold me down.

But the surface didn't come fast enough as red and blue pinpoints spread across my squinting eyes. I felt needles scorch all over my body, warm at first, then hot, then hotter. The burn got so bad I didn't think I could take it anymore. Then it suddenly faded away into nothing. Into numbness. And I let out more air. Bubbles tickled my face, while a thick glaze of unthinking crept as Jack Daniel's would across my mind. Everything was blurry, and I was so dizzy that after I broke the surface, I didn't even realize I was above water.

Even if I thought I was breathing, I couldn't tell for sure. I knew I bobbed over each wave, rising and falling on a strange tide of unfeeling. I bumped into a door, thinking how odd to find one in the water. I instinctively threw my arm over it like I would Toby's surfboard. And then I noticed all the debris as it teetered along with me. Tar paper from roofing. A trash can lid. Splintered two-by-fours. A box of Rinso and an empty litter box. Through the up and down motion of this shifting haze, I made out the shore. It wasn't the one behind Pupu Street. Out of a fog of thoughts, one lifted free. How far did I fly? And that was when I felt water splash my face. Then there was water in my ears. Were the waves trying to draw me under? I tried to move my legs, but I couldn't find them. I tried to breathe, but I couldn't feel a thing. I tried desperately to think, but everything blurred.

"No let go of dis door, Landon," I said, my body now convulsing with the need for air. "Just no let go."

When I finally dragged myself from the water, I collapsed face down on the sand. I was content to just breathe. After a few minutes, I rolled over and, even though the sky was still black, I realized where I was. 'Ewa Beach Park. Waves still thundered angrily, as the ocean roiled white with froth, like the spittle from a hungry animal. But now the rain drummed the sand next to me, no longer falling sideways. That meant a lull in the storm or maybe the eye of the hurricane. Or better yet, maybe the worst had passed. I took a deep breath and struggled to my feet. Whatever the case, it was time to get moving.

And then I saw the houses nestled along the shore. Some had cracked windows held together by tape, and others had doors blown in yet hanging on by a hinge. But some houses were far worse with sagging porches and roofs that were no longer there. As I made my way to the street, I realized the ocean might be the same, grumbling furiously as if nothing ever happened. But 'Ewa Beach was not the same. And neither was I.

All the way down 'Ewa Beach Road there was destruction. Onto Fort Weaver, then onto Pohakupuna, cars were flipped over, telephone poles tilted, and fences stretched across yards in twisted, splintered heaps like discarded fish bones. A stop sign was wedged into the outside wall of someone's living room, slicing into the wood just below a picture window. As I rounded the corner of Hailipo, in the middle of the road, I saw a mangled green street sign with white letters across it: PUPU St. I stood there, strangely amused by the absurdity of how some things could be put back together and made to look like nothing ever happened. While others, as sure as I was alive, had changed forever.

I bent down in the rain and touched the warped metal. I couldn't believe I had just tried to kill myself. How could I have been that blind? In the past year, I had been given so much. Luke, Mrs. Ka'ea, Vicky, Jason, Mrs. Kato and my G.T. teachers. They had all shown me a different way, a better way, and if I had given up underwater . . .

From now on, whatever happened between Mom and Dad no longer mattered. Killing myself seemed so silly now, so . . . juvenile. I couldn't believe I let Mom and Dad take me that low. I couldn't believe I had given anyone so much power over me. That would *never* happen again.

I stood and, since it seemed like the right thing to do, I dragged the mangled street sign up Hailipo, to the corner where it belonged. I rested the sign against a metal pole that, stripped of everything, now looked strangely out of place. I had walked by enough times to know it was missing two more signs: STOP and HAILIPO St. But then I glanced at Toby's house, and my heart sank. Almost every window was cracked or shattered. I hurried through to the backyard. Several exterior wall panels had craters punched into the paint while others had been ripped away entirely. The corner of the roof sagged. Rain was definitely getting inside. And then I saw what I was afraid of: Toby's surfboard and Jason's ankle weights were gone.

I faced the ocean and rested my hands on my hips. Gone, just like that. I took a deep breath. Funny, I had always figured that if I ever lost Toby's board it would feel like the end of the world. But the longer I thought about it, the more I realized it wasn't. It was oddly . . . okay. Seeing Mrs. Ka'ea's house in its broken condition, though, stung in a much deeper way. She'd need a lot of help in the coming weeks.

So that was where I'd be. And so would Luke. I didn't want him home with Mom or Dad anymore if I wasn't there. From now on, wherever I went, he went. And wherever he went, I went. I always thought I needed to *save* Luke. But all I really needed was to do what a big brother always should: take him with me. Even if it was just to Vicky's house, Luke would be coming from now on.

Then I remembered. Vicky. Her crystal heart. Shit. I patted down the front of my shorts. I groped at the waistband. Where was it? I folded back the flap on the inner pouch and dug inside. I suddenly wanted that heart very much. So when I finally felt it, the excitement burst through me like a pop of electricity. As I ran my thumb over the crystal, I could feel the inscription on the back of the heart. Vicky said it was the Chinese symbol for *Remember*. So that she remembered what she loved and so that I could too. I thought about all the people I came to love this past year. I closed my fingers around Vicky's crystal heart and held on tight. If there was one thing I learned tonight, it was that I didn't have to be like Mom or Dad. I had the power to choose, to be . . . different. And I would never forget it.

As I made my way back toward our house, I noticed Dad's car in the driveway. Funny, looking at his car now, I didn't feel a thing. Mom and Dad could get divorced tomorrow, and it wouldn't make any difference. I knew what I needed to do. As I walked up the sidewalk, I saw Mom's rose bushes scattered about, bodies strewn all over the yard with rust-red mounds of mud trailing each set of roots like clumps of drying blood. There were even mud splotches against the house. As I moved forward, out of the corner of my eye, I saw Dad's ham radio antenna. It was a crumpled mess of metal that no longer reached high into the sky. The bolts on the base held fast, so now the antenna appeared to sprawl face forward across the front yard, having been not only pushed over but squashed into the grass by torrents of wind.

Standing there in the rain, I inspected the house. Some louvers were missing and there were several dents in the outer wall. But no holes all the way through. Other than the rose bushes and the antenna, the house seemed okay. It could've been a lot worse. I glanced at our neighbors' houses. Next door, the Peraltas and the Higas had suffered about the same as we had. Across the street, so had the Fishers, Chings, and Gomeses. No better, no worse. It seemed curious, and even a bit unfair, that the DeSilvas would also escape the worst of Hurricane ʻIwa and come out on the other side of this okay. I chuckled to myself, imagining what our more prudent neighbors might say when they returned home tomorrow. Damn Portagees.

But when I looked back at the front of the house, I saw it: the mangled screen door. I absently reached up and felt the lump at the back my head. White, hot static shot through me. A flash, then falling. Part of me was already running down Pupu Street, away from here, away from Mom, away from what I knew could easily happen again. But I took a deep breath and closed my eyes. I forced the images back down. I had to do this. Luke was in there.

I opened my eyes and exhaled, finding myself a few feet from the front door. This was it. No more excuses. As I approached, I could hear Mom and Dad yelling in their bedroom.

"Give me my damn keys, Leonard."

There was a scuffle and the sound of a slap. "No touch me, Minerva."

"Aren't you even a little worried about your own child?"

"No even try, Minerva. Da kid prob'ly at his girlfriend's house. He not stupid. He one survivor. And I going already."

I smiled. Dad was right. I wasn't stupid. I knew exactly what I was doing. I opened the screen door and re-entered the storm.

Acknowledgments

I'd like to express my deepest gratitude to the following people:

First and foremost, Darrell and Eric, editors extraordinaire. Thank you for seeing the potential in this manuscript and then for working tirelessly on it with me. Thank you for your generosity and collaboration. Also, thank you for putting up with my stubbornness with grace and kindness.

Lois-Ann, thank you for your guidance. Once upon a time, you said one name and a cascade of words came tumbling out of me. This book exists because of your teacher's spirit. Thank you for telling me, "One day, you too."

Wendie, my fellow writing group warrior of almost a decade, thank you for the hours you sacrificed with my words. Your evaluation was always spot on. Thank you for being brutally honest. I needed it.

Aunty Betty, Aunty Sharon, Aunty Polly, and Aunty Bev, thank you for taking me in and treating me as one of your own. During a dark time, you were the light. Your kindness has made all the difference.

Ray and Donella, thank you for your friendship, insights, and encouragement. Thank you for welcoming our writing group into your home and for graciously allowing us to disturb your Thursday nights.

Feng, Summer, and Rieko, thank you for all of your hard work on the manuscript. Despite working on it at different stages, each of you had a hand in shaping it.

Joy and Wing Tek, thank you so much for all of your help. And to the Bamboo Ridge Press staff, thank you for all or your hard work, especially Wayne, typesetting and cover-art master. Thank you so much for your generosity and patience.

Kristie and Susan, thank you for your friendship, faith, and support. I have gained so much simply because you invited me into your lives so long ago. But see what happens when you feed a stray cat?

Cyn, Cat, Thomas, Yuen Ha, and Pat; Carl and Josey; Keith and Chas; Anna; Judy and Pam; John; Carene; Norman; Sandi; Nat and Jenni; Rocio, Jeannette, and Tad: thank you for respite, karaoke, volleyball, chess, movies, coffee, beach, dinner, get-togethers, lively discussion, and pure fun. I have truly been blessed with your friendship.

Christie, thank you for your partnership. Thank you for being a sounding board, a think tank of humor, and even at times, a consort battleship. Thank you for all you do.

About the Author

Tyler Miranda is an emerging writer with over a dozen publications in local literary journals. In 2009, he was awarded *Bamboo Ridge*'s Editors' Choice Award for Best Prose. In 2011, an excerpt from his novel was anthologized in a textbook produced by Pearson Publishing (New York). Miranda was raised on the under-developed west side of O'ahu, where his stories are often set. His experiences growing up in Hawai'i in a local Portuguese family have strongly influenced his writing, particularly with his Caucasian looks making him a minority in his childhood community. *'Ewa Which Way* is his first novel.